STONEHAND

STONEHAND

TALES OF SHATTERED GLASS: BOOK TWO

BARDLYRE

NEF HOUSE PUBLISHING

Stonehand
Tales of Shattered Glass: Book Two
Copyright © 2024 BardLyre

ISBN 978-1-965393-00-0

ALSO BY BARDLYRE

This one, after the hardest of years, is for my whole clan. Daine isn't the only one very lucky in the ones close to her.

CHAPTER ONE

"Mirror, Mirror on the Wall"

D aine Orban, the erstwhile Knight of the Road, sighed as she regarded her reflection in the mirror. She did not like what she saw.

The weeks since she arrived at Swinford had passed in somewhat of a blur. There had been defences to raise, militias to be trained, and a never-ending stream of demands on her time.

Although Taelsin was a more than competent Mayor, even his talents had only managed to slow the decline of this once-great City. Everywhere she looked, there was a project that would take months to bring to fruition, where they had, in reality, weeks.

Whilst the Keep in which she had been given quarters would prove a formidable bulwark, it was the only genuinely defensible structure she had seen in the City. There were whole sections of the outer walls that would provide, at best, a passive defence against a determined assault, and the less said about the troops available to hold those walls, the better.

If, as their information suggested, the King's forces were imminently expected to descend with righteous fury on the West, Swinford, in its current state, would struggle to provide much more than a token resistance.

She feared a tidal wave of slaughter awaited her and she was not sure she had such dark work in her anymore.

Daine had been tired before, of course. It was an occupational hazard for those who walked the Road. But she sensed that her current mood was something else. A bone-weary exhaustion that had little to do with a lack of sleep.

She had lost a child she had sworn to protect.

Her eyes traced over lines and creases in the face projected back at her by the mirror, and the years had not been kind. Though not in the way she thought others would judge such things, until recently, she had been content.

She could feel that the events in the Village and the schemes of the Trellecs had left wounds upon her soul that would never be healed.

She was confident that the Duskstrider would fulfil his promise and return Genoes to her. But what then? Where would she take him to protect him from the civil war that would surely tear the West apart?

And what of her own status? As a Knight of the Road, she was charged with dispensing the justice of the Goddess while on Tour. Once the King learned of her own sympathies with the rebels — indeed, that she planned to do what she could to repulse the advance of the King's army — what then?

We will cross that bridge when we come to it.

She was unsure if the words of the Goddess were especially comforting.

And suddenly, there was a flare of recognition in the gaze regarding her in the mirror. She had seen that haunted, broken look before: in the eyes of her Mentor, Gallant Stonehand.

"I am sorry to interrupt, my Lady." A servant had appeared behind her. "Mayor Elm desires your presence."

Daine nodded and stood, rolling her neck to relieve some of the tension that had become a permanent feature of her life. That she had not heard this young man approaching said nothing good about her state of exhaustion. "Trouble?"

"I don't rightly know, my Lady. Secretary Assay mentioned something about the sewers?"

Dismissing the servant, she buckled her sword and made to follow him as he backed out of her room. As she went, she glanced back at the eyes of an old woman looking sadly back.

It had all felt so much more straightforward so long ago.

*

Droughton-on-the-Water — thirty years ago.

"A mirror?"

"Yes."

"A mirror that eats people?"

"That's what I've heard, my Lady."

"Heard as in 'send urgent help, there's a carnivorous mirror on the rampage' or heard as in 'you'll never guess what hoax we're using to trick the unwary, it is the most stupid one you will have ever encountered, let's see how many fools fall for it'? There are degrees to these things, you realise."

Bayran Shareen, Priestess of the Inner Temple of Misrule, pursed her vividly painted lips and silently counted to ten. Dealing with Knights of the Road was a tricky proposition at the best of times, let alone one so wet behind the ears she was basically dripping.

There was a reason most Towns declared martial law when one of that Class passed through on their Tour. She knew her Town's garrison was filled to bursting with everyone capable of holding a blade brushing up on their combat training. To be fair, it was unlikely even a well-drilled army could do much should a Knight of the Road's ire be raised, but misery loved company . . .

She once again looked up at the figure towering over her. Tall, built like a Farmer's wife, and with all the confidence of someone who had wrestled a mountain bear and now had a nice new rug. The story went that this girl — fifteen if she was a day — had been trained by Gallant Stonehand. Considering the fate of that particular legend, whether that turned out to be a boon or a curse remained to be seen.

Bayran's early impressions were not good.

Still, you played the cards the Lords dealt you even when they were a pair of deuces.

"I believe I was given the information in good faith, my Lady, and I was tasked with passing it on to you. My Archbishop felt the presence of a mirror devouring the soul of anyone who gazes into it would be something you probably should seek to address on your Tour. Please let me know if we are mistaken in that assumption, and I will take further advice. However, should you agree with our assessment that a mirror that eats people falls within your jurisdiction as a Knight of the Road, I am tasked with giving you all the support you may require in bringing the matter to a close."

"It's a mirror. You planning to help me sweep up the broken pieces after I smash it?"

The two women held each other's eyes for a moment.

Daine Orban, newly appointed Knight of the Road, was underwhelmed by her early experiences on Tour. Apart from a rather one-sided fight with some unwise bandits, there had been precious little to exercise her sword arm thus far. That said, she was barely three months into her first ten-year Tour and had arrived at the Town of Droughton-on-the-Water a few bells before.

There was still time for things to become interesting.

However, she did not like this Priestess. She did not like her Order, dedicated as it was to the worship of the unruly children of the Goddess. She did not like her huge green eyes, artfully enhanced by elaborate black lines. She did not like her flawless, golden skin. She did not like her long black hair tied up with a pretty pink bow. She did not like the breathy quality of her voice; she should see a Healer if she had such trouble filling her lungs. And she did not like how . . . huge she felt standing beside her.

Jealousy is an unworthy emotion, the voice of the Goddess gently admonished. *You have other qualities beyond your aesthetic appeal.*

For sure, Daine thought. *It just might be nice occasionally to wear something I don't need to be strapped into.*

Bayran broke the tense silence. "Broken glass, of course. My Lady is very comical." The Priestess tossed her hair in a careless manner that nearly earned her a summary decapitation. "To return to the matter in hand, though, my Lady. Archbishop Jerule would like the matter resolved immediately and is concerned enough to have dispatched me, a Priestess of the Inner Temple, with all haste, to request your assistance in this matter. That alone should convince you of the significance of the matter."

Not quite with all haste, thought Daine. *You managed to pack quite the wardrobe.*

Strictly speaking, an Archbishop of the Lords of Misrule did not have the authority to direct Daine to as much as the washhouse. She was within her rights to ignore the request and do her business. But, to paraphrase the words of her Mentor, Old Gant, "Knights of the Road don't let people get eaten by mirrors because the person asking for help makes them feel a bit frumpy."

He'd never quite put it that way, but she was sure it as the sort of thing he would have said.

"Tell me more about this mirror. Is it eating people by, you know, a wailing and a gnashing of teeth? Or does it pull people into a different realm? Does it consume their souls, or . . ."

"I am barely more informed than you now, my Lady. If I may, can I suggest we seek firsthand experience of the artefact and then decide on an appropriate course of action?" Bayran's voice was coated with enough faux sincerity to stun a charging boar.

Daine looked past the Priestess at the long line of supplicants seeking to present their concerns to the makeshift court she had established in this courtyard. If her recent experiences were anything to go by, she would hear complaints about noisy neighbours, land disputes and egregious taxation demands for the next few hours. She doubted there would be much of interest for the Goddess here, but denying the people their chance for justice would be wrong, however minor the crimes they had to report may be.

The mirror can wait, the Goddess chimed in her head. *Justice needs to be done. It needs to be seen to be done.*

Accepting the guidance, Daine gestured for Bayran to step aside. "As you can see, Priestess, I have duties here and cannot abandon my post so readily. However, once the people's concerns have been heard and addressed, I will be happy to accompany you to deal with the danger that has alarmed your Archbishop. I gladly accept your assistance in the disposal of the impending broken glass. Perhaps the remnants will make you another pretty necklace?"

Bayran possessed just enough survival instinct not to roll her eyes at a being capable of razing the Town without drawing sweat. But, Lords, give her a Knight on their second, even their third Tour; they at least understood how the world worked. Unfortunately, this child still had all her delusions about "justice" to be knocked out of her.

"I am poised to leap into action when you feel ready, my Lady. Tell me when you believe enough local justice has been dispensed to allow you to address a soul-eating mirror." With that, she curtsied with such grace, beauty and precision that Daine had to force her hands to unclench.

Just because no one present would question her crushing the skull of a Priestess of the Lords of Misrule did not make it a good enough reason to do it. Whilst the admiration of the common folk was not part of her motivation to become a Knight of the Road, she would be lying if she said she did not think about how she would like the songs written about her to go. It seemed unlikely that straight-up murdering an unarmed Priestess for being impertinent would make for a catchy number.

"Thank you. Until this evening, then." She felt the Goddess smile indulgently at the unspoken "you bitch" in her words.

The Priestess held her low curtsey, clearly planning to stay in that position until Daine was finished.

Well, two of us can play at that game. "Now, my good sir," she said, turning her attention to the Farmer anxiously twisting his hat in his hands, "please tell me more about your oxen. Leave no detail, no matter how insignificant, unspoken. I have all day."

CHAPTER TWO

"Vim, Vigor, Piss and Vinegar"

I suppose I am just not seeing 'relocate everyone to live in the sewers' as the brilliant, tactical masterstroke you seem to suggest it is."

Tension burned in the air between the Mayor and his Secretary. All of Swinford knew the two enjoyed a somewhat informal back-and-forth, but the relationship had taken a turn for the worse since their return from the disastrous Council of the West.

Rumours of what had occurred in that Village were rife, but the fact that the West was now in open rebellion against the King could not be denied. Ensuring the City of Swinford was prepared for the storm about to fall upon them was clearly placing great strain on a previously strong relationship.

"Unfortunately, my Lord," Donal said, tapping a stylus against his impossibly white teeth, "whilst we all appreciate your sterling efforts to follow the logic of my argument, I do wonder if your time would be better spent actioning the plan as opposed to wrestling with complexities beyond you. We each have our strengths, after all."

There was an awkward silence during which everyone in the small group convened to convene at the entrance to Swinford's warren of underground sewers tried not to make eye contact.

"Master Secretary, did you just call me stupid?" Taelsin's voice was dangerously low.

"Not at all, my Lord. I merely pointed out that every moment I spend explaining and reexplaining my thinking to you is a moment lost in the protection of the City. I did not mean to suggest you were slow, merely that I am a genius."

"There was a time," Lady Gerol noted with a sniff she instantly regretted this close to the entrance to the sewer, "when the help would be executed for speaking to a Lord in that way."

"Very true." Donal beamed back at her, "I imagine that was around the time every Noble paid thirteen pounds of gold each six months for the upkeep of the City's walls. As luck would have it, I have my ledgers here. Shall I see how much House Gerol has paid in the last six months? In the last twelve? Indeed, I wonder, if we counted up all your House's contributions to the rebuild and repair of the infrastructure of Swinford for the last twenty years, if we would have enough gold to hire a particularly expensive whore. Although, if rumour is to be believed, your husband . . ."

"Enough. Donal. You will be silent." Taelsin's voice boomed around the gathering as the older woman gaped in shock. "My apologies, Lady Gerol. My Secretary does not speak for me in this matter. No one questions House Gerol's commitment to the City's well-being."

"Well, at the very least, no one questions Lord Gerol's commitment to the well-being of the City's prostitutes."

"Be quiet!" Taelsin's face reddened with anger. "Is it not enough that you disrespect me? That you thwart my will? That you undermine me at every turn? Now you must also besmirch the reputations of my oldest friends. Lady Gerol, please accept my apologies."

The elderly woman glared daggers at Donal. "I have long told you, Taelsin, my boy, that nothing good will come from consorting with the likes of this Class. Your father needed nothing more than the advice of his Nobles to run the City, and we can all agree he did a fine job."

The other Nobles in the party nodded their sage agreement. This Secretary had long been a thorn in their side in gaining influence over young Taelsin Elm. This developing fissure between them was one they were keen, nay positively eager, to exploit. "But from the first moment you let this viper poison your ear, well . . . I don't like to say it, boy, but Swinford is not the City it once was."

As if sensing the momentum moving away from him, Donal raised his voice in frustration. "My Lord, our City will soon come under siege by the King's Army. Each of us have our own sources that put the day of attack from a week to a month. But that siege will arrive, and it will be catastrophic. From what I hear, the King has placed Great General Souit in command of his forces. I am sure we are all well aware of his impressive reputation. Certainly, he has cracked harder nuts than Swinford in the recent past. Thus, we need to consider how we can best protect our population. Some of the few sections of our walls that are in decent shape are those within the sewer network. I imagine even the most venal of our Nobles would baulk at effluence swimming in the streets. If we want our people to have a chance to survive the coming assault, it makes perfect sense for us to make use of that resource."

"My Lord, do we need to listen to this drivel further? You asked us to accompany you to hear this scheme, and we have done so. I, for one, will not move one member of my House belowground. I doubt you will find a single Noble left in the City who will agree to such a ludicrous suggestion. And, what is more, I find myself unable to tolerate the presence of this . . . gentleman any further."

Taelsin glared at Donal one final time and then sighed. "I agree, Lady Gerol. Once again, I am sorry for the words of my Secretary. He had suggested this would be a solution to our problems, but I now see it as yet another opportunity for him to show off. Please, would you excuse us, and I will join you aboveground shortly."

"So, I take it we will not be moving the population belowground, then, Taelsin?" The speaker, a portly Minor Noble named Lord Olrun, barely kept the sneer out of his voice.

"No, my Lord. I am sorry to have wasted your time. Guards, close up the entrance. Nothing more needs to be done here. We shall entertain this folly no longer. Now, I must have a word with my staff. Can I please join you shortly?"

The Nobles graciously nodded their approval and withdrew to more fragrant air, leaving just Taelsin and Donal behind.

The two glared at each other in silence for a few moments.

"My Lord, you are a truly lousy actor for an outstanding politician."

Taelsin rolled his eyes. "Me? You appear to have transformed into some sort of second-rate villain from one of the more fantastical scrolls. I kept half expecting you to twirl your moustache and cackle."

"To speak plain, my Lord, I worried that should we be too subtle, the trap would not be sufficiently bated. We are not dealing with the premier intellects of the age here."

"What trap?" Both men jumped at her voice as Daine approached from the shadows. "I must say, I have just passed the smuggest group of Nobles I have seen in a long time. They are all, loudly, of the opinion Donal's days are numbered."

"My Lady Darkhelm, I trust you are well?" Taelsin dipped his head in a bow.

"You find me as well as I find you, I imagine."

Each took in the exhaustion of the other and smiled in recognition.

"I, on the other hand, am positively brimming with vim, vigour, piss and vinegar. If I may continue outlining my scheme, my Lord? My Lady? I do so love the scheming."

Taelsin sighed and nodded for Donal to proceed.

"Thank you. As you are aware, we have known for some time that the King has been far too well-appraised of our preparations for the coming siege. We had, of course, made efforts to stem the usual communication methods, but some reasonably sensitive information continued to flow outwards."

Daine rubbed her hand down her face. "You speak,

Master Secretary, as if most of those 'efforts' did not in-volve me throwing people out of windows."

"Well, quite. A startlingly efficient method of inter-rogation I wished I had stumbled upon centuries earlier. Think of the wear and tear I would have saved on knives. Well, never mind. Moving right along. Through several well-placed rumours, we have identified that the leaks must come from within the ranks of the few Nobles who have remained within the City."

"The majority of my fellow Nobles, of course, having fled at the first sign of trouble, taking with them all the food, water, and manpower they could sneak out of the City." Taelsin's voice was bitter.

"Indeed. The rats have abandoned this entirely sea-worthy vessel — see, I can be good for morale — and we must assume that those chosen to remain are either your staunchest allies or your most vicious opponents. Hence today's little game."

"And what was the outcome?"

"Well, that will rather depend, my Lady, on which of those present decides to leak news of the break in relation-ship between Taelsin and myself. Oh, and which of them gives the heads-up to the small attack squad we have iden-tified hiding on the outskirts of the City? It is now appar-ent it will be safe to make ingress through the sewers."

"I assume I am here because further defenestrations await me?"

Taelsin and Donal exchanged a look. "Not quite, Lady Darkhelm," Mayor Elm began, "we would like you to . . ." and then he stopped.

Donal rolled his eyes. "My Master feels he is overstep-ping in this request. I've explained Knights of the Road like nothing more than the opportunity to bloody some noses. He's doing you a favour, truth be told."

Daine looked at the two of them and could not help but smile. There were few people in this world — or, to be fair, the next — whom she would call friends. But she felt very close to the Mayor and his Secretary.

During their journey back from the Village, she had greatly enjoyed their company. As a Knight of the Road, she had made a virtue of her isolation, enjoying relying on no one but herself. However, in the last month, her eyes had been opened to a world of friendship she would be loath to leave behind. These two, Kirstin, Eliud and, of course, Genoes. They were the new family she had forged for herself, and there was very little she would not do in order to keep them all safe.

"Taelsin, what would you have me do? I promised Eliud that Swinford will still be standing when he returns with Genoes, and I mean to keep that vow."

At the mention of the Duskstrider, a touch more vibrancy entered Mayor Elm's eyes. "Have you heard anything from him? We know he entered the Capital, but our spies have very little else to share."

"I am afraid not, my Lord."

"The Goddess . . . ?" Donal asked delicately.

"Is being Her usual ineffable self. The best I can say is that She does not seem overly alarmed by the current situation. If anything untoward has happened to Eliud, Kirstin or Genoes, then She is not worried about it."

"That is not really as comforting as could be hoped."

"Welcome to my existence."

Donal shrugged. "Well, worrying about it won't make much difference. We're waiting for the Pendragon to appear and pull our feet from the fire. Any situation he has encountered with which he cannot cope is going to be beyond our ability to help. We'd be wiser to focus on our own problems and hope he gets here in time."

Daine nodded. "I told him to meet us here. I am at your disposal."

Donal clapped and put a hand on Daine's shoulder, leading her towards one particularly aromatic grate. "Excellent. Well, if our little charade with the Nobles has worked as we hope, we are probably going to need someone of your Skills in the very near future. The big question is, I guess, whether we can find any watertight clothing in your size."

CHAPTER THREE

The Broken Tankard

Droughton-on-the-Water — thirty years ago.

aine had noticed the increasing sparseness of houses and stalls the further they walked. She sensed they were approaching a less reputable part of Town.

Her understanding had been that Droughton-on-the-Water was one of the more prosperous places in this part of the world. However, she was learning it was not uncommon for the most beautiful lights to cast the darkest shadows.

As Daine and Bayran walked, the dilapidated houses appeared to swallow them in a hungry embrace.

Humble dwellings, their wooden frames groaning under the weight of years, huddled together in desperate solidarity. Once proudly whitewashed walls were now adorned with layers of grime, the graffiti of destitution etched in their decaying facades.

"It would seem that your Order should be more present in this part of Town, Priestess. Do not the followers of the Lords preach that everyone should have the chance to improve their lot? Where are your Hostels? Your Lower Priests ministering on these streets?"

"There is more than enough to occupy us in Droughton, my Lady. We do what we can to alleviate suffering. Some people . . ." Bayran indicated shadows peering at them from windows. "Well, there are those you can save from everything but themselves."

They had been walking for several bells before they reached a solitary inn, its sign weathered and faded, standing at the heart of the desolate district.

Bayran, with a rolling of the eyes that amused Daine, accepted a pause in their journey. The inn was called "The Broken Tankard," a fitting name for an establishment that had seen better days. Its windows had been colourful stained glass, once upon a time, but were now shattered and patched with ragged boards.

The door, once sturdy and welcoming, creaked on its hinges as it swung open, a haunting dirge that greeted those brave enough to enter. The air within was thick with the mingling scents of stale ale and despair, the sounds of muted conversations buzzing against the peeling wallpaper.

"Two ales, Barkeep." Daine's voice boomed out in the dark room.

"One ale and one water," Bayran corrected. "One of us should keep a clear head."

"Priestess, the ale will be cleaner than the water in such

a place. No one needs a sharp mind whilst experiencing dysentery."

When the drinks came, Bayran dipped a finger in her mug and muttered a few words, then grimaced at whatever was the outcome of the spell. She pushed it away from her. "My gods may approve of gambling — I will bank my Luck for now."

Daine guffawed and looked around her. The other occupants of the inn were a motley crew of lost souls slumped over their drinks, eyes haunted by the trials of existence. Men, their faces rough and lined with worry, nursed mugs of watered-down ale, seeking solace in the fleeting embrace of forgetfulness. Women wearing gowns tattered and threadbare whispered secrets to one another, their laughter laced with bitterness and longing. Their faces told tales of shattered dreams and broken promises, etched with the lines of disappointment and defeat.

"Cheerful place."

Bayran laid her hands on the counter and stared ahead. "My Lady. Life has been hard for many years for the poor in Droughton. And that was before the coming of the mirror and all it has wrought. These people do not deserve your scorn."

She gasped as Daine took hold of her arm and pulled her roughly to face her. "It is not these people I scorn, Priestess. You sit in your perfumed, beautiful robes, with slippers that cost more than the building, and make pronouncements on a 'hard life for the poor.' I say again, I am shocked at the indifference of your Order to the suffering I see here. I well know where my scorn is directed."

They sat in silence as Daine finished her drink. Each fostering growing resentment for the other.

*

Towards the back of the inn, unseen by either Knight or Priestess, engaged as they were in their own private bickering, a solitary figure slipped outside and began moving with purpose. Clad in rags, his weathered face hidden beneath a tattered hood, he moved through the streets with determination.

He knew every nook and cranny of this forsaken place, every hidden crevice that held the whispered secrets of a bygone era.

In the fading light of dusk, as the last vestiges of daylight cast long shadows upon the crumbling walls, the figure came to a halt before an ancient, vine-covered structure. The remnants of a grand cathedral stood before him, its once-towering spires reduced to crumbling stone. He stepped through the shattered doorway, his footsteps echoing in the cavernous space. The air was heavy with the weight of the past, and he could almost hear the ghostly chants of forgotten prayers.

Here, in the heart of the derelict Town, he sought solace and purpose amidst the ruins.

He brought his master great news.

*

They had left the tavern shortly after Daine's third drink. She did not especially like the ale — her Class ensured alcohol had no impact on her — but she enjoyed annoying the Priestess.

Daine recognised there was something she was missing about Bayran's attitude towards the mirror. The Priestess acted as if their mission were exceptionally time-critical, but the mirror had been active for several months, if she believed the woman. There seemed little need for such urgency in their pursuit of it.

"Remember, boys and girls, only stupid people set traps. So stands to reason only stupider people get caught in them," was one of Old Gant's favoured maxims. She was all but certain the Priestess was leading her into some sort of deception. She just did not understand why — tangling with a Knight of the Road was a shortcut to a beheading.

And then she sensed a group of people loitering up ahead.

"Can you fight?"

Bayran stopped in her tracks and wrinkled her nose at the Knight's terse tone. "Can I what?"

"Fight. You know" — she drew her longsword from its sheath on her back — "with a sword."

"Why on earth would I . . ." Bayran frowned up at her companion. "Are you challenging me to a duel, my Lady?"

Not for the first time, Daine was reminded that not everyone was blessed with her enhanced senses. "There's a group of six or seven people waiting for us around the next bend in the road. It might be more. It's hard to tell. There's something strange about the way they smell. I'm asking because I need to know if you can hold your own or if I need to protect you whilst fighting them."

It had been a long and frustrating evening for Bayran. She knew her gambit with the curtsey had been childish, but she had not expected that the Knight was equally capable of such juvenile behaviour. Daine had, somewhat vindictively to the Priestess's mind, continued to answer any and all petitions that came her way for three hours afterward. She was surprised she could still walk.

And now, far later than she had planned, they were making their way through the dark streets of Droughton.

She was disappointed in how she had handled the awkwardness in the tavern. Bayran felt she had, in some way, failed a test with the Knight. And now this insane child-barbarian was talking about engaging in some light swordplay.

"My Lady, I don't know how they do things where you are from, but here in the Town, we do not assume every group approaching us has nefarious intent. In the civilised world, we try discourse before swinging the sword." To underscore her words, Bayran swept past the Knight, calves screaming at the extra speed demanded of them, and turned the corner.

This would have made for quite the exit had she not instantly reappeared, running as fast as her sore legs could carry her. Daine stepped forward into the middle of the street to cover the Priestess's retreat as several figures lumbered round the corner after her. The Knight's eyes flickered in excitement as a horde of undead shuffled forward, their decaying limbs creaking like rusted iron.

"That's more like it," Daine grinned, taking up a classic guard position.

Catching her breath a short distance beyond Daine and drawing two wickedly sharp daggers, Bayran muttered vicious curses. "Yes. I can fight, my Lady. Just give me room to work when you are floundering around with that great heap of metal."

"Any idea what they are?" Daine used the length of her longsword to mark a semicircle in the air through which she intended nothing to pass.

"Soulless. Mirror-taken. You remember the mirror, right? Or did that slip your mind with all that serious business of corn boundaries and fence heights?"

As a putrid stench of death wafted through the air, Daine twirled her blade, catching the dim light of flickering torches. It gleamed with a polished sheen, starkly contrasting with the murky darkness surrounding them. "You spoke of a mirror that ate people. I mayhap would have led with the existence in the Town of groups of Soulless waylaying people on the street. I would have stopped at two drinks if you'd been clearer as to the danger."

Bayran shot her a withering glance. "My Lady, if you had taken your duty seriously at the time and followed my suggestion, we wouldn't be here in the darkness, knee-deep in undead."

Daine lunged forward, her sword slashing through the air with little precision. There was no need against a foe that took no evasive action. The movements of Soulless were clumsy, but their numbers could be overwhelming if the Knight let them bunch up. As she had suspected, there were far more than the seven or eight Daine had initially expected. Was there something about the undead that made them more difficult for her to sense? That could be troubling.

As she thought through the implications, Daine dodged and hacked at hands and arms seeking to entrap her, her large form moving with surprising, agile grace. "Do not fret, Priestess. Nothing I cannot handle. No need to risk ruffling your dress with such things."

Bayran's lips tightened into a thin line as she watched the Knight hold the centre of the street against such high odds. No matter how many times you heard about the efficacy of these warriors, seeing them in action was, annoyingly, impressive.

Mindful of the criticisms back in the tavern about the inaction of her Order, she was not content to hide behind the Knight's sword. She channelled divine energy through her daggers and started casting spells to protect her erstwhile companion. Her voice was heavy with scorn as she muttered incantations, the holy symbols around her neck glowing with a gentle radiance. "You can jest all you want, my Lady, but remember, my prayers are the only reason you're still standing!"

Daine chuckled, her laughter mingling with the cacophony of groans and hisses from the Soulless. "Sad as I am to deprive you of the chance to show off your miraculous powers, Priestess, you will find your charms don't work on me. If you wish to be helpful, you will need to get your hands dirty. Or, which would be my preference, stay back and let me finish my work."

As the battle raged on, Daine's blade cleaved through rotten flesh, sending limbs flying and bodies crumpling to the ground. Anxious not to be left out, Bayran abandoned her spells — she had known the Knights were resistant to all forms of magic and was frustrated to have misstepped — throwing herself into the middle of the mindless assault. With each swing of their weapons, their bickering intensified.

"Your aim is as off as your faith, Bayran!" Daine shouted as she lopped off the head of a skeletal creature.

"At least my aim doesn't rely solely on arrogance!" Bayran shot back.

The clash of metal against bone, the cracking of skulls,

and the desperate moans of the undead filled the night air, drowning out their verbal sparring. For a moment, as they fought back-to-back, their quarrels became a mere backdrop to the chaos surrounding them.

As the last of the Soulless fell, Daine wiped the sweat from her brow, a weary smile playing on her face. "Not bad, Priestess. Not bad at all. There might even be a thing or two you could teach me with those daggers of yours."

Bayran replaced the blades in their sheaths. "My Lady, these creatures did not find their way to us unaided. Someone must be alert to our direction. We need to keep moving before something you cannot defeat is sent in their stead. From my information, the house containing the mirror should be just ahead."

If Daine saw the final incantation Bayran cast on the Soulless as they turned to keep moving, she did not mention it. She would come to regret not doing so.

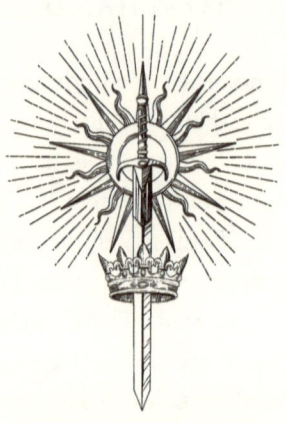

CHAPTER FOUR

"The Joy of a Well-Constructed Agenda"

Donal shuffled through the papers on his desk.

It seemed to him that if he could just find a different order, there might be a way in which they could sit that would make the future look a touch more palatable.

But no.

Regardless of how he considered things, the end was very much nigh. In a few days, the armies of the King — under the direction of General Souit, no less — would begin scouring the West. Of all those Towns and Cities that had seceded, Swinford would be at the very top of the list of those to be pacified. Quite apart from the propaganda victory in the capture and, presumably, execution of Mayor Elm, most of the trading routes to the Capital ran through their lands. The longer Swinford stood in rebellion, the less money flowed into the King's coffers. That would be a powerful motivation to crush this uprising at birth.

Donal blew out his cheeks and brushed the papers away from him. He flattered himself that he was no minor talent, but in the face of this approaching doom, even his box of tricks looked increasingly bare.

Across his long life, this was certainly not the first time he had found himself marshalling the defence of a City under the approaching shadow of overwhelming forces. Although, he acknowledged, it was somewhat of a unique situation to find himself objectively on the "right" side of the argument. It was troubling that the outcome looked much on the same track, though. That did not seem quite fair.

Still earnestly searching for potential solutions, he cycled through the Class Abilities he possessed. As a Secretary, he was an outstanding administrator — with exceptionally high Intelligence and no little Wisdom upon which to call. Moreover, he had <Perfect Recall>, little need for sleep and a talent for enhancing the teamwork of any group he was part of. Alongside these Skills, he had, over the years, supplemented his usefulness with a knowledge and capacity for runes that was rarely gained through a traditional scholar's apprenticeship. Some may think that was cheating; he merely considered it making the most of what he had.

Considering his long and exotic history, it still surprised him to how much he had liked being a Secretary.

He enjoyed the feeling of power that came from a carefully constructed agenda and the judicious use of minutes. From behind a desk, he had been able to frustrate assassinations and bring down great Lords with little more than a flourish of his quill. The attraction of soft power was great for a man who had spent much of the last century elbow-deep in the blood of heretics.

But, he feared, his time in this Class was coming to an end.

No matter how carefully he rearranged and ordered things, the gaps in Swinford's walls would not be closed any faster. His skill with a ledger could not conjure additional troops from thin air, nor could he ensure the forces they had were appropriately fed and equipped.

Ignoring the three figures looming over him, he stood and pottered towards the window that looked out on the courtyard of the Keep. From this vantage point, he could see the Lady Darkhelm preparing for her task beneath the City. She had insisted on undertaking the mission alone, for which, secretly, Donal was very grateful. Had she wished for support, he had no idea where he would have found the men to accompany her. Suicide missions were hardly attractive for anyone but a Knight of the Road.

Now, that was a thought. Would a second Knight of the Road be helpful for the City in the coming strife? He possessed the necessary prerequisites to make that Class change, of course. And it had been a while since he had fought on the front line.

Don't you dare!

He smiled at the hurried distaste in the Goddess's voice. It had been a while since a deity, at least one from this realm, had directly addressed him. "Don't worry, my dear. I wouldn't force you to be my patron. As much as I think the Darkhelm would welcome the comradeship, I fear I must turn my talents elsewhere."

If there was any response, he did not hear it.

No. As attractive as the thought of a young, strong body was — with a suitably long sword, of course — Swinford would need something different from him in the coming weeks and months.

Taelsin had disagreed when he had explained his plan to swap Classes. Of course he did. It was one of the benefits of youth that the man had not yet seen enough to completely shed his cloak of idealism. The Mayor felt sure they had not exhausted all other options and wanted to maintain their current dynamic.

Donal, on the other hand, with regret, knew differently.

Sighing, he turned away from the window and looked back at the cosy room that had been his office for all these years. Yes. He had enjoyed his time in this Class. Things had been so much simpler.

"Well, Master Secretary?"

The three armed figures who had burst through his door a few moments earlier were starting to feel anxious. There were many responses to the sudden, and unwelcome, appearance of masked assailants, and this trio had thought they had seen them all.

Complete and utter indifference was a new one.

In answer, Donal flashed his brilliant white smile. "I'm sorry, sirs. I was miles away. I believe you may have asked me a question?"

"Yes, sir. As we explained, you have been summoned by the Council of Nobles to brief them on the state of the walls. There have been allegations you have been profiting from the sale of stone and such things. We are to escort you to them with all haste to allow you to explain yourself."

"Summoned, is it? That sounds nicely official. And am I to take it that during my journey from hither to thither,

I am likely to experience an unexpected catastrophic accident? Will I slip and fall from the walls, perchance? Will a passing cart veer out of control and trample me underfoot? Or, and this was always my personal favourite, so please do accept the advice, will I accidentally impale myself, repeatedly, on a passing blade?"

The speaker for the group frowned at Donal's verbiage and brandished his club. "Now, none of your jibber jabber, Master Secretary. The Council of Nobles requires your presence, and we're to make sure nothing happens on the way."

Donal nodded thoughtfully. "Well, your arrival has certainly been timely, and I must thank you for making my mind up for me. I had thought to eke out another day or so in this Class, but there's not much this form can do against such lusty youths as yourselves, is there? Not unless we can decide things with a game of chess? What say you? A quick mental challenge? I prefer to play black?" He indicated a chess set that sat ready under a small pile of parchment.

The second man, lacking the social graces of his companion, brought his hand down with a crash, scattering paper and knocking chess pieces flying. "Quit your yammering! You're coming with us now!"

"Oh dear." Donal's eyes flashed at the spilt documents. "Now that was not very friendly, was it?"

And his Class shifted.

Few people, especially outside the great Training Schools of the Kingdom, had ever witnessed a Class change. In a society whose cornerstone was the rigidity of its Class structure, it was an unusual enough event to be almost legendary. And fewer still had ever seen it undertaken with so little ceremony.

For those like the Knights of the Road who sought to ascend from a base Class to something greater, it was a long-term, grueling process by which a patron god was wooed by feats of arms to accept the change.

What happened in this small room, however, was nothing like that.

One moment, the three hired killers faced a kindly-looking, stooped old man who clearly posed them no martial threat. A Secretary might be clever, but no amount of pretty words would save his neck when the wringing started.

But in the next . . .

Donal felt momentary regret as some of his Intelligence drained away — not too much, of course, that would be unhelpful in the coming troubles — but enough that things that were crystal clear suddenly became a touch more indistinct. The knowledge was still there, but no longer as blindingly obvious amongst a wider thread of possibilities. Still a genius, then, but no longer a once-in-a-generation mind. That was a shame. However, that pang of disappointment was a fleeting thing as, with a surge of pleasure, all sorts of other things suddenly became possible.

He was pleased that he had kept much the same body; he wouldn't want his change of capabilities to be too noticeable, after all. It would be far to their advantage if General Souit's spies had nothing remarkable to report about the leadership of Swinford. Mind you, when you stood next to a Knight of the Road, you could probably grow a second head without anyone noticing.

With eyes growing wide, each of the men who had accepted three gold coins apiece to rid the City of this troublesome administrator took a half step back. The figure in front of them was, objectively, still the same man. The same face, the same bent back, and the same comically bright teeth. But whereas before he was nothing so much as an elderly functionary, a terrifying aura now pulsed from him.

"Oh, yes. I must say, I have missed this."

Donal's mind whirled as he considered the problem of the oncoming army from a wholly different perspective. He still had access to the memories of his Secretary Class, although he could not quite follow some of the extrapolations he had made whilst in that form. But that mattered little in the grand scheme of things. He now had a wholly new way of looking at the world.

Speaking of which . . .

"My dear young things, I'm afraid events have rather overtaken you somewhat. I suppose, for form's sake, I should give you the opportunity to rethink this course of action?" Taelsin would expect that of him, of course. And, he was pleased to realise, despite the change of Class, he was still content to serve that extraordinary young man. He had worried about that. When he had been in this Class before, he had often felt the need to . . . restructure things.

The three interlopers bunched together for a moment, sensing the proximity of their end, and then, in desperation, they chose to attack as one.

The Dark Warlord smiled, white teeth now noticeably sharper and opened his arms to welcome them into his embrace.

CHAPTER FIVE

"Needs Must when the Demon Drives

The hairs on the back of Daine's neck were suddenly standing to attention, and she whirled to face the imminent threat. On instinct, she had drawn her greatsword, sweeping it with both hands in a wide arc to the guard position.

The sight of a Knight of the Road preparing for combat had a suitably chilling impact on the others milling around the Keep's courtyard. In a blind panic, the various squires, merchants and armourers fled the area, shouting their displeasure at being so unceremoniously displaced.

"Is there something wrong, Lady Darkhelm?"

Daine's eyes met Donal's and then swept past him to take in the three imposing figures arrayed behind him. For sure, they were intimidating enough in a squat, brutish way, but not at all concerning enough to have elicited such a primaeval response from her. Indeed, now she looked at them properly, there was something profoundly cowed about them.

No, these three were not the source of her . . . well, "fear" was probably the only word for it. It was the aura of some terrifying predator that had so raised her hackles; she cast around for where it may be lurking.

And her gaze returned to Donal.

"Ah. I worried this might happen. Could I have a moment to explain before the hacking begins?"

She took a step forward, seeking to bring it — whatever it was that had taken Donal's form — within her sword's reach.

He stumbled back, the three bruisers slipping past him to stand between them. "Lady Darkhelm. Daine. If we could just take a beat so that I might explain things?"

Daine flat-batted the largest of the three out of the way with her sword before closing on the erstwhile Secretary and lifting him off the ground with one hand. "What are you? What have you done with my friend?"

What happened next was something of a surprise to all concerned.

Donal, sensing an inevitable escalation in the Knight's fury, brought both fists down on the forearm attached to the hand suspending him aloft. Daine's eyes widened at the colossal impact, the effect being she let the thing that looked like the old man drop to the floor. However, rather than fall to the ground in a heap, Donal fell into his shadow and then entirely vanished.

There was a pause, and then the two remaining brutes threw themselves in a fury on Daine.

That, at least, worked out exactly as could have been expected, and within moments, all of them, with fewer limbs attached to them than previously, were lying in a pile on the ground.

Donal's voice came from behind Daine. "Apologies. That is on me. I should have found a way to lay some groundwork and introduce my transformation. Do you think I could go get Taelsin, and we could try all that again? Don't mind my minions. They'll pull themselves back together in no time."

*

"You can change Class at will?"

"Well, not quite 'at will.' It is much more complicated than that and requires me to have achieved all sorts of preconditions and feats of amazing derring-do and . . ." Donal's voice trailed off under Daine's blank stare. "At will. Pretty much, yes."

"And you knew about this?"

Taelsin shrunk back as Daine turned to him. She had yet to put up her sword, and waves of suppressed tension rolled off her. "I have always been aware that Donal had capabilities far beyond the average Secretary, but it was only after the attempt on his life by the Order of Iskent that he began sharing more of his history."

Daine regarded him silently for a moment before turning to look at the three "minions" that were stood guarding the door. As Donal has said, their arms had reattached. Her mind flashed back to her encounter with Soulless during her first Tour in Droughton. The similarity in the stance and vacant look was unmistakable.

"Who were they?"

Donal smiled broadly. "Oh, just thugs some of the Nobles sent to kill me. I acted entirely in self-defence, I promise you. I even, and I think you will appreciate this, gave them a chance to back out of it once they realised they were outmatched."

"So why are they still . . . moving?"

"Well, their appearance rather tipped my hand. I had been preparing to move my Class into Great Marshal."

"Yes. I distinctly remember that being the plan," Taelsin added, his voice wry. "In fact, I could have sworn we specifically discarded your desire to move into Dark Warlord, as it was so manifestly evil. Someone very wise even said the words,'I imagine the Lady Darkhelm will have a hard time reconciling herself to the presence of a Dark Warlord.' I wonder which good-looking, eminently sensible Mayor thought that?"

"Needs must when the demon drives, my boy. There I was, frail and alone, confronting my imminent demise. Who knows what these three could have achieved should I not, in a moment of terror, have chosen a Class with more . . . claws."

"Please answer my question." Daine's voice was low, but Donal felt the undertone. "Why are they still moving?"

"Ah, yes. Well, one of the minor talents of which a Dark Warlord can make use is the ability to, briefly, reanimate those who fall in battle. Depending on the Willpower of the individual — and, as you may expect, I have quite a lot of that — the effect can be quite wide-range and can last for some time."

Taelsin, watching Daine tighten her grip on her sword, hastily spoke up. "Donal, I think what the Lady Darkhelm would like to clarify is that your, erm, minions are not suffering."

"Oh, Goddess, no. They're dead as can be. Necks broken and euthanised quite appropriately. In many ways, it may be considered true that, having moved them on from this vale of tears, I have released them from their mortal suffering. I've implanted a few motor functions in the cores, but there's nothing cognitive firing there. Think of them as mobile furniture."

"No. I don't think I will." Daine finally sheathed her sword and took a deep breath. "Master Secretary . . . apologies, how should I address you?"

"I've always quite fancied being known as Oh High Eldritch One."

"Donal, do you think you could try to take this a little more seriously? Lady Darkhelm is a crucial ally in the struggle to come. I would hesitate to choose between the two of you, but should that necessity come to pass, I will very much not be on the side of the person keeping animated corpses around to play with and . . . are you wearing a cape?"

Finally, Taelsin's words made an impact, and Donal appeared to pull himself together with a visible effort. "My apologies, both. A side effect of this particular Class is that my impulse control is not quite as sharp as I would like. I will work particularly on restraining my more . . . baroque inclinations."

"Sir, I will ask you this once, and then we will draw a line." Daine's voice was quiet. "Can I still trust you?"

Donal opened his mouth to speak, paused, and then closed it. He looked over to his minions, and they fell to the floor as if they were marionettes whose strings had been cut.

"Lady Darkhelm, I am sorry about how this has been brought to you. I tell you in truth that should I have been able to stay within the Secretary Class, that would have

been my preference. You both know I am exceptionally long-lived and, during the years, I have rarely existed
within a Class that gave me such honest pleasure. It is
thus with deep regret that I needed to move once again
into this form." He held his hands towards her, palms forward. "These are not the hands of a good man, my Lady.
I have washed more blood off them than you could possibly comprehend — both literally and figuratively. And,
of course, each drop left a stain. Should I have believed
there was any path remaining for us that did not require
me to wade anew into crimson rivers, I would most heart-
ily have taken it." Daine flinched at those words. Eliud had
said something similar when she had petitioned him for
help against the Trellecs.

Donal continued. "But we all know the powers ranged
against us. And I would not have you fall in the strife to
come. My soul can bear the weight of this Class and not
break; it has done so countless times before. Things that
you may baulk at will need to be done in the coming strife,
and I would ask that you let me spare you the strain. Can
you trust me, Lady Darkhelm? You can trust me to do
what needs to be done in your best interests."

Daine looked at Taelsin. "You're comfortable with
this?"

"Goddess, no." The Mayor was shaking his head,
"Given my druthers, I'd have him back as my Secretary immediately. But we have days, maybe only hours, before we
are at war. If Donal thinks this Class will give us an edge,
I'm willing to take it. I trust him, my Lady."

Daine closed her eyes and reached for the Goddess.
She had been a distant presence of late. Daine's questing produced mild distaste from her patron towards the

form Donal had assumed, but nothing more than that; as if he were a child who brought something particularly foul-smelling in from the fields.

"So be it, Donal. No more needs to be said save, sir, I swear that should you let our cause down, I will remove your head from its shoulders, burn your corpse to ash and fling you to the four corners of the world in a storm."

"It is just that sort of careful, nay obsessive, attention to detail that makes you such a valuable ally, my dear. Proper belt and braces stuff there. Decapitation, immolation and a scattering. Never let it be said you do not do a thorough job, my dear. Now, whilst tempers are running just a little cooler, can I check our position on blood sacrifices? For example, is there a line to be drawn between using the blood of innocents — 'clear no-no' — and the blood of people we don't care that much about — 'take as much as you like'?"

Daine closed her eyes and sighed. She sensed she was in for a long night.

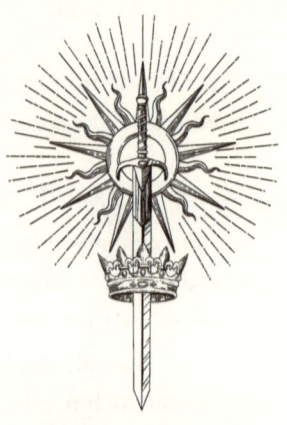

CHAPTER SIX

Mutually Assured Survival

Captain Haydyn Kettle was of a phlegmatic constitution.

This set him apart from his more fiery and impulsive comrades and was, as is the way of things in the army, the cause of much ribaldry at his expense. With his robust, solid build and air of calm serenity, he quickly earned himself the nickname "Cattle".

In many ways, his measured approach to life was the key to his slow but inexorable rise up the ranks. As was the case for Kettles back to the beginning of time, he was a Guardsman. And what those in that Class lacked for in Inspiration, they more than made up for in bloody-mindedness. Where Cattle was different, though, was that unlike those who charged headlong into battle, revelling in the thrill of the fight, he would be found doing his share but more than happy to let others take the glory.

This, as may be expected, left Cattle standing amongst the unwounded of an engagement more often than not.

As the years rolled by, if he noticed the faces of those around him becoming younger and younger and increasingly looking to him for leadership, he simply took it in his slow, measured stride. Gallant Stonehand himself had once said that if he had gotten his hands on Cattle young enough, he "might have made something special of you, my lad." But if the Guardsman felt he had missed out on something, he never mentioned it. In the same way, if he was pleased with the constant stream of promotions and commendations that came his way, it was difficult to tell. And if he was dismayed to be ordered to lead the infiltration of the Swinford sewers, no one would have known it.

His men felt somewhat differently.

"Why's it always us that gets this sort of job?" His Corporal, a short, rodenty-looking man called Jinks, was very much not of his Captain's disposition. There was a rumour Jinks had smiled once, but no one believed it. "It's like there's someone back at headquarters with a list of the worst jobs in the army and a big fat stamp with our names on it. And, boy, doesn't he love using that stamp!"

The rest of the company grizzled their agreement to that sentiment.

Secretly, Cattle shared their disgruntlement. It was one thing to lead an assault on some foreign city — he'd done that more times than he could count over the last twenty or so years — but it hit a bit differently when it was your fellow countrymen you were coming up against.

But orders were orders, and it was not for him, and certainly not for the likes of Corporal Jinks, to question them.

He cleared his throat and looked meaningfully at the

grate on the sewer outlet before them. His men took the hint and returned to sawing through the ancient metal grille.

Orders were to secure this hidden entry point to the City and secure it they would. They were then to make their way through the winding tunnels — of which, thanks to inside information, they had a detailed map — and establish a base for covert operations.

They would not be the ones doing the covert operations, of course — Cattle's company was good for grunt work and no more — but they would certainly be closer to the enemy earlier than most of the others in the King's army.

"Enemy."

Cattle chewed on that word for a while with distaste. He had a cousin who had moved to Swinford a few years back. It felt funny to think of her connected to such an idea. Of late, there'd been a lot of words like that thrown towards those who lived in the West. "Rebels." "Traitors." "Mutineers."

Something about it all did not sit right with Cattle, but his was not to reason why. The King had spoken, and the West was to be brought back in line. And if there needed to be some blood spilt to make that happen, then that was how it would be.

He was moved away from that train of thought by a huge crash, followed by equally loud cursing, as the grille came loose and fell to the floor.

Everyone in the company tensed whilst waiting to see if the noise attracted any attention. But no. It was as their information had suggested: no one had thought to keep an eye on this potential weak spot in the City's fortifications.

Although, Cattle had mused, it was not like there was a shortage of such weaknesses. In all his years, he had never seen a City wall so inviting for a breach. "Like a whore raising her skirts", was how Jinks had put it.

He'd heard Swinford was one of the greatest Cities in the West. If that was so, they would roll over these people like a bear on a termite mound.

"Making enough noise, boys?"

There were muted apologies sent his way as what was left of the gate was pulled aside. Cattle looked over his company. He knew the name of each and every one of the hundred faces turned towards him. They were not the best or the brightest that the King had to call on, but they would get the job done, more often than not. More than that, though, they could be relied upon in a pinch. In many ways, they were the precise model of their Captain.

"Form up. Sergeants, you know your business. Get your squads in, set up and wait for the fancy dans to show themselves when all the hard work is done and dusted. I want choke points established all the way through, and if I catch anyone . . ."

His voice trailed off as he realised no one was listening to him. With an uncustomed flare of irritation, he turned to look at what in the tunnel was so interesting to his men.

There, just caught by the edge of their torchlight, was an extremely familiar figure indeed. She was tall and powerfully built, with a two-handed greatsword strapped to her back. There was no sign of the helmet from which she took her name, but that face was familiar enough to every man who stood before her.

There were a few moments of silence before Cattle moved towards her.

"My Lady Darkhelm . . ."

*

She'd been impressed by the efficiency of the men dismantling the sewer grate. There was nothing showy about how they went about it, and, with relatively little ceremony, there was yet another gap in Swinford's defences.

Not for the first time, she had cause to question this course of action. For sure, she could personally hold these narrow tunnels until the end of time. But she could not be everywhere. Was this, honestly, where Taelsin felt she would make the greatest difference?

She had known Cattle for decades. First as a Private, then as a Sergeant, and she had been pleased when she heard he had been moved to the officer's mess. He was a sound man, and if he was never going to achieve feats of staggering heroism, neither was he the type to shirk his responsibilities.

She smiled at him as he walked towards her position.

"My Lady Darkhelm. I was hoping our paths would not cross in this business."

"It is good to see you, too. And it's Captain Kettle now, I am given to understand."

"Just doing my bit, my Lady. You know how it is. People ask, and it don't seem right to let them down."

"I know how that can be."

They stood facing each other for a time. Both of them comfortable in the silence and used to outwaiting their opponent. Eventually, Cattle broke first.

"Seems we've got ourselves a bit of a situation here."

"Seems like we do," Daine agreed neutrally.

"I guess you're not here to help my boys find their way through the sewers?"

"I am not, I'm afraid."

"You have your own orders?"

"I do, Captain. You know how those in charge like giving them."

"Honest truth. They do love them some orders." Cattle took off his helmet and rubbed a hand through sweat-slicked hair. "You see, I think we might have one of those conflicts of interest here, my Lady. I've got my orders to go into those tunnels, and I guess you've got some of your own to stop my boys doing that. That sound fair?"

"Sounds very fair, Captain."

"Don't suppose you can be persuaded to turn a blind eye?"

"I am sorry, Captain. It is not your boys with whom I am especially concerned. You will just be establishing the supply route, I assume?"

Cattle nodded. If he knew one thing for absolute certainty, it was that you did not lie to the Darkhelm. "But there will be all sorts of ne'er-do-wells coming after you to make use of the work you do. Those who are giving me my orders feel I should put a stop to that sharpish."

"So we are at an impasse, my Lady?"

"I fear we are, Captain."

Cattle replaced his helmet and looked back on his company. He grimaced and turned back to Daine. "They're good lads, my Lady. I'd ask you to go as easy as you can on them. Not a one of them understands what we're doing here in the West. Not sure I do myself, to tell the truth. If you can see your way clear to letting them fall back when the time comes, I'd take that as a personal favour." He nodded respectfully at her and started making his way back towards his men. "Never thought the day would come I'd cross blades with the Darkhelm."

His soldiers were looking at him with alarm. It was one thing to infiltrate a rebel city; it was quite another to do so with the Lady Darkhelm opposing you. Even those who had not fought at her side had heard all the songs. There were few illusions as to how a confrontation with her was going to end.

Then she called out. "Captain, if we both agree, I might have another suggestion. It would need your men to agree, though, of course."

He cast his eye over the white faces of his men.

"I'm confident in saying, my Lady, that my boys are very open to conversations as to alternative methods of conflict resolution that do not involve you killing us all."

"I always liked you, Cattle."

"Feeling's mutual, my Lady."

*

"And, quite out of nowhere, the Lady Darkhelm pulled down the tunnel's ceiling on top of you?"

"Yes, my Lord."

"Trapping all your equipment, the supplies for Captain Maretti's squad and sundry other crucial materiel on her side of the collapse?"

"Yes, my Lord."

"It is worth noting, at this point, that not a single one of your men was either injured or similarly cut off in this action?"

"No, my Lord. Extraordinarily lucky timing."

"Quite. You are aware, of course, that collaboration

with the enemy is an executionable offence, Captain Kettle?"

"Yes, my Lord. No collaborators in my company, my Lord."

A new voice, a softer one, joined in the questioning. "If that is so, how do you account for this outcome, Captain Kettle? You do not have a reputation as an ineffective leader of men. Nor as a coward. How can such a calamity occur, and yet every single one of your men walks away?"

Cattle looked the new speaker in the eye. "I am sorry, my Lord, what level of casualties would have been acceptable to you?"

There was an awkward silence.

Finally, the first speaker took over. "No apologies necessary, Captain. We are all relieved that you were able to extricate your men unharmed from a confrontation with the Darkhelm. How long do you think it will take to excavate the sewer entrance for us to try again?"

"Couple of days, sir. Course, she'll probably just do the same thing again. Heard she's stubborn like that. If you want my advice, my Lord?"

"Please," the speaker said dryly.

"You're going to need to get up pretty early in the morning to sneak one past the Darkhelm. If you don't have a plan as to how to bring her down, we might want to think about leaving pacifying Swinford for later. Maybe choose an easier nut to crack first."

The second speaker, the one Cattle didn't recognise, smiled without humour. "Well, fortunately, *Captain,* we do indeed have a solution to the problem of the Darkhelm."

The first speaker, his direct superior Major Fadarn,

nodded. "Re-equip your men and start digging out that tunnel. From what I understand, the Lady Darkhelm will soon have enough on her plate to stop her playing silly games in tunnels."

CHAPTER SEVEN

Defenestration as Therapy

Taelsin rubbed both hands over his face. He had been doing that a lot lately, as if the gesture was as if he were trying to wake himself up from a particularly disconcerting dream.

"Not that I don't appreciate the sentiment, Lady Darkhelm, but I am not sure we should so easily eschew opportunities to reduce the numbers arrayed against us."

He looked old, Daine thought.

Recent pressures had added lines to his face and grey to his hair that should be decades away. He was, what, mid-twenties? The transformation, now she reflected on it, was quite shocking. When he had walked into the room, there was a stiffness to his movement that suggested he had fallen asleep at his desk once again.

If ever there needed to be a monument to the burdens of leadership, Mayor Elm's ashen demeanour would be it.

She bit back her initial reply, mindful of his exhaustion. "I have committed to defending your City, Mayor Elm. And I shall do so to the best of my ability. But I will not carelessly slaughter men I have so recently called 'friend.' Neither, I should say, do I think you would truly ask me to do so. After all, you have your erstwhile Secretary available for such acts should they be required."

At the mention of his name, Donal glanced up from his reading. Neither Taelsin nor Daine let their eyes linger on the subject matter of that particular scroll. Some things were hard to forget once seen. "Quite. For the record, my Lord, I think the Lady Darkhelm did the right thing. We know there is much sympathy for our position amongst the common folk — our most potent asset displaying such mercy in the face of provocation will be a significant propaganda victory. If I did not know better, I would accuse our Knight of the Road of playing politics."

Taelsin grimaced. "I fear moral victories are unlikely to count for much in the final equation. You all read the same reports as I. Thousands of men will be at our gate before the week is out. And it is no secret our walls will not hold." He released a long breath and rolled his neck. "But you both make a valid point. I apologise, Lady Darkhelm. You are, of course, entirely correct in your assessment of the situation. The loss of one company in such a manner would surely have hurt our cause more than helped."

"In those circumstances, my Lord, there is all the more reason not to kill when we can show mercy. I predict we will soon need to seek the same courtesy from the King. Indeed, whilst we have been at odds of late, I congratulate the Lady Darkhelm on her restraint this day. And, my

Lord, I petition again that we open the gates to the approaching army and beseech a parley."

All eyes turned to the fourth member of this meeting: Lady Gerol.

Donal was the first to reply. "Of course, we would each agree that exploring alternative paths to success is always sensible. In that, I am agog at Lady Gerol's perspicacity."

There was a pause.

"Ah, bless her heart. She does not know what 'perspicacity' means, my Lord. Shall I explain?"

Taelsin nodded, his eyes cold. "Please do, Donal."

Donal walked towards the seated elderly woman. "It means 'insight,' it means 'foreknowledge,' it means — to speak plain — that we were all quite surprised, and rather impressed, at the speed with which you were able to leak information that the sewers were undefended."

Her mouth opened and closed as the Dark Warlord loomed over her. "I do not know what you mean, Master Whatever-you-are." She turned to Taelsin in appeal. "My Lord, am I to suffer this continuous barrage of insults? Your father would never —"

"My father is dead, Lady Gerol. A fact we all grieve. But my father loved Swinford and would wish for me to do what I could to take the freedom within our grasp."

"With your pardon, my Lord, I hazard I knew your father well. I would say this would not be the path he would choose."

Taelsin stood with his back against one of the many stained glass windows that decorated the Keep. The beauty in the profusion of light that framed him at this moment was truly quite remarkable. "My father did not like you, my Lady. He found you to be double-speaking. He thought your loyalty unsound. He believed you responsible for any number of assassinations — both political and actual. On that point, I understand you endeavoured to achieve something similar with Donal just the other day?"

Donal flapped his hands in dismissal. "I am more than happy to let that go, my Lord. After all, I would have done the same in her position."

"Generous of you, sir. What say you, Lady Gerol? Any words of thanks to our Dark Warlord for his forbearance? I am unsure many of the others we suspect you of bringing similarly low would be so kind." Taelsin's voice was oddly genial.

Lady Gerol saw her near future coalescing around her. But she had not achieved her position in life by folding at the first sign of trouble. She raised her chin and met the Mayor's eye. "I have never heard anything so preposterous, my Lord. I have worked my whole life to bring wealth and prosperity to this City. To hear my long service so disparaged is very upsetting. What would I gain from betraying Swinford to the King?"

Taelsin nodded understandingly. "Lady Gerol has an excellent point, Donal. What would she have to gain from such a betrayal?"

"A million gold bars is my understanding, my Lord. Shall I check?" Donal turned away from the suddenly cringing woman. He plucked a number of letters from a pile on his desk and started to glance through them. "Yes, yes, I was right. A million gold bars. Half now, which I understand are already in the Gerol vault, and half on . . . bear with me, I'd like to quote this bit directly." He held one of the letters up and peered at it as if he were shortsighted. "*The remainder to be paid when the whelp is dead, and the people of Swinford are brought to heel.* I must say, Lady Gerol, I speak for the people of Swinford when I tell you how deeply proud we are to have had our lives purchased for such a sum."

The elderly woman was on her feet and looking around at the faces arrayed against her with something akin to desperation. "My Lords. My Lady. I do not understand how such things can be. I swear, on my life . . ."

Donal beamed his bright smile. "Excellent. That seems like a very sensible way for us to bring things to a conclusion. One of the more interesting skills of this new Class is that I can make Oath-Contracts. Should you wish to 'swear on your life that you have not passed information to the King's forces,' I am happy to facilitate that."

Taelsin nodded along. "I am sure Donal will even sweeten the pot by noting that should his accusations prove to have no basis, he will forfeit his own life in compensation."

Donal's smile lessened a touch. "Well, I must say I am not delighted to have my life wagered in such a casual manner, but I do agree with my Lord's suggestion."

Lady Gerol's mind whirled, seeking to think of any form of words she could make as an Oath which she could survive. Eventually, though, she succumbed to the inevitable and approached Taelsin.

"So be it. I will not continue this charade any further. Yes, Taelsin, I have done what your Secretary suspects. And more. To speak the truth, I would do so again and willingly. Your leadership of this City had been a travesty. Swinford will fall because of your arrogance."

Taelsin nodded. "Your comments are noted, Lady Gerol. In response, I say that, just as I harshly view the depredations of the Crown on the people of Swinford, so too do I judge the actions of my Nobles who have put personal profit ahead of the common good. That, at our time of greatest need, you would seek to enrich yourself at the expense of the lives of my people is a crime I cannot forgive. Both the Lady Darkhelm and our Dark Warlord would have me offer you clemency in exchange for information regarding the invasion. Names of co-conspirators and the like."

Donal looked quizzical at that, and coughed meaningfully. Taelsin rolled his eyes. "My apologies. The Lady Darkhelm would have me offer you mercy for information. On the other hand, Donal suggests . . . I'm sorry, what was it again?"

"That we smear her extremities in offal, bury her in the ground and have enraged fire termites chew off a limb a day until she runs out of new things to tell us."

"Yes, cannot think why I let that slip my mind. The point is, Lady Gerol, that I have listened to the thoughts of my advisors over what to do with you next."

"And what did you decide, Mayor Elm? Only you will need to be quick about it. By my reading of the landscape, your head will be on a pike this time tomorrow morning, and the army of the King will march onwards to purge the rest of the treasonous West."

"My thoughts exactly, Lady Gerol."

And with that, he opened the window and pushed her through it. After several seconds, there could be heard a loud thump.

"And?" Donal was peering through the window at what remained below.

"Yes, you were quite right. It pains me to say so, but I

do feel somewhat better. Now, to the next order of business. How do we best make use of a half-million gold
bars?"

CHAPTER EIGHT

Class Beats Attribute

"They will never stand," Daine said flatly, looking over the ragtag collection of Townfolk below her.

"You'd be surprised, my dear. When you have nowhere left to run, you can stand pretty damn firm."

Daine turned to narrow her eyes at the Dark Warlord. "When did 'my dear' become a thing, sir? I liked you better when you showed appropriate respect."

"No, you didn't."

Ignoring him, she stepped forward to address the men and women who had been gathered to defend the north wall. She had similar inspections planned throughout the day and was not anticipating seeing anything more impressive than what she was looking at right now.

Still, it was not their fault. Their nervous chatter stilled as they sensed she was preparing to speak to them. Their eyes grew wide as they took in her armed form and, instinctively huddled together as a response to a threat. That was an excellent way to get themselves killed in the first salvo, she thought.

"I am not one for speeches, ladies and gentlemen. Indeed, I fancy I have already said more to you this morning than I have a hundred of my sworn companions."

That raised a few smiles. The taciturnity of the Darkhelm was, quite literally, the stuff of legends.

"But what need you of speeches? We all know the task we will face. An army will soon seek to enter your city, and it is for us to stop them. They will aim to break down these walls, and we will force them back. They will endeavour to kill those beside you, and you will stop them. The West has decreed that it will be free, and we will do our uttermost to make it so."

Daine had not expected a cheer, and, in that, she was not disappointed. Hundreds of scared, haunted faces looked up at her. They were clearly not soldiers — of course they were not — but she had hoped to see some flaring spark of defiance in their eyes. They looked beaten already. Most of them were not even armed, and for those who were merely brandishing the tools of their Class. She could see Butchers with their knives, Labourers with giant shovels and Farmers with pitchforks.

"Goddess," she whispered under her breath. "This is going to be a massacre."

Her mind cast back to a time long ago, she might have been nine or ten, when Old Gant was — as was his custom, a few drinks in — explaining the ways of the world.

"Now, your average Blacksmith, you see, he has more Strength than your common-or-garden Spearman, right. Big arms, you ken? Huge biceps, bigger than tree trunks.

They come with the Class. So you'd think, wouldn't you, that, in a scrap, it would go badly for the poor Private in the King's army?"

They had all mutely nodded at his question. One of the first things you learned at Gant's School was that, whilst the majority of his questions were rhetorical, it did not pay to fail to respond. Broken ribs and jaws encouraged quick learning, even for those who healed as quickly as his students.

"But it rarely does. Doesn't that make you think? What about this? An Armourer can have two, sometimes even three times the Strength of the mouthy Sergeant who keeps needing his sword bending back into shape. Two or three times! But damn me if doesn't keep a civil tongue in his head each time he repairs it because he understands the truth of it."

"The truth of what, Master Stonehand?"

"I'm glad you asked. Class beats Attribute, boys and girls. Every day of the week and twice with a belt on a Moonday. Consider our Sergeant with his bent sword. He's got some Strength, to be sure, but nowhere near what the Armourer possesses. He's probably got less Constitution and definitely less Dexterity. So why is the Armourer 'yes-sirring' and 'no-sirring', rather than giving him a piece of his mind?"

There was an awkward silence. Then one of the older boys grasped the nettle. "Because Class beats Attribute, Master Stonehand?"

"Exactly. Extra rations tonight for your squad. Class beats Attribute. The Armourer's Class gives him all sorts of perks that are perfect for hitting pieces of hot metal. He might even have a skill like <Fire Shield> or <Shatter>

to call upon, depending on how talented he is. Useful things like that when you're working in a forge. Crucially, though, what he won't have is anything that can do much to counter a Sergeant in, say, a <Stone Combat> stance. Our hammer-swinging friend can have all the advantage in Strength he likes, but that ain't doing him much good against a <Bull Rush>, you get me? Class beats Attribute. Every. Single. Time. And Classed soldiers versus Classed civilians only has one outcome. And it ain't pretty."

Stood atop a crumbling wall, looking down on a host of nervous defenders, Daine sincerely wished she had not recalled that memory.

The silence had stretched too long, and the crowd were shuffling awkwardly. Donal cleared his throat. "I am aware I am still finding my feet in this new Class. Thus, I accept I might not be reading the subtleties of body language or the atmosphere here quite correctly, but — and apologies for my impertinence — I think you need to get the stick out of your arse."

"Pardon me, sir?"

"These people are scared, Lady Darkhelm. They have no idea what to expect in the coming days and are looking to you to make sense of things for them. None of them have ever been in a real scrap before, but they are willing to stand the line and protect their homes. They deserve some respect for that, and — much more than that — they need you to tell them it is going to all be okay."

"But it is not all going to be okay, sir. There's an army of soldiers on the horizon, and Class beats Attribute every time."

"Begging my pardon, my Lady — see, I remembered — which colossal moron told you that?"

She was so staggered by his words that her reply caught in her throat.

"Because, as someone who has experienced more than his fair share of Classes — I daresay I would be one of the foremost experts in this area — that is the single most stupid thing I have ever heard. Class beats Attribute? Consider that to its logical conclusion, my dear. You were born with exceptional Strength, yes?"

"Indeed, sir. I was born into a family of Farmers."

"And someone — the fabled Gallant Stonehand? — recognised your potential in that Attribute and with, I presume, torturous training, built upon it to the extent you qualified for a Class change?"

Daine nodded.

"And you caught the eye of the Goddess, she became your patron and triggered your evolution into a Knight of the Road?"

She nodded again. To hear her history so condensed was . . . uncomfortable.

"So, my Lady Darkhelm, just focusing on your own experience for a moment. Which came first — the Class or the Attribute? Or, to think of it another way, if Class always beats Attribute, how did a Farmer rise to be one of the most storied warriors of our age?"

Daine was so unused to questioning the shibboleths of Old Gant that she had no response to Donal's words.

"I am the last person to tell you that Class does not matter. My whole existence has been built around the shedding of one Class for another; always seeking the most appropriate tool for the job in hand. So, I agree that Class matters. I am more able to help defend Swinford as a Dark Warlord than I was when in the form of a Secretary. But each Class is built upon a foundation of, not separate from, each individual's core attributes. If what I say is false, then surely every single Knight of the Road would be have identical capabilities. Tell me, is that true?"

She pursed her lips. Those who shared her Class — those who were left, in any event — were as different as grains of sand on the shore.

"So, and I will cease my lecture after this final, devastating point, if all you see when you look down on these people are irrelevant Attributes within useless Classes, then, for sure, you are looking at sheep ready for the abattoir."

The small crowd continued to stare upwards, clearly aware that the two figures were discussing them. Craning their necks, they looked nothing so like birds awaiting worms from their mother. The simile did little to brighten Daine's mood.

"I hear your words, sir, and I shall think upon them. The world may, perhaps, have more complexity than I have been taught to believe. However, theory does not displace reality. You are right that I see nothing but a disaster waiting to happen to yonder folk. Tell me, what do see?"

Donal grinned wolfishly, the expression somewhat incongruous on his elderly face. "I see potential, my dear. Lots and lots of untapped potential."

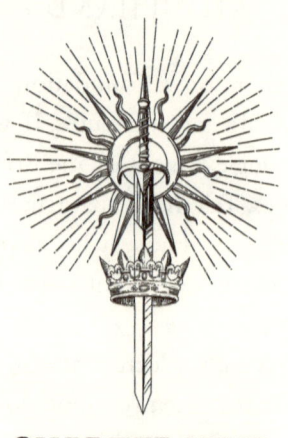

CHAPTER NINE

Tricks up Sleeves

Daine organised the defenders into pairs and assigned each unit a section of wall to defend. As she moved them around, their hushed conversations and furtive glances did little to change her opinion of their stoutness. Siege warfare was not for amateurs; she saw little likelihood of them repelling even a modest, probing assault.

Things improved somewhat after the Dark Warlord drew a rune on one of the crumbling battlements. As he completed the final line, the arcane drawing started to emit a sinister green light. This had the effect of those on the wall standing up straighter.

Daine raised an inquiring eyebrow.

"Calm down, my dear. It's a classic siege rune. 'Stiffen Sinew,' if you want to know. Every major assault since the beginning of time has used some version of it to help boost defenders' morale."

"I flatter myself that I have been involved in some significant clashes in my years, sir. I have never heard of such a rune. Certainly" — she frowned at the sickly glow emanating — "I have never seen its like before in a siege."

Donal grinned, an expression the Knight of the Road was rapidly learning to treat with suspicion. "Fair enough. I may be exaggerating as to its commonality. Ever so slightly. But I'm sure more people would use it if they knew about it. Besides, I've barely adapted it at all."

Daine looked at the men and women on the wall and, she had to admit, noted that their nervous energy had largely dissipated. It had been replaced with a calm, steely resolve that she would have expected to see from veterans, not untested civilians.

"So it has removed their fear?"

"Sure." Even to his own ears, Donal could hear the evasiveness he injected into that one word. He quickly expanded his explanation as Daine made to move towards him. "The rune's primary function is to improve the courage of all within its range. Think of it as providing a magically augmented backbone for everyone around it. It does not encourage them to suicidal bravery, if that is what is worrying you. Each and every one of our brave warriors is still perfectly in possession of their own judgment. They're just much harder to rout when the going gets tough. And I am sure I do not need to remind you that the going will soon get very tough indeed."

"And that is all this rune does?"

His smile was back. "It also has a few other effects that may prove useful."

"Such as?"

"My dear, I swear on any deity who may be listening

that I mean no harm to these people. Anything and everything I do here is to improve their chances of surviving this encounter. Do you think there's one of them that would turn down any help I could provide?"

"So why the equivocation, sir? If yon rune is entirely benign, why not explain its effects to me? Why the evasiveness?"

Donal eyes flashed, and Daine felt an overwhelming need, quickly quashed, to run and hide. When he spoke, his voice lacked its usual geniality. "I took you at your word, Lady Darkhelm, that we had drawn a line under your suspicion of me. I can do no more than swear, and swear again, that whilst my current Class may be disquieting to you, my motivations and intentions should not be. I do not foresee how we will survive this siege without access to the unique powers and talents of the Dark Warlord Skillset. I have been charged with assisting you in the City's defence, and in this, I will not let Taelsin down. But if you will not let me play my part, my full part, I do not see a hope for our success."

He speaks the truth. As he perceives it.

Daine wished the Goddess had not added that second sentence.

"I apologise, sir. I am not finding adjusting to the foibles of your new form easy."

With that, she nodded awkwardly and moved to address the defenders. When she was out of earshot, he found himself muttering, "Neither am I, Lady Darkhelm, neither am I."

*

"If you forget everything else I am about to tell you, please remember this: defending a wall is much easier than attacking it. All you need to do is hold your section and protect your partner." Daine was unnerved by the expressions on the faces turned towards her. Gone was any hint of fear, replaced by determination. She had feared they would run at the first engagement; now she was worried they would seek to hold when there was no chance of survival.

"We stay low, and we stay quiet. We keep them guessing where we are positioned. No one pops their head up to have a look at what is coming. That is my role. Unless anyone else here can heal from a bolt through the throat, of course?" She had hoped to break the tension with a smile or two, maybe even a laugh. Their silence, though, was disconcerting. Donal's attempts at helping through manic giggling and ostentatious thigh-slapping were likewise not especially welcome.

"For those with a bow, wait for the right shot and make it count. No wasting arrows; we need to spend our resources wisely."

"If I could, Lady Darkhelm?"

Frowning at the interruption, she gave the floor to Donal.

"Let's talk about arrows for a second. Do we have any Carpenters here?" One hand raised. "Let's talk about your talents. What you got?"

"I'm afraid nothing unusual, my Lord. My family have never been blessed in that way."

"I don't need unusual, I need you to have something like <Efficient Splinters> or <Frugal Shaving>. Even <Improvised Materials> would work."

"I have <Frugal Shaving>, my Lord. I'm not sure . . ."

"Excellent. Now, where are my Labourers?" Four or five hands were raised. "Anyone with <Double Bubble>?" Heads shook in response. "Blast, I suppose that would have been too lucky. How about, I don't know, <Clean and Jerk>?" With puzzled expressions, two burly men stepped forward.

"Now we're talking. Sorry to make changes to your carefully considered formations, Lady Darkhelm, but can we get Master . . ." He looked at the Carpenter expectantly.

"Mount, sir."

"Master Mount, if you can set yourself up a little way behind your brave fellows with you two" — he pointed at the Labourers — "there in support."

All eyes turned to Daine, and she nodded approval. She was not sure what the Dark Warlord had planned, but she had already expressed her lack of faith in him once this day. To do so again would be churlish.

Donal had taken a quiver off one of the archers, an old Poacher, and tipped out the arrows in front of the be-mused Carpenter. He sketched a rune at his feet, which again glowed with that sickly green light.

"Can you see any improvements you could make to any of those arrows, Master Mount?"

The Carpenter looked down at the pile in front of him. Clearly, they were all self-made and were somewhat of a hodgepodge. He bent to pick one up and held it in his hand, checking for balance. His nose wrinkled with dis-taste, and he quickly removed a whittling knife from his belt. After a few strokes, he rechecked it and seemed satis-fied. He held it out, uncertainly, to Donal.

The Dark Warlord shook his head and indicated for

him to pass it to the biggest of the Labourers. "From what I understand, this won't work if I touch it."

The second the arrow passed from the Carpenter to the Labourer, the rune's green light intensified. The big man holding the arrow suddenly swore and dropped it to the ground. Yet it was not one arrow that clattered to the stone, but three.

"Excellent. I had hoped for five, but let us not allow the pursuit of perfection to become the enemy of the good. Gentlemen, that all seems to be working as intended. Now, while we see what other surprises we can prepare for the King's army, please ensure our Archers are well supplied. I am sure I do not need to state the obvious, but make sure there is always one arrow left in reserve to be improved. Oh, and Master Labourers?"

The two big men's eyes grew wide, turning to look at Donal. Something about his demeanour transformed, and they physically shrank back. "Should Master Mount fall in the assault, your usefulness to our endeavour reduces dramatically. Please make sure he is well protected." They stammered out their reply, and, in seconds, the little group were churning out packets of arrows that were quickly dropped off next to grateful marksmen.

Daine watched them work briefly before shaking her head in wonder. "As I was saying, Archers, please fire indiscriminately. Let them have it as soon as anyone is within anything close to your range. I want to see pincushions climbing up their ladders."

She met Donal's eye and smiled. "Now, before we discuss how we will conduct the defence further, sir, I assume you have other such tricks up your sleeve?"

He returned her smile. "Like you wouldn't believe, my dear. Like you wouldn't believe."

But, the sudden sound of horns wiped all smiles from faces. For the army of the King had appeared on the horizon.

CHAPTER TEN

Chaos and Chimaeras

Droughton-on-the-Water — thirty years ago.

Daine flinched at the blaring of the horns. She could not comprehend a Town that thought this was an appropriate way to mark the passage of time.

No wonder everyone was always on edge.

With a deep breath to still her nerves, she cast her eyes back to the building which, apparently, represented the conclusion of their long walk.

"It's a house."

"Yes. Yes, it is."

"A normal house. Door, chimney, windows. A house."

"You have described it artfully, my Lady. Never let it be said you do not possess a poet's soul. A house, it is."

Daine sheathed the sword she had instinctively drawn when the Priestess had announced, "We're there." She was unsure what she had expected, but it was far more than this.

"And it is within this house that, your Archbishop be-lieves, there resides a mirror that eats people. A mirror that has transformed numerous dwellers of this Town into Soulless. The mirror you need me to destroy. That mirror. In this house."

"Yes."

"The house with the little old lady looking through the window and beckoning us to come in?"

"I acknowledge this is not quite as foreboding a setting as I expected, but the directions were clear."

"She appears to have baked something she is keen to share with us."

"Well, it won't be a wasted journey then, will it?"

Daine's mind whirled. She could sense the Goddess at-tempting to draw her attention to something about the place, but —

"My Lady, are we planning to stand here all night? I rec-ognise long periods staring at nothing might be your usual way of spending the evening, but I would appreciate bring-ing this quest to a halt before the advent of my fourth decade."

Daine turned to face the Priestess, and what Bayran saw in those eyes made her hastily add, "But of course, I am at my Lady's disposal. I meant no disrespect with my words."

But Daine kept looking at her, waiting for the curtsey that etiquette demanded was offered with such an apology. Gritting her teeth, Bayran dipped down, her legs screaming at returning to this posture.

Daine let her stay in position for a few agonising

moments before nodding in acknowledgement and returning her gaze to the house.

This was not the traditional conclusion to a quest for a Knight of the Road. She should be confronting fire-breathing demons protecting their hoard, not waving back to smiling old women. This evening's search for this fell mirror had been undercut by wrongness from the start. But, try as she might, neither she nor the Goddess could quite uncover what it might be.

Old Gant had told her it was often like this when the Lords of Misrule were involved. Just their very presence, or that of their worshippers, could spiral the certainty of fate into chaos. She remembered questioning why the Goddess would allow such destruction to be wrought.

His reply had not made a lot of sense at the time. "They're her boys. The things a parent will do for their children would make you weep. Wait until you have kids of your own, Darkhelm. Then it'll all make sense." Gant had gotten particularly drunk that night.

She was pondering those words when the front door of the house opened and a tiny old lady stepped outside. In her hands was a freshly baked pie.

"Weary travellers, would you like to step inside to rest your feet? I have pie."

*

Bayran crammed another mouthful of delicious goodness into her mouth and wondered why she had never tried this flavour before. It was so good she was even beginning to find the Knight's behaviour less irksome. Marginally.

She gestured towards the plate with her knife. "Why are you not eating? You are being impolite, my Lady."

Despite the cajoling, Daine continued to push her food

around with her finger, something seemingly stopping her from taking a bite — a deep frown embedded across her forehead.

"My Lady —"

"Will you cease your interminable chatter!" Daine's temper was at breaking point. Her mind felt like it was churning earth — with something important seeking to rise from the depths against a force seeking to keep it below. From the moment she had entered this house, she could barely hear the voice of the Goddess. But what she could make out seemed uncomfortably like a warning.

The small, ancient woman who kept bringing them pies was called Brigid. She had told the two about her history at length, but for her life, Daine could not remember what she had said.

Indeed, by her reckoning, they had been in the house for at least two soundings of the horns, and Daine could not recall anything specific that had been said in that time.

The only thing of which she was clear was that there was something profoundly wrong about this old woman.

Bayran continued wolfing down platefuls of pie like she had never eaten. That was strange, was it not? A Priestess of the Inner Temple would not usually commit such gluttony, would she? Particularly not in that dress.

The old lady, her silver hair cascading in gentle waves, continued to serve plates of the pie with trembling hands, the tremor hinting at something more than old age to Daine's mind.

She frowned at the full plate in front of Daine and said something to the Knight, but the words seemed to warp in the air. Daine shook her head to clear it, but with little positive result. The Priestess, oblivious to the Knight's unease, accepted another dish with gratitude, unaware of the danger that was about to explode into life.

No. This was wrong. There was something of great power here. Strong enough to interfere with the perceptions of a Knight of the Road and to withhold the words of the Goddess.

She made eye contact with Brigid, and suddenly there it was. She could connect with and confront the sense of wrongness.

A ripple of energy coursed through Brigid's body, her small form shuddering with anticipation. The transformation had begun. Slowly, imperceptibly at first, her appearance shifted, the lines of her face stretching and contorting. Her once-soft skin grew rough and scaly while her limbs twisted and elongated, morphing into grotesque shapes. Her eyes glowed with an otherworldly light, revealing her true nature as a harbinger of chaos.

Bayran, clearly sensing the peril, pushed herself away from the table, drawing her daggers in a desperate bid to defend herself. But Brigid's complete transformation exuded a primal power, a fusion of delicate grace and formidable strength. She batted the Priestess backwards to crash against the wall. Daine watched as her companion slid to the floor — leaving a dark-red streak behind her.

Brigid's arms sprouted feathers, sharp talons replacing her fingers. Wings unfurled from her back, broadening and casting a flickering shadow over the room. Her mouth stretched into a wicked grin, revealing rows of razor-sharp teeth, each glinting with an unholy hunger.

Undeterred, Daine drew her blade, ready to face this abomination that had replaced the seemingly kindly old lady.

Brigid's wings beat the air with a thunderous roar, the Chimaera lunging at the Knight. Their clash reverberated throughout the house, the walls shuddering and fragile belongings scattering in their wake.

The old lady's feral instincts melded with her newfound form, propelling her to strike with a deadly combination of speed and savagery.

The Knight parried her onslaught skillfully and precisely, her sword meeting claws with resounding crashes. Each clash echoed with a symphony of steel as they danced a deadly waltz, their movements a flurry of calculated strikes and desperate evasions.

The Chimaera's wings beat the air, stirring up gusts of wind that threatenined to extinguish the flickering candles. Tipped with a barbed stinger, her tail whipped through the air like a venomous serpent. Daine, undeterred, dodged and countered, her blade seeking openings.

The battle raged on, both pushing their limits, neither yielding an inch. The inside of the house now bore the scars of their clash. Splintered furniture and shattered crockery littered the floor.

In desperation, the Knight's eyes locked with the Chimaera's glowing gaze. Determination burned within her, a fire that refused to be extinguished. She gathered her strength, channelling it into a flurry of blows, her sword slashing through the air relentlessly. The Chimaera, caught off guard by the sudden attack, faltered for a fraction of a second. It was all the opening Daine needed.

Her blade found its mark, piercing a vulnerable flank. A searing cry of pain erupted from the creature's twisted maw as she recoiled and stumbled backwards. Blood, a dark and viscous ichor, stained the floor.

But even in the face of defeat, Brigid did not yield. With a surge of primal fury, she lunged at Daine one final time, her talons slashing through the air.

The Knight barely managed to parry the attack before, in one swift motion, she delivered a devastating blow, her sword slicing through the Chimaera's neck with satisfying finality. The creature's body collapsed, twitching and convulsing before finally falling still.

Silence settled over the house, broken only by Daine's heavy breathing. Brigid, her transformation undone in death, lay before her, her true nature revealed in the wake of the battle. Daine knelt beside her, a mix of awe and sorrow washing over her as she surveyed the remnants of the conflict.

In that moment, she first realised "the price of victory", as Old Gant had described it. The toll taken in the clash of light and darkness that had been spoken about so often during her training.

And now she understood it. Or at least was beginning to.

A groan from Bayran pulled her out of her morbid revelry, and she moved to stand above the Priestess.

"Can you stand?"

"What happened?"

"We were ensorcelled and then set upon by a further trap laid by whoever sent the Soulless to attack us."

Bayran took Daine's proffered hand and pulled herself upwards. "The mirror? Have you found it?"

"No. Because it's not here. As I think you well know."

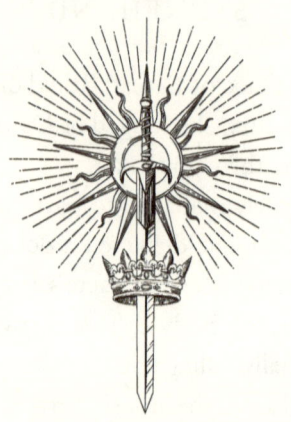

CHAPTER ELEVEN

"Scorched the Snake, Not Killed It."

"I must say, now we are here, it hardly seems worth the effort to have marched all this way." General Souit lowered his spyglass and turned to the others behind him on the hill. "One good firm push at the northern wall, flood the breach with regulars, and we'll all be having tea and crumpets with Mayor Elm before nightfall."

A few glances were exchanged between the General's staff before Major Degralk, a Pikeman who had risen, improbably, through the ranks, decided his time had come. If anyone was to risk the General's displeasure, it might as well be he. Not that the others would thank him for his sacrifice, of course. "My Lord, there is the matter of the Lady Darkhelm . . ."

Souit barely kept the sneer from his face as he regarded the burly Major. It was beyond his comprehension that the King indulged such specimens. You were born to a role in life, and in that position, you should stay. It was how it always had been in the Kingdom and, to his mind, was how it should always remain. As far as he was concerned, this modern fashion the King supported for "appointing by merit" was the thin end of a sizeable wedge. He had no doubt the Major could stand his ground and hold a long, heavy piece of metal aloft. Good for him. He was to be praised for his obduracy. But to raise him to a level far beyond his capacity and capability was unkind and unnatural.

After all, was he not preparing to raze a City to the ground precisely because those within had ideas above their station? Secession from the Crown. Never had he expected to hear such things considered, let alone enacted. But was such treason not the logical extension of allowing Pikemen to advise Lords? He hoped when all this unpleasantness was done with, there would be an opportunity for His Majesty to reflect on some of his rasher decisions of late and their far-reaching consequences.

"The Lady Darkhelm, sir? And what is your concern? You haven't been listening to all those tavern songs, have you?"

The other members of staff — though not all, by any means — laughed dutifully.

A lesser man would have shuffled uncomfortably under such a wave of scorn, but Degralk has stood his ground against far more imposing foes than Souit or his weak-chinned enablers. If these buffoons thought a sarcastic tone and some mild braying would wither him, they needed to spend some time facing down a determined cavalry charge.

"Never had much time for taven songs, my Lord. Too busy fighting. But I'm not the only one to have seen the

Lady with sword drawn. We'd be wise to consider how best
to counter the threat she will pose to any assault."

Souit gestured to the army forming up in front of the
gates of Swinford. The horns within the City that had
started to sound when his skirmishes had crested the hill
had fallen, mercifully, silent. "Sir, I have no doubt she is a
formidable warrior. But she is one woman against thousands. Had Swinford been in possession of strong, high
walls, I may have indulged your concern. But — see!
There's barely a span of stone worthy of defending, and
even then, our sources say they lack the men to do so with
any surety. I could bring this City to its knees with a third,
nay a quarter, of the forces I have available."

"But the Lady Darkhelm . . ."

Souit grew red-faced. "You forget yourself, sir. This
may be appropriate conduct in the ranks, but a gentleman
knows his place on my staff. I have listened to your worries, and I tell you the Lady Darkhelm is a minor concern
in the forthcoming engagement. The tall tales of the abilities of one Knight of the Road are not enough to cause
me to reconsider our order of battle. We will proceed as
planned."

Degralk shrugged. He had executed his duty to share
his concerns and could do no more than that. His reading
of Souit was that the man needed to be hit in the face by
reality before he acknowledged it existed. He only hoped
not too many of the men needed to die before that happened. "Apologies, my Lord. As you note, I am no gentleman. I speak as I find."

"And we are so very grateful, sir, for the benefit of
your advice and experience in such matters." Souit's tone
dripped with insincerity. "Now, provided no one else is

soiling their breeches at the thought of one Lady Knight, why don't we quickly test the mettle of the defenders?"

At his sign, a trumpet sounded, and four elegantly dressed Mages stepped up from within the ranks of soldiers. They were quite some distance apart, arrayed so that each faced a different section of the northern wall.

"Nothing too dramatic, I think. Just let them know we're here for now."

The trumpet sounded again, three short, discordant notes, and the Mages began weaving their spells.

Souit nodded to himself, well pleased with his morning so far.

*

Daine eyed the Mage who was standing almost directly opposite her.

She had, once the King's army had crested the hill and begun forming up for an imminent assault, left the disposition of the defenders to Donal. By their grins and excited chatter as they moved around her, she was sure there were a host of malevolent surprises in store for the attackers.

She just wished she could share in their newfound confidence.

An immediate strike by the besiegers was not unexpected but was profoundly unwelcome. That whoever was in charge down there had determined the weakness of the walls was such that no further preparations were needed spoke of arrogance but also — sadly — was a reasonably accurate assessment.

"You seem rather troubled for a commander whose archers have limitless ammunition, my dear."

Donal was at her side, leaning over the battlement to regard the Mage.

"Had I a thousand archers, I would indeed feel my troubles float away on wings of joy. I fear this handful will merely sting the beast to greater fury rather than stop it in its tracks."

But Donal did not appear to be listening. "Interesting," he said, "the spell she's casting is really quite loose."

"Loose?"

"Sorry, that does not explain it well. What I mean is that she — I presume she is a Fire Mage with some sort of Battle aspect — has not tethered the fireball she is preparing to her soul space. It is . . . 'loose' is my best word for what I am seeing, my dear. It is quite a sloppy way to work with an element that could literally blow up in your face if you lose concentration. In the normal run of things, of course, I am sure this would not be a problem. She is stood considerably out of bow range, after all. In the normal run of things."

Their eyes met, and Donal winked.

"Shall I see if I can find you a bow, my Lady?"

*

Souit tried to make sense of what had just happened.

One moment, his Mages were preparing to soften up the walls of Swinford and the next . . .

"Sir, we need Healers and a fire team down there right now. Sir? Can you hear me, sir?"

He was aware of someone pulling at the sleeve of his jacket. But he couldn't tear his eyes away from the sight of the left-hand side of his army in flames.

His attention had been drawn to an archer standing on the top of the north wall, a vast longbow in their hands. He had snorted at the temerity — did these Westerners genuinely believe he would be so foolish as to allow his Mages in anything close to range?

But then they had released, and amusement had turned to horror. The arrow streaked into the air and then fell, crossing an astonishing distance, in a parabolic arc directly into the chest of the Mage to the extreme left of the formation.

That was calamity enough. The King had particularly exhorted him as to the importance of protecting the Mages he had been afforded. But then, as the Mage fell, the spell she had been casting tore loose and expanded in a way he did not understand to engulf the soldiers formed behind her.

The sound of screaming and the smell of burning flesh were like nothing else he had ever experienced on a battlefield.

"Sir, what would you have us do?"

Braggart he might be, but Souit had not been placed in charge of this expedition on connections and patronage alone. He quickly recovered his composure and began issuing orders, and, in no time, the blaze was under control, burns were being treated, and the army had withdrawn, slightly, further back from the walls of Swinford.

"I don't know if you noticed, my Lord . . ." An unwelcome voice came from behind him.

Souit turned to regard the inscrutable face of Major Degalk. "Noticed what, sir?"

"The archer, my Lord. They appeared to be wearing plate armour."

Despite the events of the last bell, Souit found it within him to summon up untapped reserves of scorn. "I think you should try to keep your flights of fancy to yourself, sir. An archer in full armour! Who ever heard of such a thing?"

As he stormed off, he chose to ignore the additional, "I imagine their helmet would be pretty black, too, my Lord."

*

They watched, in silence, as fire consumed scores of enemy soldiers.

Daine had thrown the shattered bow down over the parapet. No matter how good the Carpenter, she had turned it into kindling with that one shot.

"Few cheeky Runes of Combustion on the arrow shaft, if you're wondering, my Lady."

"I assumed."

"They seem to have interacted fairly explosively with the fireball the Mage was preparing."

"That they did, sir."

"Not sure I quite expected it to cause such a conflagration, though."

Daine let that lie hang in the air for them both to recognise and acknowledge.

Donal broke the silence first. "I imagine you are probably feeling a little conflicted about what has just happened." He was watching her face carefully. "I am of the view that we need to make the price of taking Swinford unpalatable to the King. Burning hundreds of his soldiers alive will certainly make it taste less appetising."

"You mistake me, sir. I am entirely reconciled to the value of a brief, violent example. We have bought our preparations at least a further few bells, maybe even a day before they try us again."

"Then what is the source of your ambivalence?"

"We have scorched the snake, not killed it. I fear the lesson they will take from this is not to leave us be, but rather that they need to come at us all the harder."

Daine cast her eye over the devastation left behind. "I doubt there was room for compromise before. But now? Now we have caused a substantial loss of face. Now we will have to be crushed. And they have the men to do it."

They exchanged no further words as they watched the flames flicker and die.

CHAPTER TWELVE

The Dexterity of Milkmaids

D aine had been right.

The slaughter by flame of the King's army had bought the defenders of Swinford a whole day to make further preparations. Donal, in particular, had used the time well. If, that is, thought Taelsin, what he understood of the horrific plans that had been put in place could be called "well."

"But let us not forget that General Souit will have used this time equally productively. This delay is not simply because his nose is bloodied and he sits sulking. There was a plan to overwhelm us immediately. That has been repulsed, and a new plan will now be enacted."

"You give a man who lost hundreds of his soldiers to a single arrow too much credit, my Lord."

Taelsin raised his eyebrows. Since Lady Gerol's unscheduled exit through a window, the remaining members of Swinford's Nobility had been noticeably quiet during Council meetings. It seemed that brief, blessed hiatus was now over.

"Do not proffer scorn to anyone who has the misfortune to fall foul of the Lady Darkhelm, Lord Mindus. It may be beneficial to the morale of the common folk to believe the King has placed an ass in charge of his army. I would like to assume none of us are quite so foolish."

"Oh, burn!"

All eyes turned to Donal, and Taelsin clicked his tongue in irritation. "Let us all remember," Taelsin continued, that General Souit is one of three Great Generals in the Kingdom. A Class, I may remind members of this Council, we had hoped to call upon ourselves had not circumstances played out differently."

Taelsin saw Donal consider whether to quip a response and then, wisely, recognise that there was merit in silence.

"I merely note, Mayor Elm —" Lord Mindus apparently did not possess a similar instinct — "that the reputation of this Great General seems to have been much exaggerated."

"The Siege of Marek City. The Battle of Finis Pass. The South Riesen Campaign. The War of Beauran Succession." With each sentence, Daine drummed her fingers on the desk. "General Souit has well earned his position leading the King's army. Had it not been for an overconfident Mage and our Dark Warlord's instinct for mayhem, I doubt I would have been able to hold the north wall. The strategy he had prepared would have overwhelmed us."

Taelsin let that sobering assessment hover in the air above the Council.

"I presume you have not called us together for us to collectively rend our garments in despair, my Lord?"

Taelsin smiled at Lady Stelton, one of the few Council members whose company he genuinely enjoyed. He knew, of course, she would depose him in a moment if she believed it was for the good of Swinford, but that made him respect her all the more. His father had courted her before choosing to marry Taelsin's mother, and he had grown up viewing her as something akin to an eccentric aunt.

"You are correct, Lady Stelton. I have more to discuss. Primarily, I wish to discuss the evacuation of the City."

If he had expected his words to have an impact, Taelsin was destined to be disappointed. The remaining Lords and Ladies around the Council table nodded thoughtfully at his words.

"You mean to surrender, Taelsin?" Lord Mindus looked positively ecstatic at the news.

"Don't be an arse, Tomas" — Stelton's voice was withering — "he's talking about the noncombatants. You are, are you not? You have not recently received a devastating blow to the head?"

"I can confirm I am perfectly in control of my faculties, my Lady. And yes, I think we would do well to evacuate the civilian population."

"Well, not all the civilians. Just those who are not essential to the defence of the City."

Daine rumbled her disapproval. "Our definitions of 'essential' are somewhat at odds, sir. I fail to see, for example, why you have commandeered most of the Dairy District's Milkmaids."

Donal waggled his eyebrows. "Exceptional Dexterity, Lady Darkhelm. You would not believe, with appropriate encouragement, the things they can do with their fingers."

Taelsin stilled the shouts of derision from the Nobles

with a curt gesture. "Sir, whilst we appreciate you are struggling with the impetuses of your new Class, you will endeavour to remember where you are and to conduct yourself accordingly."

The Dark Warlord grimaced and nodded his agreement.

Seeing there was to be no further comment, Taelsin pressed on. "I believe that General Souit will not contest the evacuation of our civilian population. Would that be your reading of the situation, Lady Darkhelm?"

Daine ran her fingers through her short hair. This environment did not suit her, and she was increasingly irritable. She needed to be on the walls, not debating with Nobles. "If he was planning on a traditional siege, no. He would want us to split our resources to feed the population. By his actions yesterday, it would seem Souit favours a speedy resolution to proceedings. We were fortunate to forestall his initial assault, but we can expect overwhelming shock and awe tactics on the morrow. However, despite his reputation as a hard taskmaster, he has no history of putting Cities to the sword. I would imagine he would welcome us expelling our noncombatants. The King wishes to be seen to be putting down a rebellion, not massacring erstwhile subjects."

"And what would the classification be of civilians? Would you allow the Nobility, for example, to access such free passage?"

"You really are a spineless toad, Tomas. Does your wife bemoan your absence of penis?"

Taelsin smiled at Stelton's words and was about to soothe the arguing Nobles when he noticed the horrific cast of Donal's face. The man's eyes had transformed into orbs of silver, no white whatsoever, and his lips were drawn back into a rictus grimace. Daine, noticing the direction of Mayor Elm's attention, looked over and immediately took to her feet to run to the Dark Warlord's side.

"Sir, what ails you?"

With great effort, Donal forced the words through gritted teeth. "A portal. A portal inside our walls."

*

Time was absolutely of the essence.

That single fact had been drilled into her over and over again whilst she prepared for this mission. From the moment the portal was torn open, it was just a matter of time before it knit shut, and when that happened, it was not going to be pretty for anyone still in its jaws.

"Move, move, move!" Her eyes were glued to the ragged edges of the portal as she pushed her squad through. She did not need to be the last one through — that sort of chivalric impulse was for the graveyard — but it did not hurt her reputation to be seen to be careless of death.

About half of them were through when the wound leading into Swinford flared and began to contract. She quickly stepped through, narrowly avoiding catching her knee on the shrinking circle. The man behind her — Olean — tried to stop himself but could not in time. When the edge of the collapsing portal touched him, his flesh instantly melted. Fortunately, his screams were cut off as the hole in reality squeezed shut.

She quickly counted the numbers that had passed through. Twenty. More than she feared, less than she hoped.

A glance at their surroundings showed they had materialised in what appeared to be a rundown warehouse district, pretty much exactly where they had planned.

"I know. Makes a change, right?"

She glared at the speaker, a lean dark-skinned Blademaster called Grisin. "Did I ask your opinion, scrub?"

"No, my Lady."

"Then shut up."

A few of the other members of the squad smiled, but stopped when her eyes swept over them. They knew better.

Well, now was as good a time as any other. "Ladies and gentlemen, you all know your targets. Get in. Get it done. Get out. Don't get comfortable. Comfortable people make mistakes. There's not enough of us to make mistakes. You understand?"

"Yes, my Lady."

"Twenty of us. That's double the share we had planned. Get in, get it done, get out. I couldn't care less if I ever see any of you ever again, but I'm sure your mothers love you, and I'd rather not break their hearts. Do the job and survive, people. The army will come through the walls tomorrow, and they'll have our backs. Until then, this is Swinford, ladies and gentlemen. And the Lords will not save you. They know we are here and they want our blood. Take your time, take care, take lives."

She looked around and saw resolution in the eyes of those of her squad who had made it through.

"I love you all, you Lords-damned degenerates. See you tomorrow. All of you."

Her men saluted in response and then scattered.

She watched them leave and then took a deep breath. She could do this. And she could get them all out.

The Hyena and her Cackle were loose in Swinford.

*

Donal gasped and slammed forward, his head striking the edge of the Council table.

Blood poured from the wound as he stood and looked over at the Knight of the Road. "Daine. Lady Darkhelm. We have a problem."

CHAPTER THIRTEEN

Of Soulknives and Slaughter

I n less than a bell, what passed for Swinford's military structure was almost entirely decimated.

Report after panicked report rolled in telling of the unexplained deaths of those responsible for marshalling the City's defence. There simply was no time to organise any sort of counteroffensive before all of those who would be involved in such a mission were no longer responding to attempts at contact.

The accuracy and depth of the intelligence these strikes must have possessed was almost as devastating to Taelsin as the impact of the losses themselves.

He had believed the removal of Lady Gerol would staunch the flow of confidences leaking to the King's Army. However, some of those murdered this night had only been in place since that traitor's untimely "fall". The realisation of further highly placed spies within his walls was hugely unwelcome.

As the Mayor, with Donal's frenzied assistance, pored through their records to identify further quislings, Daine paced the room like a trapped animal. Every instinct she possessed was to take to the streets and hunt down those who had invaded the City.

"I am sure that is exactly what the Great General has planned, my dear. It strikes me that the only reason there have been no attempts on our lives this evening is that they are waiting for you to leave."

The Knight of the Road stopped walking and leaned against the stone wall. "Or has he predicted I will stay within the Keep, protecting you, and his agents will thus have a free hand to enact chaos?"

Lord Mindus cleared his throat. "Speaking for the Nobility, I would support the continued protection of the Lady Darkhelm within this room. Swinford's leadership must survive this assault."

"Because Goddess help the population without your inspiring presence, Tomas?"

Forced proximity was not improving the collegiality of those in the room.

With a frustrated growl, Donal sketched a rune in the air and the stack of papers he and Taelsin had searched through burst into flames. "There's no one who has access to all these new postings. Had they stood a Shadowspy behind me for the last few days, they couldn't have had better access than they are demonstrating."

There was a knock at the door, and everyone in the room tensed.

As had become their procedure since news of the

attacks filtered in, Donal empowered the Runes of Annulment he had carved into the stone around the door's wooden frame, and Daine moved forward to open it.

Even before she lifted the heavy metal bar, she felt her health begin to plummet. Goddess help the Messenger on the other side if she was so affected.

Wincing, Daine cracked the door and hurriedly accepted the bundle of papers thrust into her hand. A white-faced boy stumbled backwards into the arms of the Healer, who channelled her most potent spells to keep him alive whilst under the influence of Donal's spell. The two women nodded to each other before the Knight retreated, rebarring the door.

Breaking the seal and untying the bundle, she then scanned the latest updates, shaking her head as she read.

The notes spoke of further disaster.

The tide of death had continued to remove key defence personnel and was now spreading out to encompass vital support staff. The speed of progress and the scale of the organisation was astonishing. As was the lack of any casualties amongst the attackers.

She passed the papers to Donal. "Mayor Elm, I cannot stay here any longer. Unless the City hits back soon, no one will be left to contest a strike in the morning. All our preparations will be for nought if we do not have anyone alive to enact them!"

"And if you leave, Lady Darkhelm, and these forces focus upon this room? Should we all fall, that will be the end of Swinford." Taelsin's voice was even. Like her, he could feel the knife edge on which things now stood.

"Honest word, my Lord? If we do not stem this critical loss, Swinford is lost."

Taelsin glanced at Donal, who shrugged. "It's not like I have any better ideas, my Lord. And it's not like we're exactly helpless in here, should the worst happen. I suggest we release the Darkhelm on whoever is killing our people."

The Nobility, with the notable exception of Lady Stelton, protested vociferously, but the decision had already been made.

Taelsin quieted the arguments with an irritated gesture. "Ladies and gentlemen, the Keep is our most secure structure. This room is accessible by one door, and there are guards enough outside to reassure us all. The Lady Darkhelm is quite correct; there will be no need to remove the leadership of Swinford if we have no one left to lead. We cannot hoard our most potent asset for keeping us safe when such a disaster is befalling."

Nodding her thanks to Taelsin, she lifted the bar and passed it to Donal, who sagged under its weight. "Don't open this door to anyone but me. No matter what anyone says, this door stays closed. Do you understand me, sir?"

"I doubt I could lift this again should I try! This Class is lacking in Strength, I fear. I would wish you 'good hunting,' but I fear this is exactly the move for which those attacking us are waiting. Look after yourself out there, my dear."

Smiling grimly, she rested a hand on his shoulder. "I will put an end to this night of death, sir, I promise."

As she pulled open the door, it was unclear who was the more surprised: the Knight of the Road or the three assassins in the middle of slaying the Healer and her guards.

*

In many ways, thought Ciellia, the mission had been a disappointment. When the Hyena had pitched the job to her

Cackle, it had seemed an endeavour worthy of their reputation. Infiltration of a besieged City — through an unstable Blood Portal — under the eyes of a Knight of the Road? Sounds interesting. How much gold! Yes, please.

That so few of them had made it through the portal — she shivered at the memory of that journey — made the contract even more lucrative.

The reality, though, as with so many things in her life, had proven much less exciting than she had been promised. She had removed her list of targets well ahead of schedule. Only one of them, a Man-at-Arms with unusual Speed for his Class, had been a challenge, and that was more from her overconfidence than anything else.

She had met up with Balyn and Alanna at their rendezvous point, at which stage they voted to try for their secondary objective. The Hyena has been clear that the capture of Mayor Elm was a desirable goal, but only after completing their individual missions.

"I've had more fulfilling evenings," Alanna muttered as they phased through the gate of the Keep.

"Someone thought it was worth it to employ us to remove these people," Balyn said as he, with one hand, tore out the throat of a servant who had the misfortune to be standing in front of them as their forms solidified.

"I don't disagree," Alanna sighed. With a wave, she cleaned the blood off her fellow Soulknife. "This just feels like the definition of 'overkill.' Who hires the Hyena to kill a bunch of middle-ranking functionaries?"

Ciellia checked the map. Their information was that Mayor Elm was currently up two flights of stairs at the end of a defended corridor. "Let's remember there's a Knight of the Road around here somewhere. Think about what that might mean before you get too cocky. Did you see her take out that squad with one arrow?"

"No one's spotted her yet. I heard she's been charged with holding the sewer entrance. As they've nearly cleared the tunnels, maybe she headed down there this night? Wouldn't be the first time we've got lucky. Four Heavy Swordsmen round the next corner."

The three did not speak again as they tore their way through the Keep, closing in on the room that housed the meeting Nobility. Few of the guards they encountered had even heard of Soulknives, much less could they conceive how to fight assassins who could teleport short distances at will.

"Weird to have a Healer *outside* a room, isn't it?" Ciellia was peering at their destination.

"Maybe meetings of Nobles get fractious? They threw that snooty bitch out the window, after all."

Ciellia shrugged. It did not really matter, after all. But the position of that Healer was curious. "Let's get this done. Balyn, take care of anyone who is not Mayor Elm. Alanna, he's your responsibility once we go through the door. You have clearance for anything short of killing him; he needs to be alive for us to claim the bounty. I'll alert the Hyena once you have him and channel the Homing Beacon. Agree?"

The other two nodded, and in a moment, they flowed outwards. The guards beside the Healer were down in seconds, and Alanna's hand was in and out of the woman's chest — emerging with her heart — before a single spell could be cast.

Ciellia just had time to puzzle at an unconscious boy lying on the floor next to the Healer, before the door behind them opened, and a very familiar and entirely unwelcome figure stepped through.

"Lords, help us," she whispered, and the Soulknives struck.

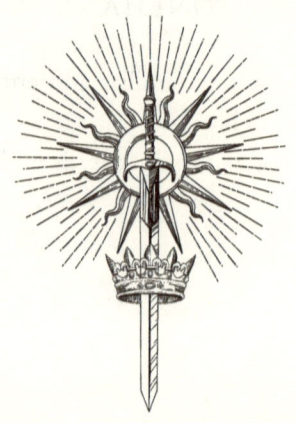

CHAPTER FOURTEEN

"Shredding Cabbage"

The figures with knives were upon her in an instant. It was the sound of three sets of rolling dice that first alerted her to the unusual nature of these assailants. That, and when the tallest of the three — the only male — vanished and reappeared beside her, plunging his dagger towards her throat.

Soulknives.

If this Class did not quite have the legendary status of the Knights of the Road, then that was merely because it was tricky to write rousing songs about assassins. The two Classes actually came a bit closer than might be assumed.

The stability of the Goddess was, of course, best demonstrated in the form of her chosen avatars, the Knights of the Road. Unchanging, unyielding solidity. The proverbial immovable objects. An Advanced, Evolved Class with the maximum levels of Strength and

Constitution witnessed in humans. Or "particularly resilient cockroaches," as Daine's Mentor had famously described them.

Soulknives, on the other hand, were sworn to the Lords of Misrule. If the Goddess's Knights were the embodiment of constant maximum power, then the shifting, changing nature of the Soulknives was their direct opposite. The power of their Skills waxed and waned during confrontations at the whim of the dice of their Lords. This made them terrifyingly unpredictable opponents.

Thus, when Balyn found his <Phase Jump> taking him to the Knight's underdefended flank and he stabbed for her throat, he could have every confidence that his Lords' eyes were on him.

And things would have worked out very poorly for the Lady Darkhelm had it not been for one significant fact.

She had faced Soulknives before.

Well, someone whose Skills were very similar, anyway.

Daine had, more regularly than any other, stood in the blood-soaked circle of sawdust against Gallant Stonehand during her years at his school. More often than not, of course, this would result in a beating that led to a hospital bed, to which a drunk and remorseful Stonehand would later come visiting. She had lost count of the times she would return to consciousness with the old man's hand in hers and whispers of his previous life tumbling from his lips.

Until their last meeting, when he confided in her about his time as a Blade of Ruin, she had always assumed he had once been a Soulknife. His stories, and her painful lived experience, spoke of uncanny Speed, a capacity to conjure bladed weapons, and strength in telepathic assaults. She had learned everything she could about the Class, hoping to be able to put it to use in their duels.

This was how, when Daine saw these assassins and heard the dice rolling, she knew what to do.

Balyn did not follow the blur of Daine's hand as she caught his wrist, broke it, and disarmed him. He just had time to register one of the Lords tutting, as if in disappointment, as the knife was driven deep into his heart.

Across the corridor, Alanna watched, barely comprehending, as the powerfully built woman in the doorway dispatched Balyn in a flurry of movement. As he fell to the floor, she experienced that moment of cognitive dissonance that came with seeing the full power of a Knight of the Road for the first time. Surely no one that big could move that quickly? She shook her head to clear her thinking and instantly threw both her daggers at the Knight.

Sensing they would not hit anything critical, Daine took both blades to her chest, her healing capacity easily overcoming the initial damage and the subsequent Bleed Effect. In response, she threw the knife she had taken from the dead man at her feet. It took the short assassin in the right eye, the force of the throw propelling her corpse backwards, to hang pinned against the wall.

And then there was one.

Ciellia stepped forwards, conjuring a psionic blade in each hand. She knew the sensible move now was to run, but she could hear her dice still rolling, and she knew her Lords would not look positively on ignoble retreat.

Where would be the entertainment in that, after all?

Watching the assassin warily, Daine plucked the two knives from her chest and carefully flicked her blood off their edges. She could still hear the sound of rattling dice, as if someone held them in a cup, not quite prepared to cast them yet.

Then the Soulknife lunged, her psionic blades slashing through the air. Daine parried with one of the salvaged knives and cut back with the other. Ciellia jerked her head away, avoiding the flashing edge, and pivoted to counter. Daine blocked each of the strikes with impeccable timing, a dark expression on her face as she kept forcing the Soulknife back to avoid her counterattacks. Her borrowed blades grazed Ciellia's left arm, then her right, leaving deep gashes behind. Blood flowed freely to drop on the floor, and both women kept glancing downwards to avoid the chance of a slip.

Undeterred by her wounds, the assassin concentrated her psychic energy into an external form. When it was ready, with a mental command, she launched a barrage of flying psionic blades at the Knight.

Sensing the need to avoid some, if not all, of these attacks, Daine jumped backwards and away. However, her trailing foot touched the edge of the growing pool of blood, and she lost her footing just as some of the projectiles hammered into her.

Seeing the hoped-for opening, Ciellia charged forward, closing the gap with the now-vulnerable Knight. With precise strikes, she delivered a flurry of blows that left deep wounds in the older woman's body. Whilst Daine's healing ability allowed her to weather most of the attacks, the relentlessness of the assault quickly began to take its toll.

Ciellia saw fatigue settle in the Knight's eyes. Their parries become slower, and her strikes repeatedly find their mark. Finally, with a decisive swing, she plunged both blades deep into the Knight's chest.

Daine's eyes widened in shock, and she gasped for breath; the psionic blades dissipated into mist now that they had done their damage. She dropped to one knee, her doomed defence having led her back into the doorway.

The Soulknife drew one of her conventional blades and stepped forward to deliver the coup de grace to the fallen Knight. She could see huddled forms of Nobility inside the room and grinned at the prospect of completing the mission.

But then Ciellia recognised something was not quite right: her health was dropping alarmingly. She knew she had taken wounds, but nothing explained this. Quickly, she pulled a health potion from her inventory and downed it, but after a momentary boost, her health started dropping like a stone again. She swayed. Poison? No, all her Resistances were maxed out.

What was happening?

In a daze, she was dimly aware that an elderly man had appeared in the doorway and was helping the Knight to her feet. "You know, my dear, it strikes me that you could do worse than invest in a good-uality shield? It would save the wear and tear on clothing, if nothing else. I cannot help but think you are taking the words 'meat shield' a little too literally."

The Knight laughed. She laughed? Ceillia did not understand what was happening. That woman had been moments from death. How was she standing, much less laughing? "It has been mentioned, sir. Now, if you want to be able to ask this assassin any questions, I suggest you disable those runes before it is too late."

"You forget, my dear, death is no longer any barrier to me asking my questions. No barrier at all."

Ciellia was dimly aware of solid hands grasping her under her elbows and lifting her to her feet. Her head lolled to look at how it all was. Alanna, but with a terrible wound on her face, was on her left, and Balyn, his chest bathed in red, was on her right.

She barely registered that her dice had stopped rolling before the darkness took her.

*

The Hyena was bending over the body of what she had been told was one of Swinford's premier Blacksmiths when a wave of nausea hit her.

One of her twenty in the City had fallen.

Then again. Almost immediately afterwards. A second presence . . . gone. She staggered and fell into a pile of scrap armour.

Her sense of those in her Cackle was imperfect; she could not tell who had fallen, just that their end had been violent. She was returning to her feet when a third death rocked her — but this one was not like the others. Whoever passed this time was unnaturally torn from the world.

The pain this inflicted made her vomit.

But that was as to nothing compared to what happened next. The three presences were suddenly back in her sense of her team, but changed somehow.

And with them came an awareness of something else. A voice.

And that voice was speaking directly to her head.

"Good evening, I'm just leaving a message for, erm, I'm told you call yourself the Hyena? Is that right? Good for you. Branding is, after all, so important in your line of business. Now, where was I? Ah, yes. I seem to have been able to connect to whatever strange psychic network you and your . . . what did she say they were called? Oh, yes. A Cackle. Excellent. You really have gone all in with that concept, haven't you? Well done, you. What? I know, I'm getting to it, my Lord! Have some patience. Do you have any idea how difficult this is? Fine. Have it your way. This is a message for the Hyena from Mayor Elm of Swinford. End your attacks on our citizenry immediately or my agent — I guess that means me — will cast <Rend Mind> across the psychic network you and your team are linked by. I am sure you know what that means. Should you be amenable to this suggestion, we are quite sure we can find a way of compensating you for any loss of business. Plus, you know, you won't have your mind shredded like last week's cabbage. The choice, as they say, is yours. You and your Cackle — I do like that collective noun. Can see it on all manner of advertising material — should present yourselves to the Keep within one bell. Or, you know, the cabbage-shredding begins. Hope to see you soon."

The Hyena took a moment to gather her thoughts and then recalled her forces.

The three who had died and then returned did not, she was somewhat relieved to see, respond to the summons.

CHAPTER FIFTEEN

Lessons to be Learned

"I had been led to believe that our method of communication with our infiltration team was foolproof?" Souit's voice was, as it had been since the abortive first assault on Swinford's walls, somewhat frosty. "Did I misunderstand your briefing?"

Spymistress Stein shuffled uneasily in her chair. She was not enjoying her time outside the Capital.

After decades submerged in the shadowy world of palace intrigue, she jumped at the King's "suggestion" to join the punitive expeditionary force to the West. The opportunity to see the rest of the Kingdom and strengthen her wider network was simply too good to miss. In her eightieth year, and by the grace of the Dark God with many more to come, she had eagerly looked forward to a reinvigorating experience from which she could return triumphant and energised.

The reality, sadly, was proving to be more sobering. Travelling in close quarters with a marching army was better enjoyed when young, wide-eyed and, preferably, without a sense of smell.

"No, sir, you did not misunderstand. The psychic network enjoyed by . . . I shall call them by their professional title, 'the Cackle,' but I hope it is understood the distaste I have for such explicit showboating?"

Souit glared back at the old woman.

He had complained bitterly about the imposition of the Spymistress within his forces. He did not have anything against her personally — anyone who survived as long as she had in a role where occupancy was measured in weeks rather than years deserved respect — but he saw her presence as an unnecessary complication. He liked straight lines, clear plans and open communication. The world of creatures such as Spymistress Stein was one he wished never to lower himself into.

"I do not care what you call them, Mistress. We both know about whom we are talking, so call them 'kittens,' for all I care. I likewise acknowledge your distaste for their overt and showy marketing but note that, as you employed them — at great expense, I should add — we should accept it worked."

Stein smiled thinly back. "Indeed. As I was saying, the psychic network of the, ahem, the Cackle is an entirely closed loop between its members, saving the access the Hyena granted my agents before their ingress a few hours ago."

"How many of your agents?"

Stein frowned. "I hardly see the relevance, my Lord?"

"You are briefing me about a foolproof, closed

communication system which has gone dark. In your explanation, you note that your 'agents' were given access to said 'foolproof, closed communication system' after which, in short order, it stopped working. If you truly fail to see the relevance of my question, Spymistress, I have a number of follow-ups to make about your professional capabilities."

To cover her momentary wrong-footedness, Stein sipped her cup of hot water. All of her reports had stressed that Souit was a solid military leader, poorly suited to life at Court. As a Great General, he had an almost prescient grasp of strategy and tactics on a battlefield but was viewed as lacking tact and diplomacy in formal settings. She had, unfortunately, extrapolated from that data to make assumptions about him that were coming back to bite.

"I have complete confidence in my agents, my Lord."

"I am happy for you. All I know about them is that they are my prime suspects in an act of malicious sabotage. How many?"

"Five."

"Thank you. You will pass their names to my Adjutant, and they will be put to the question."

"My Lord!"

"That is my last word until I am satisfied as to their innocence or otherwise in the matter. Now, what are the military consequences for us of losing touch with the Hyena and her Cackle?"

Stein seethed. Souit's actions would cause her a tremendous loss of face with her people. But it was more comprehensive than that! He was publically demonstrating a lack of trust in her leadership, which would make her work all the more challenging. However, and this is what caused her the most irritation, he was entirely right to do so. In years gone by, she would have executed, never mind put to the question, those five the moment they lost touch with the Hyena's group. In her world, loose threads existed to be cut, not coddled.

She was getting old. Old and soft. She idly wondered if that was why the King had insisted on her going out into the world. Was her replacement already in place back home?

"Mistress, I am unused to asking questions for a second time."

"Apologies, my Lord. The military consequences are limited. We are confident that nearly all the primary targets were eliminated. Should there be any remaining lines of communication in the Swinford military, they will be haphazard at best. Their orders, once these targets were removed, were to lie low and subsequently join up with our conventional forces once the walls were breached."

"I sense you are selling me a used horse, Mistress. So far, I have heard all the positives with not a hint of a downside. All targets were met, and a team of highly capable irregulars are embedded behind enemy lines, awaiting mobilisation to cause further chaos. If I were in your shoes, I would not have thought to burst in here in such a state of dysregulation over a temporary loss of communication. When are you planning on showing me this nag's teeth, Mistress?"

Stein considered all the ways she could kill this man.

She could hear his irregular heartbeat and had in her possession the precise, untraceable herb that would turn that into something instantly catastrophic. Likewise, the stiletto up her sleeve was thin enough to go in and out the pupil of his eye in a moment, leaving him a paralysed, drooling fool for the rest of his days. She could even conjure documents of unquestionable veracity into the man's wife's possession that, experience told her, would ensure the imminence of his death was quite assured.

But . . . no. Such thoughts were beneath her. The Great General was within his right to draw attention to her obfuscations. If nothing else, this humiliation had taught her a great deal about the man. She intended to learn the lesson.

"It appears, sir, that just before the network closed, it was . . . overwhelmed by the presence of another."

"I wonder it has taken us this long to get to what sounds like a fairly critical point, Mistress. But let us not bemoan the journey; let us embrace that we have now arrived. By 'presence,' I assume you are alluding to whatever magic user has been making a nuisance of themselves throughout the early exchanges of this conflict."

Stein could see that blunt honesty was to be the way forward. "I do not know, my Lord. My agents explained it as feeling as if they were being dismissed."

"Dismissed?"

"As if they were 'naughty boys caught peering through windows they should not,' was how one described it. The dismissal was . . . summary and comprehensive."

Souit raised a hand to smooth his eyebrows. "Mistress, far be it from me to tell you your business, but can I suggest that you make it a high priority to determine the Class of whoever is secretly involving themselves in the defence of Swinford? Much of our planning has been made on the assurances that, apart from the Lady Darkhelm, we will encounter nothing exotic in this assault. I have already lost good men to a curious set of coincidences, and now we seem to have misplaced a rather expensive mercenary company."

He abruptly stood and made his way outside the command tent. Stein scurried to follow in a wholly undignified manner, making her reconsider her previous decision not to poison the man's drink.

"My Lord, is anything wrong?"

Souit had halted and was silent momentarily, staring at the City he had been commanded to recapture. This was the first step to pacifying the West, and it seemed like he was already stumbling.

"I had hoped to achieve my goal quickly and painlessly, Mistress. But at each turn, this desire has been thwarted. First, ingress through the sewers was denied me. The Lady Darkhelm was in the right place at the right time to collapse the tunnels. A quick assault to take the north gate was foiled in an explosive, yet interestingly fortunate, fashion. The archer that fired the key quarrel was none other than the Lady Darkhelm. And now I find that the forces sent to decapitate the command of the City have, surprisingly, fallen silent. I am not a betting man, Mistress, but I feel my coin would be safe should I hazard on her involvement."

Stein was unused to being outside for quite so long and shivered in the cold morning air. "Apologies, sir. Is there a point to all these musings?"

Souit smiled thinly. "The Lady Darkhelm is a warrior unmatched in our world. She is a doughty opponent and, clearly, a fine enemy. But she is not a military genius. She has now been placed in our way three times. You are to uncover who is making free use of this most effective of resources."

"And when I do, my Lord?"

"I am sure you will think of something. Perhaps secret herbs, sharp stilettos and devastating compromising material, Mistress?"

They held each other's eyes for a few moments, each now understanding the other far better.

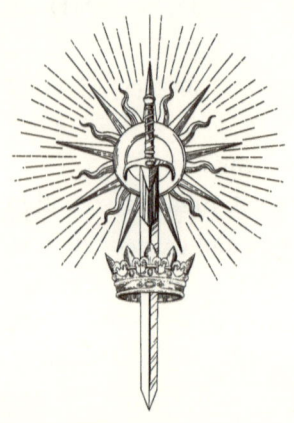

CHAPTER SIXTEEN

"Swords to Ploughshares"

The early morning mist was just starting to burn off as the King's Army formed up outside Swinford.

Mindful of the impact of the Knight of the Road on the abortive assault on the north wall, Souit had divided his forces to completely surround the City in a wide circle.

This was, undoubtedly, not his preferred manner of attack; he felt there were simply too many moving parts in such a formation. The level of coordination required across the army to make such a push coherent was considerable, and the logistics for an attack on this scale were, on paper, wholly daunting. However, as a Great General, he more than had the capacity to overcome such minor challenges.

No, it was the irksome necessity of committing so many of his forces against such a fragile enemy that was ruining his morning.

"This Knight of the Road may be able to hold one wall on her own. Let her. We will bring the others down around her ears," was how he put it to his command staff.

However, privately, he worried about such a comprehensive attack being counterproductive. Souit did not intend to occupy Swinford. Rather, he had organised this campaign to, at great speed, sweep across the lands of the West, pausing just long enough to pacify the local population as he went. As it was, he was already falling behind schedule and was beginning to doubt his boast to pacify the West in one season. If he were forced to reduce Swinford to rubble . . .

Weeks and months spent rebuilding a functioning city were very much not on his agenda.

It was thus a finely balanced thing: the City must fall and fall quickly, but he needed to achieve it with the minimum amount of damage to its infrastructure whilst also overwhelming a Knight of the Road.

Fortunately, he reflected, he had the numbers to manage it. After Swinford, he anticipated no further roadblocks, and — other than some unusual reports the Spymistress had brought him about the nondescript village in which the so-called Great Council of the West was held — he could afford to commit all his resources to one all-out attack.

He was troubled, though, that the ring of steel that surrounded the City bristled with restless intent. There were strict standing orders about how Souit required his army to conduct itself once they entered Swinford, but there were soldiers who had lost friends in the fire that thwarted the first assault, and there would be consequences for that.

As he prepared to give the signal for attack, Souit

considered his best-case scenario. If the Lady Darkhelm would make herself known defending one area of the walls, he could thus concentrate his forces elsewhere, achieve a speedy breach and immediately petition for Mayor Elm's surrender. What he knew of that man, he liked. He was not a fanatic who would risk the slaughter of his people on a point of principle. He was sure when the inevitability of defeat became manifest, they could come to an agreement to avoid the sacking of the City.

Nodding his head at the soundness of his reasoning, Souit ordered the ring of men surrounding Swinford to contract.

*

It was Man-at-Arms Fidoral who first noticed something odd was happening. He was on the front line opposite the eastern wall — *call that a wall! I've seen more secure structures on a pig farm* — and was keeping a close eye out for the much-feared appearance of the Darkhelm.

All the talk of the previous evening was that there was, really, a one-in-four chance of coming up against her this morning. The expert military strategists amongst the regulars had debated back and forth on which wall she would most likely defend, with most thinking she would be found where the original assault had foundered, at the gatehouse to the north. Those involved in the assaults on the other walls had slept a little better that evening, whilst those who were now gloomily approaching the main entrance to the City had spent the night organising their affairs.

However, no one took anything for granted, and all eyes were peeled — at all points of the compass — as the army tightened its ring formation around Swinford.

It was during this vigil that Fidoral noticed the heavy chunks of crudely shaped wood, joined to metal points, being tumbled down over the wall to land in front of him. He shouted in alarm and then realised his call was being repeated across the front line.

At least a hundred of these oddly constructed things were being hurled by unseen hands over the wall to land a long way short of the advancing soldiers. If the intent had been to strike those below with the objects, it was a lamentably timed effort.

Fidoral, keeping his shield raised for any further shenanigans, peered over its rim at the wooden object lying nestled against Swinford's eastern wall. It looked very familiar. Just very out of place.

"Is that a plough?"

*

Souit dismissed the messenger with a curt nod. He turned to the rest of the command staff. "Is there not some proverb or other about turning swords into ploughshares? It means the arrival of a time of peace, does it not?"

"Damned odd way to surrender, if you ask me," Major Fadarn noted gruffly.

"Quite." Souit tapped his lips thoughtfully. "The Mages sense nothing from them?"

"No, my Lord," one of his seemingly endless interchangeable aides confirmed.

"They are not going to, I don't know, explode once we get closer?"

"They are entirely as they appear, my Lord. They have no runes on them nor any magical signature. They are ploughs. And hastily constructed ones at that. Those with more experience than me in such matters were quite . . . critical of the workmanship."

Souit nodded, and the functionary vanished back into the sea of their fellows.

"I do not suppose our informants from within the City have shared any thoughts about the purpose of these objects?" All eyes turned to the Spymistress, who smiled thinly.

"No, my Lord."

"Pity. I imagine this sort of event is precisely why the King suggested you accompany us."

"Indeed, my Lord."

"Could we try to make this the final time there is a colossal failure of intelligence, Mistress?"

If looks could kill — and considering the various talents and Skills of the Spymistress, they very much could — all present were surprised Souit remained hale and hearty.

"The day is wasting, ladies and gentlemen. In lieu of absolutely any information to the contrary, I can see no reason to postpone our assault. Any dissenting thoughts?"

All eyes subtly turned to Degralk. *Nope,* he thought. *If the General's mood was sour enough to publically shame the Spymistress, I'm not being the naysayer again.*

After an awkward silence, Souit nodded. "Very well. Sound the advance."

Barely had the final note of the trumpet faded away before a general hubbub arose from the ranks.

"What now!" Souit's frustration at the continuing delays was starting to bubble out of control. "Have the defenders found some hoes to throw at us? Are we intimidated by garden shears now? Tell me, what is the latest agricultural calamity to befall us now!"

*

"What on earth?" Fidoral heard the man at his shoulder exclaim, and he hurriedly dropped his gaze downwards from the battlements, stopping his search for the tell-tale helmet of the Knight of the Road. His eyes alighted on the plough, which had, of its own accord, arisen, and was making its slow way towards him, digging a deep trench behind it.

He looked left and right to confirm all of the ploughs were doing the same thing. They were. He braced his shield for an impending impact, then laughed and somewhat relaxed. It would be some time before it reached him at the speed it was moving.

He assumed there would be some orders from those above before it did.

*

"I'm trying very hard not to meet the eyes of whoever told me there were no magic signatures on those ploughshares."

A somewhat nervous young woman stepped forward. "The Mages are clear, my Lord. Those ploughs are not being operated by magic."

They watched, in silence, as hundreds of ploughs, apparently entirely of their own volition, moved at a snail's pace towards the first line of the encircling forces.

"So, what is happening? Anyone? Speak freely, damn you. Is there a danger here?"

"It occurs to me that there are numerous Skills, my Lord, to assist Farmers in their work," Degralk offered.

"Skills?"

"Yes. I am no great authority, but my wife is of Farming stock. I have heard of Farmers who possess an ability such as, I don't know, <No Oxen>, which could operate a plough in the absence of a healthy animal."

"Fascinating." His tone made Degralk wince, but Souit quickly added, "Genuinely. I have never heard of such a thing. Farmers with Skills? Whatever next?"

Souit turned to regard the slow-moving charge. "So, it is possible Swinford's Farmers are, what, seeking to provide some form of martial support? To what purpose? How deep are those furrows?"

One of the aides was quick to answer. "Our estimation is a hand's breadth, my Lord."

It made no sense to Souit. He could see no tactical use for such implements nor the benefit of so shallow a trench. "Have one of our Mages destroy one. Just one, mind you. If there's something untoward being planned here, let's not fall into their trap."

In seconds, a small ball of fire was released from the lines facing the northern wall. It streaked towards one of the ploughs, destroying it in a puff of smoke.

The impact on the other ploughs was immediate. They stopped their ponderous move forward and leapt into motion, streaking towards the front line.

The Mages took the initiative and destroyed scores of ploughs before the remainder hit the line and vanished inside the press of men.

Souit watched silently as the ploughs rippled through his forces, men and women moving sharply out of their way and out of the crowd. He turned to watch as the ploughs exited the encircling soldiers to appear behind him, at which stage they turned ninety degrees to continue digging their furrows in a wide circle around the army.

The Mages began their bombardment again once the ploughs emerged from the soldiers, and, before long, none were remaining.

If the army was disconcerted by what had occurred, it was nothing compared to their reaction to the sudden loud cry from within the walls.

"Milkmaids, make ready!"

Souit raised his eyebrows at the Spymistress, who shrugged in response.

"I have no idea, my Lord."

Grimacing, Souit eyed the walls of Swinford. He could not conceive what his enemy was preparing, and that suited him ill. Since achieving his Class Evolution, there had not been a moment on a battlefield he had not been able to interpret and understand.

This feeling of uncertainty was hugely troubling.

Fortunately, he did not have to wait long for answers.

CHAPTER SEVENTEEN

"Growing Pains"

Daine thought there was something almost childlike in Donal's behaviour during the defence of Swinford.

She had always liked the former Secretary's irreverent demeanour. On Tour, she often encountered hostility — or more regularly, fear — when meeting with those holding civic responsibilities. Of course, she had long reconciled herself to the fact that this made perfect sense. It was a rare Noble, after all, who would welcome the interference of a nigh-immortal, divinely anctioned, wandering judge in their business.

With Taelsin Elm and Donal Assay, though, she had always felt welcome. They were friendly without being unctuous, genial without imposing and, in Donal's case, more than happy to treat the world with the ridiculousness it so often deserved.

Since his Class change, though, that instinct to poke

fun had been given an even freer rein. She was not yet sure whether such unrestrained liberty was refreshing or alarming.

She smiled at the memory of him positively skipping with joy when Souit surrounded the City.

Of the assault scenarios prepared for since the interrogation of the Hyena — or "a full and frank exchange of views and colossal sums of money," as Donal put it — their biggest worry had been an all-out assault on the north wall.

"We must remember," Taelsin had noted, "that there is a physical limit to the numbers the Lady Darkhelm can occupy at once. If Souit commits his entire force, with Mage support, I cannot foresee her holding back that surge."

Daine disagreed, but not for the reason Taelsin was suggesting. She knew she could defend the north wall until she died of old age. However, there was a limit to the slaughter she conceived herself inflicting on common-Classed soldiers. An arrow through a sloppy Mage and the resulting collateral damage to make a point was one thing. Massacring wave upon wave of those who were just following orders was not something she was willing to do. In the event of such an assault, she had already determined to hold the line until the defenders risked being overwhelmed and then cover a fighting retreat back to the Keep.

Nevertheless, that Souit had followed the strategy the Hyena had suggested as the most likely was encouraging as to the veracity of the other information she had shared.

"Remember, we're not looking for your finest work," the Warlord had exhorted the Carpenters, as they fashioned plough after poorly built plough. Their collective disgust at the pile of crudely constructed objects made clear how they felt about their bizarre assignment. "We just need enough of them to ensure the completion of the trench once the inevitable destruction of your creations commences."

As the Carpenters toiled, a handful of Farmers walked up and down the construction line, adding whatever help-ful Skills they possessed. Whilst only a few of them had <No Oxen>, which Donal saw as the key to this strategy, there were others with lesser versions such as <Rolling Rolling> or <Lazy Boy>, which, for the short distance re-quired, would probably serve.

"We would have to get very unlucky indeed, Lords and Ladies, for the inevitable attacks on these brave ploughs to remove all the most important ones."

Daine thought back to the sound of rattling dice in her fight with the Soulknives and chose to keep quiet.

And, bizarrely, the plan was working thus far. At a min-imum, the various trenches needed to reach the centre of the formations arrayed against them. From what Daine could see, they had easily surpassed that.

"So far, so good." She nodded at Donal.

He grinned his increasingly maniacal grin and encour-aged the Labourers to keep piling all the confiscated wine-skins on the veritable mountain that stood near the foot of the wall. She knew that similar mounds were growing across the City.

"This is not even the fun part, my Lady. I must confess, I am quite looking forward to how the Great General will react. Is the first act nearly completed?"

From her vantage point on the wall, she risked a glance over the battlement to check on the progress of the ploughs. They had all emerged from the back of the army and were now being picked off by the Mages.

"Any moment now, I would have thought."

"Then pardon me, my Lady." He turned away from her and sketched a glowing rune over his throat. When he spoke again, his voice boomed across the City. "Milkmaids, make ready?"

Six or seven young women in, to Daine's mind, unnecessarily skimpy clothing considering their professions scurried forward, and each selected a wineskin from the pile.

They then sat on stools and held the wineskins on their laps so that the spouts pointed towards the wall.

Donal was speaking again. "Interestingly, the stool is required for the Skill to trigger properly. It occurs to me that when this is all over, I would like to study such things in much more detail. There is so much we do not know about the way in which Skills work for the common-Classed. Libraries are filled with information about, saving your presence, the capabilities of Knights of the Road, but precious little is mentioned about Chimney Sweeps."

"I suspect, sir, that if you have your way, such oversights of knowledge are unlikely to remain following this siege?"

Donal grinned again. "Oh, indeed, my dear. I fear, for poor General Souit, ignorance will not be bliss."

*

At Donal's signal, each Milkmaid squeezed the neck of her wineskin, and a jet of clear liquid spurted out to hit the wall. Or, rather, it would have hit the wall if they were not aiming for a carefully drawn rune which flickered when struck and allowed the liquid to pass straight through the stone to spill on the ground outside the City.

The Milkmaids had quite a range of Skills connected to their Class. Those who Donal prized the most — and he made sure at least one was in each group around the City — had <Double Squirt>, which did exactly as its name suggested. Then there were those with <Filling the Pail> who would need to replace their wineskin less often, and <Rapid Teat> that significantly increased the speed at which the "milking" took place. But outside of those three critical Skills, there were all sorts of minor versions and variations.

All this meant was that, before too long at all, several small pools were building up outside Swinford that inevitably began spilling into the trenches and running towards the army.

Children hurried between the Milkmaids and the pile of wineskins, replacing the empty ones with full ones and throwing the empties onto the backs of carts, which Labourers then transported away.

Daine marvelled at the economy of effort and movement of all concerned. She recognised that she was as guilty as anyone in her ignorance of the Skills of the common-Classed. She did not even know the Skills her own parents had possessed.

"Well, this is, and pardon the pun, going swimmingly," Donal nodded as the liquid continued to flow into the trenches. "I think we are nearly ready for the next stage. Would you like to do the honours, my Lady? The others will follow your lead."

Daine nodded, resolving to ask Donal to look into the Orban family history. She now felt it oddly disrespectful not to know something so intimately important about her mother and father as their Skills.

She accepted the longbow, selected an arrow with its

payload securely attached, and fired it towards the army without really aiming.

Donal was bouncing excitedly on the balls of his feet. "There she goes!"

*

Souit held the gaze of the messenger. "There is no doubt it is water?"

The messenger shrugged his shoulders. What more was there to say? "Eowyn confirms precisely what the other Mages have found. It is just water."

Souit grimaced sourly and let him go.

He had been so convinced. When the liquid began to spill through the walls and into the trenches that had been dug throughout his army, he was sure it would prove to be some sort of accelerant. That was the only way he could make sense of his enemy's actions thus far. Cover the ground in a flammable substance and drop in a fire arrow. It fit with the way in which his previous attack had been repelled, after all.

Thus, the moment the liquid had started to ooze outwards from Swinford, he had ordered the casting of every flame-retardant spell his Mages possessed. And now it turned out that the City was merely trickling water towards them; it made no sense at all.

"'Ware arrow!" Souit's gaze snapped up as a single arrow, oddly weighted, flew above the north gate to fall near one of the trenches.

The bundle tied to the arrow exploded on impact, spilling its contents.

Other arrows started to fly outwards, all carrying similar small packages. It took but a moment for the Great General to see through the ploy and begin to react.

"Mages, burn those bundles!"

"Sir?"

"Burn them! They need to be destroyed immediately! Do not let them hit the ground!"

"But, my Lord . . ."

"What!" White flecks flew from Souit's mouth as he turned on the speaker.

"You ordered an Aura of Retardation cast over the army. Nothing will burn for quite some time."

Souit worked his jaw. Had he ever been so comprehensively outthought? "Order an immediate retreat."

"Sir?"

"If I have to repeat myself again, I will have your ears removed. There is to be an immediate retreat of all forces. All men are to regroup at their second marker."

"By the Goddess!"

At the exclamation of one of his staff, Souit forced himself to turn and look at the battlefield anew. Or what would have been a battlefield if, from everywhere an arrow had landed, rapidly growing vegetation were not already reaching for the skies.

"Is that corn?"

Souit watched, in weary disbelief, as large sections of his army disappeared in an instant. "Does it matter? Damn an orderly retreat. Signal a general rout."

He turned away and stalked back to his command tent.

CHAPTER EIGHTEEN

"Forlorn Hope"

Following the unexpected appearance of a twenty-foot-high cornfield ringing the City, the siege of Swinford entered a new phase.

It took the best part of a day for Souit's forces to reconvene at their designated markers. The speed of growth of the corn had been such that unit cohesion had almost totally collapsed in the retreat. The canopy's density and the rows of close-knit stalks had led to significant disorientation in an army already in an unusual formation and then commanded "to rout." Navigation within such an environment was complex, and troops inadvertently clashed with their allies due to the challenges of distinguishing between friend and foe.

When the last remnants of disintegrated squads stumbled free of the maze, morale was exceptionally low.

In response, after an evening of not-so-quiet

contemplation, Souit divided his forces and sent three battalions under solid, if unremarkable, Colonels onto the army's next targets. He could not allow the stalled momentum at Swinford to snarl up the whole campaign. Their orders were simple: an offer of surrender, followed — if refused — by an immediate assault with no quarter given.

It had occurred to Souit that his opponent in this siege appeared to be playing for time. Well, if Swinford sought to string things out expecting relief from its neighbours, he would choke off that hope. Whilst the Great General did not hold with taking civilian lives unnecessarily to make a point, the appearance of a giant cornfield was helping him reconsider that point of view.

But it was not just the cornfield that was sapping at his forbearance. Further attempts to infiltrate the City by the sewers had been firmly rebuffed, and news had reached the Spymistress that the Hyena had cancelled their contract and returned all the gold — plus hefty compensation for the failure of their gambit.

"I have never seen the like" — Stein's voice was sombre — "the woman was terrified. That does not fit with her reputation."

Souit shrugged. "Mercenaries. What do you expect? I expect they paid her off."

"For sure. But that raises two interesting points. The first is that such an action's reputational damage to the Cackle will be insurmountable. The King will ensure they never again pick up contracts within our territories. Thus, that payment would need to be colossal."

"And secondly?"

"If she was that afraid, I assume those within the City had the capacity to kill her and the rest of her Cackle."

"So?"

"So why spend an insane amount of gold rather than simply do so?"

Souit nodded thoughtfully and indicated for a servant to refresh his cup of water. The command tent was quiet this night, most finding the company of the Great General to be increasingly unwelcome. Considering how he had publicly shamed her, it was to the Spymistress's credit that she still sought him out. That or she was planning to kill him.

"It would seem to me, Mistress, that our opponents are not eager to take lives unless they have to."

He had pondered long on this. His miscalculation with the corn had not been unreasonable. It would have been a much more effective move from the City to have sought to destroy his army in an epic conflagration. Whatever method had been used — and he still did not understand how it had been achieved — there were far more lethal ways to make use of such a tactic. If not as some sort of accelerant to be ignited, then, for example, the water pumped into the trenches could have been poisoned.

No, if the destruction of this army was the goal of the people within Swinford, there were far more effective ways to attempt it than growing a massive cornfield.

Stein watched as the Great General stroked his chin. She had long reconciled herself to her first reading of the man being wrong. She had assumed his lack of Charisma was a flaw, that his build was in some manner incomplete. However, she increasingly saw his lack of social graces as a boon. No one ever needed fear they did not know where they stood with Souit — it was forever written on his face.

After a lifetime spent second-guessing the feelings of

those opposite her, often at significant personal risk, she found it almost restful to be in his company.

She nodded for her own cup to be refilled. "And is there an advantage to be gained from such a realisation?"

And then, for the first time since the siege of Swinford began, Souit smiled. "Do you know what, Mistress? I think there just might be."

*

Captain Kettle lowered his machete and wiped the sweat from his brow. The air in the cornfield hung heavy with the stench of unclean men. Each stalk seemed to whisper mockery at him, adding an eerie accompaniment to the dull thud of boots crushing the earth beneath. As his company advanced, the giant trunks swayed, according to Corporal Jinks, like mourners paying homage to the damned, urging the soldiers deeper into the heart of this vegetal labyrinth.

He had not believed that rodenty man to have such a poetic soul.

Finding his breath was back, Cattle pressed on cleaving through the vegetation. He had no Skill to make such work easier but was damned if he was going let someone else take the lead on this damned fool expedition.

"One company, sir?" he had asked in disbelief.

His Major had shrugged in reply. Always the sign of a man across the detail. "Orders right from the top, I'm afraid. One company, your company in particular, is to cut its way through the barrier and then assail the east wall."

"Is everyone else tired or something?"

"Yours is not to reason why, Captain, yours is but to do . . ."

The Major paused, his brain catching up with his mouth rather too late.

Cattle had merely saluted and gone to gather up his men. There really was not much more to say to that.

So here he was. Once again in the middle of something disastrous, trying to plot a way through. His soldiers followed, their eyes darting nervously from side to side, anticipating the inevitable ambush that never seemed to come. It was as if the corn were biding its time, patiently waiting for the right moment to ensnare the unwary in its leafy embrace.

Sergeant Drult, his uniform as soaked through as Cattle's own, muttered under his breath, "If there's Westerners lurking in here, sir, they must be corn-fed bastards."

He shot Drult a wry glance, the corners of his mouth twitching slightly. He'd known the dour man for what felt like forever. "Aye, Dru, they must be. Perhaps we'll find them seasoning themselves with butter and salt, just waiting for us to walk into their boiling pots."

The men around them chuckled softly, the sound swallowed by the rustling corn. Their laughter was a desperate attempt to drown out the growing sense of unease that clung to them like a second skin. The cornfield seemed endless, a cursed expanse that dared them to venture further.

Only the promise of what awaited them on the other side made the journey bearable. A single company charging a City wall? It was madness.

They had all witnessed the charge of a Forlorn Hope during the latter stages of a siege. Sometimes, it worked, and most times it did not. But it was always volunteers who did the charging, and the promised rewards for success were commensurate with the insane danger. None of them had ever heard of such a suicidal attack being ordered upon men like this. It was the sort of thing that made you question the intelligence of your betters.

Matching their increasingly black mood, the cornfield began to take on a sinister personality as the company trudged on. The rows of stalks appeared to close in on them like bony fingers. It was as if the earth itself conspired with the enemy to devour them whole, leaving nothing behind.

Eventually, Cattle raised his hand, signalling a halt. His men, their nerves frayed and patience waning, gathered around, eyes searching for a glimmer of hope amidst the suffocating green. He gestured ahead where, Goddess be blessed, there was a thinning to the growth. Somehow, they had reached the very edge of the cornfield. "Keep your wits about you, lads," he murmured, "they think they're all safe and snug behind all this, and that's our best chance. You've all seen the state of those walls. If we're lucky, we can be up and over them before they even know we're here."

"And then what, Captain?"

His orders were for his men to enter the City and make their way to the northern gatehouse, which he was to "hold until he was relieved."

As the north wall was the last place anyone had seen the Lady Darkhelm, he was reasonably sure his men would be relieving themselves thoroughly when he shared that detail with them. For that reason, he was keeping it firmly to himself. If they survived a charge across open ground, a climb up a defended wall and an advance into a hostile City, then he might mention they were going up against a Knight of the Road.

"You want a pay rise or something, Dru? Leave the

planning to those of us with the brains for it. You just do what you're told."

The old campaigner held his eyes. "That bad, Cattle?"

The Captain nodded. "Just . . . I don't know . . . keep as many of the younger lads with you as you can. If we can, let's try to salvage something from all this."

With grim nods, the two slipped forward and, followed by their men, exited the cornfield to be bathed by the light of the moon.

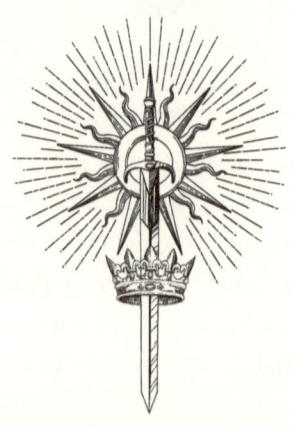

CHAPTER NINETEEN

"Nighttime Manoeuvres"

"They're bait?" Taelsin's nose wrinkled. "He's using his men as bait?"

"It's a smart plan. A good plan. It's absolutely what I would do in his position." All eyes turned to the Dark Warlord, who raised his hands in a shrug. "What? I'm just saying."

The company of soldiers had been spotted moving through the cornfield long before reaching as much as halfway to Swinford's walls. Even if they had been moving stealthily, and these men were certainly not, the flowing disturbance to the giant stalks marked their progress as clearly as if they were carrying torches.

Ignoring his erstwhile Secretary, Taelsin turned to Daine. "And what response to dangling this bait is the Great General anticipating?"

Daine sat back, unsure how best to answer his question.

The truth was, she had never before been involved in a siege such as this.

There was nothing complicated about a siege. One group was outside the walls, and another was inside. If those outside could not force their way in, then it was simply a waiting game as to who cracked first. That was usually the ones who went through their food the quickest.

However, the unusual manner in which Donal was marshalling the Skills of the common-Classed meant there was no need for any rationing. Over time, she was sure the people of Swinford would grow tired of subsisting on the basic fare being produced, but becoming bored of eating the same meal over and over again was hardly going to fling the gates of the City open in desperation.

So General Souit was not going to be able to starve them out. That only left him one other option: forcing his way in.

For that, he had the men, he had the firepower, and he certainly had the tactical expertise. Sure, there had been a few missteps thus far, but his actual losses, other than time and face, had been minimal.

Daine had watched with interest as several battalion-sized forces were dispatched elsewhere, knowing that represented a moral victory. The King's Army had expected to roll over Swinford in one push and then press onwards into the West. To have forced such a change of plan was to be applauded.

"There's no such thing as a 'moral' victory," Gant's voice growled from her childhood. "Only losers talk about moral victories. There's nothing moral about war, my lovelies. There's alive, and there's dead. And any fight you walk away from is a win."

"My Lady?" Everyone in this small room was looking at her. Apparently, she had spoken Gant's words aloud.

"Apologies. I'm getting old. It strikes me, my Lords, that we are being tested. Our response to this incursion will inform the General's next move. We are not behaving in the way he expects of a besieged City and he wishes to learn more of us. Our walls, whilst improving by the hour, are not secure enough to warrant a defence. We have lost most of our, what little there was, military organisation thanks to the work of Mistress Hyena —"

"It's just the Hyena. I'm not Mistress of anything."

Daine nodded briefly at the small, dark-haired woman. Her continued presence in the Keep, while driving Taelsin's bodyguards to distraction, was one of the conditions of the mammoth contract signed between the Cackle and the City. "This sinking ship shall keep its rats onboard, particularly its deadly ones, to ensure no further surprises" was how Donal put it. The Assassin — although Daine was not convinced that was truly the Hyena's Class — was proving to be a gold mine of information about Souit's intentions.

Putting all of Lady Gerol's ill-gotten gains to good use felt appropriate.

"My apologies. My point, though, is that from Souit's point of view, it is unclear what we are still doing stood in his way."

Taelsin was finding the discussion more than usually difficult to follow. "What does that have to do with a company of soldiers making their very slow way towards the City?"

"He wants to see what we do to them." Lady Stelton had been welcomed to their small Council of War. So far, she was proving entertainingly bellicose.

In response, Donal clapped his hands in glee. "Exactly, my Lady. He is like a cat with a scorpion caught beneath its paws. The beast is confident he can crush his prize but is concerned about the cost of that triumph. We have nipped him a few times with our claws, and he is wary about the pain our stinger will cause."

"And he hopes these poor men are to be the recipient of our sting?"

"I rather think," Daine replied to the elderly woman, "he seeks to see if we have any poison left at all."

Taelsin nodded. "Should we ruthlessly crush this incursion, he will learn yet more of our capabilities and resolve, with minimal cost to himself. And should we find a way to, relatively peacefully, send these men on their way?"

"Given the context of our other recent actions, we will be demonstrating we have no stomach for a bloody fight. We will be indicating his paws can crush without fear," Daine finished.

Taelsin sighed. "I dislike the two choices we have here."

"Oh, oh, oh." Donal was raising his hand like an anxious schoolboy.

"Master Assay, is something wrong?"

"It would strike me that when one's opponent seeks to force one of two cards on you, there is only one sensible response."

"Which is?"

"Tear up the whole deck and make him eat them."

*

Cattle reached the base of the wall first.

So far, so good.

He pressed his back to the stone and waved for the rest of his men to hurry up. He thought the conditions could hardly be worse for this sort of covert action. The moon was almost as bright and as big as the sun in the cloudless sky.

Drult hit the space to his left and Jinks to the right, both breathing heavily. His Corporal recovered first, looking fearfully upwards. "No way they've not seen us, Captain. It'll be boiling oil time any second!"

"All the more reason to get climbing, then, Jinks." He signalled for the lads carrying the ladder to make quick about their setup. Privately, Cattle agreed with the ratlike man's assessment, and it was all he could do not to cringe in expectation of a fiery death.

As soon as the wooden frame was ready, he put his foot on the bottom rung to start the climb. A heavy hand pulled him back. "Not a chance, Captain. You think I'm going to let you steal all the glory again!"

Drult squeezed past him and began climbing with a speed that belied his age, his shield held above his head. Cattle cursed and moved to follow him.

All things being equal, the section of wall they had chosen to assault could not have been more perfect. Its maintenance had been significantly lacking, and even without the ladder, the Captain felt he could have made a pretty good fist of the assault. With a decent number of men, this attack could even have succeeded.

In no time, he was levering his leg over a crumbling battlement, dragged unceremoniously up the last yard or so by Drult. Then he was on his feet, shortsword in hand, scanning for defenders.

Of which there were none.

Rather than being relieved, though, the absence of an enemy was wholly unnerving. "What's going on, Dru?"

The sergeant shook his head, not pausing in his work of dragging men up and over onto the battlements. "No idea, sir. Hang on, we've got company."

Cattle swung around to the direction Dru was looking.

An elegantly dressed elderly woman was making her way towards them, her cane tapping the flagstones as she walked. Considering the circumstances, she was such an incongruous sight that none of them quite knew how to react.

"Gentlemen, my apologies. I intended to be here before you completed your climb. Perils of my advancing years. Not as quick as I was."

Cattle found himself instinctively removing his helmet at the woman's tone. He did his best to rally. "My Lady, I must inform you we are from the King's Army. You should now consider yourself a prisoner of war. If we could have your name, we will —"

The woman's hearty laughter did little to help him recover his equilibrium.

"Sorry, that was very rude of me. Please, do continue. I haven't had a good capturing in years."

Cattle looked at Drult, who shrugged. "My Lady, I fear I am missing something."

The elderly lady's eyes twinkled in response. "If you would please follow me, I am sure all will become clear. I begged the privilege of escorting you below, and Taelsin was good enough to indulge an old lady in her whims."

She began walking back towards the stairway from which she had come. Jinks stepped forward, his face red. "I don't think you understand; we've captured you. You have to come with us!"

Stelton turned, all humour now gone. "I rather think,

young man, it is you that does not understand. Right now, the rest of your army is being treated to the rather brutal sight of you all being captured and summarily executed. I voted for crucifixion, but I believe your disemboweled bodies being hung from the walls by their own intestines won the day. I am told the quality of the illusion is quite superb, but there's nothing like a bit of reality to really sell a story, is there? Please, just say the word if that is what you would prefer."

Cattle put a hand on his Corporal's shoulder. "I think it's best we do as the nice lady says."

Jinks's eyes were huge. "Too bloody right, Captain."

CHAPTER TWENTY

"Whispers in Shadows"

Droughton-on-the-Water — thirty years ago.

Bayran's perfect face screwed up. "How would I know the mirror was not in this house?"

Daine snorted. "Priestess, we both are aware that there's no mirror here. At best, your Archbishop has been trying to distract me. And at worst, this was an attempt to assassinate a Knight of the Road. The only debate remaining is which."

Bayran frowned. "My Lady, I assure you —"

"Your spells will not work on me, Priestess. Please stop casting them; it tickles. If a Chimaera could not keep me Distracted in its own lair, how do you think you are likely to fare with whatever cantrip you are using?"

The Priestess cursed softly, then switched off <Allure>, her most potent Skill that had a Distract effect.

Almost immediately, Daine felt herself warming to the woman slightly more. As if, with the artificial means of encouraging kinship removed, she could see her for the first time.

"I'm curious. You have clearly met with Knights of the Road before. What made you think that would work?"

"You're young." Bayran shrugged. "And on your first Tour. I did not think you would likely have encountered the Skill before, much less be able to dispel it."

Daine recalled the weeks upon weeks of brutal mental training Old Gant had put her through. It was a significant point of pride for her that she was the last one of her cohort to break. Indeed, such was the level of her Mental Resistance attribute that she was surprised the Chimaera had been able to befuddle her at all. It must have been peculiarly strong. And that opened broader questions.

Nevertheless, if the wider world thought she could be beguiled by a mid-range spell, a pair of big eyes and . . . other large things, it might be wise to let them labour under that misapprehension. There were advantages to be found in being underestimated.

She batted the Priestess's words aside. "Perhaps that's true. But let us speak plainly. What is it that your Archbishop intended here?"

Bayran took a breath, held it and released it in a long sigh. She had counselled anyone who would listen, and a number who would not, that this was a foolish gambit. It was an act of the most profound stupidity to seek to enmesh a Knight of the Road in their plans. Quite apart from the immediate physical challenge these warriors presented, encouraging the involvement of the Goddess was absolutely moronic. The Lords of Misrule rarely behaved at their most rational around their mother.

Well, nothing in her creed said she needed to lie to this Knight, particularly when looking down the length of a sword. Her patrons were clear that personal survival trumped any form of professional loyalty. It was one of the tenets of her religion that most appealed to her.

"We don't know when it all began, but the first whispers of this mirror reached the Temple a little more than a month back — well, word of the Soulless, anyway. As you can attest, they are a particular menace in the Old Town, and we'd been forced to withdraw most of our Wandering Priests for their own safety."

"And the safety of the rest of the population?"

Bayran shrugged. "The Lords are not altruistic gods. Dead Priests can help no one. We look after our own first."

With difficulty, Daine pushed that to one side. "And how was there a connection made between the appearance of the Soulless and a demonic mirror as its cause?"

"Ah. Well, that starts with the Archbishop himself."

*

Archbishop Terragan Jerule sat in his gaudy study, the walls of the room bathed in the soft glow of candlelight. His eyes scanned the ancient texts and scrolls that lined his shelves, searching for something to unlock that final piece of the puzzle. Whispers of a mysterious mirror had reached his ears, a mirror rumoured to be able to uncover the hidden truths of men.

He recognised that "reached his ears" was probably a relatively benign way to describe the various tortures he had encouraged his agents to perform on the groups of Soulless they had captured. But, as he reasoned, what was physical pain to a being that had no Soul?

He did wish they cried less, though — particularly the children.

His slender fingers stroked the pile of scrolls his army of informants had sent him, seeking answers, seeking leverage. This mirror, he mused, could be the ultimate instrument of control, a weapon to be wielded against his enemies and allies alike.

He felt his patrons nod approvingly at his thoughts. If there was one thing they liked, it was when he made outrageous gambles to advance his power. Indeed, throughout his life he had become so used to the sound of rattling dice that he scarcely noticed it anymore.

A knock at the door interrupted his quiet contemplation. "Come."

Cardinal Arvid, a man of gaunt appearance and hollow eyes, entered with urgency. Jerule was aware that the Lords had been particularly capricious with Arvid of late: finances gone awry, family members lost at sea, a sudden diminishment in one of his Skills. But was that not the central peril of worshipping the gods of chaos? The poor man was at the bottom of Fortune's Wheel today, but he could wake up tomorrow with everything restored.

All on the throw of a god's dice.

"Your Eminence." Cardinal Arvid's voice was laced with trepidation. "Word has reached my ears of a mirror with fantastical properties. They say it possesses the ability to hear the very whispers of the hearts of men. And, what is more, it is said it is responsible for the recent plague of Soulless. The mirror, if we can credit it, devours souls."

A slow smile curled upon Jerule's lips. "Indeed, Cardinal. It may surprise you to know that I have heard much the same. The mirror of which you speak holds great attraction for our Lords. They see it as a tool with which we can unravel the darkest of secrets. I hardly need to stress how this would greatly weigh the scales to their benefit. They are clear we must do whatever we can to acquire it."

Arvid nodded, his eyes gleaming with a zealous fervour. He was not naive enough to believe that the Lords would reward him for being the one to find the mirror, but perhaps they might cast the dice a further time in recognition of services rendered. His Luck would have to turn at some stage. "Your Eminence, the mirror is said to be within the Town — but my sources have been unable to identify a firm location. There is some idle talk of a guardian, a Chimaera if such a thing can be believed, under whose protection the mirror lies. The exact location of the mirror cannot be scryed whilst the guardian lives."

At that, Jerule's spirits sank somewhat — even aided by the Lords, there would be little to be done against such a mighty opponent as a Chimera. But there was a journey to be travelled before reaching that crossroads. He just needed to focus on the next roll. "Find me the guardian. This is to be your highest priority. And for my ears only." With a dismissive wave, Arvid was sent on his way.

A Chimaera. If what the Cardinal said was true, then his Order would need a source of power far beyond anything that resided within this Town to deal with it. He was proud of the influence that his Priests and Priestesses wielded in Droughton, but their strength lay in the shadows, in the realm of words, rather than in martial heroics.

Although, saying that . . .

His eyes were drawn to the pile of scrolls from his various informants. Was there not something there about hints of the impending arrival of just such a person . . .

He tilted his head as a new set of dice started rolling in his mind. Interesting. A new game was always worthy of his attention. Following a pulse of his Class-specific Skill, <Kiss the Ring>, one of his more promising Priestesses arrived in a cloud of perfume.

"Bayran, my dear, in a few days, I have learned, Droughton will be visited by a Knight of the Road."

Bayran's eyebrows rose at Jerule's words. The fabled Knights drew their power from the Goddess herself. And the mother of the Lords of Misrule famously had very little time for the sort of games the Archbishop was playing in Droughton.

"Do not fret, my dear. She is new, barely more than a child and on her first Tour. Nothing, I am sure, your very particular set of Skills will not be able to handle."

"And to what end will I be 'handling her,' Your Eminence?"

"Speak to Cardinal Arvid about his search for a Chimaera. This Knight would seem to be the solution to that problem."

"A Chimaera? That would be quite a thing, even for an experienced Knight. What if she refuses?"

Jerule stroked his chin. He liked this Priestess. She reminded him of himself so many years before. "You speak the truth. Perhaps we need to be a touch more subtle . . ."

*

"Without wishing to be unkind to the quality of your scheming," Daine said, "I need to tell you that none of this has been remotely subtle."

Bayran sighed. She was doing a lot of that at the moment. "You have a singular mind, my Lady. I am not sure I could have anticipated your very direct approach to the situation."

"I assume, with its guardian defeated, the rest of your Order are urgently seeking the mirror?"

"That was to be the plan. Our most powerful adepts would have felt the death of the Chimaera and immediately began their search."

"Then I think we know our next stop. Lead on, Priestess."

If questioned whether she felt it wise to obey this Knight of the Road, Bayran would have answered — foreshadowing a certain Corporal on the battlements of Swinford thirty years hence — "too bloody right."

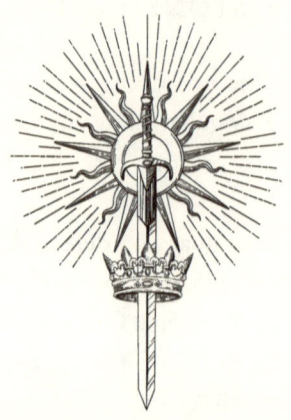

CHAPTER TWENTY-ONE

"They do it with Mirrors"

Souit, impassively, watched the brutal execution of his soldiers atop Swinford's walls. If their bloody fate caused him any disquiet, it did not show on the mask of his face.

When the final member of Captain Kettle's company was thrown over the walls to hang from a rope made of his own entrails, he summoned one of his remaining Mages.

"My Lord?" The young woman — an Air Mage who deeply regretted her brief flirtation with the King's youngest son, which had seen her dispatched on this expedition — was at his side in a moment.

"You will agree with me that was an obvious illusion, no?"

The Mage's eyebrows rose. "No, my Lord. There was not a trace of Magery there. What we saw was the reality."

"Check again."

Not for the first time, Angharad despaired at the Great General's understanding of her craft. He appeared to view her and her fellows as tools to be taken out and used when necessary rather than scholars to be consulted. "My Lord, I am afraid there is nothing for me to 'check again.' I can assure you that there was no Magery involved in what we just witnessed. The men of that company were captured and summarily slaughtered. Any Mage you asked would tell you the same."

There was a pause whilst Souit sought to make sense of that information. It was so clear to him that, as there was no possibility what he was witnessing could be the reality, the only explanation was for it to have been an illusion.

"What did you expect, my Lord, sending them to assault the walls with such little support? You sent those men to their deaths."

Souit turned to the speaker, a cavalry commander of some sort, he thought. He did not recall his name. "You will watch your tone, sir."

The man's face was red with either drink or indignation. Most probably both. "Whilst others may stand by as you make error after error, I will not let this latest folly pass. What did you hope to achieve from that sortie other than show the men the callous regard you have for their lives?"

Souit's eyes slid to the man's companions, who stood awkwardly at his side. "If you care for your friend, remove him from my sight. I will accept his formal apology no later than the third bell. Shall that not be forthcoming . . . well, there will be consequences for his outburst."

The young cavalry commander was bundled from the room, still firing invectives towards Souit.

When he was gone, the Great General turned to the

rest of his command staff. "Is there not anyone here with the sense with which they were born? Do you not all see that little performance on the walls for what it was?"

Several pairs of eyes met those of Angharad, who shrugged helplessly. What more was there to say? "We all saw the same thing, my Lord. Captain Kettle's company exited the cornfield and quickly reached the summit of Swinford's east wall. At this stage, they were captured by a contingent of Swinford's forces, who then put them immediately to death. I assure you, and I am happy for you to request the opinion of any of my peers, there was no illusion present."

"Does it not strike anyone else as strange that a City which has done everything it can to avoid inflicting casualties upon us suddenly commits acts of grotesque barbarism? That does not cause any of you a moment's pause?"

A Colonel tried to restore some reason to proceedings. "We do not doubt it has been a significant escalation, my Lord, but to argue it did not happen stands not within the prospect of belief."

"Where is your professional curiosity, sir? What benefit does our opponent gain from such a display?"

The man stepped back into the crowd, making the universal sign for "I tried" to the others. Things appeared to be at an impasse when Spymistress Stein suddenly slipped forward to whisper into Angharad's ear. The young Mage frowned at whatever was said to her and made to reply, then stopped and pursed her lips in confusion.

The Spymistress nodded towards her encouragingly. "Is what I suggest possible?"

"All things are, of course, possible, Mistress. But that

would be a very unusual application of the technique. Indeed, I have never heard it used in such a manner before."

"May I ask for you to enlighten the rest of us as to your conversation?" Souit's voice, whilst light, was tauter than usual.

"I was asking the young Mage whether it was within her capabilities to recognise an illusion if what she was seeing was, in itself, a reflection."

"Please explain."

Stein glanced to see if Angharad was interested in speaking further. The Mage shook her head. "Very well. Firstly, let me provide a brief overview of the concept I have suggested to the Mage may be in play here. Pepper's Ghost is an illusion technique that uses mirrors and particular lighting to reflect images off the glass so that what is seen appears to be a part of the physical world when, in fact, it is nothing more than a reflection. I was enquiring whether Angharad' ability to detect an illusion would see through such an application of the technique."

"And could it?"

Angharad shrugged again. "I do not know, my Lord. I do not know of any other circumstances in which such a thing would be useful."

"To summarise, Spymistress, are you suggesting that strategically placed mirrors arranged towards our watching army could reflect an illusion cast some distance away from the battlements in a way our Mages would not detect?"

"I am inquiring of the Mages as to whether that is a possibility."

Souit turned to Angharad. "I would assume, as an Air Mage, you will be in possession of any number of Skills that would make life very difficult for such mirrors, no matter how strategically placed."

"Indeed, my Lord." Angharad activated <Wind Blade> and fired hundreds of small rotating blades towards the battlements of Swinford's east wall.

There was a pregnant pause. Which was subsequently broken by the shattering of several massive sheets of glass.

*

"I told you that was too clever by half," Taelsin said ruefully, ducking down to shelter from the falling shards.

"Ah, well. Nothing ventured, nothing gained." Donal sketched a rune that projected a shield in the air. This grew to cover the minor talents they had gathered to perform the illusion of the slaughter of Kettle's company. Within the City, there were precious few who could complete such a complex spell alone. However, working in concert, and with Donal's encouragement and Skills, made Taelsin sure what had been produced would have been convincing. "If they'd fallen for it, we'd have gained another day or so at the very least whilst they worked out what it meant."

Taelsin nodded. "True. And in its failure it confirms what we know about Souit. He's good."

"But the men we've captured don't speak too well of him. I don't think things are all sweetness and light in the King's Army. And that was the point of all this, was it not? Soldiers are practical sorts. There's absolutely no way the rank and file are going to believe what they saw was an illusion their Mages cannot sense."

"No." The last of the glass had fallen, and the Mayor felt able to risk popping his head above the wall. "He's going to be stuck with an army that is absolutely convinced he's just sent a hundred men to a brutal death, and now he's trying to weasel out of responsibility by arguing some rubbish about us doing the whole thing with mirrors. I wonder how that will go down?"

*

"All I'm saying, my Lord, is that being right about this is not going to help. Everyone knows the Mages couldn't sense anything. Just knowing how it was done is not enough."

Souit regarded the Spymistress with disbelief. "You are saying that the men would prefer to believe . . ." He ran his hands through his hair and sighed. "I have had enough of our time outside of Swinford's walls. Burn down the cornfield opposite the north wall. I want everyone ready for an all-out attack. No finesse. Nothing clever. I want to be in the City by this time tomorrow."

His various adjutants nodded and dispersed to carry out his orders. The Spymisstress was also leaving when the Great General called her back.

"Mistress, thank you for your support in this."

"Of course, my Lord. That is why I am here."

"Indeed. But my thanks, nonetheless."

Stein went to leave and then paused, sensing there was more to be said. "Was there anything else, my Lord?"

"That young man who lost his temper . . ."

"Say no more, my Lord."

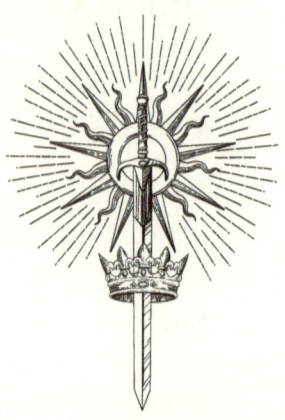

CHAPTER TWENTY-TWO

"And the Walls Came Tumbling Down."

"I've avoided raising this topic before, my Lady, but do you have any idea when we could expect the Duskstrider?"

Daine winced at the question, recognising what remained unspoken. For the first time since the King's army had appeared before their walls, Swinford was in trouble.

The thick wall of smoke that billowed from the cornfield hid the formation of the approaching forces. However, no one defending the north wall expected it would make much difference. Not now that Souit was prepared to make a determined push.

As soon as the Great General's intentions became clear, Donal switched up his plans. He had his Milkmaids stop pumping out water to feed the barrier of corn and switch to some sort of accelerant of his own design. The one that the Blacksmiths had been drooling over. The ensuing firestorm had certainly bought them a few more hours of preparation whilst Souit's Mages tried to bring that conflagration under control.

Not that anyone thought it would matter.

As Taelsin's question made clear, the defenders knew they were running out of time for the Pendragon to arrive and save the day.

"Knowing Eliud, my Lord, he will wait until the last possible moment to make the most dramatic of entrances."

Taelsin smiled at that. "Of that, I have no doubt. It just strikes me that, for the sake of my City, it would be excellent if that could occur whilst I have some walls still standing."

The Knight of the Road pursed her lips and returned to staring out from the wall at the smoke. By her reckoning, the fires that had raged for much of the last day were now starting to die down.

It would not be long now.

Movement to her right surprised her, and she found herself looking into the broad, open face of Captain Kettle. "Is there not a prison in which you should be languishing, Sir?"

"Probably, my Lady. Negotiated my . . . what do you fancy dans call it? . . . my *parole*. Apparently, as long as I promise not to escape, I can wander around as I see fit. They even let me keep my sword."

"You are not anxious to escape back to your army?"

"As far as I can tell, my Lady, me and my boys were used as bait to see what you'd do to us. It don't strike me that the certainty of our deaths was much of a dealbreaker. So, no, I'm not feeling bathed in the warm glow of General Souit's unconditional positive regard. I'll probably get over it, but for now, I'd rather be on your side of the walls than his."

Having been used in much the same way by more commanders than she could count, Daine had some sympathy for that position. Particularly as Kettle and his men did not possess any of her significant advantages.

"You could be back with them sooner rather than later. We're not sure we can hold against what's coming through that smoke."

"I doubt that, my Lady. I've never met anyone that scared me more than that old man you've got running your defences. The way his mind works? Well, let me say I'm glad I'm already captured. Wouldn't want to be marching into his next scheme. And that's without you getting involved, of course."

Daine pursed her lips again. For all Donal's confidence, that Taelsin had mentioned the hoped-for arrival of Eliud suggested she was not the only one fearing they were reaching the end of the road.

As if privy to her thoughts, a huge rock suddenly sailed through the smoke to collide with the wall to her right.

Donal's team of Professionals had laboured day and night to try to strengthen Swinford's defences, but there was only so much that could be achieved in the time available. That the projectile only caused a small crack to form down the wall it struck was a testimony to their efforts.

However, a crack did form.

And more rocks were on the way.

Daine nodded farewell to Kettle as she hurried down the steps to where she assumed the breach would form. "Please take care, Captain. I would not have you caught up in what is to come. You may well be safer back in the cells."

Kettle watched her go. Not for the first time, he felt he had somehow found himself on the wrong side of this conflict.

*

"My Lord, the Mages report they cannot keep up the intensity of this barrage. It would be best if you allowed them a pause to recharge their mana."

Souit did not so much as look at the Messenger, choosing to keep staring at what remained of Swinford's north wall. "I recall our Quartermaster requisitioning a not-insignificant number of mana potions before we made our way into the West. Am I to understand our Mages have already depleted that stock?"

The Messenger looked around for support from his fellows. None would meet his eye. "No, my Lord. But they would seek to husband those resources for challenges ahead."

Now Souit did turn to the speaker, and his eyes were aflame. "You mean they would rather squirrel those potions away safe in their inventories? That they hope to be able to slink away from this army, taking those resources with them as they go! No, sir. You will inform our illustrious Mages that they are to use all means at their disposal to turn that wall to rubble."

Stein winced in sympathy for the Messenger as he scurried away. He had not been the first recipient of the Great General's ire this morning, and she doubted he would be the last. No one else on the command staff appeared to have the stomach to countermand the man. Well, she had never found it difficult to speak truth to power. "If I may, General?"

"You may. Souit's voice was tight with tension.

"Speaking as I do, from a lay position, it would appear to me that the walls of Swinford are significantly breached. Where is the merit in exhausting our Mages in further attacks?"

"Where is the merit, Spymistress?" Souit turned to her and, like the Messenger before her, she stepped back when the anger in that gaze fell on her. "Where is the merit? Is that your question?"

"It is, my Lord. Should we not be preparing a ground assault?"

"At every step of this siege, Spymistress, I have been outthought. Do you have any conception of what that means? I am one of four Great Generals in the Kingdom, and I have been thwarted at every turn. And that terrifies me. So, yes, with a breach in those walls, my instinct is to order an immediate ground assault. But do you know what, Spymistress?"

"What, my Lord?"

"I need to fight that instinct. Whoever is commanding the defence of Swinford appears well-suited to defying me. I need to, therefore, question my impulses. So, yes, whilst it seems the height of folly to me to waste the energy of my Mages on destroying that wall, it is my hope that our opponent is banking on me feeling that."

"If I may, my Lord, I am unsure that is a sensible military strategy. The success of your Class, after all, is entirely based on a variety of Skills of intuition."

"If I am wrong, Spymistress, we waste but a little more time and some replaceable mana potions. If I am correct, however, I could be saving this army from the malign genius of whoever awaits us behind those walls."

*

"Come on! Attack. What are you waiting for, you colossal dunderhead! Our walls are breached. Our skirts are down. What are you waiting for? Come take me, big boy! Stop it! Take your hands off me!"

Unceremoniously, Donal was dragged from his position in the centre of the breach to the safety of cover.

"It will do us little merit, sir, should one of those stones crush your skull."

Ignoring Daine's words, the Dark Warlord beat ineffectually against her breastplate. "It makes no sense. What is he waiting for? Everything I know about Souit says he should have ordered a charge at the first opportunity."

Daine raised her shield over the smaller man as a shower of falling masonry collapsed upon them. "I fear, Sir, the days of General Souit doing exactly what we hope may be coming to an end. Can you hold the portal much longer?"

Donal sagged to his knees. In truth, the runes that would have portalled anyone within fifty yards back to the border had long since been obliterated.

It had all seemed so straightforward. The walls would be breached, and then the assault would be ordered. In anticipation of that tactic, Donal had expended significant energy he did not have to spare in constructing a ring of runes along the north wall, which, all things being equal, would have reduced Souit's forces in half. At least until they quick-marched their way back to Swinford.

But that plan was now, quite literally, in ruins.

A cacophony of trumpets signalled the end of the bombardment. Daine summoned one of the irregulars who comprised most of their remaining defenders. "Can you see the Dark Warlord back to the Keep, please? Do not let him persuade you to take you anywhere else. He will try." She pushed Donal towards the man and drew her sword.

It seemed the time for clever games was over.

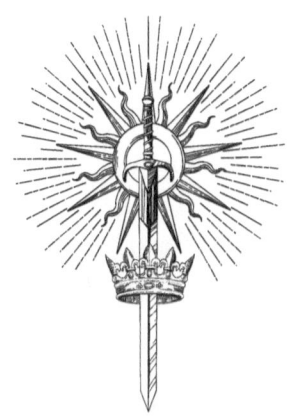

CHAPTER TWENTY-THREE

"Flood Warnings"

As the rock barrage summoned by their Mages ended, the first of Souit's infantry surged towards the breach. It defied belief that anyone could have survived such an enfilade, and they were eager to begin bringing the City to heel. The siege thus far had caused days of frustration and humiliation for which there would be a fearful reckoning.

The lead troopers had just stepped on the rubble of the remaining pieces of the northern wall when a loud voice bellowed out.

"Release!"

At that command, a thin line of archers, a motley crew of grizzled poachers, hunters and fresh-faced youths, appeared, and the advancing infantry suddenly missed a step. A twang of bowstrings sliced through the air, and the front row of the attackers was flung backwards. There was no precision. At such a range, there did not need to be. A second flurry was launched. And then a third.

Men screamed and stumbled, with the clatter of falling armour and discarded weapons adding to the chaos. Wooden shields splintered, and blood stained the collapsed stone at their feet as the attack stalled under the unceasing rain of arrows.

"Release at will. We do not let them stand!"

Daine had positioned herself in the middle of the irregulars. Unsure of the quality of aim she could expect, she had let the attackers come far closer than anyone around her was comfortable with before allowing them to shoot. At such close quarters with the enemy, she knew her presence was the only thing stopping the archers from fleeing after that first volley.

Watching arrow after arrow strike the armoured men trying to pick their way through the breach, she offered yet another word of thanks to Donal's scheming. She did not need these archers to be any good when they could release so many projectiles without worrying about running out.

"There is to be no letup. We will keep shooting until they either pull back or have all fallen."

Yet the enemy, undeterred, kept coming, a relentless tide of bodies and iron. Daine kept barking orders, urging her irregulars to nock again and again. With each successive wave, the archers unleashed their payload, their arms striving to keep up the rhythm of death, their bodies drenched with sweat at the continuous effort.

The noise in the breach was deafening: Daine's bellowed encouragement, the clash of iron against iron and the anguished cries of the wounded intertwined with the ceaseless, whistling flight of arrows.

Through the dense haze of battle, Daine's eyes never wavered, her gaze fixed on the breach she knew must not fall. She was dimly aware of some of Donal's boys and girls scampering behind the thin line of defenders, replacing empty quivers and bringing Stamina potions.

And then, as soon as it had begun, a trumpet sounded, and the assaulting men began to shuffle backwards. This was the moment Daine had been dreading. She knew what was required of her here. She needed to charge, to transform the orderly retreat into a panicked rout that would further erode the morale of Souit's army. These men, battered by hundreds of arrows, would not be able to hold against a rampaging Knight of the Road.

She just wished it were not necessary.

Reluctantly, she drew her sword and took a step forward. Then another. And then, in a rush, she was amongst them.

Swords chopped down at her from all sides, glancing off her armour. With a sweep of her right arm, she cleared a space around her, flinging men away as if they were nothing more than rag dolls. With some room to move, she barrelled into a knot of what looked to be veterans, bowling them over and trampling several underfoot. In doing so, she took an axe cut to her shoulder and, turning, wrenched it from her attacker's grasp. With one hand, she snapped it in two and hurled both pieces into the retreating press, scattering yet more bodies.

A lucky blow to her other wrist momentarily stunned her arm, and she dropped her sword. In frustration, she brought both hands together in a booming clap, crushing the man who had disarmed her into paste.

"It's the Darkhelm!" Panic took the attackers as that

shout was taken up throughout the ranks. Within moments, her actual presence became unnecessary, as far more damage was caused by the crushing frenzy to escape her.

Pausing to ensure there was to be no last-moment rally, she slipped back through the breach and resumed her place.

*

Souit nodded thoughtfully as the first wave was repulsed.

As he had expected, the Knight of the Road was to be found where the fighting was thickest, but it was the ferocity of the archery that surprised him. Surely they did not have the resources to keep up that intensity?

"Only one way to tell," he mused, and signalled the following squad to approach.

*

They held the breach for two further bells.

An increasingly frustrated Souit sent wave after wave of men to take control of the north wall. And, at each turn, Daine and her irregulars repulsed them. Eventually, though, her archers could not take any more Stamina potions without risking lethal toxicity. And one by one, they were forced to withdraw.

Thus, the breach in the wall of Swinford did not fall to an act of military genius on the part of a Great General. Rather, the defenders literally ran out of energy to contest it further.

Daine waited until the last of the archers was carried away. He had dropped from exhaustion, having fired one bolt too many. She knew it would be days before any of them could draw a bow again and worried what that would mean for the defence.

But that was for another day. For now, she surveyed the carnage before her. Not everyone hit by an arrow had been killed, of course; Souit's army had access to some of the finest Healers in the land. But there were still hundreds of bodies blanketing the ground around this wall. She had been as circumspect as possible with her own actions, but she knew more than a few of the dead had been at her hand.

Such a waste.

And it was still not over. From her position, she could see yet another line of infantry preparing to dare the breach. Souit must have noticed the decreasing volume of arrows pouring into his men and recognised the opportunity.

And now she stood alone.

Checking that everyone behind her was away, Daine stepped into the centre of the gap in the stone. She had never intended to slay so many and felt sickened at the prospect of killing more.

"My Lady?"

The familiar voice behind her caught her attention. "Donal?"

"If you would take a few steps backwards, please, I'd appreciate it. It would be awkward having to explain to Taelsin what I did with our most precious resource."

The Knight looked at the rapidly approaching soldiers. "Are you sure, sir? I can hold this bottleneck."

"But at what cost, my dear? No. This was never the plan. You've bought us enough time to reassess things."

"Time enough for what, sir?"

"You'll see. Quick as you like, my dear."

She had barely slipped inside the walls when the sea's roar deafened her to anything else.

*

A torrent of streaming water struck the approaching men and lifted them off their feet, sweeping them backwards and away from Swinford. The bodies of the fallen were likewise washed away, as well as hundreds of tonnes of rubble from the collapsed walls. It was like the City was an ocean that had sprung a leak, with an absolute deluge flooding through the breach in the north wall and surrounding it on all sides.

Souit quickly ordered his army back to higher ground, but none dared to tempt his displeasure by enquiring as to their next steps. Within half a bell, the plain around the City had become thoroughly waterlogged. A bell later, it was as if a giant lake had formed with Swinford at its heart.

"No Magery, I assume?" the General barked humourlessly.

Angharad shook her head. "No, my Lord. At least none any of us can detect."

"Have you ever seen anything like this?"

Surprised at the sincere need in the tone of the question, the Mage was momentarily lost for words.

"Well?"

"No, my Lord. I cannot conceive how this had been achieved. What is more, I am told that water is salty. It is as if, I don't know, as if a portal was opened to the bottom of the sea."

Souit shook his head and sighed. He had tried. Goddess knows he had tried. He had planned a quick, elegant campaign with minimal casualties, and he had been thwarted at every turn. Well, so be it.

"Mage?"

"Yes, my Lord."

"It appears I can no longer assault the City by conventional means."

Angharad eyed the growing moat around Swinford. "No, my, Lord."

"Thus, I fear I must ask for your assistance."

"Of course, my Lord."

"Reduce this goddess-damned place to dust."

CHAPTER TWENTY-FOUR

"Dark Pragmatism"

The night sky above Swinford was ablaze, not with stars, but with the smouldering trails of fireballs and the dark silhouettes of boulders.

As Taelsin watched, one of those giant rocks fell, tumbling over and over, to crash into what remained of a forge.

The defenders had always known this time would come and had made what preparations they could to protect the population. But there was a difference between considering the theory and witnessing the brutal reality.

Within his room in the Keep, Taelsin sat solemnly, eyes fixed on the chaos outside his window. The orange glow of fires illuminated his gaunt features, casting long shadows across the room. He peered above as another boulder arced through the air with almost leisurely menace.

In the four bells since Souit had ordered the barrage, much of the northern quarter of his City had been completely levelled. The death toll would have been cat-astrophic had they not evacuated that district some days before.

"Donal, do remind me to leave a strongly worded note in General Souit's suggestion box. His Mages' aim is atrocious."

"An excellent idea, my Lord. Parchment cuts can be quite nasty."

"Be fair," the Hyena said, sipping her wine, "they have destroyed every target we identified for them. It's not their fault you can't be trusted to play nice."

Amongst the limited options available to the defend-ers, abandoning the most strategically significant part of his City had been especially difficult. The northern quar-ter was, after all, the heart of the City's industrial strength. Should Swinford come through this siege, losing such crit-ical infrastructure would likely finish Souit's job for him.

However, with Donal's newfound capacity for mak-ing the most of the common-Classed, the choice had been made to abandon most buildings. In the short term, with the population using their Skills night and day, this would not overly imperil the defences. Essentially, if Souit thought the loss of the smithies, armouries and most of the warehouses would cripple the defence, he was going to be mistaken.

Lady Stelton drummed her fingers on the table. "This is all well and good, but if they turn their attention to the eastern district, they will start hitting residential areas, and the evacuation to the sewers is only partly underway."

Daine shook her head. "No. They'll focus here, on the Keep, next. As far as Souit's aware, the destruction he has wrought has left us militarily crippled. Effectively, this building is our sole remaining structure of any tactical value. Once the water fully recedes, Souit can bring his entire army into the City from the north. He won't need to attack the homes of civilians to achieve that objective."

Taelsin nodded. "His hope must be to move onwards into the rest of Western lands as soon as possible. He won't want thousands of displaced refugees at his back."

"He could just massacre everyone here. That would make an impressive statement."

All eyes turned to Donal, who shrugged. "I'm not saying that's the choice of a good person. Just that, you know, it would be an effective message to send."

"I think," Daine said carefully, it is safe to assume General Souit is not going to order the slaughter of thousands of civilians to make a point."

"True. I mean, it would take a really long time to do it properly."

Taelsin raised his hand for silence. "So, we are all clear that the Keep is our final line of defence. Lady Darkhelm, can you outline how you see the next day proceeding?"

The Knight of the Road stood and unfurled a map of the City. The whole of the northern quarter was blanked out, with the Keep marked in red at the centre.

"We no longer have a way of stopping the King's Army from entering the City proper. This barrage has destroyed any and all defensive structures along with any remaining runes."

Donal nodded in agreement. "The water level will start receding soon."

"In the grand scheme of things, they haven't gained much. That quarter is pretty much rubble. We've set up barricades here and here" — Daine indicated areas to the east and west — "to try to keep as much of the focus on the Keep as possible" — she tapped the red square. "We have engaged the Hyena to help shore up the defences leading to the other areas of the City. You remain confident as to that task?"

The small woman smiled, and all present became aware her nickname was well-earned. "Close-quarter fighting in abandoned streets? My lovelies live for that sort of thing. No army, no matter how big, will relish fighting the Cackle house-to-house. We've got this."

"There may be some probes towards those barricades, but if they are pushed back firmly enough —"

"Firm is our middle name." And the Hyena . . . cackled.

"That's good to hear. In that case, the focus will fall on the Keep. Donal, over to you."

Donal bowed and pushed away from the bookcase he was leaning against. "Right, about that — I have had our Seamstresses working constantly to whip up something special." He threw a swatch of brown cloth to Taelsin. "It's not pretty, but we think it will serve."

"What is it?"

"Poke it."

Taelsin raised his eyebrows. "I'm sorry?"

Donal nodded encouragingly. "Poke it. In the middle. With your finger."

Hesitantly, Taelsin did so, and his finger vanished into the material. Quickly, he pulled it out and examined the digit. "What is this?"

The Dark Warlord nodded, pleased with the expressions on the faces of those around the table. "It uses the same principle as a Bag of Holding. Most of the Seamstresses have Skills that let them copy a pattern if they study it carefully enough. I played around a little with the blueprint for the spatial storage properties of a common Bag of Holding and" — he indicated the section of cloth — "this is what we ended up with."

Lady Stelton was not the only one to look confused. "My apologies, sir. I am unsure how this is a solution to our impending problem."

In answer, Donal produced a walnut from his pocket and threw it at Taelsin. The Mayor reflexively raised his hand to catch it but was already holding the piece of cloth. The walnut hit the material and vanished.

"Excellent." Donal beamed. "You see the implications?"

Taelsin shook his head. "It has been a long and trying few days, Donal. Can you just explain, please?"

"There was a time when this group was fun. Do you remember when we threw Lady Gerol from the window? Good times."

"Sir, what is the plan?" Daine's voice was palpably frustrated.

"I'm getting to it. Honestly, you people have no sense of the dramatic." At that, he sketched a rune in the air, and the room went dark.

"Donal?"

"One second, my dear" There was a flare of light from another rune, and then an eerie green light filled the room.

"If I have to ask you to explain again, sir, I will become rather irritable."

Donal backed away from the Knight and pointed to the window. "If you look outside, my dear, all will become clear."

Daine walked to the window. At first, she thought the

glass had somehow become opaque, but then she realised there was a cloth wrapping outside it.

"Do you see!" Donal was almost bouncing with excitement.

"Have you covered the Keep in that material?"

"Exactly!" Seeing the blank looks of the others, he pressed on. "Every inch of the Keep is now wrapped up tighter than a Naming Day present. The whole structure is basically a Bag of Holding."

"And this helps us how?" Taelsin was concerned that the pressure of organising the defences was proving too much for his friend.

"Oh, come on! Surely you can see the implications!"

Daine's frown cleared, and she nodded thoughtfully. "You think it will work?"

"The theory is sound, my dear. Essentially, anything the esteemed Great General wishes to throw at this structure should be stored by the cloth. Hence, no more cracking stone. Which means no more bombardment. He's going to need to capture this place the old-fashioned way. And that will take time."

Taelsin nodded. "Time we can work with. Good work, Donal." He looked hopefully to Daine. "I don't suppose there has been any word from the Pendragon?"

The Knight shook her head regretfully, and a bleak mood settled around the table.

*

Once Donal was left alone, the customary glint in his eye faded. He was increasingly exhausted by the siege. Whilst he had initially enjoyed his cat-and-mouse game with Souit, the consequences of missteps were becoming severe.

<Skill Upgrade point available>

He suddenly sat up straighter. This was new. He could not remember the last time he had been able to upgrade one of his Skills. He was almost never within any Class for long enough to have that option. It spoke to the extreme conditions under which he was operating that, within a few days, he had already reached that stage.

As he thought through his available options, nothing immediately stood out. He felt he was already operating at the limit of his capacity, and a single point in any of his current Skills would not change the current paradigm. He would not say it aloud, but he sensed that the continued defiance of Swinford could be measured in hours, not days.

He was, with disappointment, about to upgrade <Charismatic Leader> when he sensed something new hovering at the edge of his perception.

He closed his eyes and reached towards that presence.

With shock, he realised it was a new Skill. And one he had not come across before. Hesitantly, he touched it with his mind.

<Dark Pragmatism>.

His sense of what it did was unusually hazy. There was clearly a significant percentage increase in Charisma and . . . something else. He could not be sure, but it felt like some sort of mental shielding.

With a shrug, he accepted the new Skill, feeling the welcome refresh of his mana and energy that came with expanding his Class.

He stood, all despondency now gone. Why had he been so sure this defence would end in disaster? There were all sorts of avenues to repel the attackers he had not yet pursued.

Rubbing his hands with glee, Donal made his way to the Keep's steps, a whole world of new possibilities opening up to his mind.

And from the shadows came the sound of the Dark God laughing.

CHAPTER TWENTY-FIVE

"You Have Your Orders"

Stein sighed and switched off her <Spyglass> Skill.

She had seen the same thing in each of the seemingly inviting avenues into the wider City their scouts had identified.

"Another death trap, I'm afraid. And on this occasion, I mean that literally. I have never seen such a short stretch of road be quite so liberally sprinkled with lethal traps. If I did not know better . . ."

Souit looked up. "What, Mistress?"

Stein waved a hand. "Apologies, my Lord. I was merely going to speculate that the quality of mayhem planned here would be entirely consistent with reports I have read about the work of the Hyena and her Cackle."

"Damned mercenaries. So, they've done more than just cancel their contract with us. They've joined the traitors."

Stein pursed her lips. Souit had been using the word

"traitor" an awful lot since establishing camp within the City. She feared he was trying to psychologically distance himself from the defenders. In her long experience, there was usually only one reason commanders of armies did that. And it was not because they were considering peacefully moving on. She needed to do what she could to avoid that.

"At this stage, my Lord, I would advise that we have three choices."

"Please." He gestured for her to go on. "I would welcome your thoughts."

Ignoring a snort from the back of the group — for several days now, Souit had ignored any and all suggestions made by the rest of his staff — Stein took a sip of water from a saddlebag.

"Firstly, we have the option of clearing the streets and pressing forward into the City. You must be clear that I would anticipate such a course incurring significant losses. Indeed, if Mayor Elm has contracted the Cackle, I would not like to speculate as to the extent of casualties. I would also note that such a full-scale invasion would most likely need to pacify the population house-to-house, which would take both time and resources."

Major Degralk shook his head. "Begging your pardon, my Lord. I do not see that as a viable option."

"Explain."

Ignoring the superior grin on the face of the Great General, Degralk pressed onwards. "That sort of warfare takes it out of you. There's not a soldier down there that wants to spend a moment more in this goddess-damned place than we have to. Nerves are tight enough without announcing we're gearing up for street fighting."

"Are you suggesting the men will defy orders?"

"No, sir," Degralk added quickly. "What I'm saying is, after seeing what happened to Cattle's company, we will struggle to keep unit cohesion if we take that route. If you have any hopes of a clean in and out with minimum civilian casualties, I need to counsel you that's not going to happen with this approach."

"And if I do not care for the wellbeing of Swinford's residents?"

There was a long pause during which a number of significant glances were exchanged between Souit's officers.

Eventually, Degralk shrugged. "As long as you are comfortable with such a significant loss of life to noncombatants."

"Comfortable, sir? Of course I am not 'comfortable.' There is nothing I would like more than to accept this City's immediate surrender and march onwards to our next target. However, you might have noticed that the traitors of Swinford are not suing for peace. Indeed, they offer us battle for every inch of their land. It is not I that am endangering the lives of the noncombatants of Swinford. Should they not wish to be placed in harm's way, they should take it up with Mayor Elm. But I, sir, have my orders, and I will fulfil them."

As his booming voice died away, Stein sought to reduce the tension. "As noted, I can foresee two other courses of action that do not require us cleaning Swinford's streets door-to-door."

As if exhausted by his previous speech, Souit merely nodded for her to continue.

"It seems clear, from their preparations, that the defenders seek to draw us towards a protracted struggle for their Keep. It appears to me that we are no longer able to assault that building through magic?" Stein raised her eyebrows at Angharad, who was now the *de facto* spokesperson for the remaining Mages.

The young woman shook her head. "We cannot explain it. It is as if the building absorbs anything we throw at it."

"You can still sense no magery, I assume?"

"No, my Lord."

"It is by the by, of course, but I do suggest you and your fellows spend some time considering how you are being thwarted through entirely mundane methods. You are expensive to maintain and if your usefulness during this siege is a sign of things to come, it might be sensible for me to simply send you home."

"Quite, my Lord. I can assure you we discuss little else."

The improbable defence or going home, Stein wondered silently.

By the look on his face, Souit had picked up on that subtlety too. "Please continue, Spymistress."

"Well, if we cannot bring magic to bear, then we will need to storm it traditionally."

"And what would be the downside?"

"The Lady Darkhelm."

At her name, Souit's face darkened. "Are we anywhere close to having a solution to her?"

"If we were, my Lord, then I know of a dozen Kingdoms that would be delighted for us to share that secret. We must recognise that seeking to take control of a military building that a Knight of the Road is defending will be . . . difficult."

"It will be a complete nightmare." Degralk was leaning into his role as a resident doomsayer. "If a full-scale invasion will cost us blood for every foot we take, then taking that building will cost us the same in inches. Assaulting Swinford's Keep is not something to be considered lightly."

"Your third option, Spymistress?"

"We move on."

There was a murmur throughout the group. Stein raised her hand to forestall it. "We need to consider the benefits of our continued engagement here. Swinford's walls are in ruins. In choosing to flood the surrounding plain with saltwater, they have ensured that farming in this region will be compromised for a generation. To have engaged the Cackle, they must have beggared their treasury. And the Lady Darkhelm will not stay within that Keep forever. This siege has been successful in all but name."

All eyes fixed on Souit.

The Great General gazed into the distance, accessing several of his Skills to try to parse the future of any confrontation. He was troubled because he could identify no clear path to victory. And it was not just the Knight of the Road that was disturbing his equilibrium. He could sense an opponent within the Keep who, if he were less secure in his capabilities, would be starting to intimidate him.

The lesson he had learned from the pseudo-destruction of Captain Kettle's company was that the mind leading the defence was at least his equal. And in the face of that brilliance, he was not wholly sure he could trust his instincts.

"My Lord?"

"I concur with the Spymistress's assessment. We have three ways in which to bring this to a close. I propose we follow all of them."

The Great General turned his horse to face those behind him. "Spymistress, you are to have every resource you require to dismantle the Cackle's defences. Mage, you and your colleagues are at the Spymistress's disposal. I do not wish to read reports of the indiscriminate slaughter of civilians, but neither will I tie your hands behind your back. Do I make myself clear?"

"You do, my Lord."

Souit turned to Degralk. "Major, I must confess I find you tiresome. I find your constant naysaying to be a thorn in my side. I, bell by bell, question the King's insistence that a man of your background has a place on my command staff."

Degralk coloured. "My Lord, I apologise if . . ."

Souit waved his words away. "I have not finished. But it occurs to me that, more often than not, you have been correct in your assessment. You have been correct where I have been wrong. Our opponent seems peculiarly well-suited to thwarting me, so I must take myself out of the equation. You are to command the assault on the Keep."

Degralk felt the irritation of the officers around him. "Sir, I thank you for your confidence, but there are many men around you more suited to such a role than I."

"Do not take your role as my licensed fool too far, sir. I have given you your orders, and I expect *everyone* to adhere to them." He glared around at his command staff. "Are we clear?" There were muted voices of agreement. "Once the Spymistress and Major Degralk have identified the resources they require for their tasks, I will turn my attention to the rest of the campaign. We should shortly be hearing news from those we sent ahead of us into the West. Assuming they have not experienced setbacks, we may well not be too far behind schedule."

The Great General met the eyes of each person in the room. "This has not been our finest hour, ladies and gen-tlemen. However, we will come out of this all the stronger."

A resolute tone entered his voice as he made use of <Inspiring Words>. All around him stood a little taller. "You have your orders. Do not let your King down."

CHAPTER TWENTY-SIX

"Storming the Temple"

Droughton-on-the-Water — thirty years ago.

G uarding the entrance to the Holy Temple of the Lords of Misrule in Droughton was not considered an especially prestigious post.

To be sure, there were roles for lower Priests that were objectively far more challenging and much less appealing. The members of the Order maintaining the acres upon acres of grapevine that served the Temple's bars, for example, often had cause to curse their lot in life. Likewise, those poor unfortunates who swept and cleaned the floors of the Gambling Houses after major festivals were rarely much envied at parties. And, he thought with a shudder, the less said about the Priest whose sole job was maintaining the hundreds of oubliettes that spotted the compound, the better.

But, that being said, there was still something about standing stock-still, in full armour, in the sweltering heat, in front of a big stone building that made it a pretty uninspiring way to spend your time.

He felt <Imposing Presence> time out again and quickly refreshed it. If there was one thing worse than being on guard duty, it was being on guard duty with no one being afraid of you. The tips of his ears smarted as he remembered last week's debacle when he'd forgotten to switch his Skill on.

Washerwomen could be very unkind.

Of course, some days were more interesting than others.

Today, for instance, was shaping up to be quite memorable. After all, it was not every day a Knight of the Road strode up to the gatehouse and demanded the Archbishop present himself for judgment. That was undoubtedly a novel event. However, if he was pleased with this break in the monotony of his watch, Caleth, Priest of the Outer Temple, was hiding it well.

"I beg your pardon, my Lady. What did you say you wanted?" A thin smear of sweat appeared on his face as he realised her aura had completely overwhelmed his Skill. Had that ever happened before? He tried to refresh it several times before she tapped him on the nose.

"Don't keep fiddling with that Skill; it's annoying. The Archbishop. Here. Now." Daine drew her sword. "Chop-chop."

His eyes widened and he felt the tip of his ears begin to burn again. This was shaping up to be a Washerwoman-scale fiasco all over again.

Sensing they were not getting anywhere quickly, Bayran slipped past the Knight and put a comforting hand on Caleth's shoulder. Daine tutted as the Priestess pulsed some enticing thought or other into the poor boy's mind. "Brother, the Lords know there is little worth in seeking to defy this woman. For your sake, I suggest you send Cardinal Arvid a message immediately. And then we could, perhaps, speak further and in a more intimate setting."

Caleth's armour suddenly weighed even more heavily upon his slender frame. He really was not cut out for these sorts of games. A young man scarcely out of his adolescence, his air of nervous apprehension clung to him like a tattered cloak. He was, at best, a reluctant sentinel, and right now, he felt thrust into a role for which he was ill-prepared. He must have been absent if there had been a discussion of how to play this sort of situation in basic training. In desperation, he sought to trigger his Skill again but had that boost to his Charisma immediately squashed. This hardly felt fair, all things considered. His unassisted spirit was clearly not suited to barring the way to a Knight of the Road and a Priestess of the Inner Temple.

His eyes darted about anxiously, scanning the face of the girl — because that was, after all, what this Knight was. He knew, intellectually, she could tear him limb from limb without thinking twice, but it was hard to credit such power to someone who looked so very much like his baby sister. Although, thinking about some of Monda's towering rages, maybe not . . .

His fingers gripped the hilt of his sword, knuckles whitening under the strain. The blade felt heavy and unfamiliar in his grasp, as if it possessed a weight that belied his feeble strength. The Knight caught that gesture and raised her eyebrows. He quickly released his hold and turned his attention back to the Priestess.

"I will not abandon my post, Senior Sister. The Archbishop has forbidden entry or exit to anyone whilst the conclave is in session."

Daine exhaled noisily and examined the door to the gatehouse. It looked solid enough, some sort of hardened wood with iron supports running up and down it. She had seen much worse in her time. Around it, though, the brickwork was much less well-maintained. Old Gant had always said that sieges usually succeeded when the attackers ignored the doorway and took a more direct route. Taking that advice, she would probably try to go through the wall when push came to shove. A part of her, and she was self-reflective enough to know it was a big part, hoped such action would be necessary. She had enjoyed tangling with the Chimaera.

The Priestess was losing her temper. "You cannot forbid me entry to my own Temple!" Bayran cried, the hand on his shoulder becoming a repeating prod to the chest. "Do you not know who I am? Do you truly think the Archbishop would not want to hear the news I bring? And what of this 'conclave'? As far as I am aware, nothing of the sort has been planned."

Caleth's mind swirled. Yes, it was the incident with the Washerwoman all over again. Only this time, he was being confronted not by a woman who refused to stop when asked, but two beings more than capable of destroying him with no more than a thought. His eyes nervously sought a distraction in the bustling street beyond the Temple grounds. Anything to look at that was not this

very angry, very attractive Priestess or, of course, this terrifying Knight of the Road.

"Senior Sister, I do know you, I assure you, and I recognise your authority. But the Archbishop was clear. No
entry or exit on pain of death. He was quite insistent on
this point. It is not within my power to countermand that
order."

He had heard tales of the fates of those who disappointed Jerule, whispered rumours of hellish tortures and
long-forgotten rituals enacted to end lives in screaming
torment. Right now, though, he was unsure whether the
promise of such punishment in the future outweighed the
immediate danger presented by the two women before him.

"Brother, stand aside." Bayran had given up subtly trying to influence the boy and was now openly channelling
<Allure> towards him. It was seen as bad form to ensorcel
fellow adherents in the Order, but she had endured quite a
day of humiliation at the hands of the Knight of the Road.
She was unwilling to accept further scorn heaped upon her
through a lesser Priest barring her entry.

Caleth did his best to avoid a pair of eyes that seemed
suddenly much bigger and more enticing and gazed upon
the carved reliefs that adorned the Temple gates. But the
Lords, it seemed, were deaf to his pleas. Most of the images on which his eyes fell were rather more carnal in nature than he remembered. He imagined his gods were
enjoying the entertainment of watching him suffer.

With a substantial mental effort, he pushed back against
Bayran's casting, shuddering at some of the images she was
projecting into his mind, and answered in the negative. "I
cannot allow that, Senior Sister."

At those words, the night settled around him, enveloping

the space around him in an eerie stillness. Caleth's breath quickened, his pulse thrumming in his temples as he battled against the pressure of Bayran's Skill. He cast his gaze inward, seeking the ember of resolve that still smouldered within him. He would not abandon his post.

Caleth, young and nervous though he may be, would face the darkness that threatened it with trembling but steadfast courage . . .

Beside him was a crash as Daine, bored of waiting, simply walked through the stone wall and into the Temple beyond. The two members of the Order of the Lords of Misrule watched her brushing dust out of her hair, walking into the compound.

She did not so much as look back.

"By the Lords, I hate this woman," muttered Bayran, running to catch up.

Caleth looked at the hole in the wall next to the gate he had heroically held against all pressure. He was unsure the Archbishop would view it that way.

As he pondered, he thought he could make out the sound of dice being cast.

CHAPTER TWENTY-SEVEN

"The Hyena and the Spider"

Sitting up, Stein shook her head to try to clear the ringing in her ears. At the blinding pain that came from the motion, she quickly stopped and pressed a hand to her forehead. It came away wet. Blinking owlishly, she took in the red stickiness that covered her palm; she appeared to be bleeding quite profusely.

Looking around, she could see she was not the only one so beset. Lying all around her were the remains — quite literal — of the small squad she had been leading to dismantle the various barricades thrown up across Swinford's streets.

Someone pulled at her sleeve, and she turned to the side. A young man was talking to her, but she couldn't hear the words he was saying. She pointed at her ears and shook her head, then winced. She needed not to be doing that many more times.

The man frowned and then held up his hand, which immediately glowed golden.

"— fall back, Mistress."

"Could you please say that again?"

"We need to fall back to our lines, Spymistress. I think we're the only two left."

He — why could she not remember his name? — helped her to her feet and cast another healing spell on her. She winced as something popped and then reconnected in her back. "What happened?"

"If you don't know, my Lady. I surely don't. Hurry now."

He was pushing her backwards and away from the chaos, helping her to step over the bodies of those left underfoot. She slipped in a pool of blood and clung to the man's arm in panic. He looked down at her and activated his <Bandage> Skill once again.

"I daren't use that more than three times on you, my Lady. I can patch you up, but you need a proper Healer."

Stein tried to access her own Skills — she had several that could temporarily boost her Attributes — but found herself too hazy to trigger any of them. "Agreed."

Leaning heavily on her rescuer, she turned to glance at the scene of the ambush, and the memories came flooding back.

*

It had all been going largely as she had anticipated. The barricades that blocked each and every street had been put together by someone who knew their business. So much so that it had taken some time for her to decide on a path through them all.

The first of the barricades she led her men towards

loomed in the dimming light, a patchwork of lumber and scrap. But it was the traps that demanded her attention. Feeling fifty years younger — maybe there was something to be said for getting out of the Capital — she approached them with a predatory grace, the rest of her company fanning out behind her like the wings of a dark angel.

In her youth, she had ensured she did everything possible to raise her passive Perception. Indeed, at the height of her powers, it had been rumoured she could detect someone even thinking about causing the King harm. Her true abilities were not quite so alarming as that, but she enjoyed the notoriety that came with such a reputation. It had undoubtedly not harmed her rise to power.

Nevertheless, regardless of the slight exaggeration, she only had to look at the first barricade for each of the traps contained to light up in her vision thanks to her Perception. The first device was crude, a tripwire connected to a makeshift explosion. It was designed to go off with the force of a blacksmith's hammer at the slightest touch, intended to take the hand that brushed it. It was precisely the sort of thing she would have planted herself. Not deadly but loud, messy and destined to cause casualties. Activating <Disarm Trap>, she quickly traced the wire to its anchor, a pin precariously holding back the tension. With just her forefinger and thumb, she eased the pin free and threw the now-safe device to one of the men behind her.

"This is a good one to study. Nasty as you like."

Next, she spotted a snare hidden beneath the detritus strewn about the street. Whichever devious mind was behind this had used razor wire to build a noose that would tighten with a victim's own struggles until the whole foot would be sawn free. Nodding in appreciation, she used a hooked rod to coax the loop open, disarming the threat with a flick of her wrist.

There were seven or eight similar traps within this barricade alone, and it was the work of at least a bell before she was happy to let her men approach. Given the all clear, they worked with crowbars and hands wrapped in cloth to mute their efforts. Boards were pried loose, and nails squealed in protest until the obstruction began disintegrating under their methodical dismantling.

Every motion was precise, with no energy wasted. The barricades were reduced to their component parts: harmless piles of wood and metal scattered across the cobblestones.

At that stage, things began to go wrong.

One of her men saw a figure crossing the road. A buxom, attractive woman in a highly revealing red dress. With a shout that mingled lust and triumph, he and a group of others broke away from those working at the barricade to run and accost her.

Stein instinctively knew there was something wrong with the image. Who, in the middle of a siege, took the time to dress in such a manner? She doubted Swinford's brothels were doing a roaring trade as the King's Army swept through the streets. She caught the sense of a Skill — some version of <Allure>? — being used. Her insistent shout stopped her men in their tracks, but by then, it was too late.

Crossbow quarrels poured from windows above them, each bolt punching through a victim. Cursing, Stein activated <Dwell in Shadows>, quickly hiding herself and her surviving men in a deep artificial darkness.

Silence.

Whilst Stein channelled that Skill, there would be no way for any observer to track them. They could slip away and rejoin the men she had left a few streets back. Assuming, that is, they had not already heard the commotion and come running.

Then, from the rooftops above, several filled buckets appeared, and with one heave their contents were thrown into the cloud of shadows the Spymistress had conjured. Stein and her men appeared to have been covered with some sort of silvery dust. Channelling her defensive Skill was a significant drain on her mana pool, so she had called out to one of the others to <Identify> the substance that was now all over them.

"I don't know, Mistress. It says 'lepidolite.' I've never heard of it."

"Lepidolite?" Stein's face frowned in confusion. "That's used in the glazing of pottery, isn't it? Why would they . . ."

She had no chance to complete that thought before Donal's Milkmaids switched their buckets for their waterskins and flooded water atop them.

It turned out that lepidolite dust plus water had a very violent reaction indeed.

*

Leaning on the man who had saved her — she still could not remember his name — Stein stumbled through the dark streets. It was a testament to how disorientated she felt that she could not track their progress. Surely they should be near the rest of her men by now? The Spymistress reached again and again for her Skills and, at each stage, felt them slip away. She was worried that she was suffering from a concussion, if not something much worse.

"Is it much further?"

Her guide did not reply but pulled her down into an alley. He urged her past him with a gentle push, and she walked a few steps before realising she was looking at a dead end. She turned back to her saviour, but he was no longer there.

Even through her injuries, she retained all the instincts that had kept her alive at the heart of the Kingdom for decades. Two stilettoes were immediately in her hands, each coated with extremely unpleasant substances.

With a flick of her wrist, she sent one towards a suspicious patch of darkness to her left, and was rewarded with a curse and then a horrifying scream as the poison got to work.

Something ,moved quickly towards her from the other side, and she slashed with her remaining knife. Her balance, though, was all wrong, and she stumbled where she would have once gracefully pivoted. The woman, for she saw her attacker was a woman, batted the knife out of her hand and punched her hard in the stomach.

Stein dropped to her knees.

Stupid. How stupid. After all these years, it came to this! A standard bait and switch in a dark alley. She stayed bent low, drawing in long, ragged breaths. She made a final attempt to access her Skills, but they remained stubbornly beyond her reach.

So be it.

She idly wondered how Major Degralk was doing assaulting the Keep. Somehow, she feared he would be faring even less well than herself.

"I must say, I'm disappointed."

Stein looked up into the eyes of the small woman who had struck her.

"The Hyena, I presume? I should have recognised the smell of purchasable integrity."

The woman nodded. "The one and only. I must say, I had expected more from the Spider. If I'd known you were going to be this easy, I'd have let Jorick kill you back at the barricade. This is hardly worth getting my shoes dirty for."

"Sorry to disappoint you, but well done. You've beaten up an old woman suffering from a debilitating head injury. Truly an achievement for the ages."

As she spoke, Stein cracked the false tooth — the one she had always hoped never to use — and drank down half the liquid that spilt out.

The Hyena saw the telltale clench of the jaw and moved forward to stop her, reaching out to grab her by the throat. However, once she was in range, Stein spat the rest of the substance into her face.

The last thing she heard in this world brought a smile to her face. The screams of their leader brought the rest of the Cackle running. "Won't be slipping unseen through the crowds anymore, my dear. Enjoy the scars."

And with that, Spymistress Stein, the Dark Spider at the heart of the Kingdom's political games, breathed her last.

CHAPTER TWENTY-EIGHT

"The Keep"

Major Degralk stood alone in front of Swinford's Keep.

He imagined that many years before, it would have been an imposing sight. Indeed, the Keep still seemed indomitable from a distance, its silhouette a dark crown against the dying light. He could well imagine, in ages past, a commander in his situation would feel little more than despair should they have received the order to storm it.

However, it did not take much close inspection to uncover the crumbling shambles of the outer walls. The stones, though massive, were disjointed, bearing cracks almost large enough for a man to pass straight through.

To a certain extent, the thin fabric that had appeared outside the building — and had so confounded the Mages — hid the Keep's decrepitude.

He heard a pair of slow footsteps approaching from behind him, and then Souit was at his side. "It is a sorry sight, is it not, Major?"

Degralk did not answer. He was not wholly convinced the Great General wished for him to survive this assault. Rumours of the death of Spymistress Stein were rife around the men's campfires, and more than one sympathetic grimace had been directed his way. If this was a suicide mission, he was damned if he was going to be polite to the man who had ordered it.

"I have reviewed your strategy for the attack. It is certainly interesting."

Degralk continued to stand motionless. He had tolerated the amused condescension of men like Souit his whole life. They always thought they knew better than the jumped-up Pikeman from the ranks. Never mind his years of hard-won experience. Never mind that everything he had achieved was by his own hands, not a fluke of some inherited Skill or — and he side-eyed Souit here — a Class gifted by the King.

The Great General did not seem put out by Degralk's silence. He continued to stand next to him, observing the Keep in an almost companionable silence.

"I have some suggestions, if you would like to hear them?"

That got Degralk's attention. "Suggestions, sir?"

"Nothing dramatic, I assure you. Your tactics are entirely sound. It is just, regardless of what you may assume, I would rather not lose another member of my command staff to this City."

"I would welcome any thoughts that might add to the well-being of my men, sir."

"I sense from reviewing your order of battle you do not have much experience in taking a building of this type."

Degralk clenched his jaw. "Sir, I would hazard I have seen more engagements than any solider in your army."

Souit put a hand on the Major's forearm. "You misunderstand me, sir. I do not question your service. Merely state that fighting in the open field comes with a very different set of challenges to your current mission. Your proposed strategy is entirely sound, but there is a difference between the theory and the practice. Having led more than my share of this type of engagement, I would share my experience."

"Should you wish the honour, my Lord, I am entirely happy to relinquish command." Degralk was not speaking entirely in jest.

Souit winced. "Indeed. Do not think I have not considered it. However, it has come to my attention that the defenders can preempt my decision-making. I am, therefore, seeking to be less predictable."

"I am not sure Spymistress Stein would applaud the success of this strategy." There was a pause when Degralk realised he had probably massively overstepped the mark. "I am sorry, my Lord, that was not appropriate."

Souit shook his head. "No, sir. You are quite right." He sighed. "If we did not have bad luck, I doubt we would be having any luck at all. Do you have a god, sir?"

Degralk turned to face the General. "My Lord?"

"A god, sir. Do you worship any of the pantheon in particular?"

"The Goddess, I suppose. Can't say I ever give it much thought."

"Until my Class Evolution, I had always felt pulled

towards the Lords of Misrule. You see, I was quite the gambler in my youth, sir. There were no games under the sun I would not hazard coin on."

Degralk nodded awkwardly, unsure how to respond to the unexpected direction.

"But, when the King chose to evolve my Class — do you know what I was before my elevation?"

Degralk nodded. "A Baron, I believe, sir."

"Indeed. My family had developed decent Attributes and a strong Skillset to pass down through the years. I'd used what I'd inherited to do well in the wars in the South and come to the right people's attention. Not unlike yourself, sir, now I think on it."

Degralk nodded. He knew all about military success and getting noticed. It struck him that Baron Souit of Finnistown probably received a far warmer welcome to the corridors of power than Tomas Degralk of nowhere in particular. He realised the man was still talking.

" — and when the King made it known that I was to be considered for evolution to Great General, I felt the hands of the Lords on my shoulders, willing me to play the game. So, I did what I could to ensure I was chosen to command the King's Armies. But do you know what, sir?"

"What, my Lord?"

"This Class is absolutely the antithesis of the creed of the Lords of Misrule. The Skills I now possess are all about certainty, considered tactics and long-term strategy. There is no longer room for anything so mundane as 'luck' in my world. In truth, I have the capacity to plan it out of existence. And because of that, I have found myself wondering why my gods were so keen I pursued the change. And do you know what this siege has made me realise? What every bizarre setback and undercut to my careful plans has shown me about where I stand with my gods?"

Degralk was unclear what, if anything, was required of him in this conversation.

"What, my Lord?"

"I fear they are finding the whole thing utterly hilarious."

*

Once the Great General had unburdened himself — and was not Degralk delighted, on the eve of his assault, to be told his commander feared the gods were taunting him — they had moved on to discuss tactics.

Grudgingly, the Major accepted that many of Souit's suggestions were entirely sensible and changed his orders to encompass them.

All that was left was the attack itself.

"I really don't know what you want from here."

Degralk had requested Mage support for the assault and was dismayed to see Kulor amble his way over to the forming ranks. Of the remaining Mages, this tall, fair man would have been the absolute last of his choices.

"What I would like, Mage Kulor, is a way to enter that building."

"Major, we have repeatedly told you that we can do nothing to its walls. Watch." With a flick of the wrist, a fireball flew towards the Keep. However, where it should have exploded against stone, it touched the material that lined the walls and vanished. "Goddess knows what that cloth is made of, but every man, woman and child of Noble birth will want to buy the secret once we drag it from the minds of the defenders. Imagine it! Clothing that makes you invulnerable!"

Degralk was somewhat more concerned about his

impending charge towards a building with an impregnable covering.

"We'll have to take the door the old-fashioned way, Mage. I need you to cover us from whatever is going to rain down whilst we are doing so." He pointed at the arrowslits that spotted every few feet of wall and some rather unfriendly-looking structures that hung from the battlements.

"That shouldn't be too difficult. I have some Skills connected to the air that I should be able to chain together. <Gust> and <Swirling Wind> will keep you safe enough, I'm sure."

"Us."

"Excuse me."

"Will keep 'us' safe enough. You will be standing right in the middle of our formation."

"Ah" — the Mage's face was suddenly ashen — "in that case, I may supplement those spells with some channelling of a shield Skill. And perhaps I could use a few of my higher protection runes to keep everything shipshape. Yes, that would be a proper belt-and-braces approach to the situation."

"I thought it might."

*

The crash of the battering ram had become almost background noise to the defenders. The monotony of its regular collisions with the door had an almost lulling effect.

Almost.

Donal stood atop the Keep, looking down at the activity below. The attackers had been at it for some time, and he was, he had to admit it, pretty impressed with their resilience.

The Dark Warlord had assumed that when he'd "emptied" the cloth covering the walls on top of them, those men would lose interest in assaulting the door. Or breathing. Or very much else at all, to be honest.

But they had someone down there who had, by hook or by crook, been able to defend them from the massive number of projectiles he'd expelled from the pseudo-Bag of Holding down on them.

He was pretty sure, though, that whatever Mage was holding it all together down there must be running pretty low on mana. The last thing they would be expecting would be . . .

*

At a strange squelching noise, Degralk turned and watched in horror as Kulor turned inside out.

There was no warning. There was no scream of pain. There was no time. One moment, the weary Mage was sucking down yet another mana potion and complaining bitterly about the headache that awaited and then — well, Degralk was comfortable in saying a headache was the least of his problems.

"Shields up!"

With the death of the Mage, all the rocks, fireballs, arrows, and other projectiles spilling out of the walls of Swinford's Keep now fell directly on his troops. Metal clanged as shields slotted together to catch and hold the weight falling upon them.

They were so close. Just a few more bone-jarring collisions, and they would be through the door and into the building proper. He could even see, when the battering ram hit the cracks in the door, the pale faces of irregulars lined up to defend the hallway.

Not a soldier amongst them.

Just a few more moments, and they'd be in.

*

Donal pressed a hand to his forehead and frowned. He felt drained. It was like he had just activated an especially potent spell. He looked down and saw that something had clearly happened to the Mage below. The protections they had weaved around the attacking force had wholly fallen away.

Had he just done something?

Whoever it was down there, they'd been good. It would have taken something . . . exotic to have incapacitated them so completely.

Then the pressure in his head was gone, and he was moving towards the stairs. The King's Army would be through that door in moments; he needed to ensure all the surprises he had prepared were fully operational.

As he walked down the stone stairwell, <Dark Pragmatism> hummed happily in the background.

CHAPTER TWENTY-NINE

"The Gatehouse Has Fallen."

With a final heave of the battering ram, the heavy wooden door to the gatehouse shattered and collapsed inwards. The figures stood in a thin line of defence, activated whatever Skills they possessed, and began to pour arrows into the press of soldiers that surged through the breach. In front of the makeshift archers, men wearing heavy armour lowered pikes to impale the onrushing attackers.

Much to their concern, the King's men suddenly found themselves trapped between the falling masonry outside the walls and the killing zone established on the other side of the door. As the losses mounted, the bodies of the wounded began to foul up the progress of those crashing through the broken wood.

Crucially, vital momentum began to stall.

Degralk thought back to Souit's words the previous

evening: "Your first key challenge will come once you breach that door. You must get your men through and into the gatehouse as quickly as possible. Get stuck, and you are as good as dead. You will be ground to dust if the initial charge is halted."

Fearing they were in danger of failing that challenge, Degralk put the first of Souit's suggestions into action. He cleared his throat and bellowed: "Front row, duck and cover!"

The men desperately striving to charge through a hail of arrows stopped and crouched behind their raised shields.

"Second row, prepare!"

From behind a now-solid wall of shields, all the waiting attackers drew javelins from quivers on their backs and readied their aim.

The defenders holding the long pikes were suddenly aware of their extreme vulnerability. With panicked shouts, they pulled back and away from danger. As they did so, though, they reversed into the archers, and the cohesion of the defensive lines began to degrade. It was impossible to keep up the steady stream of arrows with their own stumbling back into them.

"Throw at will!"

At such close range, the flurry of javelins had a devastating effect.

Despite Daine and Donal's work of the preceding weeks, these men and women were not professional soldiers. They had been carefully drilled in their specific roles and had achieved something astonishing in holding the breach against the might of the King's Army.

It was all that could have been asked of them. And more.

However, none of them had the experience to cope with a sudden change of tactic.

When Degralk saw the defenders' resolve shake, he urged his men forward, painfully aware of the losses racking up behind him. He was swept along by the tide of his men, releasing his shortsword and stooping to pick up a pike dropped by a defender as he passed. The familiar weight felt good in his hands, and he smiled with genuine pleasure. If he was going to be in a fight for his life, he would take every advantage he could get.

The defence rapidly crumbled. Shaken by the unexpected projectiles and now hurried by the rapidly closing soldiers, Swinford's irregulars broke. For anyone who chose to run, Degralk ordered them let go. A swarm of routed, terrified civilians fleeing backwards would have far more impact on the rest of the siege than a mound of slaughtered bodies.

Enough, though, chose to stand and die that the Major found himself in the thick of the action, liberally using his <Immovable Object> Skill on his borrowed weapon.

As one of those who refused to run barrelled towards him, he felt his senses sharpen in that old, familiar way. He noted his attacker's poorly maintained armour clanking discordantly with each step, glaringly contrasting with his lighter, more flexible gear. Muscle memory transferred his weight onto the back foot, angling his pike's tip towards the oncoming man. He triggered his Skill and waited for what he knew would happen next.

As a badly aimed sword slash flew towards his head, he manoeuvred his pike with both hands, leveraging its length as he had done for so many years. The tip of the pike, aimed with precision, slipped through the narrow gap where helmet met breastplate, finding the vulnerable throat beneath.

The impact was a sharp jolt that rattled the wooden shaft, but Degralk's Skill held it steady. The attacker's momentum worked against them, driving the pike deeper through their neck, severing arteries. With a swift, practised jerk, the Major withdrew his weapon, the dead body toppling forward to land beside him.

But there was to be no respite. Another assailant appeared, this one more agile, darting in with a knife. Degralk adjusted his grip on the pike, shortening its effective length for closer combat. As the blade swiped towards him, he deftly tilted his weapon, its shaft knocking the thrust aside. In a fluid motion, he stepped sideways, exploiting the enemy's momentary imbalance. He thrust the pike's butt end into the attacker's stomach, winding her, then swiftly reversed the pike to deliver a finishing thrust.

The second corpse fell to land on the first.

Spinning the pike back into a defensive position, he looked around, prepared to receive another attack. But that seemed to be that.

For all the preparation on both sides, it was already over.

The first clash was theirs, and the rest of his men were pouring through the secured breach.

*

"The gatehouse has fallen, my Lady."

Daine nodded at the news, not looking up at the frightened messenger. Uncertainly, the young girl bowed and then withdrew.

Without pause, the Knight of the Road continued to slowly oil the length of her greatsword.

Not long now.

*

As the adrenaline began to drain away, it felt as if time had slowed. Intellectually, Degralk knew his men were carrying out his orders as fast as they could, but, in his state of heightened awareness, they appeared to be doing so as if underwater.

He took a breath and tried to calm down his heartbeats. The first objective was completed. Now they needed to dig in and prepare for the assault on the central tower itself.

Golden light flashed throughout the ranks as the Healers moved about ensuring all was as well as possible. Looking around, Degralk was pleased to see he still had so many of his initial force available to him. For all the sound and fury of the fighting, the losses on either side were not particularly material. Perhaps a hundred of his own men had fallen, the majority of those being crushed outside the Keep. The defenders had lost maybe half of that.

But, of course, he had far more he could afford to lose.

He watched as dead bodies were passed through the broken door, clearing space for the forthcoming charge.

Looking out over the open courtyard space that led to the tower door, Degralk could see this would be hot work. Souit had stressed they would be assailed from both sides. From behind, as those who had defended the walls now turned their attention inwards, and then from above as those in the tower sought to repel them.

And that was assuming there were no forces that would seek to contend with them outside the tower itself. An image of a large figure wearing full plate swam into Degralk's mind, and he pressed it quickly away. He knew that, at some point, he would be forced into conflict with the Darkhelm.

He was counting his blessings that she had not seen fit to contest the gatehouse.

He glanced at the stairways leading up to the battlements above. His initial plan had been to swarm those battlements and take command of the external walls, but Souit had dissuaded him from that course of action. "You must remember that Mayor Elm is the mission. Once you have him, that will be the end of all resistance. You should seek to get through the external walls and immediately try to take that tower. Do not let anything else delay you. After all, if they couldn't keep you outside the walls, they don't have enough power to be worth worrying about."

"Whenever you are ready, sir."

Degralk started at the voice. One of his Captains — Goddess, he couldn't remember the woman's name — was saluting smartly. He replied in kind.

"I am sorry, Captain. What did you say?"

"Our fallback position is established. I think it is fair to say that the boys and girls are ready to press onwards."

Degralk nodded, his eyes scanning the empty courtyard before him. Would it remain so? "Then it would be rude to keep them waiting. Give the order to form up."

And should Degralk have glanced upwards at that moment, he would doubtless have noticed the sickly green light that suddenly burst from a complex rune drawn on the ceiling of the gatehouse.

However, he did not, and the opportunity to avoid what was to come slipped through his fingers.

Back in the command tent, Souit's head jerked upwards as he heard the sudden rattling of dice.

It was no coincidence that, in response, the fingers of a corpse with a catastrophic chest wound twitched and then bunched into a fist.

CHAPTER THIRTY

"A Memory of the Soulless"

Droughton-on-the-Water — thirty years ago.

"Where is everyone?"

Daine and Bayran had been walking around the Temple for quite some time and had yet to encounter another soul.

Corridors stretched out in complete silence. The soft echo of the footsteps of the two women was the only sound to disturb the stillness. Halls and courtyards stood empty. They had even passed a fountain around which eight pairs of shoes were carefully arranged, with their owners nowhere to be seen.

This was not the epic confrontation against hordes of zealous defenders of the faith Daine had imagined. Had hoped for, if truth were told.

"I do not know, my Lady. By my count, we've passed

four empty guard posts. It is unheard of for this sanctum to lie so undefended. And that is without considering all the Brothers and Sisters that should be out and about this close to compline."

Bayran was nervous. Nothing about the plans for this day had worked out in the way she had imagined. From that very first interaction with the Knight of the Road, she had been wholly off-balance. First her humiliation at the courtroom, then the confrontation with the Unsouled outside the tavern, to being nearly killed by a Chimaera.

And now to find the Temple deserted, having been forbidden entry by a Lower Priest?

She was well aware that her gods enjoyed their games, but she had hitherto found herself alongside of those pulling the strings. Realising that she now appeared to be on the other side of the curtain was disconcerting in the extreme.

Her mind wandering, she nearly walked into Daine's back when the Knight suddenly paused outside a closed door. It looked identical to all the others they had strolled past, but Bayran immediately felt the same sense of wrongness that clearly had captured the other woman's interest.

There was an oily, unclean aura behind that door that was quite at odds with the broader atmosphere of the Temple.

The two exchanged glances before Daine pushed at it but found it locked. She then put some weight behind her shove and popped it straight off its hinges.

As the door crashed inwards, both women saw what was within and took shocked breaths. Everything within the chamber was cloaked in a sinister green light that seemed to seep from the walls themselves. The air was heavy with the stench of expelled mana, an acrid tang that offended their senses.

But that was nothing compared to what was in the centre of the room.

Clustered together in a defensive circle stood a congregation of Priests, their faces drawn and haggard. Although standing, these people were clearly no longer alive, their eyes dark, lifeless pits devoid of any spark.

What stood before Daine and Bayran were little more than hollow vessels.

The bodies stood rigid and unmoving, like statues frozen in eternal torment. Their unnaturally thin skin clung to prominent bones. Indeed, there were more than a few cases where the skeleton beneath had torn through. As if mirroring the degraded state of the bodies, tattered robes draped over their emaciated forms, once-beautiful cloth reduced to nothing but rags.

The sickly green light was coming from a series of runes, Daine realised. One on each wall, the ceiling and the floor. Despite her Class Resistance to all forms of magic, she could still feel a slight tug on her health from them, but nothing to explain what she now saw. Whatever had reduced the Priests to this state was much more potent than whatever had been drawn here. She looked over at Bayran, who was glowing with some sort of Healing Skill.

"You okay?"

Bayran was shocked by the sight of what had befallen her brethren but nodded nonetheless. "Some sort of passive drain. But it's very minor. I can channel through it without much mana cost."

As horrific as the scene in front of them proved to be, the sense of wrongness that had drawn the two women to the room went further than some dead Priests. There was something else.

Daine turned to look at her companion. Did she trust this Priestess? She was obviously shaken by what was in this room, so she was comfortable that the woman was not part of whatever was happening here. That did not, of course, mean she could rely on her. Therefore, perhaps the more pertinent question was, did it matter if she was betrayed by her?

Daine did not think she had anything to fear from the Priestess as an opponent, but if Gant had driven one thing into her, it was to "hope for the best, but plan for the worst."

She turned back to regard the group in the centre of the room. The flickering light of the runes cast grotesque shadows upon the chamber's walls, accentuating the twisted features of the Priests.

Their hands, once raised in prayer and supplication, now hung limply by their sides, devoid of purpose or meaning. Voices raised in praise of the Lords of Misrule had been silenced, replaced by a silence that hung like a deathly pall.

"You roll the dice and take your chance" might be the creed by which this Order lived, but Daine did not think these Priests would appreciate how their Luck had run out.

Or maybe it hadn't.

Again, there was that nagging feeling that there was something else going on here. In this chamber of souls laid bare, despair mingled with the faintest glimmer of hope. Though the Priests now stood as empty vessels, defiance lingered, a stubborn refusal to yield entirely to the darkness that had consumed them. In the depths of their vacant eyes, a flicker of their former selves persisted, a whisper of the souls that once burned bright with devotion. But now, trapped within this chamber of shadows, their prayers went unanswered, lost in the void that had become their existence.

Daine stepped forward to touch one of the runes. Again, the slightest pull to her health but nothing else. She did not recognise the script which appeared to have been painted with blood. "If I had to guess, I would say your Archbishop has begun feeding your Order to the mirror. What was it the guard said? No one in or out."

"But that's —"

"I know." Daine turned away from the rune and moved through the chamber, trying to find any other evidence of how the transformation had taken place. The Runes had not drained these people, but they were clearly keeping the Priests in some sort of stasis. It must have been the mirror for which they had been hunting that had caused this — these men and women of the Inner Temple had been turned into Soulless.

But did the mirror need to have contact to pull out the soul? She did not think so; these Priests looked like they had all been taken unawares.

So, simple proximity.

Did the Archbishop have it placed in this room and then send these victims to their doom? Perhaps the mirror left its victims with just enough life force to be animated, which the runes constantly drained. A brutal but effective way to empower the mirror without having rampaging hordes of Soulless to contend with. That seemed most probable.

But, if that was the case, where was it now? And how much more powerful could it become? How many Priests would it need to consume before she needed to worry about her capacity to destroy it?

The prospect of needing to call for support did not appeal. Old Gant had been clear that while, in theory, she could call upon help if needed, there would be consequences. There were stories of those Knights on Tour who could not carry their own water.

They were not complimentary.

Daine Orban had plans for how her legend would develop, and they did not include running home for the big boys.

"Priestess, I know this is horrifying, and I am sorry for you to see your fellows in such a state, but I need to know more of this 'conclave' of which the guard spoke. Is there somewhere your Archbishop may seek to assemble large numbers of your Order? This was the only room we have passed that gave me such a sense of wrongness; I cannot believe there are too many chambers filled with similar horrors."

Bayrun was pale as she considered the implications of what the Knight was saying. "There is — the Great Hall of Chance. At a push, the whole Order can be accommodated there. But he couldn't possibly . . . To do such a thing!" She looked again at the Priests in their frozen, deathly state. "I cannot conceive the Archbishop would do such a thing."

Daine moved towards the door. "I fear, Priestess, that when the prospect of power is involved, few lines remain uncrossed. Please, could you lead us to the Great Hall?"

And that would have been their next destination.

That is, should the green runes not have suddenly blazed into light and the Soulless Priests not have become animate and attacked them.

CHAPTER THIRTY-ONE

"A Step Too Far"

S ouit was the first person in the main army to recognise what was happening.

But even he, when a large force of enemy combatants suddenly reared up and attacked his men from behind, was momentarily lost for words. Had they been hiding somehow? Perhaps in tunnels that Degralk had missed when securing the walls? But, no, after that initial moment of shock, the true picture became clear.

"Necromancy," he yelled, turning to any messenger he could find. "Get me my Mages here now!"

*

Though Souit was the quickest on the uptake on the command staff, it was Private Geerdon who had first contact with the army of the dead. Or rather, it was the fist of the corpse of Corporal Drall that made contact with him.

Lethally.

In many ways, Geerdon was quite unfortunate. The risen Soulless was not moving quickly, nor was there any great power behind the blow that was made. However, the element of surprise, followed by an unlucky, staggering step on uneven ground, meant the young man slipped and hit his head on an inconveniently placed stone.

The last thing he heard as he died was the sound of hundreds of pairs of dice rolling.

*

As the sickly green light leaking from the runes on the gatehouse ceiling intensified, more and more of the fallen of both sides rose to attack Degralk's men. And a series of unfortunate and unlikely coincidences played out the length and breadth of the battle.

The Major watched, appalled, as the corpses of his men and those of the Swinford defenders began shambling about, swiping and lunging at anyone in range. Beyond the instinctive horror at what was occurring, he could not understand how such seemingly weak attacks were causing casualties far above their apparent threat level.

He drove his pike into a headless corpse drifting towards him, and was rather disconcerted as the body placed both hands on the shaft sticking through it and began dragging itself down the length towards him.

With a yell, he swung the Soulless off his weapon and was satisfied that when it crashed into the wall, it did not rise again.

Looking around, he could see that an enterprising group of soldiers had lit a bunch of torches and were using them to drive the animated corpses backwards.

Degralk took a breath to encourage others to do the same — everyone knew fire and the undead did not mix — when a horn sounded from the Keep, and, of course, at that moment, archers let loose upon his men. Those remaining defenders on the walls of the battlements — the ones he had thought he should ignore — likewise took the opportunity to add their voices to the mix.

Trapped between the horror of the attacking Soulless from behind and the rain of arrows from the front, Degralk felt the bottom drop out of his stomach.

He did not know what to do to salvage this.

*

"I do not want to hear any excuses. We need to reduce the pressure on the men inside. I do not care how you do it, but I need those Soulless gone. Now!"

The remaining Mages attached to the army were not enjoying their life on the Road. Whilst they had been able to rationalise away the death of Haran on the day of the first attack — she'd been told repeatedly to tighten up her elemental control — the fate of Kulor was quite different. They had all felt the astonishing wave of power that had killed that arrogant young Mage, and not one of them still alive was interested in attracting the attention of its source.

As had become their custom, they all looked at Angharad, who sighed. "My Lord, we are not anxious to act until we understand more of the players involved here. There have been too many unusual uses of power during this siege for us to throw spells out and hope for the best. Consider what we have seen: The fire that took Haran. The growth of that cornfield. The illusions that were not. The never-ending flood. That word of power that killed Kulor. And now this. There is no Mage within Swinford, of that we are certain, yet we look at all that has happened and are sure of the involvement of a High Mage. We see an army of Soulless, which suggests the involvement of deep Necromancy, and yet know that is not the case. In short, my Lord, we do not know what to do."

Souit drew his ornamental shortsword and levelled it on the Mage. "Did I stutter? I need those Soulless gone. And now. This is not a theoretical exercise; my men are dying down there." He raised his voice above the sound of rattling dice, then realised he was the only one who could hear them.

"Whatever it takes, Mage, you must relieve the pressure on Degralk's command. Immediately."

Angharad glanced at her fellows, all sharing the same sentiment about the mental well-being of the Great General. There was precedent, of course, for removing an insane leader in the field, but she certainly had no wish to assume command and, since the death of the Spymistress, did not think there was anyone else with the experience to make a decent fist of it.

Knowing the King's mood around the Western Rebellion, she doubted he would look kindly on frustrating the war effort. Indeed, removing a Great General in the middle of a siege could look rather like treason in the wrong light . . .

Ignoring the blade inches from her chest, she turned to consider the problem. The other Mages backed away, either giving her a respectful distance to work or ensuring they would not be caught up in any retribution from the Keep.

A little from Column A and a little from Column B, she assumed.

Thinking through her range of Skills, Angharad activated <Life Drain>. It was one of her lowest-levelled powers — she found anything that took its power from the Dark God to be distasteful — and she hoped it would be beneath the notice of whoever had obliterated Kulor.

Questing out towards the Soulless, she planned to lightly tug at whatever life force these beings still possessed. In theory, that should be that. However, when her power reached the outermost edge of the shambling, undead force, it passed straight through them.

There was nothing to drain.

Frowning, she tried again. She knew her level in <Life Drain> was low, but if anything, that should mean she failed to drain all available life force, not that she could not find any to latch on to.

She tried several more times, ignoring the growl of frustration from Souit as the undead foe beset more and more of his men.

No. There was not a drop of life force to be found. So, not Necromancy. Which she knew anyway. So, what was animating these bodies? Switching from <Life Drain> to <True Sight>, she zoomed in on the gatehouse.

It was chaos. Degralk had split his army in two. One half, with shields raised in a defensive turtle formation, faced the tower and tried to weather the hail of falling arrows. The second, in a square formation, was engaging the Soulless to the rear. The situation looked like it would get out of hand at any moment, especially with the appalling bad luck that she had seen curse the King's men repeatedly.

But no time for that. There must be something in the gatehouse providing "life" to the undead. Some sort of artefact or . . .

Her Skill locked onto a complex rune carved into the gatehouse ceiling. It was emitting a pale green light that she instinctively recoiled from. Capturing the form of the rune in <Perfect Recall> for future study, she conjured a <Fireball> and launched it at that spot, guiding it above and through the throng of men to strike at its centre.

*

The impact was immediate.

As soon as the rune was destroyed, all the Soulless collapsed and returned to their lifeless state.

Degralk did not need a second invitation. "Pull back. Everyone returns to the first staging position."

It stuck in his craw to abandon this position, especially considering how hard-won the gatehouse had been, but he needed to take a beat to assess the damage. Besides, the door to the gatehouse lay open. It would be easy enough to return once order had been established.

As he forced soldiers past him, encouraging the speedy retreat, he shook his head to clear a strange rattling noise bothering him.

*

Donal felt the tentative questing of the young Mage.

Good on her, he thought. He had been singularly unimpressed by the quality of Magery from the other side, so was pleased there was finally someone showing a bit of moxie.

Such a shame to have to snuff out that sort of enterprise.

His eyes darkened as he focused on the core of her power. All he needed to do was pierce that, and the flood of unrestrained power would consume her and anyone within a few hundred feet.

He recognised it was distasteful to do so — he was pretty sure he had once written a scroll about how this was one of the most unforgivable misuses of power — but he couldn't have her interfering again, could he? Needs must, and all that.

*

Angharad suddenly doubled over in pain.

It was like someone had stuck a needle into her heart. No, not into her heart. Her soul.

She activated every defensive Skill she had, but nothing seemed to make a difference. A white-hot sliver of pain was piercing the centre of her being again and again. She had never felt such a profound violation of everything she was and hoped to be. And, what was worse, she could do nothing as her power started to leak through the wounds.

Desperately, she looked around at the people crowded about her in concern. "Run!" she gasped.

*

"Nearly there," he muttered happily, batting aside the girl's pathetic attempts to deflect him. "All be over soon. No need to draw this out."

"Master Secretary?"

Cursing, Donal broke his focus and turned to the voice. He was moments away from finishing. He had probably done enough damage as it was, but he did so like to make sure.

Nevertheless, it did not do to ignore the sudden appearance of a Knight of the Road, especially when they had their sword drawn.

"My dear, terrible timing as always!"

Daine rested the tip of her sword on the stone floor. "I am sorry for that, Master Secretary. Nevertheless, I fear there are matters we must urgently discuss."

His black-filled eyes met hers, which, he realised with

a sinking feeling, were glowing gold with the power of a summoned Goddess.

"Ah. Oh dear."

And he struck out at her with everything he possessed.

CHAPTER THIRTY-TWO

"Friendly Fire"

A dark aura of shadow exploded out from Donal and filled the room. Momentarily startled by the change of light, Daine then focused on two orbs of glinting blue opposite her and advanced, sword raised.

"This is not what I want, Donal."

"Well, I am afraid that is rather too bad, my dear. We so rarely get what we want in this life. And I should know."

His voice was behind her.

Ignoring what she had thought were his eyes, she swung her greatsword, one-handed, in a wide overhead arc. Considering the oversized nature of the blade, it was a ridiculous movement to witness — even knowing the extraordinary Strength of the Knights of the Road — and the tactic took Donal by surprise.

Spinning with the weight of the strike, she saw the Dark Warlord fly back to the very corner of the room, black armour appearing around him that seemed to absorb what was left of the light, making him appear as a part of the shadows. Out of the darkness, a thin dagger formed in his hand. The length of the blade shimmered with runes of the same ugly, rotting glow from the gatehouse and, Daine recognised, from so many years before in Droughton.

Those long-forgotten memories pulled at her focus for a moment, but she stilled her mind and stepped forward to attack the man.

Do not kill him.

Daine paused to cock an ear, eager to see if the Goddess had any further words of wisdom . . .

But no. That appeared to be the extent of her vision.

Her mission was to somehow subdue a man with millennia of tricks up his sleeve and a somewhat worrying recent power-up. And, of course, there was no word of explanation as to why or, perhaps more pertinently, how.

Rolling her shoulders, ignoring the increasingly familiar pops and cracks of age, she stepped forward into the shadows.

I'll do you a deal, my Lady: I'll try to leave enough of him alive at the end of this for it to count as not killing him. Best I think I can do, in the circumstances . . .

The two combatants circled each other for a few moments. Donal was the first to move, his blade darting forward in a thrust aimed at Daine's chest. She was prepared for such a move, stepping aside with a fluidity that belied her armour's bulk, and crashed a heavy mailed fist down into the side of the Dark Warlord's head.

In her long experience, that really should have been that. So it was disconcerting to watch her erstwhile friend merely shake his head a few times to clear his vision and grin back at her.

"Was that really the best you can do? I'm disappointed. If I didn't know better, my dear, I'd say you were pulling your punches." As he spoke, his knife darted out to quickly score a rough rune on her chestplate. "I do so hope you don't regret that generosity."

With that, his body became incorporeal and vanished back into the shadows at the edge of the room.

Daine moved to follow before realising the area around the rune scratched on her armour was becoming very warm indeed. The steel glowed first red, then white in a widening circle, burning the cloth and skin beneath.

Grimacing, Daine sought to block out the pain. In the middle of a battle, there was nothing to be done but to endure it. This was one of her favourite pieces of armour, too.

"Are you really sure you wish to do this, my Lady? You would not be the first Knight of the Road I have needed to vanquish, but, in all honesty, you would be the first to whom I would regret doing so."

"Counterpoint. I have always enjoyed bringing down Dark Warlords, and I cannot say I care very much about you either way right now."

Ignoring the burning pain, she lashed out with a blow that would have cleaved a lesser opponent in two. Donal, however, twisted away to the other corner of the room, the edge of her blade missing him by mere inches and creating sparks that flashed as she cut down the edge of the wall.

Then the Dark Warlord returned at her with a series of strikes aimed at the softening metal of her chestplate, each faster than the last, his blade a blur of motion. He punched hole after hole through the once-resistant armour. As if being empowered by his attacks, all around the room, dark runes, each humming softly as they unleashed their power, surged into life and began to drain her.

"I've known this moment would come since you followed us back from that blasted village. Did you really think, when the time came for this confrontation, you would so easily be able to bring me down?" Shadows coiled around his arm, extending his reach, his knife striking from impossible angles.

"Donal, you appear to have spent an awful lot more time thinking about me than I did you. And that does not seem like the sort of thing you would be doing with Swinford under threat if you were quite yourself. Sir, you are not in your right mind. This was not the preamble of an attack upon you. I intended nothing more sinister in coming here than discussing the latest manifestation of your Class. I wanted to discuss with you that I have seen Soulless used in this way before. And it was not to the benefit of anyone."

There was the flicker of something on the man's face, but his attacks continued. Daine tried to meet each of his strikes with her sword, but her range of movement was hampered by the searing heat burning her skin. Her strategy, usually, was to use her Strength to end confrontations immediately. But under direction from the Goddes not to kill him, she found herself forced to try to get Donal to expend energy by dodging and parrying her powerful blows. Ideally, when he was exhausted, she would find him far more manageable to subdue than he was proving at present.

Holding on to that thought, she advanced, pressing the

older man backwards, her massive sword an improbable whirlwind of movement he could not dare to clash iron with. But, dodging each strike, Donal leapt onto the room's central table, then sprang off onto a wall and back again, his movements erratic and unpredictable. He was no longer just fighting Daine; he was using the layout of the very room as a weapon against her.

Even when seemingly cornered, the Dark Warlord continued to unleash a flurry of rune-enhanced strikes from both his knife and the runes he'd carved around them, each emanating dark energy that exploded from the walls to pull at Daine's life force. She absorbed each attack, but the sheer number of blows began to take their toll, her body trembling with the effort her <Self-Heal> Skill made to keep her functioning.

There will be an opening. Shortly. I must stress, do not kill him.

Then, in a sudden shift, Donal changed his tactics. Rather than seek to avoid contact, he began to focus his attacks on Daine's armour, looking for weaknesses.

He feinted high, then struck low, only to spin and deliver a backhand strike at the centre of her breastplate. The superheated metal completely lost its integrity under the strike, and Daine shrugged off the pieces that remained, the heat causing her far more pain than it was providing support.

However, in the absence of any further protection, the rune-covered dagger pierced her skin and plunged inwards into her heart.

As it did so, Daine was disturbed by the expression on the man's face. There was nothing left of the mischievous, kind man whose company she had grown to value over the last few weeks. In its place was a pallid mask of hate.

"Got you!" The voice had nothing of Donal in it either. It seemed to be both very young and extremely old at the same time.

As it tore into her heart, the runes on the dagger activated, and Daine was alarmed as she felt her health halve, then halve again and again.

I hope this was the opening you meant . . .

Seizing the initiative, she clamped both her hands around Donal's and locked them around the handle of the blade embedded in her chest. Her health continued to decrease at an alarming degree, but, as she had done throughout her life, she trusted in her patron Goddess.

And, a tiny part of her thought, if this was to be the end, she was not wholly horrified at that outcome.

Sensing something was wrong, Donal activated all the runes in the room; Daine met the onslaught with a roar and held him locked in her tight embrace.

Just when she could not stand the pain any further, she felt the Goddess manifest within her. Just as when she was delivering judgement within a court, that power swelled within, healing all her wounds and flowing into Donal's dagger like a reverse waterfall.

As the tide of energy surged into Donal, the man shrieked, and the shadows around him burned away. His skin blistered and split in much the same way as Daine's own.

You are not welcome here, my son. Return to your own domain.

If there was a reply to the Goddess's words, Daine did not hear one.

And then . . . it was all over.

Donal slumped to the floor, a golden haze covering his body. Daine carefully caught him and lowered him down, pulling the remains of the knife that had connected them out of her heart.

"Thank you, my Lady. Do you want to tell me what that was all about?"

Daine was unsurprised to receive no response from the Goddess and mentally shrugged as she felt her fade from this realm.

What was a surprise, however, was the sight of something she had not seen since her final days with Old Gant.

At the corner of her vision, she appeared to have her first Class notification in almost thirty years.

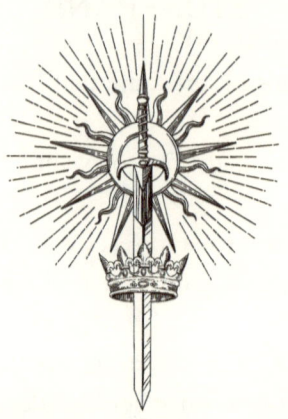

CHAPTER THIRTY-THREE

"Class Evolution"

D aine did not know how much time had passed since
noticing the invitation to evolve her Class.

She stared, as if into space, as a whole gamut
of emotions and fragments of memory swam around her
head.

She was aware that Donal was lying at her feet, unmoving but breathing softly. She had managed to keep her
promise to the Goddess, in any event.

"Don't rush it," Gant growled in her memories. "I haven't put all this effort in for you to fumble things at the
last. When the moment comes for you to evolve your
Class, take a beat. You have time."

And there she was back in the training yard, her senses
overwhelmed by the coarseness of the sand, the stench of
blood and sweat and the blinding light of the midday sun.
How many times had she nearly died in this place? And

how many times had the man standing in the centre of the ring, hands on his hips and a sneer on his face, been the cause of that?

Gallant Stonehand, the Kingdom's premier Mentor, stared balefully back at the small group of children before him. As if finding their very appearance disgusting, he spat messily into the sand.

"Evolving your Class is a choice you need to make with your whole heart. In front of me, I see a bunch of Farmers, Labourers and Bakers. Sure, I've beaten some fight into you. Most of you can now handle a blade. And you can all take a kicking and ask for more. But all I've really done so far is put lipstick on a pig. You're going to need to take the next step yourselves."

Daine remembered the sense of anticipation in the air that day. The Goddess had already begun courting her for the Road, and she knew a few of her — well, not "friends". Say "acquaintances" — had been visited by other members of the pantheon. But there were as many sitting in front of Gant who had no idea what awaited them as there were who did not.

"When offered a Class Evolution, you are given a chance to fundamentally change who you are." Gant had grinned then. "And a new personality can't come fast enough for some of you."

No one asked any questions. Of course they did not. That lesson was one of the first battered into you at Old Gant's school.

Heroes were to be seen and not heard.

"Our training has been aimed at passing the various thresholds in attributes that we believe the gods use to decide who to offer Class Evolution. It's not an exact science, of course. Divine beings don't converse with the likes of me. But I know a little of my business, and it's a rare scrub that can make it this far on the journey and can't impress one deity or another."

It took a collective surge of will for the audience to not look as one towards the small graveyard behind the training yard.

If he noticed, and of course he did, Gant pressed on regardless. "So, when you tickle the fancy of some god or other, they'll reach out and offer you a Class Evolution. Some may woo you first" — did his eyes glance her way? — "but most will expect you to drop to your knees, take what they give you and praise them for the opportunity to serve."

As Old Gant had spoken, she had become aware of the voice of the Goddess in her mind, and she had quickly transferred her focus. Gant sought to make her pay for her inattention later in the training circle, but by then, she had completed her Class Evolution from a Farmer to a Knight of the Road, and the bout did not quite go the way he had expected.

He had still, eventually, beaten her black and blue. But the look on his face whilst he did so was priceless.

And now, thirty years later, she was being offered the opportunity to progress again.

By thinking about the notification, she became aware of what it said. They were not words to be read as such, but she understood them with all her being.

Knight of the Road → Templar Ascendant

The Templar Ascendant embodies decades of rigorous training, discipline, and mastery in the art of war. This Class emerges from

the ranks of Knights of the Road who have dedicated their lives to
the Goddess and have completed deeds she recognises as heroic.

Daine was unsure how to react.

She had never heard of Knights of the Road "evolving". The wording of this notification suggested it had
happened before, but if that was so, it had never made it
into any of the records. To be honest, she had the sense
the Goddess was playing a little fast and loose with some
fundamental rules of the game here.

She just was not sure why.

Considering things more deeply, she could tell that the
change would increase all her Attributes exponentially. If
she had been hard to kill before, she could not conceive
what it would take to kill her if she chose to evolve. On the
other hand, she remembered how long it had taken her to
get used to functioning normally with her current level of
Strength. At her time of life, did she really have it in her to
go through all that again? She did not think the furniture in
the Keep could stand it . . .

The Skills that came with this Evolution were certainly
interesting, though. As a Knight of the Road, she had been
quite lacking in that department beyond <Intimidation>
and <Self-Heal>. Although she was unsure too many of
the foes she had crushed, decapitated and otherwise dispatched over the years would shed too many tears for her
over that. "Please tell me more, oh immortal warrior, about
how sad it is you lack exotic Skills."

Should she evolve, she could see that she would gain
two additional Skills designed to bolster the abilities of any
group she was in. Considering she had spent her life essentially travelling alone, she could not but think her patron

was being a little arch with this offer. Nothing said "you need more friends" better than Skills that were only useful when activated within a team. She could not but think there was something fairly convenient about <Rallying Cry> and <Righteous Resolve> suddenly becoming available to her in the middle of a siege.

Daine had never read too much about the various tiers of the Classes. She knew enough to recognise that Knights of the Road were considered to be on the Epic scale, whereas Eliud's Pendragon was most certainly judged Mythic. It felt to her, at least initially, that a Templar Ascendant would have a chance to hold her own against the Duskstrider for a little while. That was a proposition that made her smile.

Donal murmured at her feet, and she looked down at what seemed like some pretty clear foreshadowing about the dangers of the path before her.

Sometimes, the ends did not justify the means.

Had Donal's new Class not been selected precisely because it would help hold the defence of Swinford together? And look at the devastation that had wrought. Evolution was not a danger-free choice.

Could she genuinely decide to walk down the exact same route and hope for a different resolution?

That felt like a perfect opening for the Goddess to swoop in and reassure her that this was all part of a carefully considered plan. However, as with most occasions in her life when she had turned to the deity for answers, silence was her only reply.

Her indecision led her to the window of Donal's office. The attackers below had withdrawn beyond the courtyard and were restoring some sort of order following their mauling. However, far from retreating, they were clearly gearing up for another push. Say what you like about the King's Army, but there were some tough soldiers down there.

With Donal incapacitated, she would be needed below to hold things together at the door. Taelsin had been understanding thus far about her reluctance to be overly aggressive with the attackers, but she could clearly not allow the Keep to fall.

No matter her scruples, she needed to take every advantage offered her if Swinford was to remain standing when Eliud returned with Genoes.

"Whatever you do, though," Old Gant had said, "make sure you evolve somewhere safe. It takes each of us differently, but one thing is common. You'll be good for nothing until the process is finished."

It was hardly a ringing endorsement for accepting evolution in the middle of a siege. But if you waited around for everything to be perfect, you would not get out of bed in the morning.

That homily made Daine smile. How many years had it been since she had thought of those favoured words of her mother?

That they had come to her now felt like a sign.

Sitting down heavily on the stone floor, Daine pulled a cushion under her head and propped her feet up on an unconscious Dark Warlord. Satisfied she was as comfortable as she could make herself, she closed her eyes and took a breath.

And accepted the notification.

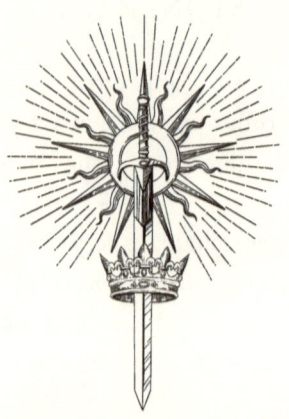

CHAPTER THIRTY-FOUR

"Going All In"

Angharad gasped as the turmoil of her agony abruptly ceased.

She lay on the floor for a moment, unsure what to do with herself. One moment, she had been writhing her last seconds away — her soul tearing apart — and now she was . . . fine? Better than "fine", actually. She felt like her entire being had been renewed. Refreshed. Reset.

That appalling violation of the integrity of her mana core had stopped as quickly as it had begun; the lingering shock of the pain was already subsiding — as if her conscious mind were locking that memory away.

Nevertheless, although the deep wounds clawed into her soul were quickly healing, she could still sense the damage that had been done. She could tell she had lost at least two Skills — there were holes in her foundation where

<Continual Flame> and <Arcane Sword> used to be —
but considering what had nearly just happened, she would
gladly pay double that price.

Although . . .

The longer she considered the damage the attack had
wreaked on her, the surer she became that there was more
to it than a few Skills ripped loose. Something had happened to her Class.

Angharad was a Mage from a long and distinguished
line. Mages of Withertop knew from the cradle that their
sole purpose in life was to master their discipline and go
out into the world to serve the Kingdom. She had dedicated every moment of her twenty-five years to that endeavour, and she assumed her parents had been proud
when she had been attached to Souit's punitive expedition
to the West. They had not mentioned it either way.

Perhaps they merely saw her as doing precisely as expected. Would you cheer for a child who learned to walk?
Angharad was dimly aware that most parents did celebrate
that achievement, but there was little benefit in dwelling on
her upbringing.

For generations unending, the Mages of Withertop had
provided "support" for the King's Army. It was not that
they lacked power (far from it. The Duskstrider himself
had noted that Angharad's mother had "a mana pool he
would like to drown in." There had been quite the debate
about what he had meant by this) but rather, they had a
broad range of Skills for the benefit of others.

This was such an uncommon attitude amongst powerful Mages — all of whom saw personal progress and ambition as the pinnacle of all achievements — that Withertop

Mages were viewed with some strange mixture of deep awe and profound suspicion. Surely no one was so altruistic as to specialise in being a generalist?

The other Mages in the Army had been happy to allow Angharad to speak for them because if anyone had to deal with the Great General, they felt it might as well be the Withertop Mage. Her type lived for that sort of self-sacrifice, after all.

Of all her siblings — indeed, most of her immediate family — her Intelligence was by far the highest. Its level was to so great that Old Gant himself had reportedly come to look her over shortly after her birth. Her mother and father did not speak much of that fell encounter, but they made clear she had not reasonably met the necessary standards for his school. Angharad was never sure whether they were pleased or disappointed by that.

Alongside unusually high Intelligence, she also had a reasonably high Constitution and — linked to her <Medium Armour> Skill — solid Dexterity. Most of the Skills she inherited from her family were various flavours of <Conjuration>, <Divination> and <Transmutation>, and she had done everything she could to raise their levels.

Thus, stood before Swinford's walls, Angharad had been the epitome of a Withertop Mage. But something had fundamentally changed under that attack.

It was not just that she had lost some Skills; she had enough of them, after all. It was more that she had become less . . . versatile. On the other hand, she seemed to have become much better at a few very specific things.

For someone who had spent their life being a jack-of-all-trades, there was something quite intriguing about potential mastery.

The others in the command tent, who had fled when her power started to leak out of her in such an unnerving way, had returned. She felt a hand on her shoulder. "Mage, are you well?"

Angharad looked up into Souit's broad face, noting genuine concern in his eyes. "I think so, my Lord. Someone within the Keep would appear to have reacted poorly to my interference."

"But you were able to drive them off?"

"Hardly. Such was its power that — if we did not know differently — I would have assumed the Duskstrider himself was behind it. However, for whatever reason, the attack ended just as my end was assured. But . . ."

"Mage, pregnant pauses are not exactly welcome at this stage of proceedings."

"Apologies, my Lord. I am trying to make sense of what has occurred. Their attack, somehow, has made changes to my build. I do not believe this was an intended effect — they surely were seeking my death — but the outcome is quite extraordinary."

"Which is?"

"I appear to have evolved into an Archmage."

*

Degralk rolled his neck and took another deep breath.

He pushed his memories of the last few minutes away. There would be time to process the horror of battling the undead. He could not let his mind, nor those of his soldiers, pause on that right now. After all, it was one thing to cut down an enemy; it was quite another to fight against the corpse of a comrade.

No, he could not think about it.

For now, he had a mission to complete.

Swinford's defenders had done what they could to barricade the door to the Keep, but he was confident they could retake the ground they had abandoned. He just had to hope there were no more unwelcome surprises.

And what was that damn rattling noise?

Looking around, he saw his Sergeants pulling the men back into something approaching an appropriate formation. There was a wariness in the eyes of the men, though. And who could blame them after what they had just been through? It would take a heart of stone to order them to attack again. But that was what he was going to do.

What he would not give for a Motivational Skill right now.

Well, the situation was not going to improve by worrying about it. He strode to the front of the forming line, turned and drove his pike into the ground.

"Well, I don't know about you, but I'm ready to get back to killing some flesh-and-blood traitors!"

There was a lukewarm cheer, with most avoiding his eyes. It was as bad as he thought.

"I know how you feel, but somewhere in that Keep is the person who has just put us through that. They think they've won. They can see us shuffling about and think they've broken us. Are they right?"

Silence.

He added an edge to his voice. "Hear me. No one should have to experience what we've just gone through. No one. All of you have just had to fight the remains of your friends. And I am so, so sorry for that."

More silence.

"But whose fault was it? Was it yours?"

A few no's chorused back.

"I said, was it your fault? Did you deserve to go through that?"

There was a louder response this time.

"How about those we had to slay again? Did they deserve to have their rest disturbed? Did they, who had so bravely fought and died, deserve that desecration?"

Men were standing straighter, and their voices barked their defiant answer of no.

"No. I don't think so either. I think I want someone to pay for that. And all I know is that person is in that building. And I would like to make their acquaintance. Albeit briefly. Any of you fancy joining me on that mission?"

Shields struck the ground in a cacophony of anger.

"Glad to hear it."

A knot released in his stomach. He was not wholly sure what to do next if they did not get behind him. A solitary lone charge, perhaps? "Pikemen, you're with me. Form up at the front. We advance in a staggered line, double-marching to that barricade. No matter what happens, we will hold that door."

He turned towards his small group of saboteurs, grim men and women who were, largely, what was left over from the Spymistress's force. They had their own scores to settle with the defenders of the City. "Sappers, you'll be coming in with us on that first push. We need swift clearing out of that debris. Be vigilant for traps, hidden dangers, and anything that smells like a rune."

They all nodded in reply, faces set in expressionless masks.

"Captain Gukrun, you have the reserve infantry. You stand ready to charge the moment we have a sufficient opening. Nothing fancy; as soon as the door goes down,

you start clearing them out. I don't want any quarter offered to anyone who tries to fight back, but neither do
I want civilian deaths. We're the King's Army, after all.
They're the traitors who've just used Necromancy. Let's
ensure everyone knows who the good guys are in this."

Gukrun raised her chin in acknowledgement. She was a
solid choice for such hot work. Vicious without being un-
controlled. Speaking of which . . .

"Sergeant Cristum, get yourself up and on those walls.
Take anyone with you that you fancy has a talent for that
work. I was minded to let those blasted archers be, but
they enjoyed themselves far too much during that last assault. I don't need any prisoners."

The rest of the men rumbled their approval.

"Listen up, everyone. We're angry. We want revenge,
and by the Goddess, I mean to get some. But the only
way that happens is that we maintain our discipline. We're
the King's Army, not a barbarian rabble. Our strength lies
in speed, ferocity and commitment. We go through that
breach swiftly and forcefully and then take it from room to
room. You all know your roles and it's going to be messy.
Maintain your formations, watch for ambushes, and trust
in your training."

He took one last moment to look down the lines.
"Beyond everything else, remember who we are."

Well, time to go all in. "And go."

CHAPTER THIRTY-FIVE

"Rallying Cry"

Daine descended the stairs of the Keep as if walking in a dream.

With every downward step, the strange novelty of her new Class was again brought home.

She could tell that her Strength had significantly increased: after all, she had accidentally ripped Donal's room door off its hinges when she left. Following her Class Evolution from a Farmer, it had taken her several weeks to be less casually destructive to Gant's fittings and furniture. She sincerely hoped she would adjust more quickly this time around. The middle of a battle was hardly the time to figure out new physical limits.

However, beyond just being stronger, she was already noticing distinct differences in other aspects of her mind and body. As a Knight of the Road, she had felt . . . there was no better word for it than "bulky". Her Orban genes already ensured she was tall, wide-shouldered and broad of beam, and then her Class had further emphasised those features, making her move with all the subtlety of a siege engine. Of course, much of the time, the situations in which she found herself benefitted from her uniquely robust frame.

When she'd asked about the physical change following her first Evolution, Gant had explained that "none of you Knights have got enough Dexterity to balance up your Strength. You're quick in a fight, aye, but there's a difference between being fast and being supple. It's why you all walk like you're carrying barrels under your arms."

But now . . . now Daine felt like she was moving with a grace quite alien to her previous experience. Indeed, the simple act of walking was proving to be a revelation. She found herself instinctively placing her foot in just the right place. With each step, she was always perfectly balanced on the balls of her feet and knew that if the occasion demanded it, she could spring forward or leap back instantly. As someone used to pressing uncompromisingly forward, it was not quite like learning to walk anew, but it was not too far away.

She was assuming a commensurate improvement to her Constitution. But she would need the coming fight to retake the gatehouse to learn more about that. Thinking of those fighting below, she quickened her — exceptionally well-balanced — steps.

However, it was in her Skillset where there had been the most radical changes. She had known she would gain two new Skills — <Rallying Cry> and <Righteous Resolve>. Both of these were considered superb — and extremely rare — party buffs. The first helped boost the offensive

Stats of all troops fighting in the caster's party. Considering its powerful effect, it had a reasonably quick cooldown, and was intended to be used to decisively turn the tide of battle. She had expected a fairly small casting area for such a significant boost, but it did not seem like that was the case. She could be wrong, but it felt like she could cast this over a substantial portion of Swinford in one go. Daine had often heard Gant swear about the "broken Skills" some Classes possessed. <Rallying Cry> looked like it might well be one of them.

Her second new Skill <Righteous Resolve> was less welcome. It appeared to be linked to drastically improving morale. It was not quite the mirror of the rune that Donal had carved into the length and breadth of Swinford's walls, but it was in the same conceptual area. From what Daine knew of this Skill, it was usually gained by the High Priests of the more fanatical cults. When triggered, it would ensure that those in its effect area — which was again very broad — would fight well past the time when injury and pain should cause them to fall. Having had to slaughter more than one cult whose members were empowered by <Righteous Resolve>, Daine was not sure she would be casting that any time soon. She felt a great distaste for what Donal had done with the fallen this day, and <Righteous Resolve> was just creating more Soulless but by another name.

However, it was not the new Skills that startled her the most, but one that had undergone a profound change.

<Intimidation> was not a Skill she had ever much enjoyed using. With her size, Strength, and reputation, it always felt like overkill when she chose to activate this aura. It was somewhat like throwing a man from the top of a

high cliff and shooting an arrow after him as he plummeted. She only tended to use it when she wanted to be left alone — which, of course, was most of the time — but she had never found it especially helpful for discharging her duties.

With her Class Evolution, however, <Intimidation> had been upgraded to something called <Domain of Law>.

Daine had not heard of this Skill, which was unusual in itself. It was one of the central tenets of the training of the Knights of the Road: they needed to be familiar with everything that could possibly be brought against them. Being Resistant to magical effects did not mean you could become blase about such things. The last thing a solitary Knight on Tour needed was to come up against an exotic Skill and have no idea how to combat it. "Those that don't study get dead" was a pretty on-the-nose bit of advice from the past that she had seen come true on more than one occasion.

Daine was aware of other <Domain of> Skills but had never heard of one that appeared to be so explicitly connected to the Goddess. Judging by its cooldown of a day, it seemed likely to have a powerful effect. But, again, it did not seem that the middle of a battle was the best time to explore it. If she hoped for her patron to have any words of advice about the new Skill, she was to be disappointed.

There was the sound of increased fighting below, and she moved even faster, again revelling in her complete sureness of foot.

Within moments, she had reached the ground floor and took in the sight before her.

The King's Army had rallied effectively, and the fighting

on the threshold of the Keep was proving too hot for the defenders. Donal and the Blacksmiths had fashioned some metal boxes for the men and women of Swinford to fight from within, which explained how they had managed to hold their own against professional soldiers for so long.

But discipline and training tended to overcome most obstacles, and noting that the defenders were sorely pressed, Daine activated the first of her new Skills and waded into the press.

*

Degralk thudded the end of his pike into a defender's head and watched them drop, as if boneless, to the floor.

The assault was taking longer than he'd anticipated, as everyone on the other side of the door seemed to be encased in some sort of metal cage. He and his fellow Pikemen were holding the doorway, but the infantry who had surged past them appeared to be making heavy weather of it. He was just preparing to lead a charge to add his men's weight in support when he heard a change in the sound of the battle.

A good commander — and he was a very good commander indeed — could literally hear the moment the enemy was about to rout. He would not be able to explain how he knew, but it was as distinct a sound as any in the world.

But on this occasion, and to his dismay, it was his own men he sensed preparing to flee.

Eager to shore things up, he shouldered his way through what was left of the door, knocking defenders flying, and cast about to see the state of things.

At first sight, his sense of impending disaster made no sense. Gukrun's infantry had established decent positions

within the Keep itself. The entryway was secured, and
there was fierce fighting around the various other door-
ways. Although those encased in the ridiculous metal boxes
were proving difficult to dislodge, that was nothing that
time and training would not resolve.

And then he saw her, taking the last few steps down
from the stone staircase.

Darkhelm.

The spreading panic amongst his men now made much
more sense.

Her very presence seemed to be transforming the
course of things, with the defenders suddenly attacking with new vigour and energy. If he did not know better, he would have thought those he faced had all, at the
same time, taken a whole host of Stamina potions. Their
movements were sped up, and their weight behind their
attacks seemed much heavier. Even those inside the
goddess-damned metal cases were suddenly more mobile
than seemed credible.

But these newly refreshed defenders were the least of
his problems.

His men around the Darkhelm were falling backwards
as if they were ice melting in the path of a volcano. He
saw Infantrymen falling over themselves to get out of her
path, and he could not blame them. He had always wondered what it would feel like to go up against one of these
appalling monsters up close. He never conceived it would
have been like this.

And she had not even raised her sword.

One of his Sergeants tugged on his arm. "Sir, it's the
Darkhelm. We must pull back. We need more support."

Degralk shrugged her off. "No. Reform the line. We

need to hold here!" He blocked a swinging axe with the shaft of his pike and dropped to a knee to sweep the attacker's feet from under them. Standing, he turned to carry on issuing his instructions, but there was no longer anyone at his shoulder. Looking back towards the doorway, he could see his men seeking to force their way back through, crushing each other in their desperation to escape.

The defenders were closing in on him, and he bared his teeth in defiance. He had no intention of letting them take him alive. And then the press of men parted, and the Darkhelm was in front of him.

He activated his Skill, pointed his pike and planted his feet. Storied warrior she might be, but he'd never been forced to take a backward step in his life. If these were to be his last moments, he was going out the way he lived.

However, with a movement he barely registered, her hand shot out, taking hold of his weapon, pulling it from his grip. She clenched her fist, splintering the heavy shaft into firewood.

He met her eyes, golden light pouring from them and framing her face in a halo.

In wonder, he shook his head. "We never stood a chance. Just get it over with."

The voice that answered him did not sound quite human. "On the contrary, Major Degralk. We are only just beginning."

CHAPTER THIRTY-SIX

"Calamity Upon Calamity"

The rushing stream of men and women fleeing the Keep did not so much as pause at the gatehouse. Despite the best efforts of those holding that fall-back position, there was simply no reasoning with those engaged in a madcap, panicked retreat. It was far more than just the expected temporary loss of discipline during a rout. Whatever had occurred within the Keep had terrorised these soldiers out of their senses.

Souit shook his head at the news. "I don't suppose there is any sign of Major Degralk?"

"He has not been seen amongst those exiting the Keep. There are, however, confirmed reports of him preparing to engage the Darkhelm directly."

The messenger was delicate enough not to add what was the assumed outcome of that unwise confrontation.

Turning to Angharad, the Great General raised his

eyebrows. "Does our new Archmage have any words of advice?"

The young woman pursed her lips in thought. "The Darkhelm is formidable, but our men have faced her during this siege without such a dramatic loss of unit cohesion. It seems unlikely her mere presence would have caused what is being seen. I did, however, sense a significant outpouring of power just before our troops reentered the Keep. I would suggest whatever has so terrified the men will be linked to that. The arrival of the Darkhelm could be a coincidence."

"I asked for advice, not idle musings."

If Angharad was offended by Souit's tone, she did not show it. An inviolable air of calm had settled around the woman since her Class Evolution. She stood slightly taller than before, her long hair released from its tight bun to flow freely behind her. These changes gave her something of an ethereal aspect, which the Great General found extremely irritating.

"My apologies, my Lord, if I misspoke. Nevertheless, I am unsure what advice you would have from me in the current circumstances. It feels somewhat trite to exhort you to uncover what happened in the Keep. We need to know what has caused our men to flee with such alacrity. However, as I am sure you will have thought of that already, I confess I have little else to add. However, I stand poised to offer any assistance you require."

Souit grunted in reply. In the space of a few days, he appeared to have lost his two most competent advisors in Stein and Degralk, but had somehow gained an Archmage. He was unsure whether this put him ahead of the game.

That same trade-off was true of his territorial gains to

date. Whilst the army had breached the walls of Swinford, he was unclear whether this actually brought the siege any closer to a conclusion.

He needed reliable intelligence from that latest clash at the Keep — but without the Spymaster, nor the man charged with leading that assault, he found himself some-what bereft of options.

"My Lord!" One of his staff appeared at his side with an anxious look on his flushed face. Souit braced himself for further calamity and nodded for the man to continue. "We have received news of Colonels Sajida and Brockland. You need to come immediately, sir."

Souit's eyebrows rose. Those two officers were in charge of the legions he — when they first became bogged down at Swinford — had sent ahead into the West. Neither was an outstanding commander, but both were effective enough in their own ways. Surely it was too soon for word they had achieved their objectives? Was it possible the rest of the West had utterly capitulated in such a short stretch of time?

He stewed over that humiliation. The insults he would have to smile at and swallow if it turned out the West was pacified by his juniors whilst he laboured to bring one crumbling City back under the King's authority. His repu-tation would not survive such a humbling. If he was lucky, the King would merely unevolve his Class and let him keep his head. And that would be the best-case scenario.

Smarting from the thought, he snapped back rather more brusquely than he had intended. "One of the ben-efits of my position, sir, is that people come to me rather than the other way around."

The unfortunate officer glanced anxiously at Angharad

for support. She stared impassively back at him. "Begging your pardon, my Lord, that will not be an option. You — you really do need to come with me. It is rather difficult to explain."

"If you are still looking for advice from me, my Lord," Angharad murmured, "I think you should go with him."

*

Two pairs of sightless eyes stared back at the Great General.

The decapitated head of Colonel Sajida was artfully arranged upon a velvet pillow lodged within an oaken box. Her face wore a somewhat surprised look as if her untimely death had rudely interrupted her day. That of Colonel Brockland, on the other hand, had been more pragmatically delivered in a hempen sack. His expression was locked in a rictus of pain, and, to expert observers, the removal of the head had not been achieved quickly nor cleanly.

Of the two, Souit knew which one he would rather have as his final moment.

The two packages had been delivered to different sentries at the foremost picket. Neither of the soldiers presented with their ghoulish prize could remember much of the man — or woman — who had delivered them, save that they wore red and gold livery. It had been insisted that these gifts be delivered to the Great General without delay.

"There was no other message?"

The two sentries exchanged glances, which did little to improve Souit's temper. "Sirs, I am not in the mood for a mummer show. Either tell your tale or begone with you."

The taller sentry, an older man whose hair had long since turned silver, rummaged in his pocket and produced two bloodstained pieces of parchment. "It didn't seem right to leave them in their mouths, sir. I served under Colonel Sajida in the Eastern campaign. She didn't deserve this. She had a good head on her shoulders." He blushed crimson at the unfortunate choice of words and began to stutter uncontrollably.

The second sentry saved him, taking one of the blood-soaked pieces of paper and passing it over to Souit. "We didn't mean anything by it, my Lord. It just didn't look seemly to bring you to them like that. It's the same message written on both."

Souit unfolded the sheet and read it, his face clouding with fury. He glared up at the second sentry. "Is this some sort of joke, sir?"

The sentry quailed under that stare. "No, sir. The papers were in both of their mouths, sir. Honest truth. We haven't messed with them or anything."

Souit thrust the paper towards Angharad, who read through it once, then cleared her throat and read the message aloud to the rest of the command staff.

"To all who bear witness, let it be known that the Free Lands of the West, aggrieved by the King's incursions upon our land, hereby declare war against him.

"The West stands united, under the leadership of House Trellec, to fight for our freedom and future. Our resolve is unyielding, our purpose clear: to drive the forces of the King from our borders.

"This declaration is not made lightly, for the horrors of war weigh heavily upon us. Yet, in the shadow of the King's despotism, we find no alternative but to take up arms.

"Our gifts to you this day are to demonstrate the

strength of our resolve and the inevitability of your destruction.

"We embark upon this path of conflict with solemn hearts and steadfast courage. May justice guide our swords and fortitude sustain us as we fight to dispel the darkness of tyranny.

"So decreed, in the name of freedom and the enduring spirit of our people."

When she had finished, the Archmage could not help smirking. "There is something about rebellion that brings out the worst of prose in people, is there not?"

Souit gestured towards the decapitated heads. "Will someone do something about them, please? I can't think with them gawping up at me. And find me the courier who delivered them. Immediately. If they're wearing red and gold, they should be easy enough to track down on the road. And double the watch at the picket; I want to know if as much as an ant makes its way towards us."

With a flurry of movement, the crowd dispersed, gossip and rumour moving far faster than mere feet could take them, leaving just the Archmage and the Great General.

"If you are still in the market for some advice, my Lord . . ."

Souit glared back and shook his head.

CHAPTER THIRTY-SEVEN

"Do You Have the Stomach For It?"

"**C**an I just check; are you really convinced all this is strictly necessary? I mean, without wishing to add to my woes, if I was still minded towards malevolence, you should know that many of my Skills are voice-activated."

Donal tried, without success, to rattle the heavy chains that bound him to his chair.

"I repeat my advice from earlier. We should have cut out his tongue," the Hyena said, sipping at her cup of wine. Despite the best efforts of the City's Healers, her face still bore the terrible scars of her confrontation with the Spymistress.

"And rob you of my witty repartee? Surely, some punishments are too appalling to contemplate in a civilised society . . ."

Taelsin cleared his throat, and the ceaseless bickering

that had bounced back and forth for over half a bell halted. With attention now all on him, he looked around the room at those who had become — by necessity, more than design — Swinford's ruling Council.

Lady Stelton was the sole remaining Noble. Whereas most of her fellows had retired to their country estates at the first sign of trouble, conflict appeared to agree with the old woman. She had been thoroughly invigorated by her role in the capture of Captain Kettle and his men. It was all Taelsin could do to keep her from taking her hunting bow to the walls.

Sat next to her, feet up on the table, a bottle in one hand and a glass in the other, was the Hyena. She had not been much slowed by her disfiguring injuries — indeed, the ferocity of her Cackle's endeavours against the King's army had only increased. Since a large section of Souit's forces had crossed into the City proper, her force had no shortage of targets for their particular brand of carnage. However, even though they were a spectacularly effective mercenary company, there were simply not enough of them. Step by step, barricade by barricade, the King's Army was spreading out and occupying the wider City.

Next to the Hyena sat two somewhat incongruous presences. Captain Kettle and Major Degralk looked baffled to be included in this meeting. Having vowed on their word of honour not to attempt to escape, both had been given their parole and freedom in the City. Taelsin, though, had insisted on their attendance at these discussions.

Next to Kettle, sitting opposite the Hyena, was Donal. As far as anyone could tell, all traces of <Dark Pragmatism> had been purged from his Skillset. However, no one was willing to take any chances. All agreed that

Swinford still stood primarily due to the brilliance of his strategies. However, few who had witnessed the rising of the dead around the Keep were sure that particular price was worth paying. The coils of chain that pinned him to his chair were mainly for show — Taelsin was convinced the Dark Warlord had the strength to break them should he wish — but it was a cosmetic gesture that felt appropriate.

The final member of the group, and the real reason why all were certain Donal would behave himself, was the Lady Darkhelm.

It did not take any of Taelsin's ability to read people to recognise that something profound had been altered about the Knight. No, not "Knight".

Templar.

Outwardly, her appearance had changed little. She was perhaps slightly taller, with a minor increase in muscle to her build. While some Class Evolutions had a regenerating impact on the age of the body, that did not seem to have been the case here. Although some of the tiredness in her eyes had vanished, she was still — manifestly — a woman in her mid-fifties. The most noticeable change, however, was that the pressure of her aura had magnified. Taelsin was not much given to religious ponderings, but if asked what it would feel like to be in the presence of a god, he would no longer need to consider too deeply.

Putting that thought, with difficulty, to one side, Taelsin addressed the group. "If I can redirect our attention away from childish squabbling and back to the defence of my City?"

All eyes returned to him.

"To my understanding, despite significant pressure, we still hold around half of the land. The earlier bombardment largely levelled the northern quarter, and the eastern quarter is hotly disputed. In response, we have evacuated anyone who cannot assist in the defence to the sewers and have barricaded every major route."

The Hyena nodded, eyes now serious. "We just don't have the people to do more than slow down their advance. We're picking companies off at the edges, but they're too wary for us to achieve much more. I'm sorry to say it, but my bag of tricks is looking increasingly bare."

"Is this a good time to enquire about the Cackle's refund policy? I'm not sure I remember reading a 'we work for you until I'm out of ideas' clause in our contract. Frankly, I'm not sure we're quite getting value for the exorbitant sum of money we paid you."

It was rather impressive that Donal managed to maintain his bright smile in the face of the Hyena's withering glare. "Far be it from me to point fingers," she said, "but I'm not the Warlord who let his walls be breached. It's generally seen as a pretty important part of siege warfare to keep the attacking army outside the City . . ."

Taelsin banged his hand on the table and turned to the scarred woman. "It is your assessment we cannot stop them from wholesale occupation?"

The Hyena shrugged. "I doubt they want to do that long-term; they're just looking to squeeze us out. Souit has an army, and he's given them orders to keep us on the run. And, damn him, he's good at this sort of thing. We're doing our best, but numbers always count in the end."

"How long?"

Another shrug. "Maybe a week. Less if I keep losing people. Of course, the Keep is the prize. If they take this building, it's over."

Taelsin turned to Kettle and Degralk. "Do you agree?"

The two glanced at each other and grimaced. It was Degralk who spoke. "Sir, whilst we are both appreciative of the mercy shown us, we cannot help you plan your defence. If you expect anything different by inviting us here today, we have to disappoint you."

"Told you that's what they'd say. Kill them. Off with their heads. Flay their innards. Consume their eyeballs."

"Donal!"

The Dark Warlord wrinkled his nose. "I'm just playing the part in which you have cast me."

"Then play it silently." Ignoring his friend's mock gasp of hurt, Taelsin returned his attention to the two soldiers. "I am not asking you to aid our defence. I am asking whether you agree that General Souit will have occupied the City within weeks. If anything, confirming that will have a negative impact on our morale and you will be aiding your cause."

Degralk hesitated and then nodded. "With the breach in your wall, I concur it is simply a matter of numbers and time. Occupation is not the point, however. The Great General has no interest in being bogged down in Swinford long-term. To achieve his aim, this Keep must fall and, saving your presence, so must you."

Taelsin nodded. "Thank you. That is our reading of things, too. My Lady Darkhelm, anything to add?"

Daine leaned forward, placing both hands down on the table. All eyes tracked the tilt that occurred with even such light pressure. "I am not sure I have much more of use to add. I am confident I can hold the Keep against conventional forces. It is my hope the Great General will be unwilling to waste too many against me, but I will hold the gatehouse in any event. However, that will pin me to this building, and I can be of no help against the wider Army. Alternatively, should this Council wish, I can take to the streets and seek to drive the Army beyond your walls, but" — she helplessly opened her hands — "I imagine I will confront the same issue as the Hyena and her Cackle. Sadly, numbers matter."

"The plan was never to defeat this army. We just needed to keep it occupied long enough for the arrival of the Duskstrider to tip the scales in our favour." Taelsin's voice became uncharacteristically bleak. "In the absence of any news from him, we must play this out. It is, though, clear to me we cannot indefinitely keep Souit at arm's length and hold the City."

He stood and began pacing the room. "Lady Stelton, I would ask you to relocate along with the rest of the civilian population to the sewers. I need someone I trust oversee-ing things there."

The elderly Noble frowned. "You aren't trying to keep me safe, are you, boy?"

"Wouldn't dream of it. I want your head next to mine on Traitor's Row if that's where this ends up." He pointed towards the Hyena. "You are to provide what support Lady Stelton deems necessary in establishing good order with the civilians, at which stage, I will consider our con-tract ended."

"Ah, the good little doggy gets to run away home. How nice for her."

The Hyena studiously ignored Donal's words. "We took quite a weight of gold from you, my Lord. I don't like to speak for my boys and girls" — Donal snorted and was, again, ignored — "but the Cackle prides itself on providing a quality service. We'll get your people all nicely safe and tucked away for you, but we'll probably hang around a little if that's all the same to you?"

"Of course, we're more than happy to have you with us. Will you wish to be based in the Keep or —"

"We're more the sleeping-beneath-the-open-sky-killing-from-hidden-nooks-in-dark-places types, to be honest. We'll just look to make ourselves a general nuisance. Maybe we'll annoy Souit enough to make him run for the hills."

"I can see how that could happen. Sorry, can anyone actually hear me? I seem to be wasting some quality material on deaf ears."

Daine reached out and rested a hand on Donal's shoulder. His eyes widened, and then he grimaced in pain, clamping his mouth shut.

"The plan is," she said, "with the civilians safe, we hunker down here and hold them off until Eliud appears in the sky, like the Goddess's own vengeance. I welcome hearing other thoughts, though."

Everyone around the table shook their heads.

Taelsin said, "I am sorry, my Lady, that we appear to be putting ourselves entirely in your hands. I did not wish for you to carry such a weight."

Daine smiled grimly. "It would be fair to say, sir, that this is not the first time I have found myself alone against significant numbers."

She triggered <Rallying Call> and was pleased to see everyone sit a little straighter around the table. All, that is, apart from Donal.

"It will be bloody business, Darkhelm. Do you have the stomach for it?"

Daine simply pressed down on his shoulder, causing him to yelp. "It won't be the bloodiest I have seen, sir. Not by a long way."

CHAPTER THIRTY-EIGHT

"The Enemy of My Enemy"

Droughton-on-the-Water — thirty years ago.

"I don't suppose you have a cleaning Skill amongst your cantrips, do you?"

When the Priestess failed to answer, Daine turned to ensure she had not been hurt in the brief but violent confrontation with the Soulless.

Bayran was staring at her with a look of profound horror. It was not just that the Knight was covered, head to toe, in gore. Nor was it that she had witnessed the savage slaughter of so many Priests who had — until their untimely transformation by the mirror — been her friends and colleagues.

No.

Her horror came from having seen the true might of Daine Darkhelm unveiled before her.

The Knight had been impressive in the skirmish against the Soulless on the streets of Droughton. Against the Chimaera — from what Bayran could recall — she had likewise shown herself to be entirely formidable. However, the clinical ease with which the Soulless within this room had been decimated was terrifying. From the Priestess's knowledge of such things, it did not appear that Daine had any great skill with her blade. After all, technical proficiency was unnecessary when the sword could be swung with astonishing Strength and overwhelming Speed.

Those two things combined ensured that what Bayran had just witnessed was less a battle than a culling.

"Are you well?" Daine stepped towards the Priestess.

"Quite well, thank you." Bayran retreated away from her and towards the door. "I have <Freshen> amongst my Skillset if that would serve?"

Noticing the new note of fear in the voice of her companion, Daine resheathed her sword and opened her hands in a nonthreatening gesture. "If you would be so kind. Anything you could do to help with the mess would be welcome."

Bayran triggered the Skill and directed it towards the young woman. Immediately, the blood and viscera that stained every item Daine was wearing evaporated, leaving the impression she had just put on freshly laundered clothing. Unfortunately, the spell did nothing for anything covering the Knight herself.

"I thank you." Daine ran her fingers through her blood-soaked hair and shook the excess this tugged free to the floor. She looked at Bayran and indicated the bow the Priestess wore in her hair. "Could I purchase that from you, please?"

Wordlessly, Bayran pulled the pink ribbon from her hair and handed it over, trying to avoid making contact with Daine's hand. The Knight fashioned a tight ponytail, tying it up with little ceremony. "Gant was always going on about shaving my head before I went on Tour. I thought he was exaggerating."

Bayran struggled to comprehend the matter-of-fact manner in which their conversation was going. Around her lay the slaughtered bodies of twenty-odd men and women, and this Knight was making grooming small talk. "Gant?"

"Gallant Stonehand. I thought I was getting one over on him by leaving it this long. Apparently not." Daine ran a hand across her face, the resulting scarlet smear doing little to improve matters. "Now, Priestess, I think it is beyond time for us to settle things with your Archbishop. If you would lead on, please?"

*

The Great Hall of Chance was silent.

That was the first thing Bayran noticed as they slipped through the open doors. That, in itself, was almost unheard of. This vast space was filled with alcoves containing every conceivable game of luck in which hard coin could be hazarded. It was commonly held that, at any one time, hundreds of thousands of pieces of gold would be changing hands amongst the worshippers in this Hall.

There simply was no greater space dedicated to glorifying the influence of the Lords of Misrule anywhere in the West.

But now its tables, wheels, boards and decks lay still.

And it was very clear why.

"Lords, protect me!" Bayran would have collapsed to her knees had Daine not caught her.

The room was a charnel house. There must have been at least five hundred bodies lying strewn across the floor. Some bore the marks of violence, but most had that same desiccated, drained appearance of the Soulless in the previous chamber.

The mirror had taken them all.

At the far end of the room, raised on the central dais, stood Archbishop Jerule. Or, at least, that's where his body was currently situated. Daine was fairly sure the soul of the corpulent man had long since fled his body. Although his eyes were vacant, his face was trapped in a shocked, agonised expression. As with so many who trifled with powers of which they had little comprehension, Jerule had realised too late exactly how small his ambitions were in the schemes of the gods.

Behind the Archbishop, dominating the back wall, was a giant mirror — easily twice the size of the man in front of it. Its frame seemed to have been fashioned from the blackened bones of a creature long extinct, and its surface was not glass but a pool of darkness, a piece of the night sky captured and condensed into a tangible form.

As Daine and Bayran watched, faces emerged from that abyss, contorted in silent screams or gazing with eyes filled with sorrow. They instinctively knew these were the souls of those the mirror had consumed, creating the Soulless the Knight had been forced to destroy.

"Priestess, listen to me." When Bayran did not respond, Daine shook her roughly. "Do you hear me?"

The Priestess looked at the Knight. Was it only a few hours earlier that she had dismissed this figure as a child-barbarian? Looking into the calm, competent eyes of the young woman holding her up, she realised how very wrong she had been. The Knights of the Road did not represent destruction. They were not irritations to be managed or monsters to be avoided. They were, instead, the last line of defence when the challenges moved beyond mortal comprehension. "I hear you, my Lady. My apologies, I was overwhelmed."

Daine waved aside her words. "Nothing is more important for us now than smashing that mirror. If we do not, by the time anyone else is available to deal with it, things could be getting out of hand."

Bayran stared at the destruction of her Order and wondered at what the Knight had seen in her life not to view this current situation as "out of hand."

"Whatever happens," the Knight continued, "no one else can be permitted to leave or enter this room. That is your role."

"I understand, my Lady. And you?"

"I'm going to handle the mirror."

"How?"

"No idea. But there's no point overplanning these things."

And she charged.

As Daine began running across the floor of the Hall towards the mirror, the countless numbers of Soulless rose to impede her progress. But they may as well have tried to hold back a relentless tide.

Although she knew those Daine slew as she moved were already dead, that awareness did little to ease Bayran's suffering as she witnessed the massacre. Against other opponents, the sheer weight of numbers of Soulless would have sufficed. No normal person would have been able to maintain any forward momentum against such a press of bodies, especially when receiving a myriad of wounds from nails, hands and teeth.

The Priestess's eyes streamed with tears as Daine's body was shredded, torn and flayed by the relentless attacks upon it. However, just as quickly, those injuries were healed, to be inflicted again. The pain the young Knight must be going through was indescribable.

And yet she kept moving forward.

And kept destroying those around her.

When Daine was halfway across the room, Bayran lost sight of her completely, so covered was she by the bodies of her Soulless brethren. The only way she knew Daine was still alive was the slow progress of a constantly moving mound of scrabbling, pulsating limbs.

You are about to learn an important lesson.

Bayran's eyes widened as she recognised the dual voices of her gods echoing in her mind. They had spoken to her like this three times over the years, on each occasion in acknowledgement of an especially audacious achievement. They had never before addressed her in such a casual manner.

And not just you, Priestess. I fear our little brother is about to be shown the significant error of his ways. Not that he will learn from the experience, of course."

Her gods spoke simultaneously, one voice slightly higher than the other. The effect was like being sung to by a tiny, wryly amused choir.

"My Lords?"

His error was not in trying to displace us as the preeminent power in Droughton, of course. We applaud his audacity. The world would be very boring indeed without such gambits as these.

There was a guttural roar, and Soulless were thrown

into the air as if by an explosion. Bayran just had time to glimpse a battered but unbowed Daine standing a few feet short of the Archbishop before the mob of Soulless dived upon her and swallowed her up underneath them again.

But with great ambition comes great risk. Mother could never approve of such a move or let it stand without deploying her new toy in opposition.

As Bayran watched, the surface of the mirror blurred and then resolved into a child's face. And yet, that was the oldest-looking child the Priestess had ever seen. He glared down at the writhing mass of bodies in which, presumably, still fought the Knight of the Road.

Ah, so unwise. He was ever unable to recognise when to cut his losses. In that way, we guess he is not so dissimilar to us.

Then Daine was free from the press and approaching the Archbishop. Jerule's dead eyes blazed with anger, and his body staggered towards her, aiming to prevent the Knight from reaching the mirror.

Bayran's mind was suddenly filled with the rattle of millions of pairs of dice. The noise dropped her to her knees screaming in pain. Daine ignored her distress and reached out for the Archbishop. She took hold of the man's head and . . . tore it free from its shoulders.

Dice began to be cast over and over again as Daine was left, alone, standing in front of the mirror. The cacophony of casts deafened Bayran, almost splitting her mind with its volume.

Daine met the glare of the ancient child, and then, after raising her torn and bloodied fist, she pounded it through the middle of the mirror, smashing it into thousands of pieces.

*

"I'd heard of your encounter with Droughton's Soulless, of course. The tavern song is rather more focused upon your companion's buxom and fragrant nature than flowing rivers of blood and broken mirrors." Lady Stelton sniffed her disapproval.

"Yes. I believe Archbishop Bayran did her best to have it outlawed."

"Which doubtless enhanced its reputation," added Donal.

"I do not think she much minded. She comes out of that song rather better than I remember being the reality."

Taelsin was watching Daine with a frown on his face. "What brought that particular memory to mind, my Lady?"

The Templar tapped a finger on her chin. "I am not sure. It just feels as if many of the same beats are being explored. I was newly awakened in my power, as I am now. The gods were, as now, in open conflict. Soulless walk the land. I do not like coincidences."

There was no time to explore that thought further as a messenger unceremoniously burst into the room, red-faced with excitement.

"My Lords. Ladies." He took a moment to steady himself and passed a sealed scroll to Taelsin. "A second army has been sighted arriving from the South. They are taking up positions as if they mean to attack the King's Army. General Souit is deploying his forces in a defensive array against them."

Taelsin opened the message and scanned its contents. "Unexpected, but doubtless welcome. The enemy of my enemy and all that. I do not recognise the sigil, however."

He passed a drawing of the banner under which the

arriving force marched across to the Hyena. She looked at it, shook her head and passed it onwards. When it finally reached Daine, she gasped at the sight and dropped the parchment as if it were a venomous snake with fangs bared.

The drawing was of a yellow banner depicting, at its centre, a shattered dagger held in a mailed fist.

"My Lady?" Donal's voice was filled with concern about her reaction.

"That flag. It cannot be."

Taelsin and the Hyena exchanged raised eyebrows. "It's probably just a minor mercenary company" she said. "It's certainly not one I recognise."

"But I do. That's a Blade of Ruin. It's the emblem of Gallant Stonehand."

CHAPTER THIRTY-NINE

"The Dark Spots on Your Soul"

In many ways, being unexpectedly attacked from the rear by an unknown assailant was a return to comforting normality for General Souit.

After weeks of gnawing frustration during the siege at Swinford, there was blessed relief in the flurry of orders and complex manoeuvring required to turn his army around to face this new threat.

He instantly determined that Mayor Taelsin lacked the numbers to lead a successful sally from the Keep. He thus put the defenders of the City out of his mind. Likewise, should the Lady Darkhelm decide to emerge and slaughter his men, he could do nothing about it. So why bother spending energy worrying?

After the horns were sounded to alert his men to the approaching threat from behind, Souit dispatched a steady stream of messengers to ensure the rearguard was adequately established. After a moment's careful thought, he triggered his <Doubletime> Skill to speed up this process. There would be a high price in Stamina to be paid by the soldiers when the timer ran out, but far better to be exhausted but in position than fresh and ripe for the slaughter.

Unit after unit quickly withdrew from inside Swinford's walls to gather themselves at the new front line. In no time at all — and Souit allowed himself a grim smile of satisfaction that hours of practice with just this sort of deployment had paid off — a thick line of bristling swords and shields was facing the arriving army.

With irritation, he bemoaned his lack of quality cavalry. Whoever was approaching under the banner of Gallant Stonehand — what a ridiculous pose! — was well-supplied in that regard. He could make out a couple of thousand horsemen on each flank — his scouts reporting a reasonably even split between heavy and light companies.

"But there's all sorts of irregulars mixed in there, sir. They just scream mercenaries to me."

"I concur." Souit dismissed the messenger with a new set of orders and turned his whole attention to the problem of the cavalry. On the open plain before Swinford — and in such numbers — they could easily cause devastating chaos. Even their presence on the edges of the main army narrowed down his options for deploying his infantry.

Especially with nothing tangible to field against them. Unless . . .

He beckoned over Angharad. "I have never before had an Archmage at my disposal. Can you please brief me on your capabilities?"

The young woman left behind the fawning group that now surrounded her at every juncture. She walked with a new assurance to stand beside Souit, looking towards the rapidly approaching force.

"And I have never been an Archmage before, my Lord. I imagine it will be some time before I can truly bring my expanded power to bear."

"Yes, yes, I understand. Brave new world and all that. But to be frank, I need something done about their cavalry. What do you suggest?"

Angharad considered for a few moments. "I do not appear to have gained any new Skills, but I had an extensive range of them before my Evolution. It more appears that the potential range and scope of their effects has increased."

"And that means?" There was more than a trace of frustration in the Great General's voice. If Angharad was not going to play a part in solving his cavalry problem, he would rather she said so so he could move his thinking onward to other options.

The Archmage read his expression accurately. "I can do everything I could do before, but better. Much better."

"How much better?"

"Exponentially so."

Souit took a beat to factor that extraordinary fact into this planning. "I am concerned that a charge from their heavy horse contingent will break our front line. Considering our many reversals during this siege, I am unsure that the men will have the resolve to hold. I, therefore, need that potential threat neutralised."

Angharad considered the distance and noted that the heavy cavalry was hovering far outside the typical range for Magery. But then she stopped. Because that wasn't true anymore, was it?

She ran through her list of Skills that might serve the Great General's purposes. She was shocked that they all appeared to have the appropriate range to reach the cavalry and that the mana cost, although insane, was apparently well within her capacity.

It appeared being an Archmage was going to be a lot of fun.

"So? Can you solve my problem?" Souit was carefully observing her face.

"Yes, my Lord. I rather think I can."

*

An expectant hush fell over the lines of the King's Army.

The dust Angharad's lengthy magical barrage had thrown up in the distance was just beginning to clear, and they were all eager to see the result. Of course, not a one of them believed she would actually have hit anything. Most of those positioned at the front were veterans of countless campaigns. They could measure — to the inch — the range of the various spells of Mages, and this girl would need a personal blessing from the Lords of Misrule themselves if she thought she'd get lucky enough to as much as scratch the fancy breastplates of the heavy cavalry.

"Good on her for trying, though," Corporal Salen grunted. "It will be hot work if those heavies get a head of steam."

No one replied.

It was commonly held that a horse would not charge an infantry square bristling with pikes. At least, that was what their Drillmasters had hammered into them during basic training. And that was the prayer running through a thousand minds right now.

And it was largely true. Against light cavalry.

Their heavy brethren, though? Their horses were huge — sometimes twice the size of those more usually deployed by Scouts — and each was armoured equally as well as the Knights that sat on their backs. These monstrous beasts were trained to drive straight into a tight press and keep on going — not caring who or what they crushed beneath them.

What was worse, flat, even ground like that which divided them was almost their perfect battleground.

Then, suddenly, cheers started to be heard throughout the army, and Salen tried to peer through the dust to make out the cause. Then he realised that was the point. He could not see the heavy cavalry through the dust because they were the dust.

"By the Goddess," he breathed. "We've got ourselves another Duskstrider."

*

Angharad was not sure how to feel.

On the one hand, she had just executed the single most potent casting of which she had ever believed herself capable. On the other, she had just reduced hundreds, if not thousands, of soldiers to ash.

"That was . . . instructive, Archmage. Thank you. Without wishing to seem ungrateful, could I point you towards the other flank? There is a similar contingent there that could benefit from . . . your attention."

Worryingly, Angharad realised she would have no issues triggering another instance of <Circle of Fire> again. Exactly how deep was her new mana pool?

However, she was prevented from exploring that further by the emergence of a swirling gold beam of energy that flew straight for her chest. It had originated from the centre of the mercenary army and was clearly being channelled by a practitioner of immense ability. Angharad managed to raise her hands in time and trigger every defensive Skill she possessed to deflect the beam away from her body and into Swinford's walls. The massive smoking hole it left behind suggested it was very fortunate she was able to prevent it from striking her.

"Belay my previous order, Archmage. I would ask that you and your fellow Mages deploy your strongest shield Skills, please."

Angharad looked to her hand, to the wall, to the direction the beam had come from. "Absolutely, my Lord."

*

"I am so sorry."

Nobody said anything.

"It's my age, you see. I just cannot seem to rely on myself anymore."

The eyes of the myriad mercenary captains gathered on the hill were wholly locked onto the ground.

"For example, I cannot even remember giving the order to return fire on that Mage."

In front of them, down the entire length of the King's Army, multiple shimmers in the air could be made out as various shield spells burst into life.

"Look at that! The exact opposite of what we wished to happen. All of our careful plans are up in smoke because of an order I cannot even remember issuing. Ageing is truly a terrible thing."

A swarthy man with long, dirty hair cleared his throat

and spat a dark-green substance onto the ground. "You gave no such order, my Lord."

"But" — a querulous tone entered the voice of the old man seated on a throne made from bone — "if I did not give the order, why would our own Mages have done such a thing?"

"Because you fool, we'd just lost half our cavalry. Would you have us watch as they obliterated the rest? I saved a few thousand men. Men we'll need if we're to defeat Souit."

"Ah. That explains it." Long fingernails were drummed on pale ivory. "Although, forgive me, Caolo, what orders had I issued regarding such things?"

The tall Mage, Caolo Wintereye, drove his staff into the ground and stared balefully into the single eye of his commander. "You ordered us to accept all losses to avoid alerting them to our capabilities. But you meant some stray shots from their siege engines, not a goddess-damned Archmage destroying half of our men. I've saved us from . . ."

The movement from sitting to upright was so fast that none of those present realised anything had changed. And then, as one, they all stepped away in alarm from the thin, bent-backed figure who now stood amongst them.

Particularly as he was holding the severed head of the Wintereye by its hair.

Gallant Stonehand raised his arm high so that he could meet the eyes of the Mage. A Mage who, appallingly, was still alive. "I'm not sure if this is the time, but you should know that the origins of my Class are quite interesting. I doubt many of you know that we were initially intended to be medics. The Dark God had discovered that rot and illness — if left unchecked — would spread and destroy the whole body. He recognised that there was a time of opportunity when the corruption could be removed to save that which remained. It was at that moment he empowered the Blades of Salvation."

The decapitated head swung gently in the age-spotted hand. Caolo's eyes were huge, and his mouth moved and twisted as if in agony.

"It was said that the first of the Blades could excise a brain tumour with nothing more than a pin. That they had a range of Skills that could ensure an amputation was nothing more than a temporary inconvenience. Indeed, at the height of their fame, there was even the suggestion that Blades of Salvation could cut a person free from death itself."

The old man giggled at that, but no smile touched the corners of his lips.

Then the Stonehand's voice dipped to a whisper, and his words became inaudible to anyone but Caolo. "But the Dark God was not satisfied with mere salvation. He wished for those he had empowered to be more ambitious in their duty. To cut out disease from not just individuals but society as a whole. Over the years, his Blades were given more and more Skills, most of which moved them further and further away from their original, medical roots. Before long, fear of the Blades of Ruin spread across the land."

Then the old man's eyes opened wide, and his face contorted in a mask of rage. He triggered a Skill and empowered his voice with <Terror>, and it crashed outwards, dropping more than one of his Captains, whimpering, to their knees. "And you should be afraid! Because I can see your corruption. I can sense the dark spots on your souls, and I will — I must — cut them out. Not all will survive its removal, but the blackness will no longer take you. It will be removed!"

Then, as fast as it had come, the anger was gone. And he was again a frail figure, looking with confusion at the head in his hand. "I don't . . . what happened to Caolo?"

One of the Stonehand's aides came forward and gently removed the Mage's head from his grasp. He watched blankly as it was taken away, his words once again a whisper.

"He's dead, but he doesn't know it. Everything that he was and had the potential to be is ended. But Caolo will not understand. Consciousness without a soul is an unfortunate thing." He suddenly called after those removing the head. "Please, find him a nice view. It will keep him calm. He deserves the peace."

"Of course, my Lord."

"Or dig a hole and bury it. It's all the same. Now, where were we?"

Gallant Stonehand, Commander of the Ruined Blades, and currently contracted for an unfathomable sum by House Trellec to scour the forces of the King from the West, turned his full attention to the army before him.

"And where is she?"

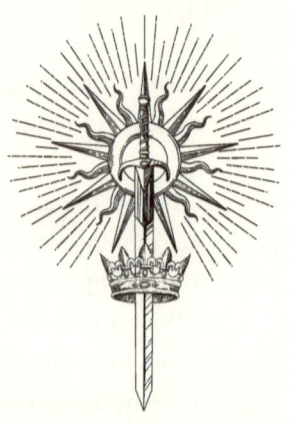

CHAPTER FORTY

"A Disappointing Welcome"

"At some stage, I'm just going to assume you're putting me on."

Kirstin slowly became aware of the voice. And that it was talking to her.

"I refuse to believe that Logan Twilight — and imitation is certainly not the sincerest form of flattery, as far as that man is concerned — is capable of an <Oblivion> spell that would keep a reasonably fit young woman unconscious for this length of time. Is it possible you are merely enjoying a good nap?"

The Archer slowly opened her eyes. There was a stone ceiling above her. Chains appeared to be hanging from it.

"Ah, so you are yet living! Come on. Chop-chop. Places to go, people to see."

Ignoring the voice — even in her less-than-wakeful state, she sensed that was likely to be a good default position — Kirstin tried to roll to the side to begin the laborious process of sitting up. However, sudden resistance to that movement and a loud "clank" suggested the chains above her were not just decorative.

"Are we . . ." Her voice was raspy, so she cleared her throat to try again. "Are we in chains?"

"Yes and no. Were we in chains? Yes. Are you still in chains? Also, yes. Have chains been invented that are strong enough to have held me once I awoke — in record time, I would have you know — from an entirely inferior <Oblivion> spell? Not so much."

"Eliud, in some cultures it would be considered somewhat rude to free yourself from restraints and yet leave your unconscious female companion trapped."

"Really? And are we in one of those cultures right now?"

"Apparently not."

Kirstin rolled the opposite way and found enough slack in her bindings to be able to sit up. Albeit uncomfortably.

Looking around, she appeared to be in a large, dark room divided into eight separate cells, four of which lined the length of each sidewall. A thin walkway led between the cells and connected the heavy iron doors at each end of the room. She reckoned that quite some care had been taken to ensure no one could reach someone standing on that narrow path from within the cells.

She said, "Remind me again what a warm welcome you were going to receive when we arrived at the Capital. There was talk of a parade . . ."

Her only answer was that the metallic cuffs on her wrists and ankles suddenly glowed as if white-hot and then melted away to the floor.

Almost unwillingly, she looked to her left to take in the grinning face of Eliud Villa, holder of the Pendragon Class, known commonly as the Duskstrider and, by any measure, one of the most powerful Mages in the world.

"I do not deny this has been a disappointing welcome. You don't need to say 'thank you,' by the way. Unless you want to, of course."

"I don't." Kirstin stood and pressed against the bars of the cage around her. "There's no door."

"No." Eliud was stood in a similiar position in his own cage. "I noticed that too. Neither has anyone come to check on us in the fifteen bells I have been awake since shaking off the effects of an especially weak and unimpressive cantrip. If I did not know better, I might worry that someone had locked us up and thrown away the key."

"Fifteen bells! We haven't got time for this. Genoes needs us to find him."

The grin on the Duskstrider's face dropped away. Without his habitually good-humoured expression, the man had a haunted look. And Kirstin did not think that was just because of his loss of the stableboy he had been charged with protecting. From hints she had picked up through conversations with the Lady Darkhelm, that reversal was simply the latest in a line of tragedies that may have driven a lesser man mad.

"We will find him, I promise. But I did not wish to rush your recovery. <Oblivion> is an unpredictable spell at the best of times. Particularly if you are not used to its effects. Truly, I'm glad to see you are well."

Touched by his obvious sincerity, she nodded back. Then panic took her. "What about Savage? Josul? Where are they?"

Eliud's smile was back. "They're fine. I doubt it was what Logan intended, but whoever he charged with incarcerating us here did not appreciate he probably would have wanted them locked up, too. I can feel them prowling around this — whatever it is. I sense they're frustrated not to have been able to find us, but neither of them is in any particular distress."

Kirstin pressed her weight against the iron bars. They did not move whatsoever. "So what do we do? Do you know where we are?"

"I am not sure. The last thing I can remember Logan saying was that the Sky Keep had been preparing for my visit for some time."

"Well, that isn't ominous at all."

"I'm not overly concerned. The Kingdom has left me alone for so long precisely because they have no conclusive way to deal with me. If the best they've come up with is a cage without a door . . ."

"So we shouldn't be worried?"

"Me? I'm golden. No worries whatsoever. On the other hand, I presume you'll be needing food or water at some stage. You might want to try calling for help whilst you have the energy."

Kirstin pressed her fingers to the bridge of her nose. "I knew I should have stayed with the Darkhelm."

*

Three more bells slowly passed by with no sight nor sound of their captors. For all his bravado in front of Kirstin, there was a growing churning feeling in Eliud's stomach.

And he could not quite understand why.

He thought it all came down to the fact that cages without doors were quite an unusual feature in prisons.

It begged the question of how Kirstin and he had been placed inside them.

And how whoever had put them in there wanted to get them out.

The obvious answer, of course, was Magery, but he could not identify that any had been used in this room besides his own. So, had the bars been mundanely built around their unconscious forms? And if so, what was the point of that? Even someone as arrogant as Logan would have to acknowledge such measures would be ineffective against Eliud.

As if to reassure himself as to that point, he rested a finger against one of the bars and superheated it with <Blaze>.

"Ah! What was that!"

He glanced to his right, to where Kirstin was hopping up and down, holding one foot and staring at the floor of her cell in utter horror.

"What's the matter?"

"I don't know. It was like my foot was suddenly on fire." She knelt down to rest her hand on the stone slabs. Finding them cold, she shook her head. "But that doesn't make any sense."

Watching the Archer carefully, he triggered the spell again. This time, he was able to follow the feedback loop that ran directly from his cell into Kirstin's. She jumped up in pain as <Blaze> transferred from the bars of his cage to the floor of her cell. What was more, he sensed that the loop effect was replicated on the floor of each of the other empty cells.

Interesting.

"I'm just going to speak aloud for a little bit. Feel free

to ignore me. I find it helps to get things out of my head. It strikes me that if I were going to design a prison to hold . . . well, me, I'd know the biggest challenge was going to be pure power. So, I'd need to do something to stop the prisoner from bringing that to bear. I'd build into my planning that the person I wanted to keep locked up had a bit of a reputation for being protective of those he travelled with. In those circumstances, some sort of sympathetic link between different cells would do the trick. It wouldn't even need to be too clever or intricate a spell. In fact, this barely needs any power of its own. All the spell has to do is channel anything I trigger in my cell into those of my companions. After that, it just relies on me not wanting to kill my friends in order to escape."

Kirstin regarded the Pendragon nervously throughout his speech. "So, if your magic is off the table, how do we get out?"

"I mean, if we're being scrupulously honest, let's acknowledge that I can get out at any time I so wish. It's just whether I'm willing to burn you alive to do it, which is the real question. In fact, I could have saved myself an awful lot of awkward guilt if I'd just let myself out whilst you were unconscious. Less screaming, you know?"

"Right. Well, considering that I am awake and that you now know that anything you do in your cell happens in mine, what's the plan?"

"I'm worried enough about coming up with a plausible story for Savage that I'd like to explore alternative solutions to sacrificing you for my own freedom."

"Well, that makes me feel simply wonderful."

"At least for a bit."

CHAPTER FORTY-ONE

"Resurrection Complete"

"I know this might not be the best time, but when this is all over, you'll have made some incredible gains in your Resistances."

Kirstin wiped the sweat from her face and tried to take a deep breath. She winced as broken ribs protested against that movement. "I think it's best if we don't talk right now."

"I can try healing you again?"

"No!"

Eliud banged his fists against the bars of the cage in frustration. He had been so sure there must be a way around the feedback loop connecting the two cells. But if there was, it was thus far beyond him. Whenever he triggered a Skill, the energy was immediately dissipated into the cages around him, causing Kirstin significant injury.

And that included any efforts he made to heal the damage he was causing the Archer.

It had been so long since he had encountered a problem he could not solve through sheer power that he was feeling somewhat deskilled. He knew he could easily free himself from captivity in an instant, but not without killing Kirstin.

"Does the sympathetic link work both ways?"

It had been a while since he had heard something from Kirstin that was not pain-fuelled cry, and he almost missed her question.

"I am sorry?"

"I asked whether this feedback loop transfers both ways. Or is it just your cell connected that way to all the others?"

"I would assume the spell's focus would be on restricting me. But it would probably work a little both ways. Why?"

Kirstin directed a powerful kick into one of the bars. It bent slightly before clicking back into shape, and Eliud doubled over more in surprise than pain.

"I suddenly feel a little better. What do we try next?"

*

Kirstin returned to consciousness for the fifth time and found Eliud pacing back and forth in his cell. Seeing her come around, he squatted beside her, resting his head against the bars between them.

"Okay. We clearly need to change things up. No matter what I try, the trigger on the feedback spell picks it up and channels it right back to you. I'm basically out of ideas at this stage. So, here's the new plan. It is not one of my best, but it is still orders of magnitude better than what most people could come up with in these circumstances."

"Eliud, I swear to the Goddess, I am so far away from finding you quirkily charming right now."

"Noted. And I am truly sorry for all this. I would never have allowed you to accompany me if I had thought there was any chance this would have been the outcome. But our only path to Genoes is if I can persuade the King to locate him for us, and I cannot do that from within this cell. I think we have explored all the obvious options for escape, and if we have learned one thing through all this, it is clear that there is no value in subtlety."

Kirstin sat up a little straighter and cracked her neck. "Subtlety. Right."

"So I am going to suggest something a little radical."

"This is going to involve you causing me a lot more pain, isn't it?"

"Actually, if everything works out how I expect, I assume probably not."

"Well, that does not seem too bad?"

"I mean, it's going to involve me straight-up killing you."

*

Timing would be everything.

After all, the true value of an unlimited mana pool was that it made almost everything possible.

Eliud had a grudging respect for whoever had designed this trap for him. The premise was sound, and, in normal circumstances, he could imagine it would have kept him tied up for quite some time.

Over the years, he had lost far too many companions. When he had first met the Lady Darkhelm, she had persuaded him to leave his self-imposed isolation following a string of disasters. He had withdrawn from the world because he had concluded he was simply too powerful to safely be around others. Particularly those he cared about.

That the outcome of his time at Court had led to yet more bloodshed — and the loss of further friends — had made about as devastating a series of events as he could conceive.

Thus, the orientation of this room was perfectly designed to play into his greatest fear: that using his power would hurt those he loved.

But to be measured against that was the fate of Genoes.

The Dark God had taken the boy for no other reason than to cause Eliud pain. And he did not find that to be acceptable.

He needed to break free from this cage, then escape whatever the Sky Keep was, find the King and persuade him to put him on the trail of the Dark God in order to rescue the boy. And they would then find out how much hyperbole there was when people described the Duskstrider's power as 'godlike'.

But to even start achieving that, he would need to kill Kirstin.

"When you put it like that, I find myself being less than enthusiastic about this plan."

"I am not saying there is no risk. I am, however, saying that waiting here until you die of dehydration is probably not an ideal alternative."

"And you are sure this will work?"

"The theory is sound. The only thing holding us here is a minor spell that diverts any power I seek to use into the other cells. So far, we've been trying to find the sweet spot where I can use just enough power to get free without hurting you too much. Turns out, that's been harder than we might have anticipated."

"That's one way of putting it."

"So the only other option I can see is we go the other way. I use so much power that I overload the feedback spell. We accept this will have consequences upon you, and I trigger every Healing Skill I have with everything I've got. Which — I don't know if I've mentioned — is quite a lot."

"The 'consequences' are going to be that the sympathetic link kills me, right?"

"Yes."

"And you think you have enough Healing Skills to bring me back? I mean, I've never heard of a Resurrection Skill and I have no interest in shuffling around as a Soulless. You're saying you've done this before, and it's worked?"

Eliud's pause was its own monologue.

"Is there any other way you can see of getting us free?"

The Duskstrider shook his head.

Kirstin closed her eyes for a moment. The faces of Jak and Genoes dominated her mind. One was a brother she had not been able to save. The other . . . well, there was still a chance there.

She opened her eyes and nodded. "Let's do it."

There was no need for any more words.

Eliud's eyes turned purple, and streaks of lightning surrounded him. Kirstin screamed as the feedback loop channelled all that power into her body, but this time, the Pendragon did not stop. He drew more and more deeply on the unending well of his power and increased his output.

The cell on the far right-hand side of the room exploded first. Then, the one on the other side of Kirstin. In moments, each of the cages was reduced to slag as the spell that drew Eliud's power away did its best to keep the Duskstrider caged.

Kirstin's burning, smoking body stopped screaming, and she collapsed to lie still on the floor — but, to Eliud's despair, his own cage still stood.

He could not trigger any Healing Skills until he was free. However, not needing to worry about hurting Kirstin further, he ramped up his casting and, for a few heartbeats, the spell syphoning away his power held. He had just enough time to reevaluate his poor opinion of Logan when the dam burst, and the metallic bars around him liquified.

In the same instant as the restrictions upon him faded, he hit Kirstin with every Healing Skill he had. This turned out to be quite a lot.

With each triggered Skill, the face of someone he had lost appeared in his mind. He had been responsible for so many deaths in his time, and there was no version of reality — in this realm or the next — where he was willing to add the Archer's face to this gallery of failure.

A constant stream of pure mana poured into the young woman, repairing the horrible burns the cage had inflicted upon her, resetting bones that had been shattered and restoring organs that had been ripped and torn.

And it was still not enough.

He roared in frustration and pushed more and more of his mana into Kirstin's body. It had been decades since he pulled so deeply on his power, and still, he needed more.

Does she mean so much to you?

Eliud recognised the voice of the Goddess and ignored

it. She had sought to win him to her side on more than one occasion over the years, and he had always refused her.

I do not make this offer without conditions. Should I save her, you will owe me a favour.

Eliud triggered Skills over and over again, but they had long since stopped making any difference. Kirstin was now the healthiest, most radiant corpse in existence. She had been right that there was no Resurrection Skill. But still he had hoped . . .

What had he been thinking? His arrogance again. No problem his power could not solve, right?

To be in the debt of the Goddess, though? That was a weighty thing. He had avoided that for so long because he well knew the possible consequences. But looking at the young woman's body, he considered his choices for barely a second. "I consent. I will owe you one favour. Bring her back."

*

The first thing Kirstin noticed when she opened her eyes was that she felt the best she ever had in her life.

The second thing was that the room they had been kept in had been absolutely devastated. There was no longer any sign of the cages and even the iron doors at either end of the path had been blown off their hinges. Eliud certainly could bring the fury.

The third and final thing that caught her attention was a notification flickering in her vision.

<Resurrection complete. Class Evolution available>

CHAPTER FORTY-TWO

"A Girl Needs a Little Distance"

"Eliud!"

The Pendragon breathed a little easier at the sound of the young woman's voice. He had no reason to believe the Goddess would have gone back on Her word; after all, She had been seeking to entrap him in such a trade of 'favours' for almost as long as he had been alive. However, it was reassuring to have it confirmed that the Archer now lived.

Although, he said "Archer" . . .

"Well, would you look at that!"

A soft, green glow surrounded Kirstin, spilling out to illuminate the corners of the shattered remains of the room. What was more, as the melted iron of the cells had cooled into a vast puddle around the girl's form, its reflective surface was flinging light upwards so that it seemed like she was, herself, shining from within.

In a way, Eliud considered, that was not too far from the truth.

"What's happened to me? I have a message that my resurrection is complete. Did I die?"

"A little. Not so much that we need to make a fuss about it."

"And you brought me back to life?"

Eliud shrugged and avoided her eye. Fortunately, she was too overwhelmed by things to notice. "Something like that."

"It says I can make a Class Evolution!"

He was not surprised. Although such a change of status might feel like a fairytale to the general population, Class Evolution — at least for the more powerful members of society — was not an especially uncommon phenomenon. In his experience, anyone going through a particularly traumatic series of events (and, of course, surviving) was likely to meet the requirements for some sort of Evolution. With the involvement of a god, and the Goddess herself had interceded for Kirstin, it was almost a foregone conclusion there would be an opportunity for the Archer to advance her Class.

Following Gallant Stonehand's descent into madness, he had himself briefly held the position of Mentor. In that role, Eliud had been charged with finding and training those for whom Evolution would be of desirable benefit to the Kingdom. However, even before his own fall from power, he had struggled to put the young people in his care through the sort of rigorous and dangerous programme required. Whilst a surprising number of people were more than willing to pay the price in torture and near death in order to evolve, he had certainly not been the right person to oversee that process.

"That's fantastic news, my dear. And all you needed to do was be kidnapped, tortured and then accidentally murdered. The world is truly a marvellous place."

That she did notice. "Are you okay?"

He waved away her enquiry. "If we are lucky, Savage and Josul will be able to locate us soon." He looked around at the room he had destroyed when overpowering the sympathetic link that entrapped him. "After all, what's the good of intelligent animal companions if they need more than a giant explosion to orientate themselves back to their Masters?"

He gestured to a large piece of fallen masonry, which turned itself over to provide a serviceable bench. He sat upon it and patted a space next to him for Kirstin to do the same. "So, let's hear about your options."

"Options?"

He closed his eyes and tried to remember how he had once explained things to the newly evolved. It was so very long ago.

"You have moved beyond the threshold of your Class. Although there is some disagreement as to the whys and the wherefores, it is generally held that actions above and beyond the 'norm' . . . Understand that I do not use that word slightingly. The world only exists because it has enough people in it who fulfil that 'norm' day in, day out. Do you understand me?"

Eyes wide at his suddenly harsh tone, Kirstin nodded.

"Good. Well, when an event, or a series of events, occurs that requires someone to move beyond those 'normal' expectations, it is not uncommon for them to be allowed to advance their Class. As you know, the Lady Darkhelm was of Farmer stock before her own Evolution."

"So I can become a Knight of the Road?"

He instinctively laughed at that, then, seeing the hurt on Kirstin's face, softened his voice. "Not a Knight of the Road, no. In all such things, there are thresholds. Daine had the genes of Farmers immemorial running through her veins. Her evolved Class needed her to have significant Strength and Endurance at its core. I am afraid it is not in your path to become one of the Knights."

A moment of disappointment flashed across Kirstin's face, and Eliud could understand that. Who would not dream of being one of those terrifying, unstoppable warriors of myth? He recognised the significant irony that he was sure that Daine would profoundly disagree.

"How can I tell what I can choose, then?"

"First of all, you need to find your calm. I cannot tell you how many people make a rash choice at this moment. For those who have been working their whole life for the chance to Evolve, when it comes, they snatch too quickly at a half-understood dream. This is a choice to be made with a sober mind and a settled heart."

Kirstin nodded and took a few deep breaths. Eliud smiled as the green glow around her intensified. For all her resurrection might prove to cost him in the future — damn the Goddess and her favours — he was not sure he would trade this moment for the return of that cost.

"What next?"

"The answer is inside you. You have been notified that an Evolution is possible. Possible, mark you. There is nothing to say you cannot decide to stay an Archer. If so, all your capabilities in that Class will be enhanced. The potency of your Skills will increase, you may even pick up some new ones, and you will, undoubtedly, become one of the premier launchers of pieces of sharpened wood by the method of kinetic energy in the whole Kingdom."

She laughed. "But I can become more?"

He winced at that. "You have the opportunity to become 'different', not 'more'. There are those who would disagree with me on that point, but I hope none of them are within this room. Do you understand me?"

Kirstin nodded. "Yes. Not better. Different. I understand."

She closed her eyes and let her mind drift. She had no idea what she was seeking, but she trusted Eliud enough to follow his advice.

And then . . .

She found herself running through a vast field in pursuit of a dark-clad figure. Her Speed as she moved was extraordinary as if blown by the wind itself. In moments, she had nearly closed the gap, and in desperation, her quarry turned and threw a knife towards her. Without hesitation, she took a step into the air, then another, and then she was floating as the knife passed harmlessly beneath her. Still hovering, she drew an arrow and shot it towards her prey — the projectile moving with an explosion of energy that far exceeded anything she had ever experienced. As the vision faded, she understood she could choose to evolve into a <Skystrider Ranger>.

Immediately, the scene changed, and Kirstin found herself perched on the battlements of a tower, staring down at the crowds beneath. She appeared to be looking for someone. But no, this was not a good vantage point. She was too high. She glanced to a house below and . . . teleported onto its roof. As soon as she reappeared, she craned her neck and continued her hunt.

There she was!

She drew her arrows and launched two shots in quick succession at a scarlet-cloaked woman striding down the street. But, as soon as the arrows were in motion, the woman seemed to sense the attack and rolled to the left, both arrows flying past helplessly. Kirstin just smiled and rewound time for a few seconds, adding a third shot to hit the target in the head as she rolled away. Her second option was to become something called a <Temporal Marksman>.

The final shift in perspective took Kirstin to the middle of a battle. She was surrounded by three men, all armed with swords, who were doing their best to cut her to pieces. She was dodging and blocking, where necessary, but was clearly overmatched. Finally, she misjudged something and a slash cut into her.

However, it did not.

At the moment of contact, Kirstin suddenly became incorporeal, and the blade passed straight through her to drive through the chest of one of the other men. Taking advantage of the confusion, she drew an arrow and fired it into the ground beneath her, causing an explosion of starlight that blinded and completely disorientated her attackers. Finally, as the two surviving men stumbled away, Kirstin drew a second arrow and, without aiming, fired it into the air. The second it left her bow, she gestured at the two men and clenched her fist, triggering a Skill. They were instantly snatched off into the air, flying behind the arrow as if tied by a leash. This final choice was termed <Celestial Harbinger>.

She opened her eyes.

"Well?" Eliud's eyes were twinkling.

"All amazing options." However, she already knew the choice. Growing up with a brother as unpredictable and aggressive as Jak, there was one thing more than anything she wished over and over again she could do. "You see, when push comes to shove, sometimes, a girl just needs to be able to achieve a little distance."

Archer → Celestial Harbringer

Kirstin accepted the Evolution.

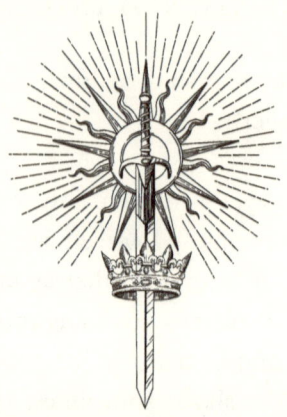

CHAPTER FORTY-THREE

"Balance in All Things"

"I demand to be heard!"

The Goddess sighed at the wheedling, peevish voice pressing at the boundary of her realm. She considered pushing him away; however, it was a rare enough occasion that her youngest son sought an audience. It would have been peculiarly churlish of her to refuse.

With a sigh, she allowed the Dark God to breach her defences and moved swiftly to meet him near the edge of power.

Yes?

"You are breaking the rules!"

Are you aware of how childish you sound?

If anything, the mild chastisement caused his volume to increase. "It is not me that insists that we conduct ourselves in this ridiculously restrained manner. If you insist that we all obey your many and varied diktats, then it is only right that you are bound by them, too!"

I sense you are perilously close to stamping your foot . . .

The Dark God's form shimmered, instantly moving through different versions of his aspect. He eventually stabilised as a young man, no older than his mid-twenties.

"Do you seek to bait me, Mother? Are you so unconfident in the rightness of your argument that you cannot win any other way?"

And you seek to blame me for your own emotional incontinence. How you respond to my words is entirely within your power to decide. That you are most comfortable in the form of a child perhaps speaks poorly to your own confidence in holding a rational conversation.

His face darkened in rage, and he opened his mouth to retort, then paused. His form blurred again, and he was suddenly a much older man, matching the presentation of the Goddess. He dipped his head in acknowledgement.

"I apologise."

Accepted. Now, what brings you to my realm with such haste?

"I think the time for games is over, Mother. You are perfectly aware your intercession with the Archer was inappropriate. The board is finely balanced, and you have sought to weigh things in your favour most outrageously."

It is not against propriety for me to grant the Duskstrider a favour. Or would you argue that such actions are not within my purview?

The Dark God paused for a moment, regarding his mother's aspect. Tall, willowy, and with just a touch of grey to her lengthy, black hair, she had remained in this form more and more of late. And he thought he knew why.

With a casual gesture, he manifested a giant stained glass window between them.

"You recognise this?"

The Goddess nodded and, he thought, frowned. He could only just make her out through the coloured glass that now divided them.

It is the current configuration of the Church of Dawn.

He nodded. "Not one of your more subtle moves, I think, to display this so prominently."

All must be clear about the powers currently in opposition in the world. As you note, balance in all things is essential.

She moved to the left-hand side of the window, and her son — instinctively — took up a position on the right-hand.

She touched her own likeness at the top of the glass depicting a blurring of her three aspects. Virgin, Mother and Crone. Her finger traced down and then around the images of the critical pieces she had put on the board for this conflict. Daine, Taelsin and Eliud.

She loved each and worried that she expected too much of them.

That emotion surprised her. What an unusual thought about these mortals! She had been spending too long in her Mother aspect. She knew her son had already noted that profoundly irritating fact.

Subtly, she aged her form.

Returning to the window, below those three, shown towards the bottom of the glass, were a range of minor players in the game. Those such as Donal, Savage and Josul. She noted that the depiction of Kirstin was currently reforming. That made her smile.

Glancing over to her son's side of the glass, though, turned the grin into something more sober.

His depiction matched hers at the top of the design — boy, young man, elder. It could be no clearer that they were adversaries.

With distaste, she made out image after image of those who had chosen to follow the Dark God. Drunnoc, Fion, that demonic Healer and the Steward who so profoundly misused his power. But there were so many more. Her son had gifted shards of his power to so many other mortals, and their twisted forms filled the middle portion of the glass. That monstrous serpent was there too, along with his own minions.

You speak of balance. She gestured to the window. *Do you genuinely claim it is I who am to be censured for my interference?*

The Dark God shrugged. "You set the rules, and I try to break them. It has, and will be, ever thus. But that does not mean you are free to do so yourself."

The Goddess paused at that. For all she might wish it were otherwise, he did have a point. It was in his nature to seek to leverage every possible advantage. Just as it was in her own power to try to restrain him from those destructive impulses.

"You see it, don't you?" His voice was almost gloating. "You have overstepped in this."

Irritation pulsed from her in a wave, cracking the glass straight down the middle. *You forget yourself.*

"I think I am the only one who remembers who they are." And then his form shifted again to that of a petulant-looking teenager. "All you ever do is break your word. You promise, and you promise, and you promise, and then you just do what you want anyway. I achieved the capture of the Duskstrider, and my prize was to be the death of the Archer. You cheated me. I demand you set things right!"

You stole his charge from him! Genoes is of critical importance to all things. Far more than your silly ambitions. Eliud deserved compensation for your actions.

As she uttered the words, she saw understanding dawn in her son's eyes. He glanced towards the centre of the window, where the crack she had caused ran through the middle of the image of the Unaligned. He grinned broadly.

"So he is important! I knew it!"

The Goddess shook her head. She had sought to inflame his emotions to destabilise him, and instead, he had achieved the same in her. She unspooled time by a few seconds to replay the scene.

". . . I demand you set things right!"

Perhaps you are right. I may have allowed myself to become too involved.

The Dark God's eyes narrowed. He sensed something had changed in the atmosphere between them, but he could not quite put his finger on what. Knowing he needed a cooler, more rational head, he moved his aspect back to middle age.

"Warm words, Mother. But what is to be the solution?"

I have broken no rules by granting the Duskstrider a favour. I will soon ask for one from him in return.

"But the Archer should have died. And now she has evolved. You have strengthened your hand in an unseemly way."

As they watched, the image of Kirstin vanished and

appeared slightly further up the window. She was now surrounded by starlight.

I accept that. What would you ask for to balance the scales?

He smiled and opened his hands. "No more than my due. A resurrection."

Impossible. You already have the advantage in power.

"And yet . . ."

She watched as his eyes scanned the window before alighting on the small, childlike figure in the middle. The Dark God frowned as he looked at that, searching for a memory that would not come.

But . . . I accept I may have acted at the very edge of my authority. You are to be allowed a resurrection.

His eyes left the window and met hers. "Truly?"

It pains me that you still feel the need to question my word.

He shifted into a toddler. "Thank you, Mama. I knew you'd see things my way."

Exhausted, she banished him from her realm. The last thing she saw was his malignant grin as it faded to nothing.

"A significant misstep, mother." Two voices speaking in harmony sounded from behind her.

It appears I need need to strengthen the walls of my defences.

"How rude."

She turned around to face the two young, bearded men. *And how have I displeased my other sons this day?*

They both laughed in synchronisation. "Not us, Mother. We merely felt you reroll your dice and were interested as to why. He will realise what he has captured soon, you understand?"

The Goddess did not answer. Of course, she knew the Dark God would recognise what Genoes was. All she could do was ensure her pieces were prepared for that gambit when it came.

The Lords of Misrule approached the window, moving so one stood on each side. "There's a saying the mortals have about eggs and baskets. It would appear our brother understands the meaning of that better than you. You have put a lot of faith into a small number of very fragile things."

And they put a lot of faith in me.

They nodded at that. "Our brother speaks of balance yet keeps his thumb heavily on the scale. You do not feel able to act, but we do not enjoy witnessing games played with loaded die. By your leave, we would . . . spread a little chaos."

That possibility intrigued her. *You have never sought to help me before.*

"And we do not now. Chaos is a double-bladed knife. It cuts the wielder as keenly as the victim. We may end up helping him far more than we do you. That is our nature. However" — they both indicated the window — "without our intercession, you will undoubtedly lose. And that thought currently displeases us."

The Goddess quested forward in time, seeking the outcome of this decision. But, as had been the case since the events in the village, the future was turbulently in motion. She saw the sense in her older sons' words. Her pieces would be crushed if she allowed the game to continue with such a weight of opposition.

But to hazard so much on the mere roll of a die.

So be it. I would welcome your input.

The Lords of Misrule laughed, and each placed their

hand on the glass that divided them. The window began to swirl then, and the rattling of dice in a cup could be heard.

Good luck, my children, she whispered, *and then grimaced.*

Because "luck" was now very much in play.

CHAPTER FORTY-FOUR

"The Potential to Be Quite a Handful"

Eliud stood guard over Kirstin as she completed her Evolution.

Not that there was much to protect her from. Despite the destruction he had wrought, there had been no influx of guards coming to see what had occurred with their prisoners. Whilst welcome, this had some troubling implications.

His concern increased when Savage and Josul dropped from one of the holes he had inadvertently punched in the ceiling while overloading the sympathetic link.

After accepting the enthusiastic welcome from one of his animal companions and the barely concealed disdain from the other, he was dismayed when they both noted that since their own awakening, they had not seen anyone else either. Both of them had been locked away in entirely mundane cages next to each other, the bars of which had not been strong enough to withstand Josul's attentions. Eliud was not altogether clear whether Savage even recognised she had been trapped.

After nodding perfunctorily to the Pendragon, the kitten had settled on Kirstin's lap, pummelling the girl's leg as her Evolution finalised. Savage gave every impression of being perfectly content with life.

"So, where is everyone?" Eliud mused, scratching Josul behind his ears. The giant dog whuffled in pleasure and leant against his master's leg. "No one really locks people up in abandoned prisons and leaves them to it. There has to be more to it than this."

"I feel weird."

Eliud's attention snapped back to Kirstin. "Welcome back. Weird how?"

The girl stood — carefully placing Savage in her customary place on her shoulder — and rubbed the joints of her fingers. "Everything feels . . . too much."

"That's all perfectly natural. Your senses have undergone a significant upgrade, which is overwhelming. You'll get used to it over time, but things will be a touch intense for a while. Speaking of which, although it can be seen as rude to enquire about another's Class, in the circumstances . . ."

"Celestial Harbinger."

Eliud whistled appreciatively. "She really doesn't mess about with Her favours."

"What? Who?"

"It does not matter." He waved away her question. "Strong choice. Excellent offensive capabilities and, from memory, some sort of phase defensive Skill?"

Kirstin nodded. "I saw a vision of being in combat, and

I was able to let a sword slide straight through me and into the attacker behind me."

"Handy. What's it called?"

She closed her eyes for a moment. "<Nebula Cloak>. Most of my original Archer Skills are still here, and there are two other new ones. <Stellar Arrows> and <Gravity Well>."

"Did your Evolution vision show you what they did?"

"The first caused a massive explosion of light which disorientated my attackers, and the second tethered them to an arrow, dragging them behind it when I shot."

"Okay, well, we better test how they both work before you use them for real."

"How?"

"Well, no time like the present. Let's spar."

Kirstin frowned. "I don't know, Eliud. They looked like pretty strong Skills. Is now really the time?"

Eliud began going through an elaborate warm-up routine. Savage sighed. Loudly. He ignored her.

"We don't know what we will be up against through those doors. We'd be foolish not to ensure you can access your full Skillset. Come on, give me what you've got."

He clicked his fingers, conjuring a longbow and a quiver full of arrows out of the air, and floated them over to Kirstin.

"Just how powerful are you, Eliud?"

"I have some game. Now" — he adopted a martial pose — "have at it."

"Why do I think this will be an opportunity for you to show off how strong you are and make me look foolish?"

Savage yawned and dropped to the floor. "Because you have met him."

"I'm hurt by that. Okay. How's this? You use everything you have, and I promise I will only use one minor Skill."

"Which one?"

"Your suspicion wounds me. Fine. <Spark>. The only Skill I will use is <Spark>."

Kirstin looked at Savage, who gave a feline shrug. "It's used to light campfires. It could be considered an extremely minor damage-over-time Skill at its worst."

Shaking her head, Kirstin equipped the quiver and tested the bow's draw. "You're wholly setting me up for something here, and it's important you know I don't forgive you in advance."

And she activated <Nebula Cloak>.

Immediately, she could tell what Eliud had meant by this being a "phase" Skill. Whereas in her vision, it looked as if her body had become insubstantial, the reality was a bit more complicated. It felt as if she had stepped slightly out of time. Not a huge amount, but enough to be effectively untouchable by physical attacks.

It was a disorientating effect, and, secretly, she was glad that Eliud had pressed the point on practice. It was hugely preferable to get used to this feeling in a controlled environment rather than in the heat of battle.

Kirstin drew an arrow and then dropped it. Physical movement in this state was going to take some getting used to. It was like her body was not entirely under control.

She lined the second arrow up on Eliud. "Are you ready?"

"I don't know, my dear. Are you going to drop it or shoot it at me?" As he spoke, she felt him trigger <Spark> on her. As Savage had said, she could feel a tiny pinprick of damage begin to chip away at her health.

She activated <Stellar Arrows> and fired at his feet. Her aim was not quite up to her usual standards — she would need to put in substantial practice wearing the <Nebula Cloak> to be able to compensate for its effects.

However, the massive explosion of starlight that enveloped the Duskstrider made a few inches either way make very little difference.

Her heart was in her mouth for a moment until her eyes recovered from the startling bright light, and she saw a perfectly healthy Eliud standing in the same ridiculous pose.

"I suppose you are going to tell me that did not hurt at all?"

Eliud's only reply was a wink. "What else do you have?"

Feeling her blood rising, she moved to her final new Skill and triggered <Gravity Well>. For a moment, Kirstin did not understand what she needed to do, and then she noticed she had in her hand a small sphere of . . . weight. That was the only way she could describe it, but that was not quite right. The sphere was no more heavy than a marble, but it felt like it had the potential to weigh a lot more. She drew a new arrow and touched the sphere to it. The tiny little ball immediately vanished, and she could feel that the arrow had taken on the sphere's properties. Interesting. That suggested the Skill was about the sphere rather than being intrinsically linked to her Archery.

She aimed directly up at the ceiling and fired.

Eliud was yanked off his feet and followed the arrow upwards to crash into the stone above. Not wanting to give him a chance to respond, she triggered the Skill again, and this time, rather than connecting it to an arrow, she threw the sphere at the floor on the opposite side of the room.

Eliud was flung, face first, downwards after to it to smash into the ground.

"Ouch." Savage grinned. "That looked inelegant."

Even though Kirstin could sense that the sphere was exerting phenomenal downward power on the Pendragon, she watched as he, very slowly, pulled himself to his feet, pointed at her, stuck out his tongue, and reactivated <Spark>.

They duelled backwards and forwards in this manner until, with a shout of triumph, Kirstin managed to land a fourth distinct <Gravity Well> on Eliud, pinning him to the ceiling by each limb in a star shape.

"Got you! Not so cocky now, are you!"

Eliud raised his eyebrows as he realised he really could not move any of his arms and legs anymore. "Very impressive. I can see quite some potential for this Skill of yours. However, before you start doing your victory dance, how are you feeling?"

She was about to bite back when a wave of nausea hit her. But that made no sense. He'd only hit her with <Spark>, hadn't he?

"Seventy-five unique incidents of <Spark>, I think you will find. I imagine you're just a few ticks of damage away from unconsciousness. If you could see your way to releasing me before — oh, blast."

Kirstin's eyes rolled up in her head as the constant, if tiny, health drain of <Spark> became too much for her. Her own <Gravity Well> Skill was cancelled the second she collapsed, and Eliud tumbled to the floor.

Josul was quickly at his side, nuzzling him until he sat up. Savage, of course, was more concerned about Kirstin.

"She'll be fine," he answered in response to the cat's

indignant yowl. "More than fine, actually. With those three new Skills and her improved Dexterity and Health, your Mistress has the potential to be quite a handful." He washed a quick <Restore> spell over the two of them, re-setting their health and mana stores.

It had been an instructive experience. But now they needed to move on. Eliud was sure there had to be more to this prison than a sympathetic mana loop cage, but at least he did not need to worry that Kirstin would slow him down.

Hauling her to her feet, he looked left and then right.

"Any ideas?"

As if in answer, a cold breeze suddenly blew from the door on the left, followed by a low growl. Josul turned and bared his teeth, whilst Savage wound herself through Kirstin's legs.

"Okay. So that's decided, then."

CHAPTER FORTY-FIVE

"The Nature of Evil"

With great difficulty, Eliud pulled at the threads of mana powering the enchanted mirrors and clenched his fists tightly. The gesture shattered the walls of glass into a million pieces, releasing his party from their hold.

His lips were dry, and he needed to take a few settling breaths before trusting himself to speak. When he finally did, his voice held a quaver he did not like. He cleared his throat and tried again.

"Okay. So what have we learned here?"

Kirstin collapsed down onto her hands and knees, eyes streaming with tears. A glance over towards Savage and Josul showed that, although they were physically fine, their heads were bowed.

"Kirstin?"

She shook her head, unable to answer.

He understood how she felt, but he needed to press the issue. "No, that's not how this plays out. We use what's just happened as a growth opportunity. Otherwise, it becomes something that beats us. So, what have we learned?"

"That whoever built this place is evil!" He was surprised by the vehemence in the girl's voice.

"Evil? That's a strong word."

With a gesture, he gathered up all the shards of shattered glass on the floor and reformed them as mirrors against the walls, albeit without their former powers.

"In my long and varied experience of such things, nothing in this world can be considered truly evil. There are good and bad actions, for sure. But evil? No. Most people view themselves as the heroes of their own little stories and, more often than not, the actions they take, they see as means that are justified by the ends. Considering the current circumstances in the West, it feels trite to note that one man's freedom fighter is another's rebel. However, the line between the two is rather more blurred than anyone would like. Do not dismiss things you do not like as 'evil.' Somewhere, a person is thinking the same about you."

He paused, taking the opportunity to quest out with his power into the next chamber ahead. This room, one that was filled with mirrors, was the sixth they had entered since breaking free from their respective cages. While, in theory, nothing they had encountered thus far had been a challenge for him to defeat, the overall experience was beginning to take a toll.

And no challenge more so than this last chamber.

The more he thought about it, the more he believed that was likely be the point. He was being worn down.

"For example, consider the Mages that designed this prison. Would I consider them to be evil? Of course not."

Josul growled at that whilst Savage hissed.

"No, hear me out. After what we have just gone through, I understand the instinct to think they must be peculiarly malevolent. However, from a different perspective, they have clearly been charged with finding a way to restrain me. In their minds, it is I who am the monster. And not just them. I doubt there are many places in the land where there is no story of the deeds of the Duskstrider used to terrify children. I do not see myself as 'evil,' but I understand why others may view me as such. In those circumstances, can you blame someone for using everything at their disposal to achieve their goal? The more I think about it, I am not sure this is a prison. I think it may be a labyrinth in which I am the monster."

*

They had stumbled into the room of mirrors after a relatively easy experience against a smaller room that had quickly filled with water the moment they had stepped within it. In response, Savage had merely dislocated her jaw and sucked in the flood faster than it was able to rise.

He never really had gotten to the bottom of where things went when she did things like that. He had once idly theorised that she represented a gateway to some sort of alternative realm. If so, those on the other side of the portal had just become very damp.

So, they had pressed forward into this room and, as the door locked behind them, were surprised that nothing appeared to happen. It had become their experience that each room made its attack almost immediately after they entered it, so the pause was somewhat disconcerting.

Then the mirrors shimmered, and the hallucinations began.

*

Kirstin had recovered some of her composure. "What did you see?"

Eliud shook his head. "It doesn't matter. It wasn't real. The sole purpose of the enchantment on these mirrors is to present each of us with our worst fears. Arrayed in this configuration, the impact was, of course, significant. But we must remember that an evil person did not design this. Just someone charged with preventing my escape. And they gave it their best shot. I asked what we learned from that . . . difficult experience, and I can tell you, it's not that the designers were evil. It was that we were able to defeat it."

Kirstin was struggling to be quite so blithe about the experience. As soon as the enchantment in the mirror had activated, she had been transported to the worst moments of her childhood. It was not one particular day or any notable incident that the mirror reflected back at her, but rather a distorted, grotesque version of her whole life.

More than anything, though, it was the sense of helplessness. All those times when Jak tormented her. Her feelings of despair and loss after the execution of her father. Her mother's slow decline to the grave. Her feelings of terror during her time in Keep Trellec. The mirrors took each moment and crafted something new, unique and horrific to expose her to.

But the worst thing was that, as the waves of terror had rolled over her, she could do nothing about it. As nightmare after nightmare rose to the surface and crashed against her, she felt her mind begin to crack under the weight of it all.

And just when she thought she could not survive a moment more, the pressure had been released as Eliud broke the spell.

She could not conceive of the strength of spirit that had taken. For him to experience his worst nightmares in a prison designed particularly to combat him and his power and then to be able to rip them all free from its embrace. She worried that her only real lesson from this room was to stay on the right side of the Pendragon.

Kirstin triggered <Nebula Cloak>, feeling much calmer when able to remind herself she was no longer a helpless child. Yes, that version of herself no longer existed. She had the power and the will to do something about such things now.

Savage yowled and batted at her incorporeal form. Kirstin dropped the Skill and picked the kitten up. "What did you feel?" she whispered, pressing the small, furry creature against her cheek. "What was it like for you before Eliud broke the spell?"

"Hungry," the cat replied.

*

Eliud had had enough.

Of course, there was to be found some intellectual appreciation in the craftsmanship of these rooms. Whoever had designed this place had put a great deal of thought into how to counter his Skills. That none of them had worked thus far did not detract from the sincerity of the effort. The mana cost in just that room of mirrors alone would beggar most Noble houses.

That thought staggered him, and he did not know whether to be impressed or appalled. It had been over a decade since he had last been in the Capital, and then he left barely alive and half-broken. How long had this place sat empty, just waiting for him to return? What destruction had they feared he would wreak to go to such lengths to contain him?

That was a thought that would fester.

However, regardless, his interest in experiencing more of this place was now firmly at an end. The tightness around Kirstin's eyes and how Josul was pressed, shivering, against his legs were enough to reconcile him to that fact.

"Does anyone have any objection if I bring this little sideshow to a premature close?"

Kirstin frowned. "You can do that?"

"Ah, little apprentice. It wounds me that you would ask." Eliud pointed upwards and channelled a thin beam of purple lightning straight through the ceiling. They all watched as the energy arced through three further levels before bursting into the open air and dissipating.

Nodding, Eliud opened his hand wide and rotated his wrist as the increased intensity of the beam began to clear a wide channel through the rock. Pieces of crumbling masonry fell all around them as he did so, requiring that he activate a minor <Shield> to cover the small group from the falling debris.

When satisfied with the tunnel he had carved, Eliud dropped the energy beam and pressed down around them all with a quick explosion of air, launching them through the gap.

Kirstin screamed as they shot upwards, holding Savage tight to her. Josul, for his part, simply stuck out his tongue and enjoyed the experience, his ridiculous, floppy ears standing in the updraft.

Within moments, they burst free of the roof of their

prison and into the open sky. As soon as they were out, Eliud cancelled the spell and used small gusts of air to guide them all down to a safe landing spot on the battlements of what appeared to be a small fortress.

However, as they landed the group was struck by two unusual things. The first was that it was incredibly cold. Savage hissed in discontent and buried herself in Kirstin's jerkin whilst Eliud quickly made more appropriate use of <Spark> than he had during his duel with the Celestial Harbinger in the cells below.

It was as they were warming themselves with that fire that the second thing became apparent. The building they had been held in was suspended hundreds of feet in the air, seemingly drifting aimlessly above the ocean.

Eliud was, despite himself, impressed. "Well, at least that answers why they called this the Sky Keep . . ."

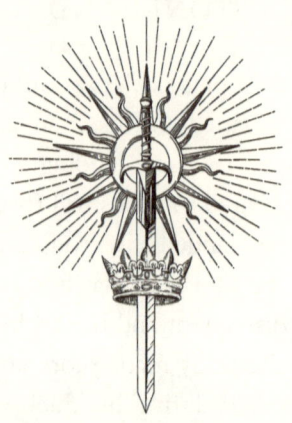

CHAPTER FORTY-SIX

"Here be Dragons"

"Well, that is a touch unexpected."

Eliud took in the wide expanse of the sea around the floating Sky Keep and quested out with his power.

Nothing.

He could sense absolutely nothing around them. He knew he could ratchet up the mana dedicated to this search, but the fact that he needed to told its own story.

"I do not think we're in the borders of the Kingdom anymore."

Kirstin, teeth chattering with cold — despite the blazing inferno Eliud had brought into being in the middle of the battlements — started at that. "We're not in the Kingdom?"

"If I was a betting man . . . which I am not because I

am invariably correct, but if I were, I would hazard a considerable sum on this being the Northern Ocean."

"How so?"

Eliud held up three fingers. "One, I cannot sense anyone for leagues around. Every other significant body of water of which I am aware is scattered with islands, trade routes and other places where I would expect to find people. Only to the North is it so desolate. Two, this simply balmy weather we are having. And three, if I were building a giant floating fortress on which I planned to imprison a powerful Mage and then send it away, I'd absolutely choose the North."

"Why?"

There was a loud shriek from above, and a giant shadow passed over them. Eliud grimaced. "Oh, you know, it is not quite as tame up this way. Let us drop down below for a bit while I figure out a way to Eliud us out of this."

"Tell me you did not just use your own name as another word for an escape plan."

"Just something I am trying out."

*

They re-established themselves a few floors down in a room set up as a banqueting hall. An exceptionally long table surrounded by chairs stood in the middle of the room, with every possible combination of food and drink laden upon it.

Kirstin was about to fall upon it when — remembering the nature of the Sky Keep — she stopped and looked at Eliud. "This is all going to be poisoned, isn't it?"

"Absolutely."

Her shoulders sagged. They had been imprisoned for

some time now, and despite her evolved Class, the lack of food and water was beginning to tell.

"However, it appears to have been poisoned in such a way as to corrupt the mana of the person eating it."

Eliud closed his eyes as he tried to pick apart the spell upon the fare on the table. "My word, this is quite horrible, actually. And, I should note, far beyond the expertise of Logan Twilight. The more of these rooms I see, the more it feels like every Mage with a grudge in the Kingdom has been involved in this place's construction."

"Why would every Mage in the Kingdom have a grudge against you?"

"You've met him. Why do you think?"

Eliud glared at Savage, who was walking down the length of the table, sniffing various dishes. "Now, now. That is not very kind, is it?"

"So I cannot have any of this?" Kirstin was starting to feel a touch of despair.

"Oh, no, it will probably be fine for you. It all seems to have been rather vindictively aspected towards me."

"Probably fine?"

Eliud waved off her worries. "If you had not evolved, you could have feasted like Savage in . . . well, anywhere, really. Now? Well, you have quite a lot of mana, but it is more to empower your core abilities than a pool in and of itself. Even if the food did taint you, I cannot see it would have much detriment." He picked up a slice of apple pie and looked mournfully at it. "Me, on the other hand? This is intended to destabilise my very being."

"What did you do to make them so angry?" Kirstin had sat down and piled a plate high. Josul had leapt up onto the table, and he and Savage were similarly gorging themselves.

Eluid smiled ruefully and collapsed into a chair of his own. "Power, my dear. And this is probably a lesson it would be good for a new little Harbinger to learn. It does not matter how benign you are, or how altruistic or — certainly in my case — how hugely charismatic you may be; people fear those stronger than them. Of course, they are pleased to call on you when the village catches fire or when the crops fail. Then, it is all 'Thank the Goddess! It's Eliud! We're saved.' But as soon as the crisis averts, they start to view you in another way." His expression darkened. "No. There's a reason you found me in a cottage in the backend of nowhere."

Kirstin's mouth was too full to give an immediate answer, and she needed to gulp it down before speaking. "But that's not everyone. I know the sort of people you are talking about. My brother was like that. Jak never saw someone stronger than him without wanting to pull them down. There's a type who needs to measure themselves, and when they fall short, they lose their mind."

She cleared her throat and took a sip of water. "Most folk don't know what to rightly make of you. Growing up, I'd heard stories of the Duskstrider. But you're spoken of in the same way as the weather."

Savage snorted at that. Kirstin frowned at the cat. "No, I mean it. The sun rises, the rain falls, and Eliud Villa is. Your coming is welcomed, but no one wants to live around you. The likes of you and Daine, you're some form of reasonably friendly natural disaster."

Eliud nodded. "Indeed. And now, my dear, I am afraid so are you."

"Hardly."

"Celestial Harbingers are a vanishingly rare Class. You

may not have the pure damage output of our friend, the Lady Darkhelm, but with your phase defence, there's not much she could do to you. Couple that with your gravity-based ability, and you can put a dent in most people's day."

Kirstin pushed her plate away. The opportunity to learn more about her Class from someone as learned as the Duskstrider dwarfed filling her belly.

At least for a few minutes.

"But what do Harbingers do with their time? Should I be joining an army?"

He winced at that. "Well, you could do that, but I imagine — at least, I hope — you would find that sort of work quite restrictive. With your Skillset, you would most likely find yourself knee-deep in assassination missions. Trust me, they get old fast. No, I think you would find yourself much more fulfilled settling yourself down in a City — maybe even the Capital, so you'd seem a little less exotic — and then advertising your services."

Kirstin's nose wrinkled in distaste. "That sounds like a recipe to become 'knee-deep in assassination missions.' Or worse."

"Not at all."

Savage yowled.

"Well, yes, absolutely. But at least you will be able to choose who receives your attention as a private operator. The King's Army frowns on that level of independence. No. What I mean is that someone with your Skillset will be able to demand an almost-unlimited fee from a motivated buyer. A few jobs where you have to hold your nose slightly will set you up for life. Then, you can be much more discerning about your missions. People like the Lady Darkhelm and the other Knights of the Road are tied to Tours and areas of the world. With the sorts of resources you could accrue quite quickly, you could become wholly independent as a beacon of hope for the Kingdom."

Kirstin's face grew increasingly sceptical as he spoke. "If that's such a wonderful life, why aren't you living it?"

He nodded at that. "Please understand, I mean no disrespect here. And, as I say, the ranks of the Celestial Harbingers are particularly scarce. However, there is only one of me. And, believe me, that is a good thing. The reason why it appears so many Mages have got together to try to create a prison that would hold me and then direct that prison to the outermost reaches of the world is not because of my winning personality."

Eliud stood and waved his hand above the table. The corruption spell within the food and drink was immediately expelled — including an amount from Kirstin — to hover in the air. It was rolled around in dark black waves like a malevolent cloud. With a click of his fingers, Eliud dispelled it.

"I cannot tell you how complex that weaving was. The years of study that Mage must have spent in perfecting that spell. It is probably the only significant Skill he has, and he was motivated to do his best work to try to kill me. I don't even really know what it is, and I can negate it. It's ridiculous. I'm ridiculous. If I were them, I'd hate me too."

"He gets bored," Savage yowled.

Eliud shrugged. And Kirstin was struck by how very sad this all-powerful man suddenly seemed.

"I get bored," he agreed. "But," and he clapped his hands together with faux-sincerity, "that is by the by.

And who can really be bored when there are Dragons overhead."

"Dragons?!"

"Yes. Ah, I probably should have found a smoother segue for that."

CHAPTER FORTY-SEVEN

"I Will Not Always Be There"

Kirstin tried to track the swarm — "Clutch, my dear" — of Dragons circling the Sky Keep.

"Does their collective noun really matter?"

"Only if you care about accuracy. As you are a former Archer, I would have anticipated that being important to you. But never mind."

Kirstin idly stroked Savage, who was doing her best to maintain a soothing purr. "If I were standing atop a massive, drifting magical prison specifically designed for me by powerful people who disliked me, I'd probably be thinking more carefully about my tone in social interactions."

"But that's where we are different. I do not bother myself with what others think about me at all."

"He's lying," Savage yowled. "You should hear him weep into his cups each evening about 'why don't people like me?' He's a rather tragic figure when all things are considered."

Eliud clicked his fingers, and Savage was portalled away. "Probably safest she stays below whilst we attempt this. All that fur; awfully flammable, don't you know."

"Whereas we are famously impervious to flame . . ."

*

They were not Dragons. On that, Eliud was clear.

"While I would not like to be too definite, I doubt any Dragons remain in the Kingdom. One of the key roles of the first Knights of the Road was to remove the shadow those beasts cast across the land. Some culls were more effective than others, of course, but over the generations, the numbers of Dragons were greatly reduced. Indeed, I believe our mutual friend was responsible for killing the last of those to be found in the West."

"So, what are they up there?" Kirstin, despite herself, was finding the lecture fascinating.

"I would assume Wyverns. Not without their own challenges, of course, but a magnitude less difficult to deal with than a single Dragon."

"What's the difference?"

Eliud slipped deeper into his teacher persona. When he was like this, Kirstin thought, it was far too easy to forget this man had the power to tear holes in the very fabric of reality. She had quickly learned he enjoyed cultivating this "absentminded professor" demeanour and was happy to play along.

"A few major and a couple of minor things. Firstly, size. The full size of a Dragon will be four or five times that of an adult Wyvern. Secondly, Wyverns have two legs instead of four, with their wings connected to their front talons.

Those two differences make Wyverns much faster in the air, which can be a pain, but you are much less likely to be wiped out by a single blow. Oh, and whereas you can hold a perfectly reasonable conversation with a Dragon — right up until it decides to eat you — Wyverns are about as intelligent as pigeons. Just pigeons that can breathe fire and want to eat you. So, you will want to keep that in mind."

"What do you mean?"

"Well, unless one of us does something about them, there's every chance they'll get it into their tiny brains they wish to attack the Sky Keep. And I really do not want to have to swim home."

"And by 'one of us,' you mean me, don't you?"

"They're Wyverns, my dear. A little below my pay grade."

*

Kirstin mentally rehearsed how she intended for this to play out.

There were seven Wyverns slowly circling the Sky Keep. They were high enough above them that if she squinted, she could pretend they were starlings. As she saw it, the key was to reduce that number to something manageable as soon as possible. She could keep track of three or four of them in a pinch, but any more than that, and she risked being blindsided. They did not need to do anything cleverer than knock her off the battlements; even giant fire-breathing pigeons could get lucky.

Fortunately, she still had access to all her old Archer Skills, as well as the more exotic ones that evolving into a Celestial Harbinger had brought.

So, she was confident in taking down one, maybe even two, before things would become spicy.

She looked over to where the Duskstrider had positioned himself, cross-legged, right in the middle of the roof. He was going to be providing the bait for their little plan.

They met eyes, and then, with a nod, he channelled a beam of light right through the middle of their wide circle. With a shriek, they banked and began streaking downwards towards his position.

The "starlings" began to get much bigger, much faster.

Triggering <Multi-Shot>, Kirstin fired an arrow at the lead Wyvern, her Skill splitting her arrow into four — four? That was new. An upgrade, obviously, from her new Class — and striking both it and the wings of the Wyvern behind.

In his impromptu lesson, Eliud had stressed the thickness of a Wyvern's hide and that it was unlikely to be pierced by mundane arrows.

Their wings, on the other hand . . .

The arrows tore through the wings of the lead two Wyverns, whose diving assault suddenly became something far less controlled and elegant. Unable to control their direction, they both flashed past Kirstin's position, screaming in terror, to vanish below.

That left five.

Kirstin grimaced. Not ideal, but no plans survived contact with the enemy intact. She hopped down from her position on top of a battlement and triggered <Nebula Cloak>. And not a moment too soon, as three of the Wyverns opened their mouths to bathe her in yellow flame.

The other two had concentrated their fiery attacks on Eliud, who simply accepted their attentions with a yawn.

She was not sure, but it looked as if he had conjured a series of marshmallows on sticks.

One of the Wyverns landed next to Kirstin and snapped its jaws towards her. She instinctively jumped backwards, forgetting the protection provided by <Nebula Cloak>, and phased through the wall of the Sky Keep, tumbling off the roof.

Panic took her.

She had never been too worried about heights, but neither had she ever been falling to her death before. As a defensive Skill, <Nebula Cloak> might well allow her to survive impact with the ocean far below, but Kirstin doubted it would do much to stop her drowning.

But she did have other Skills at her disposal.

Looking up, she targeted one of the Wyverns attacking Eliud, triggering <Gravity Well> and shooting a sphere-enhanced arrow towards it. As expected, the projectile struck the monster in the chest and bounced off, but the contact was enough to transfer her Skill to it. To her great relief, that offered her something tangible to pull down upon.

She shot upwards towards the Wyvern, phasing through the pillar of flame it was launching at Eliud and then through the surprised beast itself.

In moments, Kirstin found herself in clear air, looking down on the Wyverns, who had all turned their attention to Eliud. The Duskstrider had triggered a low-level <Shield> and was apparently entirely unbothered by the situation.

Her upward trajectory began to slow, and she prepared herself to return to the fray. As she began falling, she fired off <Stellar Arrows>, the flashes of light and booming noise causing three of them to crash into each other as they circled, sending them over the edge of the Sky Keep in a tangle of wings, legs and talons.

Switching off <Nebula Cloak> — she did not want to accidentally phase through the roof and drop into the rooms below — Kirstin landed heavily, too heavily, and rolled to a stop.

Something had cracked — her hip? — as she struck the stone, and she was unable to get to her feet. She looked over to Eliud for a heal, but from behind the silver shimmer of his shield, he stared impassively back.

The two remaining Wyverns, seeing easier prey, swooped down to land on either side of her.

Kirstin tried to trigger <Nebula Cloak>, but the pain from her hip was too much for her to summon the requisite concentration. Well, that was a rather unwelcome development. The bigger of the two Wyverns bent its long, sinewy neck and snapped at her, sharp teeth piercing her shoulder, causing her to shriek in further agony as it picked her up.

Josul barrelled forward, crashing into the monster's belly — causing it to let go — and then Kirstin was falling to the floor again.

With her remaining functioning arm, she pulled a dagger clear from her boot and slashed wildly at the Wyvern's neck as she fell.

By all rights, such a weak, unfocused attack should have had little prospect of causing damage. However, the moment the tip of Kirstin's blade touched the thick skin, there was the sound of dice rolling, and then the dagger slipped past a scale and opened the Wyvern's jugular.

Just as Kirstin hit the floor again, briefly losing consciousness with the pain, she was sure she made out the sound of two voices laughing in harmony.

The final Wyvern was briefly occupied with Josul, who snarled and jumped around its feet. It ineffectually tried to bathe the giant dog in flame but had little success, eventually deciding to ignore him and turn to the easier prey.

Kirstin lay on her back, watching the approaching jaws.

She had dropped her dagger when she landed and had nothing left of which to make use. The eyes of the Wyvern were directly above her, and in meeting its gaze, she felt repulsed by its cold, alien presence.

Eliud was right; there was no intelligence there.

She was about to be killed by a large, scaly pigeon. The absurdity of it all made her laugh out loud, lifting the pain for a moment and — surprisingly — allowing her to reach her Skills. Reaching up, she forced a sphere of <Gravity Well> into the beast's maw and pushed it upwards with such force that she ripped the Wyvern's head clear off its body.

The moment the final Wyvern was killed, a wave of healing washed over her, fully repairing her broken bones and restoring her health pool.

Kirstin did not move, lying flat on her back.

She had single-handedly defeated seven Wyverns. And yet she felt no sense of joy. No feeling of satisfaction in her own burgeoning power.

"You would have let me die, wouldn't you?"

Eliud appeared at the corner of her vision, looking down on her with a face of concern. "It did not come to that. As expected, you proved more than up to the task."

"But you weren't going to help, were you?"

There was a pause, and then Eliud sat heavily beside her. "I was not."

Kirstin sat up carefully, but her injuries were no more. She pulled her knees to her and wrapped her arms around them. "Any reason why?"

The Duskstrider did not answer immediately, and when she glanced over, she saw tears streaking his face. "Because I will not always be there." He took a breath and collected himself. "It has occurred to me, my dear, that I am the worst enemy of those I would call my friends. My power, you see?"

Kirstin shook her head. "I don't understand. You could have stepped in at any time you wanted. I should never have been in danger."

"But that is the point, do you not see? Right here, and right now, you were not in danger. But what about when I am not there in a few weeks? What then? What would you learn from me saving you today? That you do not need to fear. That Eliud will save you. *What happens when I'm not there?*" His last sentence was almost a wail.

"You would have let me die to teach me not to rely on you?"

"I would."

"That seems like a pretty intense lesson."

That raised a smile. "But, having lived, what have you learned?"

"Other than that you are a colossal —"

"Other than that, yes. What has fighting those Wyverns taught you?"

"That I'm strong enough to beat them on my own. That I do not need anyone else's help."

"Then my work here is done."

The soft sound of clapping came from the other side of the roof. Kirstin and Eliud turned to see a vision of the Goddess slowly applauding.

An interesting lesson, Eliud. For both of you, I think. And now I am afraid I have a favour to ask you.

CHAPTER FORTY-EIGHT

"You Must Not Engage the Stonehand"

"Is that —"

"Yes."

"And She's talking directly to you?"

"She is."

"And She did you a favour?"

"How about we talk about this later? Deities tend to become irritable when they are not the centre of all available attention."

Kirstin nodded and cut off the host of other questions that were crowding her mind. Instead, she stared intently at the manifested presence of the Goddess. Of course, she had heard of members of the pantheon appearing like this in tavern songs, but it was overwhelming to actually experience it.

Her first impression of the Goddess was that She was a tall woman with the bearing of someone who had seen many years. However, Her appearance, in a most disconcerting way, did not seem to be fixed.

Her hair, which at one moment seemed like the flowing strands of a youthful maiden — dark and lustrous — subtly shifted to the softer, greyer hues of a mother's experience, and then again to the thin, wispy white of an elderly woman. Kirstin struggled to focus on the constant flux.

The Goddess's face followed a similar pattern. One moment, it was smooth and unlined, with the vibrancy and optimism of youth. Then, almost imperceptibly, it gained the gentle creases and warm, knowing smile of middle age, only to morph into the deep, weathered lines and sagging skin of old age.

These changes were not drastic transformations but rather like watching shadows play across someone's face under a flickering candlelight.

It was Her eyes, though, Kirstin realised, that remained the constant — deep and insightful, hinting at an ageless wisdom that transcended all physical alterations. They were an anchor to Her shifting form, providing a sense of continuity amidst the constant change.

They were also precisely like Daine's.

"I must confess, I thought you would hold the threat of my returning your favour over me for decades to come. It's been, what, a few days? Unusually impatient of you."

You always take the most uncharitable view of my actions, Duskstrider. I cannot think when I have ever given you cause for such derision.

Kirstin found herself fascinated by the voice of the Goddess. It was like a seamless blend of life's phases, an ever-evolving melody that flowed from youthful vibrancy to maternal warmth and then to the depths of old age. It was a single song sung in three harmonious parts, each emphasising the next with a fluid grace.

The Goddess's words started with the clarity of a soprano, a fresh, lively tune that held the promise of dawn and the eagerness of new life. But as She spoke, this melody gently matured, taking on an alto's richer, fuller notes. Like a river growing deeper and wider as it travels, the sound became more resonant and nurturing, like a comforting embrace of love and wisdom gained through living.

Finally, as Her sentences concluded, the timbre deepened further, settling into the earthy tones of a contralto. This was the sound of twilight, of memories etched deep, of knowledge carved by the passage of countless years. It was a voice that resonated with shadows and the weight of history.

"While there may be a time and place for us to pick at that thread, Goddess, I do not think here and now is it. We know where we stand with each other, and that is enough. What favour do you ask of me?"

The Goddess frowned. She had never quite been able to understand Eliud Vila. He defied Her experience of mortals. With the Knights of the Road, Her chosen avatars, things were always so much more straightforward. For them, there was right. And there was wrong. Their role was to enforce justice, and She aided them with aspects of Her power as they did so.

However, there was nothing so simple with the Duskstrider.

As his title suggested, he existed in liminal space: as comfortable in the shadows as he was in the light. He had come into his power without the patronage of any of the pantheon and although that was not entirely unheard of, it was rare enough to be noteworthy. That he had survived into adulthood and not been ensnared in any wider scheme was doubly so. It was not like none of them had tried.

It did mean, however, that She had limited leverage over him. And that was a situation to which She was highly unused.

To speak plainly, in intervening to save your friend's life, I was also required to make a significant concession to the Dark God.

Kirstin opened her mouth to speak, but Eliud stilled her with a raised finger. "Whilst I am grateful for your intercession — and I thank you once again — I will not be held responsible for any repercussions you may have received. You offered to trade favours, and I accepted the offer on those terms. Those and those alone."

The Goddess narrowed Her eyes. *Have a care, Duskstrider. I afford you great latitude, but you will speak to me with respect.*

"I apologise." Kirstin winced at Eliud's tone, which clearly held not an ounce of sorrow.

As I was saying, my son argued I had overstepped by interfering in one of his schemes. He asked for compensation for that, and I felt compelled to grant his request.

"We both know the Dark God cannot 'compel' you to do anything. If you allowed him what he asked for, it is because it served your own purposes. So let us not pretend this all comes as a surprise to you. And I still have not heard anything about repaying your favour."

The weight of the Goddess's aura flowed outwards. Josul collapsed, rendered unconscious by the waves of power, and Kirstin — despite her Class Evolution — fell to her knees, head ringing and intense nausea overwhelming her.

Eliud, however, did not move.

"You have often asked me why I will not accept your patronage. For clarity, it is behaviour like this. I freely accept you are not the most capricious of the pantheon. I even allow that, at times, your presence in the world has been for the common good. Indeed, as these things go, you are largely benign. However, your 'love' is ever conditional on subservience. And I find that abhorrent."

The Goddess's form stabilised into that of a young woman who looked immediately shamefaced. Her aura receded, and Kirstin felt she could move again. She sat beside Josul and gently stroked his fur as he awoke.

Now it is I who must apologise. I am feeling unusually pressured by current events.

"And that is why I will continue to entertain your presence. You are still the only god I have met that will admit it when they get things wrong. Now, let us stop prevaricating; what favour will you ask of me?"

The Dark God has returned Gallant Stonehand to the world.

Eliud's head swam for a moment at the implications. "And you want me to rectify that?"

No. The Goddess shifted back into the form of an elderly woman. *The favour I ask is for you not to engage with him at all.*

A wave of relief washed over Eliud. Gallant had been his mentor, even his friend, towards the end. He had no idea what part the old man had to play in the schemes of the Dark God, but he was glad he would not be required to take action. In any event, he was not even sure — as strong as he had become in the years since he had last encountered the Stonehand — how easily he would be able to achieve that.

"I have no problem with that. It is a wide world. There

is room enough for the two of us to live quite happily without ever crossing paths."

I am afraid it will not be as simple as that. A tight smile appeared on the Goddess's lined and worn face. *The Dark God has brought back the Stonehand for a singular purpose. He seeks to bring about the death of the Lady Darkhelm. Even as we speak, the Stonehand has been provided with a great army and pointed towards the City of Swinford. In but a few weeks, the two will clash, and even I cannot predict the outcome.*

Eliud clenched and reclenched his hands. "But if that is the case, I need to be there. I swore to Daine I would help defend Taelsin's City!"

And you swore to me that you would repay my favour. A note of steel entered the voice of the Goddess. *You will not interfere when the Stonehand and the Darkhelm meet.*

"He will kill her! You know how she feels about him. Even if she was strong enough to fight him on equal terms, she's utterly terrified of him!"

The Goddess nodded sadly and began to fade from the realm. *Do not mistake me; I would have the Darkhelm prevail. But if she does so, it must be on her own terms. Your path lies back in the Capital. Lest you forget, there is a stableboy to be recovered.*

And then they found themselves all alone on top of the Sky Keep.

"What does all that mean?" Kirstin's mind swam with all she had heard.

The Duskstrider, though, stared off into the distance as if seeking to see right to the gates of Swinford. "It means, my dear, that I have no choice but to break my word to Daine. She — and the rest of them — will be on their own. And the Stonehand is on his way."

CHAPTER FORTY-NINE

"Chaotic Nonsense"

"If you would be so kind as to let Mayor Elm know that I am rather busy at this moment." Souit dismissed the messenger from the City without a glance and returned his concentration to the battlefield.

He could not discern what his opposite number in the newly arrived army was seeking to achieve.

There had been no real signs of aggression from that direction since the beam of powerful energy that Angharad had hastily deflected into Swinford's walls. His men were now sheltered under various overlapping <Shield> spells, and Souit was as comfortable as he could be that he would not have his army vapourised around him.

However, instead of seeking to immediately press their numerical advantage — and that was despite Souit's Archmage destroying half of the enemy's heavy horse contingent — those fighting under the ludicrous flag of the Blade of Ruin just kept adjusting and readjusting their positions.

It had been going on for so long and was taking such a significant physical toll on the troops that the only way Souit could make any sense of it all was by deciding that the enemy commander was breathtakingly incompetent.

For — as much as it pained him to admit it — if the mercenaries had sought to attack the moment they appeared, he imagined he would have had little choice but to abandon the field.

It was thus astonishing that they had given him ample time to reorder things to his satisfaction. Indeed, after a position of profound uncertainty, he was now confident — all things being equal — his forces would be very difficult to dislodge indeed.

That surely made all this posturing and reorganising the actions of an inexperienced moron. In Souit's experience, that was not at all uncommon for those in charge of mercenary outfits.

But, then again, that did not make any sense either. The heads of Brockland and Sajida he had received made that very clear. Whoever was in charge over there had enough about them to bring down two solid and capable commanders. How could he reconcile that with the chaotic nonsense brewing and churning before him?

He was baffled.

"What in the world are they up to?" After a pause, he turned to regard the remaining members of his command staff. "That is not a rhetorical question, ladies and gentlemen. I mean it. Does anyone have any idea what is going on?"

There was much shaking of heads, and as they all

watched in awkward silence as rows of spearmen swapped positions with heavier armoured troops and then, without pause, moved back again. Cavalry — both light and heavy — galloped the length of the lines and then returned to their positions. Even from here, everyone could see the horses were right at the very edge of exhaustion. Should this display carry on much longer, the mercenaries would start to incur casualties.

There was simply no rhyme nor reason to it.

It was as if a madman were constantly issuing contradictory orders. But if that was so, why were the men following? Mercenaries were not known for their unquestioning obedience to capricious masters.

It was all too strange.

"My Lord, I am afraid I really must insist."

Souit turned back to the elderly messenger from Swinford, who was lingering in a most disgraceful manner. "Are you mad, sir? I tell you, you are dismissed! Return to your lines."

"No, no, no. That won't do at all. I assured Taelsin his message would get through, and I have some ground on the trust front to make up with him."

Impatiently, Souit gestured for his guards to remove the old man from his presence. "Take him back to the breach. Drag him if need be. And sir, be glad I don't have you flogged for your impertinence!"

"Well, although that sounds quite lovely," said Donal, "now's probably not the time. To speak plainly, we have concerns as to the intentions of the army recently arrived on the field. Given a choice, I was all for letting the two of you kick seven bells out of each other and wiping out whoever was left standing. However, I've recently had it pointed out to me that my impulses might not be wholly trustworthy, and thus, other voices have prevailed. I, therefore, have been sent with a formal offer of truce from Mayor Elm until such time as this unknown threat is neutralised."

Souit's face had grown crimson as that message was delivered. "You dare to suggest the King's Army needs assistance from a bunch of cowards and traitors to see off a mercenary army?"

"No" — Donal beamed, and his teeth were unnaturally white — "but I'm going to suggest you might need the help of the Lady Darkhelm against Gallant Stonehand."

*

Such had been the chaos of switching and changing formations that the attack — when it came — took the King's forces entirely by surprise.

A long line of medium infantry advanced, much in the same manner as had happened repeatedly over the last few bells. However, rather than the slow, aimless march eventually pausing and leading to the order to retreat, the men suddenly lurched forward and picked up their pace to a light jog.

In no time at all, they began to close the gap between them and the front ranks of the King's men. Panicked orders were issued to draw attention to the sudden threat, but the response was sluggish and haphazard.

While that was going on, behind the onrushing men, a seemingly aimlessly milling company of light horse suddenly formed up on their flanks, their riders drawing bows and firing indiscriminately into the unprepared ranks of King's men.

As the <Shield> spells that had been thrown up had

been calibrated to reflect overwhelming Magery, they offered no protection against the types of fast-moving projectiles now passing through them.

Then, as the arrows were beginning to find their marks — in lieu of an organised shield wall — the advancing infantry suddenly stopped, produced javelins, and flung them in unison. Adding their greater weight to the sniping of the horse archers.

With screams, men began to fall.

As soon as the javelins were in the air, the horse archers spun away and galloped back towards their lines, with the now-defenceless infantry turning to follow them home.

The attack had come so out of the blue — and after such a long time of inactivity — that it took a moment for the various Captains, and more importantly, their Sergeants, to recognise the immediate danger. After all, when you'd just seen your friends struck by arrows, the natural inclination for any soldier was to seek out a little retribution.

And, would you not know it, there was a slow-moving, unprotected line of men just begging to have the hammer brought down upon them.

Before the order to "hold!" was bellowed out over and over again, several hundred men left their lines to pursue the fleeing infantry.

However, the second they stepped outside the protection of the myriad of <Shield> spells, the sky darkened, and beams of lightning crashed down amongst them, each strike incapacitating an individual target with breathtaking precision. The mercenaries then spun around and returned to those who had set out in pursuit of them.

As the King's Army watched in horror, each of the men who had left the protection of the shields was captured, stripped and then — in a brutal display that took the best part of two bells — beheaded in front of them.

To begin with, those killed were still insensate following the lightning strike, but as time wore on, consciousness was regained. This display then became a traumatic spectacle as soldiers begged and pleaded for their lives in the face of an uncaring enemy.

Several sallies to recover the captured men were attempted — with the same precise lightning streaking down to claim all those who stepped outside the magical protection.

Their numbers were added to the butcher's list.

Finally, when all the executions were completed, a cart of stakes rumbled forward, drawn by oxen and driven by an old man with wild, white hair.

With difficulty, he clambered down from his seat and began inspecting each and every head, throwing some onto the back of the cart, whereas others he impaled on stakes that he left facing the now-silent lines of the King's Army.

Soon, with all the other mercenaries retreated back to safety, he was the only enemy left facing them, screaming incoherently and waving the severed heads of the fallen in the air.

None dared set foot beyond the protection of the <Shield> spells,

It was during that macabre display that Souit turned to the now-sombre face of the old messenger.

"Tell your master. I will listen to what he has to say. However, I will make this plain from the outset: the moment this threat is dealt with, the truce will expire."

Donal nodded. "We would not have it any other way, my Lord."

CHAPTER FIFTY

"A Failure of Diplomacy"

Negotiations were not going well.

"Regardless of the nature of this new threat, there are no circumstances in which I will even consider integrating my forces alongside a practitioner of Necromancy."

"It was only the once, and then just a little bit. How about if I promise not to do it again?"

"You, sir, are an embarrassment."

"An embarrassment that fought a Great General to a standstill. Go me."

As the raised voices increased in volume, Taelsin beckoned over a servant with a tray of wine. With luck, the interruption would prevent Souit from spontaneously combusting.

"Perhaps it would be more profitable, Great General, for the two of us to discuss our proposed truce privately. It will prevent," and he directed this at Donal, "misunderstandings."

Souit waved away the proffered goblet and continued to glare at the Dark Warlord. "Whilst I acknowledge we were somewhat inconvenienced in this afternoon's exchanges, steps have been put in place to stop such a thing from occurring again. I have complete confidence that my forces will deal with this mercenary outfit in short order. At that point, we will return our attention to pacifying your City. To that end, I would encourage you to consider your position."

"Our position is safe behind our walls —"

"Which we have breached!"

Taelsin nodded. "Which you have — after a huge number of attempts and the waste of significant time and resources — eventually managed to breach. However, there is now a new army on the field, and you find yourself uncomfortable between it and us. I am happy to share that we do not count this force as allies. You will note that we have not taken the opportunity of their appearance to attack your rear . . ."

"I argued and argued and argued," intoned Donal mournfully.

Taelsin ignored him. "What is more, I would formally invite your men behind our walls to better repel this threat."

That gave Souit pause.

He liked this young man, this Mayor Elm. From all the reports he had read, he was a man of integrity and honour whose word could be trusted. The discussions around this table had reinforced that view. He was that rare form of Noble whom Souit felt he could respect.

Apart from him — he reminded himself — being a prominent member of the West's secession from the Kingdom and one of the key "traitors" he had been ordered to bring low.

The old man — Donal, was it? — was an entirely different matter. If he was to believe what he had been told over the last few bells, this ridiculous fool in a flowing cape was responsible for the many reversals the King's Army had experienced at Swinford. They had access to no intelligence to suggest that Taelsin's Secretary was anything other than an effective, if idiosyncratic, functionary. Therefore, either he had gotten very lucky indeed during his time commanding the City's defence or something quite significant was going on.

Since becoming a Great General, Souit had prided himself on removing "luck" from the equation. He, therefore, was most interested in the capabilities of Donal Assay. But that was for consideration in private. For now, he had a negotiation to address, and he felt like he was being played. "I can see, sir, no honest benefit to you in making me that offer."

Taelsin smiled. "For all that has happened over the last few weeks, General Souit, I do not view us as enemies. Swinford does not seek an antagonistic relationship with the King. It is, therefore, my intention to offer you the hand of friendship against a far greater threat."

"Mayor Elm, you are in open rebellion against the Crown. How can you not perceive us as enemies?"

"Do not confuse the fevered ramblings of House Trellec with the wishes of most of us in the West. We would govern ourselves, that is true, but we would not take up arms to force the issue. I offer you safety behind our walls because the threat of yonder army is the true opposition of us both."

Taelsin kept his eyes on the man throughout his speech. To his mind, it was essential he be able to distance the West as an entity from the actions of the Trellecs. He perceived an — admittedly narrow — path he could walk by which freedom for his people was achievable. And sheltering a Great General from an attack by mercenary marauders seemed a sensible way to begin doing just that.

But Souit was already shaking his head. "No, sir. The West's Declaration of Independence was clear about the state of war between us. Should you wish to disavow that intent and thereby surrender your City to me, I will use what discretion I possess regarding your subsequent treatment. But, mercenary army or not, I do not intend to combine our forces. I am here merely as a courtesy."

"You are here," a soft voice added, "because Gallant Stonehand commands the enemy in front of you."

All eyes turned to the figure of Lady Darkhelm, who stood, arms folded, in the corner of the room. There was something different about her that Souit could not quite pinpoint. It was like she was . . . bigger, somehow.

She continued, her words barely audible. "Legends of the Stonehand's effectiveness in the field are well-known. As an individual, he remains one of the most feared assassins in living memory. But as a commander . . . well, I will not bore you in listing his victories nor in counting the legion of corpses of those who have fallen to him. Indeed, if you are willing to listen to rumour, I once heard tell that the King constructed the Great General Evolution around the Skills of the man. In any event, he was a nightmare made flesh to face across a battlefield. And that was when he was sane."

No one spoke, and then Souit slapped his hands down on the table in frustration. "My Lady Darkhelm, it pains me to see you alongside these traitors."

"I've served the Kingdom loyally for over three decades, General Souit. The West is my Tour, and I still stand the Road, so take care with your words. The Goddess is at ease with my choice to be behind Swinford's walls. You attacked knowing on which side I stood, and I think you will acknowledge that I have been circumspect in my retaliation. If I were in your shoes, I would not be so quick to reject the open hand before you."

Souit, balefully, looked around the table — Taelsin, Donal, the Hyena, damn her eyes, and an older, aristocratic woman — until he spotted Angharad. "You are very quiet, Archmage."

The young woman blushed. "What would you like me to say, my Lord?"

"As the most powerful user of magic around this table" — Donal coughed loudly — "what are your thoughts as to our challenges?"

Angharad steepled her fingers and pressed them to her lips. "There are multiple Mages in the mercenary force. Most are heavily veiled, so I cannot get a true sense of their potency, but we have seen examples of extraordinary power and precision in the assaults upon us. I would hazard my new Class gives me more power at my disposal than any of them, but," and her blush deepened, "I am newly evolved. And, well . . ."

"Spit it out, woman."

"She's saying she thinks she could beat any of them in a fair fight," Donal said, stepping in to help, "but it seems unlikely they will queue up and follow Atticus's 'Rules of Magical Duelling.' That right, my dear?"

Angharad nodded quickly. The old man held her eyes briefly and then focused on Souit. The intensity of his gaze made the Great General sit back in his chair as if firmly pushed. "I have lived a long time, sir, so I will give you the benefit of my experience." Taelsin glanced sharply at his friend, hearing none of the usual jocular tone to his voice. "You are, and I recognise this as a deficit in your Class rather than your character, too quick to come to judgment. I assume you have a Skill that shows you potential outcomes?"

Souit nodded warily. "<Foresight>."

"And you have it running constantly?"

"I do. But I fail to see the —"

"Take it from someone who has learned the hard way: overreliance on such a Skill makes you dispense with nuance. You will find yourself constantly focusing on likelihood and pragmatic utility at the expense of innovation. You will be able to judge the most likely outcomes and respond to them but will overlook the unusual. I am sure that makes you formidable in command of the battlefield, where such clarity of thought is an asset, but it makes you tiresome company."

"Donal!" Taesin fired at the exact moment Souit took to his feet.

"Sirs, I have not come here to be insulted."

Donal pressed on as if neither had intervened. "You see everything and everyone in terms of how they can best serve your desired outcome. Any outcome that does not fit into that, your Skill encourages you to discard for the safety of the certain way. Such single-minded focus has its place, but — right here and now — it is putting your men at risk. What Mayor Elm suggests about sheltering behind our walls is eminently sensible, with no real cost to you, yet you reject it. The Lady Darkhelm warns you of your opponent, and you decide you know better. By the Goddess, your sense of individual omnipotence even has you snapping at an Archmage as if she were a scullery maid, not a figure of extraordinary resources in her own right." His wink at Angharad did little to improve her demeanour.

"What is your point, sir?" Souit was stony-faced, but his mind whirled at the man's words.

"My point is that you need to switch off <Foresight>, take your head out of your backside and apologise to someone who, if she doesn't stop blushing soon, has the power to melt us all where we sit."

All eyes were on Souit.

He took a breath and then released his Skill. Almost immediately, he heard a noise as if dice rattled a cup.

"I accept I may rely too heavily on that Skill. Such matters call for sober reflection. Outline for me again what you propose. And Archmage?"

"Yes, my Lord?"

"I have been made aware that I do not always speak to you with appropriate respect. I would apologise for giving that impression."

Whilst the young woman blushed even brighter, Taelsin and Donal nodded to each other. Souit was maybe someone with whom they could work.

CHAPTER FIFTY-ONE

"Mana Regen Theory"

"**Y**ou want me to do what?"

"Stick your finger in it. Trust me, you'll love it."

"Stick. My. Finger. In. It?!"

"Why are you looking at me like that? It's a perfectly reasonable request. Anyone would think I was asking you for something outlandish!"

Angharad glanced around, sure that this must be some sort of ridiculous prank.

Her invitation to the top of Swinford's Keep had appeared in her quarters without anyone seeing who put it there. Mayor Elm's Secretary — but was that what he truly was anymore? — requested the pleasure of her company to discuss the bombardment that the Stonehand's Mages had begun on the City.

It had been an unusual conversation thus far.

She knew her fellow Mages were becoming increasingly disenchanted with her as the extent of her enhanced power continued to manifest. However, this sort of revenge jape did not seem entirely in keeping with their style.

She turned back to the strange, wizened man before her, who was eager to press some sort of porous rock into her hand. "Sir, you have not explained exactly what you are looking for from me here."

Donal sighed. There was so much to do and so little time in which to do it.

From the moment General Souit accepted the necessity of moving his army behind the walls of Swinford, the defenders had been on something of a deadline.

The magical strikes of lightning, flame and pure energy that had begun to pour down upon them were surely just the precursor to something far more bloody. It could only be a matter of a few bells before Gallant Stonehand — and even thinking that name gave Donal a little thrill — decided to unleash his full wrath upon them.

In his limited time before that cataclysmic event, Donal was doing what he could to mitigate the coming massacre. But to do that, he needed the complete and utter compliance of everyone he spoke to. And people were not playing ball.

Even his rosiest interpretation of the outcome of the approaching battle had far more heads impaled on spikes than he was comfortable with. And to even achieve that much, he needed comely young Archmages with highly kissable lips and vast reserves of mana to insert their fingers exactly where he told them.

"You do appreciate you said all that out loud, sir?"

Donal shrugged. Internal monologue, external musings,

it was all the same to him. "Do I really need to explain all this again?"

"I am unsure, sir, you have explained it at all."

With a sigh, Donal tossed the porous stone in the air, caught it, and then gestured to the glittering shield dome that had spread over the City. As they watched, a handful of explosions bloomed on the outside of the defences. "You're keeping all that up by your little own self, aren't you?"

Angharad nodded. Intellectually, she recognised how ridiculous it was that one Mage could maintain a shield Skill across this wide a space, but apparently, she could. And easily. "Now the Skill is in place, I am not noticing any real drain on my mana. Even when —"

There was a brief explosion as another sunburst of power from the mercenary army crashed against Swinford's magical barrier.

"Even under such a sustained attack, my Mana Regeneration appears to outpace the Skill's usage. To be honest, I feel as if I could keep this Skill running indefinitely."

"Excellent. Aren't you a fiery powerhouse? Interestingly, most Mages overlook that Mana Regeneration is inextricably linked to maximum mana. Those that make this error in logic appear to reason that their primary goal is not to lengthen the period in which they can deliver their Skill but to render it so that mana is not a limiting factor in how often they can trigger them."

"Which does make sense . . ."

Donal tapped Angharad lightly on the nose with the rock, stunning her momentarily into silence. "Ah, but Mana Regeneration is derived from maximum mana. Thus, having a deeper mana pool dramatically increases your Mana Regeneration. Say you had 100 mana before your Class Evolution, with a Mana Regen of 1.75 mana per second. Increasing your mana pool by 12 percent leads to a Mana Regen of 1.96 mana per second. A once-per-second, 10-mana Skill can be used eleven times before you would start running on empty. On the other hand, that extra 12 percent max mana means it can be triggered fourteen times."

Donal fumbled in his robe and produced a ring with a bright emerald stone. "When worn, this trinket increases Mana Regeneration by 100 percent. It's actually one of my more sought-after artefacts. The people I had to kill to get hold of it. Good times. Now, if I had given the you with 100 mana this ring, you would have achieved 3.5 Mana Regen per second. If I then slipped you another ring with 50 percent Mana Regeneration, we could have gotten you to 4.375 per second. Not too shabby. However, if we decided not to beggar our treasury and simply added 25 mana to your pool, we'd see the exact same absolute regeneration rate. For a fraction of the resource. What is more, each maximum mana point is more effective per cent of increased regeneration. Indeed, the value of max mana increases the higher your Regen is!"

Angharad's head swam. None of this was particularly unusual magical theory, but it was the first time she had been lectured on it, in the middle of a siege and by an old man who kept tapping her in the face with a rock. "Sir, I thank you for the information, but what does this have to do with —"

"With you sticking your finger in this?"

"Yes!"

A further explosion hit Angharad's <Golden Dome>. She frowned as it dispersed her power more effectively than previous impacts. She restrengthed the Skill and smoothed out the damage.

Donal was watching her carefully. "That one nearly got through, didn't it?"

"Not at all. I just lost focus for a moment."

"Aha!" Donal tossed the rock and caught it. "And that's my point!"

"It is?"

"Well, no. Not yet. But that's because I haven't made it yet. But it will be. As far as we can tell, you have an insanely deep mana pool. Yes?"

"Yes." Angharad watched, alarmed, as Donal capered backwards and forwards on the battlements.

"And your Mana Regeneration well outstrips your current power usage. Yes?"

"Yes."

"So, if that is true, why does one explosion bounce off and one make a more significant impact?"

Angharad thought about it and then shook her head. "I don't know."

"Concentration, my dear! Even if it is not a drain on your resources, you still need to concentrate on the Skill to ensure it works as well as it can. And this, finally, is where my little stone comes in."

He threw it to her, and she caught it with one hand. "What is it?" she asked.

"A critical failure. A complete and utter disaster. The single worst piece of coloured glass that poor Glazier has ever, or will ever, achieve. I tell you, we had to work extremely hard to make something this bad."

Angharad rubbed her hand over the rough piece of blackened stone. It had the texture of coal but the porous nature of some sort of sponge. "This is glass?"

"It was. And now it isn't. It has been produced in such a catastrophically bad way by a Glazier adept with the <Refract> Skill that it actively inhibits energy leaving it rather than allowing light to pass through."

Angharad went to give the rock back to Donal. "This is all very interesting, sir, but I do have other things to . . ."

"You are not listening." The power of whatever mental Skill the man unleashed struck Angharad like a physical slap. "You are an Archmage. That is an extraordinarily rare thing. We will need all of your power in the coming confrontation. However, without your <Golden Dome>, everyone within this City would already have been reduced to ash. But maintaining that Skill is taking up all of your concentration. Even my blathering about Mana Regeneration percentages reduced your focus enough for the shield to somewhat falter. You thus cannot be expected to maintain this shield and aid us in the coming fight. Cleverly, with this sporadic bombardment, the Stonehand is effectively neutralising someone who could be a key offensive measure."

"But if we need the shield, I must maintain it."

"Nope. Not at all. You see, the shield isn't failing because you do not have the mana to keep it going — far from it — there's no power shortage. Rather, it fails when you shift your mind to something else. So all you need is an anchor point for your power, which will lock your power in place without you needing to think about it."

Donal was walking away from her now, and she scurried to keep up with him. He turned the corner of the battlement and vanished out of sight.

"And that's what this rock is?" With her pace quickened, she nearly ran into him as he came to a halt.

"That? No, don't be ridiculous. That is just the charging point. That is the anchor." Donal said, pointing up at a huge, metallic obelisk in the centre of the Keep's roof.

*

"So, you did what he asked?" General Souit regarded the Archmage gravely.

"Well, yes. He made a convincing argument. If I empowered the . . . rock with enough mana to charge the <Golden Dome> Skill and then tied it all off to the metallic anchor, I would be able to free myself up to concentrate on the attacking forces. Do you think I did the wrong thing?"

General Souit turned to stare down at the approaching mercenary army. As soon as his men were behind the walls, the Stonehand had brought his forces forward within striking distance.

Although the magical bombardment continued to rain down on Angharad's shield, somewhat inhibiting their ability to see beyond its protection, there was no doubt that a more significant attack was imminent.

In many ways, he was glad that his Archmage would be available to assist in the defence. The lines and lines of heavily armoured, clearly well-trained men and women preparing to assault the walls — and the breach he had worked so hard to punch in it in the first place — greatly concerned him. He did not need <Foresight> running to be able to predict how ferocious would be the coming fight.

On the other hand . . .

"Now you have empowered that shield, are you able to turn it off?"

"No, sir. That's the point. It is now operating entirely independently of me."

"So, after we defeat this attack and return to assaulting Swinford, they will also have your shield as a defence?"

Angharad was quiet for a moment. "He played me, didn't he, sir?"

Souit's eyes wrinkled into a smile. "I doubt you were the first, and you certainly will not be the last. But we can deal with that problem when the time comes."

And then he stood up straighter.

Because, to the sound of blaring horns, the Stonehand's army had begun its assault.

CHAPTER FIFTY-TWO

"It Will Get Gnarly"

The mercenaries' magical bombardment eased as the first row of the Stonehand's infantry closed on the edge of the shield.

Souit had assumed that the mercenaries would swarm straight for the breach his army had opened in Swinford's walls, and had, thus, positioned a large section of his forces there to meet them. It certainly appeared he had read the situation correctly, as several thousand men were marching directly for that gap.

Amongst them, Souit had been delighted to learn, he could include Major Degralk and Captain Kettle. Taelsin was not wholly sure, but he would swear he saw the stony-faced General give the slightest smile when they, and the men they commanded, were released from their parole to his keeping.

It was not clear, though, that the feeling was mutual.

"I dunno, sir," Sergeant Drult said, tightening the strap on his gauntlet, "I can't help but feel we were safer in the cells than out here and in these things."

While he undoubtedly agreed, Captain Kettle chose not to reply.

Truth be told, he did not like the look of the mercenaries — he would not call them soldiers — who were marching towards them. For as disdainfully as such men and women were viewed by those in the ranks, the reality was they would be in for a rare old scrap here. To make it in a mercenary company, you needed to be fairly sure you would make it through an engagement alive to claim your fee. Therefore, unlike the army, which accepted any waif and stray who needed three square meals a day, mercenary groups tended to attract those whose talents ran to the exotic.

Therefore, while Cattle and his men could probably call on one or two fairly mundane military Skills between them, there was no telling what could be coming their way.

A few years back, whilst clearing out a pirate nest, Cattle had found himself one-to-one against a full-blown Lightweaver. That sort of thing would make a fellow wary of the unknown.

And that did not even take into account the disparity in their kit. He was not the only one looking with substantial envy at rows upon rows of polished breastplates, elaborate helms, and epic-quality weaponry coming their way.

"Still, sir," Drult murmured sarcastically, "at least we've got these nice, snug metal boxes."

"Quiet, there!" Degralk barked, walking the length of the defensive line. He glared at the box containing Drult briefly before winking at Cattle and moving on. The two had found much in common during their captivity and had struck up an unlikely friendship.

The Sergeant waited until Degralk was out of earshot and continued with his theme. "I mean, are you happy with this arrangement, sir? Inside these things, we can barely move. Once the boys need to do anything much more flexible than stand and fight, it will get gnarly."

"It's like I told you, Captain," Jinks chimed in, "they don't trust us to hold the line."

Cattle banged his mailed hand against the edge of his own box — he would not think of them as cages, that way madness lay — and waited for silence. "You heard the Major speak about how hard it was going up against civilians encased in these things. You telling me you're afraid to do something a bunch of Weavers and Merchants were up for?"

No one answered.

Privately, Cattle could not blame his men for their anxiousness. He, like them, was currently tightly wedged in a metallic cube. Each of them had been adjusted to fit the individual soldier within them, and then they had been affixed together the length of the wall breach in one long line.

The boxes each had a hole to see through —— covered by a thick place of remarkably transparent glass — and holes for each man's arms to push through, which were then covered by some sort of chainmail attached to the box itself. The boxes were positioned on a slant, and there was just enough room for each to hold his spear and shield in a standard configuration, but it would undoubtedly be an oddly restrictive way to fight.

The old man who had introduced the men to these devices was certainly enthusiastic about them. "Nothing short of a Juggernaut will be able to cut through!" He had held forth on the various bonuses these boxes offered those who fought in them for some time.

Those under Degralk's command who had been captured assaulting the Keep spoke darkly about how challenging it had been to engage those fighting from within them. That had gone some way to calming the complaints of the rest of the men.

The mercenaries were now crossing the shield's edge and had moved into what Souit had designated the "killing ground".

A horn sounded, and arrows poured down from Swinford's battlements. Cattle did not understand the mechanics, but the Westerners had apparently devised a way to provide their archers with unlimited ammunition. They had not shared the exact details of the secret, but they were happy to equip the King's men with everything they needed to pepper those trying to assault the walls.

If Cattle had hoped this would stall the assault, though, he was disappointed. With an easy movement that spoke of hard training and extensive experience, the moving line of mercenaries shifted into several turtle formations, with each heavy shield snapping into a precise place amongst the whole. Thus, when the torrent of arrows hit those shields, they largely bounced harmlessly away.

If that was not impressive on its own merits, that their advance barely slowed as they did so certainly was.

"By the Goddess!" Jinks whispered.

"Hush, there. That's easy enough to do when the alternative is being turned into a pincushion. Motivates you like nobody's business." Drult's voice was a low drawl. "We've done that a hundred times."

Maybe. But never as smoothly, Cattle thought. And certainly not without casualties.

Despite its lack of impact, the arrows continued to crash down — with unlimited arrows, there was no reason not to — but now was the time for the Mages to begin their work.

*

"Not yet, Archmage." Souit rested a hand on Angharad's arm as he felt power swell within her. "We do not show all our cards just yet."

Although she knew this was the plan, the young woman's frustration was palpable. She had been unnerved what little the archery bombardment had done and was anxious to see some material change come upon the mercenaries' advance.

The other Mages that the King had attached to Souit's forces — those who still lived, of course — opened up with the full range of their offensive Skills. She could sense their frustration at her rapid rise in prominence (Mages were nothing if not hierarchical) and none of them were holding back now that there was a chance to show they were more than just her support staff.

From their positions high above the "killing ground" on the walls and in the towers of Swinford, they delivered death upon the mercenaries in great swaths. <Fireball> after <Fireball> lanced down to explode within the turtle formations. These were followed by multiple casts of <Blizzard> that struck superheated shields to crack them into pieces through which the nonstop tide of arrows poured.

Souit nodded in satisfaction. So far, so good. The space between the barrier's edge and Swinford's walls was now littered with the dead and the dying.

But still, the mercenaries did not break. The advance, although slowed, did not stop, and they would make contact with his own men within moments. The discipline required to absorb that punishment and keep moving forward was almost inhuman.

Souit raised his spyglass, seeking out his opposite number. It was at such moments that he truly missed Stein. He doubted he would be scrabbling around trying to spot where this Gallant Stonehand was positioned should she still be at his side.

Nevertheless, it did not take him long to alight on the throne made out of bone, which appeared to be the preferred spot of the leader of the mercenaries. But when he did, he found the ancient man with the flowing white hair staring straight back at him.

Souit jerked the spyglass down, something about the man's intense glare profoundly unnerving him.

"Are you alright, sir?" The Archmage's face was filled with concern.

Souit cursed. It did not do his reputation any good to be seen to hold such fancies. The old man was simply staring into space, that was all. He could not possibly see him at this distance. "I am perfectly fine. A bothersome fly, that was all. It took me by surprise."

He raised the spyglass and found himself once again looking straight at the Stonehand. That gaunt face was pulled into a rictus grin, and he appeared to be excitedly mouthing something — the same few words over and over again.

There were just a few moments before the battle started in earnest, but Souit took the time to pass the spyglass to

Angharad. "Their commander seems to be saying something, Archmage. Can you make it out?"

The young woman accepted his gift sceptically and pressed it to her eye, reacting similarly to Souit when first meeting the Stonehand's gaze.

Her lips moved as if trying out the words she saw repeated on that man's terrifying face.

"Well?" Souit asked as she lowered the glass.

"I can't be certain, sir, but I think he is saying — well, screaming, really — 'Where is she?'"

And then the front row of the mercenaries crashed into Swinford's defenders.

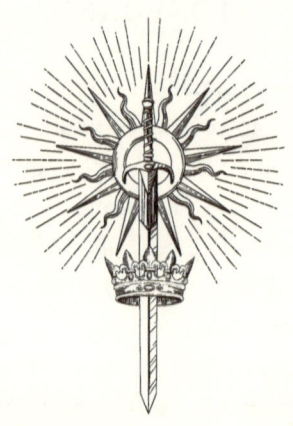

CHAPTER FIFTY-THREE

"Truly Hot Work"

Charging a shield wall was hot work.

In theory, pure momentum meant the attackers would have an advantage when the two sides engaged. However, in practice, attempting to motivate men to run with any conviction into rows of shields and protruding spears was a fool's errand. What happened more often than not was a lot of early noise and enthusiasm that waned away as the distance closed. This usually meant that the initial first contact when it occurred would, at best, be at a walking pace.

The Stonehand's infantry, though, hit the line of defenders at full pelt.

In the normal run of things, thought Cattle — his shield arm absorbing a ferocious strike from a battleaxe and going momentarily numb — they would never have been able to stand against such a collision. If it were not for the heavy metallic boxes in which he and the men around him were wedged, they would, quite simply, have been blown aside by the rabid commitment of these mercenaries to their charge.

As it was, although the men who defended the breach in Swinford's walls shuddered under the force of the attack, they held their line.

Cattle slammed his shield into the face of the Axeman, leaving him momentarily exposed for Drult to place the tip of his spear through the man's throat with an economic jab. Exactly as they'd done countless times before on hundreds of battlefields.

Say what you want for fancy armour, Skills and all the Magery in the world. Nothing beat good old-fashioned experience.

"That's it, lads," he called, his voice oddly magnified through the glass plate in front of his face. "It's all fun and games until someone loses an eye. Let's see how much they really fancy it!"

With that, the charge abruptly halted, and the second row of mercenaries arrived to reinforce the first.

It was then that the truly hot work began.

*

Souit nodded as the initial assault on the breach in the walls foundered.

"It seems your confidence in your metal boxes was well held, sir," he offered to Donal, not meeting the man's eyes. "I thank you."

"As was yours in the prowess of your men, Great General. After all, a tool is only as good as those that wield it." The magnanimity in the old man's words was somewhat undercut as he immediately turned to Taelsin and added: "That was the sort of thing you wanted me to say, right? Was the tool metaphor appropriate? I'm not sure he understood it. Did he get it, do you think?"

"Donal, why don't you go and see how our shield barrier is holding up?" Taelsin's smile was a touch fixed.

"Oh, it's fine. Our beautiful Archmage, as well as having a quite lovely smile, has power to burn. She has ensured that the reflective core has been thoroughly well-charged. I cannot imagine anything short of the intervention of a god could punch through at the moment. Good girl. Pretty. Sort of catch a young Mayor might do worse than have on his arm, if you know what I'm saying."

Angharad blushed bright crimson. Taelsin put his hands on his friend's shoulders and spun him around. With somewhat undignified haste, he unceremoniously guided him towards the stone steps leading away from the section of wall on which the command staff had positioned themselves. "Places to go, Donal. People who are not us to see. Why don't you ensure all your little surprises are locked and loaded?"

Donal took the steps downwards, two at a time. "Don't mind me. I know when I'm not wanted. You want her all to yourself, don't you?"

"My apology, sir. Archmage. Since his Class Evolution, he has become a little irreverent." Taelsin paused, considering. "I mean, I say 'since' . . ."

"And you are quite sure it was that man that plotted out your defences? There is not a hidden mastermind behind it all?"

"No," Taelsin said, avoiding looking at Angharad, "that was all him."

"Extraordinary.

All eyes turned back to the breach.

*

Swinford's archers continued to pour a nonstop barrage onto the fighting below them. In the normal run of things, once the close fighting was joined, it was not seen as especially sporting for commanders to order flurries of arrows to be shot towards their own men.

However, the strength of the metal that Donal's craftsmen had been able to produce — combining their Skills and his runes in an unheard-of fashion — made friendly fire concerns much less pressing. While no one was ever going to refer to them by Donal's preferred name of "Murderboxes," they were certainly having an impact on the nature of the combat.

The defenders were not having everything their own way, however. Although the metal casings were withstanding fearful punishment — far above what even the most expensive plate armour could weather — those in the breach could not easily press home an advantage. Their restricted manoeuvrability was such that once the initial shock of the line holding wore off, things settled into a stalemate.

Stonehand's men had arranged themselves into tight assault groups, with those at the front engaging the defenders, the ones in the middle holding broad, interlocking shields overhead to protect from projectiles, and those behind resting for a while before swapping out with those in the front row.

It was an impressive display of teamwork that was designed to outlast an opponent who did not have the luxury of taking a break. And Cattle's shield was already weighing extremely heavy on his arm . . .

Then, suddenly, the pressure was released, and the whole of Stonehand's infantry took, in concert, a step backwards, revealing hooded figures raising their hands towards the defenders.

"Mages!"

*

"I think that's your cue, Archmage."

Angharad nodded, took a deep breath and activated <Shadow Walk>. The Skill immediately transported her in front of the line of defenders, facing perhaps twenty dark-cloaked Mages.

"Well, at least that worked as intended," she said to herself, throwing up a broad shield in front of the men holding the breach.

The storm of Magery that struck the barrier a few feet before her was significant — she would have melted where she stood had she attempted this before her Class Evolution.

However, that was the old Angharad.

She smiled broadly as she absorbed the attack. Who would have thought she would have been able to wield such power? It was wholly intoxicating. The <Circle of Flame> she had used to destroy much of the enemy's cavalry was one thing, but this was quite something else. This felt like the sort of thing she had only read about in books. There were twenty of them arrayed against just her!

The Mages opposing her shifted the nature of their attack — activating Skills for which she had no name — but it made very little difference. The Archmage could almost see what they were going to do before they attempted it, subtly adjusting her shield to respond to whatever they tried.

The experience was so invigorating — so all-consuming — that she did not sense the opening of a black portal behind her.

*

It was Jinks swearing a blue streak that brought Cattle's attention to the sudden appearance of an old man with long white hair directly in front of them.

But before they could do anything — even shout a warning — the man blurred across the short distance between them and drove a knife into Angharad's back.

She screamed, activating <Quick Heal> and spinning around to face her attacker. A second knife was in the man's hand, cutting and slashing across the young woman's body.

Angharad attempted to trigger whatever protective Skills came to her mind, but the Stonehand's speed left her no time to think. She had all the power in the world, but no experience encountering such brutality. Defensive Skills formed and were shattered in the air between them, with the knife repeatedly finding its way through to plunge into her flesh.

The men in the breach were frozen in horror — trapped within their metal boxes — none able to move forward to help the young woman who was being cut to ribbons in front of their eyes.

And yet, despite her panic and pain, Angharad was somehow holding the shield protecting the defenders from the opposition Mages. Those men and women intensified their assault, seeking to take advantage of the Archmage's plight, but to no avail.

As she fought for her life, Angharad kept the defenders safe.

But the assault was taking its toll. Each strike from the Stonehand against one of Angharad's Skills was met with a burst of splitting arcane energy, causing the ground to rumble and lightning to flash from the sky. Spectral flames flew up into the air, dancing around them as they fought, but they did little to deter the relentless onslaught of the Stonehand. If she could have had a moment to think, there were any number of ways Angharad could have channelled her power to combat this attack, but she was simply too pressed.

She was paying too much attention to maintaining the shield, to somehow keeping the blade deflected away from her pain-wracked body, on not losing her footing on the increasingly blood-sodden earth.

The blitz attack had been so sudden and so ferocious that only now did Souit perceive the danger. They — he — had never anticipated a move like this. After all, what commander chose to attack an Archmage one-to-one?

But before he could order any countermeasure, it was over.

With one final, brutal strike, the Blade of Ruin drove his blade through a floating golden shield into Angharad's chest. Her cry of agony was eclipsed by yells of anger and violation from the men she continued to protect, even as she sank down to her knees.

The Stonehand withdrew his blade and cocked his head, observing her in a strangely absent way. It was as if he could not quite remember who she was and why they had fought. He raised a finger to brush the hair from pale face, staring intently into her eyes. Then, without warning, his hand clenched into a fist, pulling her hair upwards and exposing her neck.

He beheaded her with one swing.

As her body hit the ground, Angharad's shield failed, and the myriad of attacks from the Mages streaked forward to engulf the men holding the breach.

The light of that conflagration flickered in Gallant Stonehand's eyes as he scanned up and down the line of metal boxes wilting and melting under such a force of mana.

He raised the head of Angharad, looking into her dead eyes and whispering, almost affectionately. "Where is she?"

No one noticed him slip back through the portal. They had concerns of their own.

CHAPTER FIFTY-FOUR

"A Terrible, Terrible Idea"

"It worked. I have gained access to the Stonehand's portal." In the dark of the sewer tunnels, Donal's voice was unusually sombre.

Daine let out a breath she hadn't known she was holding and triggered <Rallying Cry>. They had decided it was best to wait as long as possible before making use of it. There were no definitive accounts of how Blades of Ruin locked onto their prey, but it seemed sensible not to announce Daine's presence by pulsing out such a noticeable Skill. She hoped they had not waited too long to aid in what sounded like a fierce battle for control of the walls.

Fretting, her mind lingered for a moment over the second of her new Skills, <Righteous Call>. However, she could not bring herself to use it. It may well help with the battle she could hear raging above, but it simply seemed immoral. Empowering those who had received grievous wounds to fight on long after they should have been dead was not something Daine was comfortable doing.

If there was one thing the reappearance of the Stonehand had taught her, it was that the dead should stay dead.

The Hyena whispered instructions to the two of her Cackle she had selected to join her and Daine on this mission. Azam was a short, friendly-faced man with dark skin and darker hair. If Daine had not read the reports of the carnage he had inflicted on the King's Army during the running battles in Swinford's streets, she would have believed him to be a Teacher or suchlike. The truth was rather more unusual. As a Bombardier, his Class was relatively rare and particularly suited to his chosen life of sabotage and mayhem, for Azam had access to an extensive range of Skills which caused things to explode.

"You should see their faces when I use <Last Resort>," he had said, grinning at her. "They think they have me cornered and then . . ." He exploded a small ball of energy he had formed in his hand.

Apparently, Azam's <Last Resort> was used rather more frequently than its name would suggest.

The second figure joining them was a nondescript woman whose Class — Stepper — Daine had never heard of. She had tried to engage this woman, this Jessica, in discussion about her Skillset, but the Hyena had unsubtly interceded. Even for Daine, with all her resiliences, it was still somewhat disconcerting to stand near an assassin of whose capacities you were unaware.

And then there was the Hyena. Her fighting spirit had not been quelled by the injury the Spymistress had inflicted on her. Indeed, the ferocity of her knifework had seemingly increased.

Satisfied with what she saw in her companions, Daine turned to Donal. "Do I want to know how you managed to gain access to the path of Gallant's portalling Skill?"

He looked back at her, and something about the hollowness of the gaze struck her. "No, my Lady Darkhelm. You truly do not."

*

The plan was very straightforward.

At Donal's insistence, they had not included any of the members of the King's Army in the discussions.

"If you are going to have me make use of incredibly rare and forbidden techniques, the very least you can do is do me the courtesy of not having me show my arse in public!"

"I can concur," Taelsin had added dryly, "no one wishes to see your arse in public."

As the Dark Warlord had explained it, Donal would, using the Blade of Ruin's own movement Skill against him, channel a portal through which Daine, the Hyena, Azam and Jessica could pass and seek to eliminate the Stonehand.

Of course, only Daine would seek to fight him directly. The three members of the Cackle would be there to dispose of any bodyguards and to dissuade anyone from interfering with the fight whilst the Darkhelm, in the words of Donal, "took care of business."

"Are you sure you can handle him?" Taelsin had asked, his eyes filled with concern. He was not used to seeing the woman so . . . skittish. It was like seeing a mountain offer an apology.

"No," she had answered honestly. "I do not even understand how he is out there. When I last saw him — her memory flashed back to the crying, broken figure she had walked away from — "he was near the end of his life. I cannot see how he has recovered to be in the field again."

She had sought to ask the Goddess about Old Gant's reappearance, but their connection stayed cold as if she were deliberately being ignored.

"However," Daine had continued, "I am the only one of us who has any chance of defeating him." She hoped she sounded much more confident than she felt.

"There is no need for this confrontation," the Hyena had spat out. "You are of better use against the main army. A few hours of you slaughtering his men, and he won't have the numbers to take the City."

But Daine had already been shaking her head. "Gallant Stonehand will not be interested in capturing the City. It won't matter to him if we kill all of his men around him. He will keep coming and coming until everyone in front of him is dead. No. The only chance Swinford has of still standing when this is all over is if I get to him first and end it."

It was then that Donal had theorised that he should be able to follow the path of the Stonehand's portal ability if he were to manifest it close enough to the City. "We'll just need to put on a good-enough show that he might want to come and have a look. Once he does, he'll open a door we can follow all the way back to his command tent."

"And you have an idea for what that 'good-enough show' can be," Taelsin had asked.

Donal's eyes had strayed to the Archmage for a moment before returning — somehow looking slightly darker — to the small group. "You know what, I just might," he said cryptically.

*

Daine checked her gear for the final time.

Not that she thought it would make much difference if she ended up in a drag-out fight with Old Gant.

Even thinking about him in those terms brought heat to her face.

She recognised she had a complicated relationship with the man. More father than teacher. More mentor than drill-master. But then, of course, more bully than friend. How many times had he nearly killed her when she was nothing but a child?

She knew — of course she did — that had it not been for the beatings, she would never have been able to make her initial Class Evolution. He had taken a Farmer's daughter, broken her down, and transformed her into a Knight from legend.

But the experience had left deeper scars than could ever be healed.

And now she was going to kill him.

She'd wished him dead a hundred times. A thousand. But had she ever really thought she would be the one to do it?

Daine rehearsed what would happen in her mind.

They would step through the portal, her first, the others following closely in her wake. Anyone around the Stonehand was the Hyena and her Cackle's problem. Daine would make straight for him and seek to end things with one blow.

Suppose it took more than that? Well, then all bets would be off.

Donal, his face still unusually gaunt, gestured them over impatiently.

"If we are going to do it, it must be now. Just so we are all clear — because no one else seems to agree with me that this is a terrible, terrible idea — this is a one-way trip. I can rip open enough of the residue of his Skill to push you in his wake, but I simply do not have the power to pull you back. Once you go through, you will be on your own."

The Hyena laughed and tapped Jessica on the back. "Don't you worry, old man. The Cackle have got in and out of tighter spots than this. You concern yourself with getting us there, let me worry about getting us out."

Donal's mouth tightened, but then he shrugged. He turned to Daine, and his voice was soft. "Don't hesitate. Not for a second. He's not the man you knew. Whatever means have been used to bring him back have turned him into a mad dog. What stands at the end of the portal is not Gallant Stonehand. It is not someone you used to know. All that awaits you is a broken, tortured thing that is merely wearing his face. As somewhat of a connoisseur of such things, I can tell you — categorically — that killing him will be the kindest thing you can ever do for him."

Daine did not reply, merely drawing her greatsword in preparation.

They lined up in front of Donal, the three members of the Cackle tucked in behind Daine. The old man looked like he might say something else, but then he smiled broadly and clapped his hands together, then moved them apart, creating a dark tunnel in the air.

"Go get him!" he shouted, and then pushed the portal outwards.

It hovered between his hands and then expanded,

swooping out to envelop the four figures. In an instant, they were gone.

Donal stood alone for a moment, the smile collapsing in on itself until only remnant remained.

"Please make it worth it," he said. Eyes filling with tears.

CHAPTER FIFTY-FIVE

"Unstoppable Momentum"

Daine stepped through the portal, taking a moment to orientate herself.

Her first glance took in the expansive interior of the covered structure they had stepped into. The sheer size of the tent was striking, easily twenty feet across. At its centre, a robust wooden table grabbed her attention, laden as it was with a schematic of Swinford and various documents, surrounded by a handful of portable stools and benches.

Daine assumed the portal had manifested them directly into the Stonehand's command post.

So far, so good.

Donal's worst-case scenario had been for the attack group to appear at the precise moment the Blade of Ruin was addressing the entirety of his troops. Despite everything, Daine felt a slight — an ever-so-slight — easing in her tension at seeing that had not come to pass.

Looking up, she judged that the tent's roof was at least three again of her height, supported by a sturdy wooden frame. The heavy canvas walls were etched with complex runes. At least some of them were presumably fire-retardant ones, considering the plethora of open flames dotted around the space. The flickering light from these candles and oil lamps cast long, sinister shadows across the floor and against the walls.

To one side, there lay a modest bedding area with a cot and blankets, surrounded by wooden chests and leather pouches, presumably for storing scrolls and supplies. Daine's mind flashed back to an ill-advised visit to Old Gant's sad little room when it had become clear he was near the end of his life. It was as if someone had frozen that memory in time and moved it wholesale to the corner of this tent. The accuracy was eerily precise, even down to the empty bottles of whisky piled by the cot.

The tension that had somewhat released its hold on Daine returned with a vengeance. Any doubts she harboured about whether this was actually her old master vanished.

Daine felt the others join her and begin to spread out.

In the final moment before their plan was implemented, she felt a gentle draft from the high placed ventilation flaps brush her face. Instinctively, she lifted her chin, letting the coolness run through her hair, the fresh breeze countering the warmth generated by the lamps. And easing the white-hot terror blooming inside her at seeing her target.

Old Gant stood directly ahead, facing away from her. His long, white hair spilt down the length of his back but looked flecked by streaks of red. As had been his custom when training his students, he wore a simple outfit of a black leather tunic and trousers. At his waist, in matching sheaths, she could make out his twin daggers. But if Daine knew her man, others would be secured under his arms and more again strapped around his thighs.

Daine shifted her gaze downwards. Gant appeared to be holding something in his right hand. Was it a ball wrapped in string?

Her eyes slid away from that strange sight to the other occupants of the room. There were, as expected, two guards at the tent entrance, one on either side, and they were facing outwards, away from the portal. Again, that was about as good an outcome as they could have hoped.

However, there were five others — three with outlandish weapons strapped to their backs and sides, and two who were clearly Mages of some sort — looking directly at them. Well, that was why there were more than just her here. Ignoring everyone else and trusting her companions to do their part, Daine charged towards the Stonehand.

Without any communication necessary, the Hyena and Jessica ran past her, each making directly for a Mage. Azam paused for a moment — as if weighing up the distance — then generated one of his spheres of explosive energy and threw it directly at the guards at the entrance.

The first of the Mages had just enough time for her eyes to open wide in shock before the Hyena leapt on top of her. The assassin's legs wrapped around her waist, momentum propelling the two of them to the floor in a muddle of flailing limbs. In a blink, though, the Hyena was sat on top of the Mage, plunging repeatedly downwards into her chest with thin stilettos.

Jessica vanished, then reappeared behind the second Mage — a tall, bearlike man — and looped a thin metal cord around his neck. The two of them disappeared, then returned again and again in different parts of the tent as the Stepper viciously garroted him. Despite the bigger man's increasingly panicked efforts, the assassin eventually sawed straight through his thick neck and removed his head.

"No matter what else you find when you get there, you kill the Mages first," Donal had drummed into them over and over again. "You shatter a glass cannon long before it gets a chance to fire. Once that danger is removed, then you see what else needs to be done." In the time is had taken them to die, Daine had taken no more than two steps towards Gallant.

And yet, for all his legendary reactions, the man had not moved.

The sound of an explosion, followed by appalling screams, at the entrance suggested Azam had completed the first stage of his mission. He had successfully cut off any further immediate support. The flickering light of those roaring flames and the billowing smoke added to the growing chaos in the tent.

And still, the Stonehand did not react.

Daine adjusted her grip on the hilt of the greatsword and swept her arms backwards, just two short steps away from him being within reach.

Now that the Hyena and Jessica had finished with their first victims, they had moved to engage the other three figures in the room before they could intercept Daine's assault on their commander. The Hyena threw a bottle of something foul-smelling at a man reaching for a crossbow — he quickly lost interest in doing anything other than screaming — and began duelling with a swordswoman who had drawn a long curved blade. The assassin's knives flicked and deflected the wild swings of her target, seeking to close the distance as soon as possible.

Jessica made for the final other figure in the room and cracked out a whip to ensnare the axe he was bringing to bear. She tugged on it, seeking to disarm him, but he was too strong, and she was forced to release her weapon. She vanished and reappeared a few steps further back, reassessing her options for attack.

Daine could not spare any further attention for her companions, though, as her sword completed its backswing and began to career forward, the white-framed head now finally within her range.

Her slash chopped onwards, empowered by every moment of fear, of anger, and of pain that this man had ever caused. The attack was fuelled by the nightmares of a young girl, by the Strength of a Knight and the determination of a Templar. It was the most potent attack she had ever launched, and she knew in her heart that nothing could possibly turn it aside.

Her sword sang through the air, streaking towards its destination with unstoppable momentum.

And still, the Stonehand did not move.

But then, at the moment the blade kissed his neck, Daine became aware of the rattling of dice in a cup in her head. The noise lasted no more than a moment, and then it was followed by a throw. She heard the cast clatter as if across a stone floor and come to a halt.

The Goddess gasped.

And Gallant Stonehand, her friend, her mentor, her horror, was no longer in the path of her sword.

He was not stood before her at all.

He was instead behind her, twin daggers licking forward to drive and twist deep into her back, severing her spine in two places. He left the blades in place, preventing her from healing and repairing the damage.

Then, her legs no longer her own, she was crumpling downwards with just his whispered words in her ear. "Still too slow, dearest Daine. Too slow, by far."

*

Alone in the sewers, Donal felt the casting of the dice.

He tried to offer to trade in every one of a millenia of favours to any deity who would listen. None were willing to intercede. He reached out with every power he possessed — and many he should not — to seek to alter the course of that cast.

But his efforts were rejected, and the dice came to a rest.

He did not hear the gasp of the Goddess, but he surely made out the laughter of the Dark God.

And then he felt the twin blows bisect Daine's spine and foresaw all their doom.

"*Taelsin*," he mentally sent to his friend and master, "she failed. Tell Souit to move immediately to the evacuation plan and let Lady Stelton know the portal in the sewers is open for the civilians to flee. I've left enough power there for them to all get through if they're quick." He thought of what would be appropriate final words to a man — in his more unguarded moments — he liked to pretend was his son. But there did not seem to be any. "Take care, Mayor Elm. I hope this buys you enough time."

Donal ran his hands through his hair and smoothed

down the collar of his cape. It was so important to make a suitably dramatic entrance, after all.

And, as the last of its energy dissipated, he stepped through the Stonehand's portal and into the command tent.

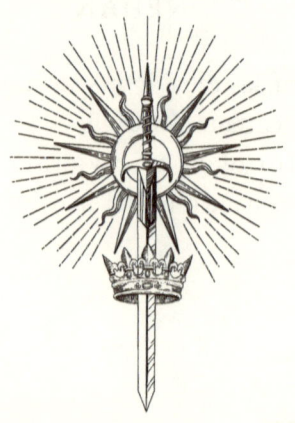

CHAPTER FIFTY-SIX

"A Lion in Winter"

Donal stepped through the portal and took in the scene before him.

Despite everything, he felt a little spurt of triumph that it seemed most of what he had predicted had come to pass.

Near his feet, the corpses of two berobed figures suggested the Hyena and Jessica had followed his advice and taken the spellcasters off the table with alacrity. Those two were currently engaged with the only other enemy occupants of the room, and whilst the fighting was fierce, Donal did not feel any intervention would be necessary.

Azam was standing in the middle of a fire blazing away in the tent's entrance, tossing further balls of energy out into the night. By his loud laughter and shouts of encouragement to those outside, if he was worried about what was happening behind him, he was hiding it well. The screams from those beyond had a panicked quality, suggesting an organised and concerted effort to charge the tent was still quite some time away.

Everything was going exactly to plan.

And then Donal turned to the centre of the room, to the thin figure of an elderly man standing over the motionless body of the Lady Darkhelm.

Well, all apart from this bit, he thought. Can't win them all.

With that, Donal reached into the pockets of his robe and withdrew — quite literally — his trump cards. He clutched a deck of cards in each hand, but these were far from the typical collections of numbers and pictures used in card games. Each was etched with a rune — some already glowing faintly with arcane energy — ready to be employed in this last, desperate gambit.

Across his exceptionally long life, Donal had always been fascinated by runes. No matter the Class he inhabited, nor the role he sought to play, he was always careful to dedicate time to further his appreciation of the art. And over the centuries, he had developed quite the unusual collection.

Most were entirely trivial, quality-of-life runes. The sorts of things that an effective functionary might etch around a castle so that its latest Grand High Lord was never without light, heat or a space in which no one could eavesdrop upon his latest torture victim. Indeed, Donal had spent many happy hours in Swinford using his encyclopedic runic knowledge to forestall some of the depredations of time on the fabric of that once-great City.

Of course, during his study, he had also come across other runes, such as the Dark Words of Ash — one of which he had been forced to use outside the village, all those months ago, when fleeing from the Trellecs — whose use was now wholly forbidden in this more civilised age. The fact that several shadowy organisations were explicitly dedicated to eradicating those who held such knowledge was a significant reason Donal had receded to the shadows in recent decades.

Most of the most helpful combat runes Donal possessed needed intense preparation, careful arrangement, and a colossal amount of mana to activate correctly. And the idea that the Stonehand would allow him the time and space to make use of any truly powerful runes was for the birds.

That was why he had not initially accompanied Daine and the others on this little assassination mission. By the time Donal felt he would be able to be useful to the confrontation, all their projections suggested it would already be over.

One way or another.

But what good Secretary would not have a backup plan for his master in case the very worst of all outcomes occurred?

With the tent's interior illuminated by Azam's ferocious blazes, Donal began to scatter his cards with reckless abandon. Each flick of his wrist sent the cards spinning through the smoky air.

The cards — each inscribed with a rune — landed haphazardly around the tent. Yet despite the chaos of the flames, it seemed that each card found its way to the floor with eerie precision; those that were already glowing with a green light provided a stark contrast to the orange and red hues of the fire. As more and more cards began to activate, their runes pulsed with a quiet power, creating a network of magical energy amidst the destruction. The tent's fabric shuddered under the strain of conflicting energies — the raw, destructive power of Azam's fire starting to lick up the sides of the tent against the controlled, mystical force of the runes.

Then, with a shout of triumph, the Hyena slid one of her blades under the chin of the Swordsman facing her. She had barely watched him fall before throwing her other knife at the Axeman who was leaving Jessica hard-pressed. The latter was struggling to make an impression on her target, with only her ability to vanish and reappear a few feet away keeping her from being dismembered by his wild swipes. Jessica had abandoned her whip and was trying to deflect his attacks using two small duelling canes.

The Hyena's knife took the Axeman in the shoulder but did not leave a mark on him. Setting her mouth in a grim line, the Hyena retrieved her knife from the Swordman's neck and ran forward to join her colleague's fight.

There was a cry from the tent doorway, and Azam staggered back, three crossbow bolts in his chest and stomach. He triggered his primary Skill, <Last Resort>, and turned into a pillar of white-hot flame, the arrows melting in the intensity of the heat. The assassin had explained that this Skill had some healing properties while he channelled it. Donal hoped it would prove to be enough.

With the final card leaving his hand, Donal stepped back, his eyes taking in the precarious nature of the situation. The space was degenerating into a chaotic blend of fire and magic: unpredictable, dangerous, and teetering on the edge of collapse.

And at its heart, the Stonehand still stood above Daine.

His lips were moving as if he were speaking to her, but the noise in the tent was far too loud for Donal to make anything out.

Well, he had done what preparation was possible.

Time to roll the dice.

At that wording, Donal cocked his head. It was rather unusual for him to express himself in terms of gambling metaphors.

My Lords, if you're hazarding on the outcome of this game, I hope you lose your shirts, he thought, and then raised his voice into a shout. "Gallant!"

At first, he thought the old man did not hear him, but slowly, the Stonehand's head turned his way.

The old assassin's face was a landscape of time and fury. His skin, weathered like ancient leather, was pulled taut over high, prominent cheekbones. The overall impression was of looking at an animated skeleton.

His eyes were sunk deep into their sockets and burned with an ungodly rage. The mad fire that flickered and danced within matched the intensity of the heat building around them. They were the eyes, thought Donal, of a man who had seen too much and forgiven nothing. These were eyes that had stared down death itself and never, not once, ever blinked.

Around his face, Gallant's long white hair — flecked with the blood of an Archmage and a Templar — flowed from his scalp. It cascaded over his shoulders in stark contrast to the darkness of his clothing. To Donal's mind, it was like a ghostly veil that framed his gaunt face.

When he opened his mouth to reply, his thin lips split — dry in the heat of the tent — blood bubbling out to give him a predatory cast. When he spoke, it was with a voice that seemed to rumble up from the depths of his tortured soul.

"Do I know you?"

Donal opened his now-empty hands wide in a disarming, welcoming gesture. "Not as such. But it would be fair to say our paths have crossed multiple times over the decades."

The Stonehand's face remained blank. His expression was as if Donal had not spoken. Then he frowned and spoke again. "Who are you?"

Donal made a slight gesture with his left index finger, and one of his cards detached from its place in the intricate network and swooped to hover in front of the Stonehand. Once it settled, the card crumbled away, transforming into a moving picture of a battlefield. The image was largely transparent — Donal could still see the old man through it — but was visible enough.

Gallant's whole body turned towards the picture, shifting away from Daine. Every fibre of Donal's being wanted to move to assist his fallen friend, but he couldn't allow his concentration on the old assassin to waver. Not even for a moment.

The Stonehand was staring in wonder at the projected image. He raised one bloodied finger to point at a figure moving quickly amongst the detritus of war. "That's me!" The voice was filled with so much childish joy that Donal's heart broke anew.

The events of this day had left him emotionally raw. His necessary — but no less painful for that — sacrifice of Angharad. The deaths of all those men in the breach when her protection failed them. The inevitable fall of the Darkhelm. Now, this desperate gambit.

And yet the innocent pleasure on the Stonehand's hard, lined face as he watched his younger self twirl and pirouette in combat on some distant plain was almost the hardest to bear.

What had been done — over many years and by many different people — to this man was abhorrent.

And then, as its mana ran out, the image faded, and a vicious snarl replaced the beautiful pleasure. "Where did it go? Bring it back!"

The Stonehand jabbed his finger towards Donal and stepped forward, further away from Daine.

"Do you remember that? It was the first time I saw you."

"Bring it back!" Gallant roared, baring his teeth. With his white mane of hair, he looked every inch the lion in winter.

He took another furious pace forward.

It took every bit of Donal's considerable discipline not to glance at the configuration of his runic cards. Not to look down at the feet of the Stonehand that were so close to crossing the nexus point.

Surely, it would be just one more step . . .

He gestured, and another card left the complex array to transform into a moving image. It reduced the overall power of the working Donal had prepared, but what would the potency matter if he could not make Gallant trigger it?

"You had infiltrated our lines — I never found out how — and were running merry riot in the baggage train. The Duke, my Master, had ordered all his children held there. He thought they'd be safe."

The look of serenity was back on the old man's face as

he watched his casual slaughter of guards, of servants and then of children. "I was so perfect," he whispered.

"I had been supporting an assault on the King's left flank when the screams began. I didn't make it to them in time." Donal was keeping his voice level. Matter-of-fact. He needed this man to just move towards him once more. "Do you remember how this ended?"

The card began to flicker, and Gallant frowned, half turning back towards the body of the Darkhelm.

Who still had not moved.

Donal summoned a third out from the arcane network — would it still hold? — and re-engaged the old man's interest. The image now showed two figures, one the younger Stonehand and the second a Knight with a drawn greatsword who could have once been Donal.

Gallant's eyes flicked from the moving image and up to the now-familiar man opposite him. "You?"

The confusion in his eyes was palpable.

Donal replied with a broad smile and a beckoning gesture. "Yes, me. Bring it in!" He opened his arms wide as if encouraging an embrace.

Hesitantly, the Stonehand took another step forward.

And then the tent erupted.

CHAPTER FIFTY-SEVEN

"Not Meant to Be"

The Hyena's eyes shot open, and she gasped for air.

There was a moment of disorientation before she realised her <Rise and Shine> Skill had triggered. This unusual talent ensured she regained consciousness faster than anyone else in the vicinity. It was a Skill that had saved her life on more occasions than she could count.

She rolled over, looking around to try to unpack what had happened. Azam had also recovered quickly. His Skillset — built around the giving and taking of vast amounts of explosive energy — was almost ideally suited to tanking . . . whatever had just happened.

It did not appear the others in the command tent had been so lucky.

The Axeman who had been causing Jessica such trouble had been reduced to a smoking ruin. His body appeared to have shielded the Stepper from the worst of the

explosion, though, as whilst unconscious, Jessica seemed
to be breathing.

Whatever had happened had sucked the air out of the
room, putting out the flames that had been in danger of
running riot. The unexpected pause in the fighting meant
the Hyena was taking her first look at how the second half
of the mission was progressing.

Her heart sank at the sight.

Donal was here — or at least she thought she could
make out his unmoving body. The two of them had discussed the circumstances in which he would join them in
this assault. None of them resulted from everything working out precisely as hoped.

"Well, I guess that explains the explosion," she murmured, pulling herself to her feet and casting around on
the floor for any of her discarded blades.

She'd been able to retrieve one before she caught sight
of Daine lying facedown with two knives embedded in her
back. Well, that would be the fairly clear reason Donal had
made an appearance, was it not?

Cursing, the Hyena scanned the room, but there was no
sign of their principal target. However, with the light extinguished and broken furniture lying in chaos all around, that
was hardly surprising.

The Hyena moved cautiously towards the fallen
Templar, keeping low to the ground, eyes alert. She had
various Skills that improved her eyesight and general senses
in the dark, but she suspected any that Gallant Stonehand
possessed would be by far the superior.

She was about halfway towards Daine when a hand
touched her back. To his credit, Azam did not flinch as she
abruptly spun to kiss her knife against his neck. He winked

at her, generating a small fireball in the palm of his hand. The soft illumination made it easier to understand more about the current situation.

The inside of the tent was utterly devastated. Whatever Donal had done — and the Hyena had no doubt the Dark Warlord was responsible — it had been wholly catastrophic.

Azam pointed a finger at a smoking patch on the floor, shaking his head in wonder. "That's the point of origin. But it's like the explosion focused . . . inwards?" He whistled. "I couldn't even begin to do something like that. The layers of power . . ."

Azam might have his own obsessions, but the Hyena only cared about one thing. "Is the Stonehand dead?"

The Bombardier shrugged. "Put it this way, if the focus of whatever that was is in less than a million pieces, we must get out of here. There will — literally — be nothing we can do to it."

Through the ragged remnants of the tent's canvas, the Hyena could see figures cautiously gathering in the darkness outside. "I think we do that anyway. We're going to need Jessica. And fast."

"On it." Azam moved towards the unconscious Stepper, popped the cork on a vial of smelling salts and wafted it under her nose.

The Hyena took the opportunity to creep to Daine's side and put her hands on the handle on the first of the knives. It was embedded beyond the hilt and had clearly severed the spine. In normal circumstances, she'd never consider removing it without taking instructions from a Healer, but then the Lady Darkhelm was anything but normal.

"My Lady, can you hear me?"

There was no response.

"My Lady Darkhelm. Daine. We have to retreat. What would you have me do?"

Silence.

Uncertain, the Hyena sat back on her heels, looking around. Jessica seemed to be awake, which at least suggested the Cackle had a way out of this mess. But what to do about Donal and Daine?

"Well, it's not like I can make things worse, is it?" And she reached to pull out the first of the knives.

The blow she received across her face cracked her jaw, dislodged numerous teeth and sent her spiralling — head over feet — across the tent.

Seeing his commander's unexpected flight, Azam rose to stand, balls of energy filling his hands, and then stumbled, clutching his chest, the hilt of a blade protruding.

In a panic, he prepared to trigger <Last Resort>, but a second knife flew through the air, taking him in the throat, and he dropped, lifeless, to the floor.

Emerging from the shadows like a monster from fireside horror stories, Gallant Stonehand stood, swaying, above Daine's prone form. He had ripped his twin knives free from the Darkhelm's back to throw at the Bombardier. Glancing down, he smiled to see no spurt of blood had followed their removal.

She was finally dead.

In the corner, he could see the smoking remains of the old man who had shown him all those pictures of his past. Gallant felt a little tug of sorrow for that man's passing. It had all been some sort of trap, obviously, but he would have liked the opportunity to have explored that talent a bit further. There were so many gaps in his memories that someone who could entice the air to retell his story was a resource to be treasured.

But, no. It had not been meant to be.

As with so many things across his long life, the Stonehand was forever cursed to be let down by the fragility of others. That thought spurred him to look down at Daine again, and he spat on her corpse.

None worse than that girl. Bitch.

There was a noise from his left, and the other assassin — the woman with the scarred face — was back on her feet, stumbling back towards him. She was game, he would give her that.

Without a word, the Hyena lunged forward, her knives flashing in rapid, jagged arcs. Despite her broken jaw and the dizziness the astonishingly hard blow had caused, her movements remained fluid.

She had triggered every Skill she possessed — there seemed little point keeping anything in reserve — and aimed a flurry of stabs and slashes, targeting the Stonehand's torso and face. Her unarmed target moved backwards with an incongruous grace that, in other circumstances, she would have marvelled at.

Despite the speed of her strikes, he sidestepped and parried with his forearms and hands, accepting countless injuries by diverting her blades away from their intended directions. The Hyena increased the intensity of her assault — tapping all her reserves of Stamina — and felt a burst of satisfaction as the Stonehand sustained deep cuts on his arms and several gashes across his cheeks.

However, despite the pain the wounds must have caused

him, Gallant's movements remained economical and precise. Indeed, he remained eerily calm under the onslaught, starkly different from the Hyena's frenzied aggression.

As she feared it would, the Hyena felt her enhanced Speed begin to wane as her Skills timed out and their cooldowns began.

At precisely the worst moment for her, the momentum changed. Gallant reached out and caught one of the Hyena's wrists, twisting it sharply, forcing her to drop the knife it held. She winced in agony, then again as the Stonehand began to rain blows upon her — a sharp elbow to her ribs, a knee to her abdomen. Each strike was methodical, designed to break bones and disorientate without expending unnecessary energy. In reaction, the Hyena's breath became ragged, her defence less coordinated, as pain and exhaustion set in.

It was over.

They both had known it even before it began.

The two's eyes met, and Gallant leered across the distance between them. Then, with a swift motion, he disarmed her of her remaining knife and grabbed her by the hair, pulling her off-balance. The Hyena gritted her teeth and tried to pivot away, but her movements were sluggish, hindered by her injuries and Gallant's overpowering strength.

Then the Stonehand blurred, moving faster than the Hyena's eyes could follow. Until she felt a sharp pain to her chest, she did not even realise he had swooped to pick up her dropped knife.

It was driven deep into her, and the Hyena's eyes crinkled in resignation as her body went limp.

The Stonehand supported her as she fell and lowered her almost reverently to the floor.

"You were good," he said in his gravelly voice. "but not good enough."

"Didn't need to win," the Hyena whispered back. "Needed time."

The Stonehand frowned. "Time? For what."

He missed her following words as blood bubbled to her lips. He brushed the liquid away from her mouth and leaned in close. "Time for what?"

"For me."

And Daine Darkhelm struck him with everything she had.

CHAPTER FIFTY-EIGHT

"Domain of Law"

"Most fights," Old Gant had said, "are over before they start. Opponents are rarely evenly matched — either in terms of gear, talent or experience — so it's just a matter of time before those advantages tell."

They listened in silence. They'd all been there long enough now to understand their instructor was at his most dangerous when sounding the most lucid.

"Thus, when a mouse finds itself in a fight with a lion" — all eyes turned to the broken, bleeding figure of the ten-year-old girl lying at his feet — "the only chance the mouse has is to take the lion by surprise. It may be very unlikely, but there might be one opportunity to forestall the fated tide of battle."

Old Gant squatted on his haunches and reached out to pull the girl's head upright towards him. Her eyes fluttered open. "One shot, you hear me? The mouse and the lion have an inevitable outcome. It is just a matter of time. Your only chance is to make that one shot count."

He caressed her hair for a moment, then drove her face into the ground, rendering her unconscious once again.

With that, Old Gant stood, dusting down his hands. "No food for Orban until I see a significant improvement in attitude and technique. Anyone I catch sneaking her food will take her place."

Of course, no one risked the Stonehand's wrath. It was ten days before Daine was granted an evening meal.

But by then, she had learned her lesson.

*

The Lady Darkhelm drove her mailed right fist into Gallant's face.

He had turned slightly at her voice, and the blow caught him flush on the cheek. There was a gruesome crunch of breaking bone, and dark blood spurted into the air as Gallant's head snapped back.

It was a blow that would have killed any other man. The force of the punch — carrying with it the weight of decades of anger, pain and trauma — would have felled an oak tree.

And yet, though he staggered, the Stonehand did not fall.

Daine lunged forward, closing the gap before her target had a chance to recover, and followed up with an elbow that caught him on the jaw. Shards of teeth, like broken pearls, scattered across the floor.

But she did not stop.

She raised her clasped fists high to bring down a

two-handed strike on the top of his head, simultaneously bringing her knee up into his nose.

The Stonehand took his extraordinary punishment in complete silence; the only sounds in the tent were Daine's breaths coming in heated snarls and the thud, crack and metallic chorus of the Darkhelm's armour as she struck and struck and struck.

But as fast as Daine was able to deliver the damage, the Stonehand overcame it. His skin resealed, and his bones reknit within moments.

Soon, she realised any advantage of surprise she had held was long gone, and the grinning face of her nightmare was simply, passively, infuriatingly letting her strike him.

She drove one more fearsome punch into his stomach and then stepped back, sucking in air and flexing her fingers as her own broken bones healed in her hands.

"You finished?" The old man's smile was sardonic. "Glad you got that out of your system. How many times have we played out this little scene? But it always has the same conclusion, does it not? What do you truly see happening next? I beat you black and blue again and withhold your supper? I am afraid we're a little past that."

"I agree. We are both too old to keep playing the same roles."

He frowned, not understanding her words. Nor liking the expression on her face. He was used to seeing the girl angry. He enjoyed seeing her afraid. However, whatever emotion she was currently showing him was wholly alien to his experience.

"So what makes this little farce different this time around?"

Daine smiled. "I have brought friends." And she triggered <Righteous Resolve>.

Azam stood first, pulling the blades from his body and tossing them towards the Hyena. She caught them — one in each hand — whilst still lying prone on the floor and then acrobatically flipped upright, all signs of her wound gone.

Daine nodded to the pair solemnly as they took positions around the Stonehand. They smiled back, oddly at peace with what was happening. They had not been healed, they completely understood that. When the countdown on <Righteous Resolve> ended, they would return to the realm of the dead. That was how things should be, and they accepted that. You lived, you fought and — eventually — you died. What more could anyone wish for than to die fighting alongside good companions?

However, right here and right now — before returning to that eternal rest — they still had a final job to do.

Jessica moved to stand between the other members of the Cackle, swirling her whip back and forth. If she thought it strange that her two companions had been resurrected from lethal wounds, her face did not show it. She did, however, phase in and out a few times as if testing that her Skills remained accessible.

Azam smiled and filled his hands with giant spheres of boiling energy. "Not much point me keeping anything in reserve, is there?" he whispered to the Stepper. "You, however? You need to get out of here alive to take the story back. You hear me?" When Jessica did not answer, he shot a little burst of fire her way. "Do your bit, but no more, you get me? There's enough of us here where it doesn't matter either way. No heroics, Jess." The young woman bit her lip but nodded grimly back in reply.

"Well, isn't this a collection of fell powers?" Donal asked, moving stiffly to stand on the other side of the Hyena. The Stonehand's eyes narrowed when he caught sight of him.

"You dead too?" the scarred woman asked bluntly.

Donal winked bank, sketching a few runes in the air that glowed dully. "It's a bit more complicated than that. After all, what do we truly mean when we say 'dead.' Philosophers have long argued . . ."

The Stonehand roared — a terrible, atavistic sound that had no place in the throat of a human — reducing them all to silence. There was some sort of Fear Skill there, and despite at least two of the party having nothing left to fear, its impact upon them was noticeable. In response, Daine triggered <Rallying Cry> and was pleased to see the group stand just a little taller as if a hair more relaxed.

Looking around, she grieved the loss of the Hyena and Azam. They were both tough and uncompromising warriors she had come to respect during their time in Swinford. They had discussed the inevitability of their deaths should Daine fail to put down the Stonehand, and they had accepted that as part of this mission, but seeing them in this liminal state — not dead, yet not alive — was profoundly painful. Still more deaths on her conscience. More examples of being too little and too late.

But this was not the time for sorrow.

Looking over at the Dark Warlord, she was unsure what to make of his revival. Physically, he looked like he had merely been out for a brisk afternoon walk. Indeed, other than the blackened scorching covering his robes, it would be difficult to say he had experienced any inconvenience at all. Daine raised her eyebrows at him, and he gave a "maybe/maybe not" gesture with his hand. She was unsure what that meant.

The group encircling the Stonehand exchanged one last look, and without another word, they attacked.

*

Azam kicked things off, hitting Gallant with ball after white-hot ball of energy. The Stonehand's clothes and hair caught fire, and an overpowering stench filled the tent as the old man screamed and burned.

Ignoring the flames, Daine stepped in close, seeking to keep Gallant's focus on her to give the others freer rein. She threw another huge right hand, but despite Azam's constant bombardment, the Stonehand had enough of his wits about him to move to the side, and the fist sailed past.

He turned to follow her momentum and was about to strike at Daine's unprotected flank when the Hyena sailed in, knives flashing. Gallant took a number of cuts as he reached out to grab her by the throat, lifting her into the air. Daine brought a thundering chop down on his arm, and he released the assassin, who slid down and around his legs, seeking to hamstring him.

At the same time, Jessica's whip flicked out into the Stonehand's face, causing no damage but distracting him for the moment Daine needed to grab hold of both of his wrists.

Gallant and Daine met eyes as he sought to break her grip, and she battled to maintain it. As their war played out, Azam continued to throw fireball after fireball into the man's back while the Hyena slashed and slashed at his legs, avoiding his wild kicks and stomps.

*

Donal watched on with a distant look on his face. This was a curious fight. Two near-immortals locked together, almost as if in an embrace. For all her Strength — and that so greatly increased since her Class Evolution — Daine was obviously at the disadvantage. And yet she held on as, inch by inch, this unstoppable force broke the immovable object's restraints on him.

Puffing out his cheeks, Donal was in the curious situation of not really knowing what to do. He had hit the Stonehand with a pretty innovative — even if he did say so himself — runic array that had seemingly done very little.

He had, of course, no end of tricks left up the smoking remains of his sleeves, but if that complex working achieved nothing, were any of them going to be remotely productive?

Well, no point standing around like a spare part, he thought. Following Daine's lead with <Righteous Resolve>, he triggered his own version, <Minion>, to reanimate the bodies of those slain by the Cackle. He doubted they would do much good — unlike the Hyena and Azam, these would not be sentient — but in his experience, more meat shields were all to the good. The bodies of the seven corpses shambled to life and walked towards the Stonehand.

*

Sweat poured down Daine's face.

It took every ounce of her resolve to hold the Stonehand in place, and she could feel him slipping free. In her mind, she could see the next few moments of the fight playing out.

With a jerk, he would throw off her grip, then reach down to catch the Hyena — nearly through to the bone with her frenzied strikes. A few blows to the head would break <Righteous Resolve>. He would then take the Hyena's two knives and, well, Gallant Stonehand with blades was a far more terrifying prospect than trying to fight him unarmed.

He would kill the others first. Because he knew that would cause her the most pain.

Then they would fight for the final time. And — as he had done so many times before — he would win.

The fury of the unfairness of that bloomed in her, and she strained to pull his wrists back together.

His eyes were on her, mocking. As if he were letting her play out this little game until he tired of it. "What happened to you!" Daine shouted directly into his face.

She was shocked to see the impact of her words. Gallant's face went slack, and his eyes opened in . . . was that fear. "I don't know." All his resistance to her hold vanished, and she was able to clamp his wrists together. He pressed his head forward as if to whisper a secret in her ear. "I can't remember, girl. There's gaps. So many gaps. Sometimes I don't even know who I am."

Then, as soon as it arrived, the moment passed. A snarl replaced the trembling lip, and he burst out from her restraint with an explosive movement.

*

The Hyena felt the change in the battle above her and cartwheeled away. Shaking her head when the wounds she had inflicted healed as soon as she ceased her assault, she retreated out of the Stonehand's reach — they certainly did not need him getting hold of her knives — and moved next to Azam. By the slowing of his attacks, the Bombardier was clearly nearly out of mana.

"You ever seen anything like this?" Despite everything, Azam's tone was even. "Can't remember the last time something I hit didn't stay down."

"We're hardly the ones to talk," the Hyena replied, preparing to renew her assault. She paused as the bodies of those the Cackle had slain at the start of this ill-fated mission rose up and moved to attack the Stonehand.

Jessica phased next to them. "I've rarely felt so redundant. I'm not sure he even knows I'm attacking him!"

Azam and the Hyena shrugged. "We'll keep the pressure on while we can. Remember, no heroics!" Azam said sternly to the young woman, then watched in horror as the Stonehand tore his former guards and Mages apart. "This isn't a place for heroes."

*

The sacrifice of Donal's minions bought Daine a moment to reassess. The Stonehand was simply too strong, too fast, and healed too quickly. She couldn't conceive of what it would take to defeat him.

Gallant ripped his former bodyguard in half and moved towards Donal — correctly identifying him as the cause of that latest gambit.

This was not right, Daine thought.

And, with that thought, did she hear the faint rattling of dice?

Gallant was always powerful. But not like this. She thought of all the times she had faced him in the arena. He had always won, of course he had, but she knew she had hard-pressed him at times. Three decades on, how was he more formidable? She knew the decline of age was on him when the King had changed his Class into Mentor. So how was he still capable of wreaking such havoc?

Daine grabbed at Gallant's shoulder and spun him around. Azam hit him again with a fireball, and his skin blackened and then healed in an instant.

"Whatever happened to you is not right," she said, head swaying back to avoid a thrown fist. "No matter what you did, no matter who you were, this is not justice."

The Stonehand raged at her, spittle flying from his mouth. The words he yelled were barely comprehensible, just a string of invective. All against her.

The noise of rattling dice increased. Daine could sense she was supposed to do something — to decide on a course of action — which would set the dice in motion.

He leapt at her, fingers clawed into talons to gouge out her eyes. Daine blocked and then tried to push him away. But one of his hands locked around her throat, squeezing.

Still, the dice rattled, waiting for her.

Daine reached to the Goddess for aid but found a pair of eyes looking sadly — helplessly — back at her. *I don't know*, the Goddess whispered in her mind. *I can never see beyond this moment. I don't know!*

He was a monster. But what had been done to him was monstrous.

There needed to be justice for what he had done. But he, in turn, deserved justice of his own.

Without knowing why, Daine activated <Domain of Law>.

And the dice were cast.

CHAPTER FIFTY-NINE

"Fixed Moment in Time"

All colour bleached out of the world. It was like reality had become a shadow play on a linen screen. All sound beyond the tent was muted to be replaced by a dull hum. A soft breeze added to the sense of unreal desolation.

Gallant sneered. "Was that it? After all this, *that* was your final move? Someone was not paying particularly close attention during our lessons. How many times? If you save your best and last until the very end, it needs to be worth it." With that, he ripped a hand clean from Daine's grasp and struck her a blow to the face that echoed around the oddly silent grey landscape. Her head snapped to the side with the impact but immediately swivelled straight back to meet his surprised gaze.

"On that, we can agree to disagree. It seems pretty worth it right now."

And Daine struck him back.

Throughout their long association, Daine had hit the Stonehand many times — not least in the hammering she had inflicted bare moments ago. The sheer depth, breadth, and range of his healing capacity, though, made any amount of damage essentially meaningless. Eliud had once described to her how — during the first meeting with the man — he'd hit him with his full elemental power, melting Gallant to the bone. But the Stonehand had merely laughed as his tissue and skin reknitted to his bones.

So, Daine had experienced the transient success of rocking the man back.

This time, however, it felt different. Indeed, the look in Gallant's eyes told her that he felt the difference. He stumbled backwards a few steps, raising a hand to his split lip. A drop of grey blood appeared at the corner of his mouth, and as all in the tent watched, the cut did not close.

"Oh boy," whispered Donal," someone is in trouble . . ."

You have just a few moments, a voice echoed in Daine's head. *<Domain of Law > gives ME complete dominance over the immediate area. No other God can interfere, and all empowered Class Abilities — other than those I have bestowed — are temporarily blocked. But there is a cost.*

Daine could feel the Skill draining her Stamina reserves at an extraordinary rate. She would have already bottomed out if her pool had not substantially increased during her Class Evolution.

"So, he's normal?"

Gallant Stonehand is not, and has never been, one of mine. Whatever malign influence has twisted this man into what stands before you no longer has a say, until the Skill runs out.

Daine needed no further urging. She stepped forward

and crashed one fist after another into the old man's body. The Hyena stepped forward to help, but Donal rested a hand on her forearm and shook his head.

"Not this time. Leave it to the lady."

With all the colour leaked from the world, the Stonehand's blood flew from him in strange grey gouts. Daine drove a kick into his knee, snapping the bone in two and following up with a backhand to crash him into the floor.

Kneeling over him, she continued to pound blow after blow into his head until the man stopped seeking to defend himself. Sensing it was at an end, she grabbed the front of his tunic, lifting him upwards for a final, decisive strike. As she coiled her fist backwards — flooding her body with every dormant Skill she possessed — Gallant's remaining eye flickered open, and his mangled mouth crooked upwards in a macabre grin.

"Always knew it would be you. To end it. Good on you, girl!"

Daine struggled against all her belligerence draining away. That voice — with none of the mocking cruelty — was one she remembered too well. Because it had not just been beatings and horror, had it? There had been times, near the end, when they had connected differently. When they had been able to talk more as equals rather than combatants.

"Gant?"

The Stonehand turned to spit out a glob of blood, flesh, and bone. "Seems that way. Some of me is still in here. But it's all a fog, you ken me? Sometimes, I can swim forward, but more often, a younger me has the reins. I don't have the strength to hold him back."

Daine fought to keep her anger from flaring. "I suppose none of this was you? That you're not to blame for any of this?" Her fist remained drawn back, poised to deliver the final punch.

The destroyed face laughed, further splitting wounds open. Grey rivers flowed down Gallant's face, staining his long white hair. "It was all me, girl. No matter how you view it, I haven't done anything here I haven't done a thousand times before. You thought I was a dragon at school? That was an almost mellow version of me. The Class, you know? The King understood. He saw I was on the brink and gave me an escape. Whatever this is" — he tried to gesture towards himself, but his arms hung broken — "I was on the cusp of being. Someone just let it have the reins."

Daine felt a hand on her shoulder. Donal. "My lady, I don't know what Skill this is — I have no access to any of my powers — but even without them, I can feel your energies waning. If it is to be the end, it must be now."

Daine stared down at the Stonehand. What he said was right. He was a mad dog that the King had put a leash on, only for someone to let this horror free. Was it justice to put him down?

I cannot help you with this. Whatever you choose to do within your <Domain of Law > will be just. It has MY sanction. But you must choose. And choose quickly.

"You're leaving it all to me?!" Daine could not keep the anguish from her voice. "I am supposed to enact your will. He deserves to die. If I don't kill him, so many others will suffer. It must be right to kill him. That was our plan!"

Do not be childish. There is no greater 'right'. There is no 'wrong'. There is just what you have the power to enforce. Will the world be a better place without a resurrected Gallant Stonehand raising chaos? For sure. Is the trade-off of having you as his executioner and breaking your mind worth it? I doubt it, but I do not know. This is a fixed moment in time; I cannot see beyond it. This may be the moment a terrible stain on the world is removed. It may be the opportunity to turn the tide against the Dark God. It may save Swinford. It might save the West. Or it could do the opposite. The death of Gallant Stonehouse may cause the King to let slip the dogs of war. Indeed — and believe me when I say there are far fouler presences than this old man at Court — this may be the catalyst for all-out war. And — and I worry most about this — it may be your undoing. I do not know. But it would be best if you chose a path.

The Stonehand had slipped into unconsciousness. By the extent of his injuries, Daine suspected he might well die without her doing anything else. But no. That would be a dereliction of duty. And she had forever done her duty.

A cry from her left caught her attention. It was Jessica the Stepper. She was looking down at the bodies of her two companions. <Righteous Resolve> had run out.

Daine called out to her, "The Hyena said you were our way out." The girl did not respond. Her attention was fixed on Azam and her fallen leader. "Girl, do you hear me? Can you get us back?"

The girl rallied. "Yes, I have short-range portal abilities. I can move us back behind the walls in twenty, maybe thirty steps." Then she blinked in alarm as she tried to access the Skill. "It won't work."

Daine raised a hand to calm her. "That's just temporary. As soon as I drop <Domain of Law >, you will be able to cast it." She nodded towards the bodies." Do you want to take them with us?"

"It's not our way." Jessica shook her head. "You lie where you fall."

"My lady." Donal's voice became urgent. "You have gone a very unhealthy shade. I may suggest you are now drawing on your health pool. This is not a situation that can continue. In the words of my long-lamented first master, it is time to defecate or leave the chamber. Or words to that effect."

Daine raised her fist again, looking at Old Gant's face. One punch, and it would be all over. The threat of this man would be gone forever. She felt everyone holding their breath as she smashed her fist forward with a colossal impact. There was a beat of silence, and then she cancelled <Domain of Law>.

Donal was the first to speak. "Ah. So, it would appear you missed."

Daine leaned low and whispered into Old Gant's ear, his wounds already healing. "You were a monster, no doubt. But who you were does not define who you can be. I beat you, and I let you live. But I don't ask anything of you but to start anew. I did not know you as a Blade of Ruin. I can't say I care for what you've shown me you were like back then. I did not care much for you as a Mentor, but I doubt I'd be where I am now — for good or for ill — without you and what you did. Whoever bought you back wanted the early version of you. I'm reminding you of who you became. You weren't much better, but people said your name out of respect, not terror. Next time we fight, I'm taking your head. Make sure you remember that."

"As somewhat of an expert in blood feuds, this seems unwise." Donal's face was still. "I may remind you, we are still under siege from this man's rather more than enthusi-astic army."

Daine moved away from the Stonehand and crossed to-wards Jessica. "We never intended to hold Swinford this long. We were merely delaying until Eliud came to our rescue. What Gallant has done — slaughtering Souit's forces — will raise the ante with the King. This is no lon-ger a minor secession crisis; it's a full-blown civil war. And we cannot fight from behind Mayor Elm's breached walls."

"So, what do we do? We have the Trellecs, the Stonehand, and the King at our heels. There will be blood, and we are caught in the middle."

"The evacuation has started?" Donal nodded in reply. "Good, then we take the only road left open. We run."

CHAPTER 60

"Epilogue"

The Dark God raged.

Of course he did. He raged at his mother, for giving her favoured instrument a Class and a Skill that could — however temporarily — negate him. He raged at his brothers for interfering in their chaotic way. He raged at the Stonehand for not being able to live up to his reputation for clinical destruction.

But most of all, he just raged.

Genoes watched him carefully, his eyes still in his calm face. He knew he should be terrified of the situation he was in. He had been kidnapped by a literal god. No matter how the deity chose to manifest himself — most often in the body of a ten-year-old boy — there was no denying the destructive power he possessed.

Genoes had no idea how long he had been trapped in this realm. He suspected time passed differently here than it did back in the real world. Indeed, the only way he had to mark the passage of the days was by the periods of ecstasy and despair in which the Dark God rose and fell as he schemes unfurled.

From this latest outburst of wrath, Genoes took it that his friends still lived. The Dark God had been so smugly satisfied that Daine and the rest were doomed, and this was a significant relief.

"What are you smiling at?" The Dark God's eyes were now fixed upon him, ablaze with fury.

"I am not smiling," Genoes answered levelly. "And you need to stop shouting."

The grass on which the two stood instantly turned brown, and birds fell from the sky to crash onto the dying Earth.

"You don't tell me what to do! You are nothing! You hear me? Nothing. They've forgotten all about you, you know? Despite everything they said about never resting until you were recovered, do you know how little they mentioned you? Should I show you?"

Images of Eluid and Kirstin walking through a series of rooms — Savage and Josul with them — flashed before his eyes. They seemed . . . content. Then pictures of Daine, Taelsin, and Donal followed. All were seemingly going about their everyday lives.

"They don't miss you, Genoes. They have more important struggles with which to concern themselves."

There were more moving visuals now — Eluid in chains. Kirstin fighting . . . was that a Dragon? Daine and Donal fighting each other, murder in their eyes. Taelsin stood above his City, looking down at the smoking remains of one of his broken walls.

"You are nothing!" the Dark God spat at him. "I took you because I thought it would cause them pain. Well, guess what? It didn't. Poor little Genoes. The Orphan no one wants!"

Genoes felt tears prick his eyes, but he willed them away. He would not allow himself to fall into this boy's trap.

"They're all still alive, then? Thank you for telling me." He gave his broadest smile back. The Dark God gave an incoherent scream, and a rain of dead and dying birds fell from the sky. Twisted roots forced themselves upwards from the earth, tearing great swaths of ground away. Lightning flashed, striking the ground around Genoes.

Through it all, Genoes stood still, letting the anger of a god explode around him. As it began to subside, he bent down to pick up three stones. Turning his back on the still-raging god, he began to juggle. He'd always been able to do it for as long as he could remember.

When he got his rhythm with three, he added a fourth, then a fifth, enjoying the tumbling movement. He had eight moving in a smooth parabola before he realised the sun was back out and the only wildlife around him was fit and healthy.

"How'd you do that?" There was a soft, almost feminine voice behind him. "Is it a Skill?" Genoes let the stones drop and turned to face the god, who was now in the form of a much younger boy of perhaps six or seven.

"I don't want to play with you if you lose your temper. It isn't nice." Genoes's voice was firm.

There was a moment when he feared the blazing fury in the child's eyes would burn out of control. But then it faded, and the god smiled.

"I'm sorry. I don't mean to."

There was a silence as the two regarded each other. Then Genoes sat cross-legged and indicated that the god should do the same. "Okay. But I don't like it when you're mean. If you want me to play, stop it. Now, the trick is to get two into the air at once. You do that, the rest all falls into place."

And as the two settled down to play, a pair of glowing, golden eyes watched them at the edge of the Dark God's realm.

And She was pleased.

*

The retreat from Swinford was brutal.

Even though many of the civilians had passed through Donal's portal whilst the battle raged at the walls, it was still taking far too long for the rest to escape.

After Angharad's death, those fighting at the breach were quickly overwhelmed. Souit dispatched the rest of his Mages to help manage the retreat, but they fell to the more significant number arrayed against them. Thanks to Donal's planning, though, enough of Souit's men extricated themselves from the mess for the King's Army still to be a force. At least on paper.

Degralk had been charged with holding the increasingly thin line covering the retreat to the portals. Cattle and his squad had joined them in those efforts — at least those of them who had survived the conflagration at the walls.

"How far?" Cattle called over his shoulder, thrusting out with his sword and stepping backwards before any response could land.

"Not far!" Jinks was doing his best to cover his Captain's flank, but the street was too broad, and their numbers were too low. "If we turned round and ran . . ."

"And that's why I get paid the big coins," Cattle said, wincing as he took a glancing blow on his helm. "The only way we make this is step-by-step to that portal. We aren't going to be able to run faster than those guys." Cattle nodded at the cavalry pacing towards the back of the press of mercenaries harrying them.

"Don't need to run faster than them, Captain," Jinks murmured. "Just need to run faster than your fat arse!"

"Be grateful for my girth, lad," Cattle replied, catching a downward slash on his blade and pushing it away, "it's the only thing between you and those nasties."

"Front row, kneel!"

Degralk's voice came from behind and was weighted with such authority that those at the square's front had knelt before their conscious brain kicked in. Even then, it was only just in time to avoid the flurry of quarrels that flew over their heads to obliterate those attacking them.

"Now run!"

Cattle waited until the last of his men stepped through the purple portal before taking his eyes away from the approaching mercenaries. "You first," he said to Degralk. They were the last remaining members of the King's Army in Swinford.

"Not on your life."

"Got a reputation to maintain, sir. Spent years developing it. First in, last out, and all that."

"You were captured on my watch, Captain Kettle. That's not going to happen again. Once I know you're safe, I'll be right behind you."

"Appreciate the sentiment, sir. But not sure that was rightly your fault. Now, if you would be so kind to get moving, they seem to be regathering themselves for another a push . . ."

"Charming as this is" — Donal's head appeared from the other side of the portal — "maintaining this portal is the mana drain equivalent of a sucking chest wound. It would simply be marvellous if we could all agree that you both have enormous members, and I can close this off."

He'd barely finished speaking before the mail-plated arms of the Lady Darkhelm reached through and dragged them to the other side. The portal snapped shut behind them.

*

"A Mayor without a City?" Taelsin said, staring off into the distance. "Whoever heard of such a thing?"

Donal looked up from the man he was healing — he had switched his class to High Druid to better support the retreat — and shrugged. "Not sure I've much time for a pity party, sir. If you're looking to brood, there's a Great General who hasn't spoken to anyone all day I can direct you to."

Taelsin looked over to the small group of riders to the left of the refugee column which marked the presence of General Souit. That man was taking his expulsion from the City about as well as the Mayor was.

They were not sure where Donal's portal had sent them — "Definitely to the east of Swinford. Maybe the south-east, but no further than that, I'm sure!" — but Taelsin was comforted that if they did not know where they were, it seemed likely neither did the Stonehand. Or the King. Or the Trellecs.

My, what a number of opponents I have at my door, he thought, and then laughed as he did not have a door anymore.

"If I were a wiser man," Donal began. "No, wait. I am a wise man. This is going to be golden. As a wise man, I might point out that a City is merely the stone and mortar around a people. I still see most of those under your care before me."

Taelsin nodded. Five thousand men, women and children. All of those who had not been able to flee when news of the approaching army was shared.

"We have you, my lord. More importantly, we have me. And we have the remains of a pretty solid fighting force under the command of a Great General who I will assume is pretty motivated to win his next engagement."

"But where are we heading, Donal? Who is going to take us in?"

"Sir, and I mean this with all love," Donal's eyes danced with stars, an after-effect of his most recent Class change, "let us not borrow not borrow trouble. Swinford held until it could hold no more — far longer than any of us had truly anticipated. That chapter is closed and a new one begins. There is the story of the West to be written and I can think of no better way for that to begin than with desperate people led from chaos into the promised land. Under the banner of a great Lord, with the advice of a charming, attractive genius protected by the swords of those who used to be his enemy. To be honest, sir, if we hadn't lived through it, I would be suspicious this is all a little too perfect."

Taelsin, thinking of the friends who had not made it through the portal, wrinkled his nose in distaste at that. Then his eyes fell on the lone figure in the distance at the back of a column. He frowned as she bent to touch the Road.

*

Daine's hand brushed the dirt of the King's Road.

This had been her Tour for thirty years. She knew every inch of the West and shed blood to keep the King's peace in every Town, Village and City she visited, and now . . .

Why did you not kill him?

Daine ignored the Goddess. She had repeatedly asked the same question since they had escaped the Stonehand's command tent, but Daine did not think She was owed a reply.

And, to be honest, she did not know the answer herself.

She knew that within the <Domain of Law>, it would not have been a just execution. And such things mattered greatly to her, perhaps more so since supporting the rebels.

The ground beneath her shifted, and Donal stepped up from the dirt. He was enjoying the Skills of his new Class far too much. "How is it looking?" he asked without preamble.

"Was there a 'my lady' in there somewhere?" she replied, only half joking.

"Probably. So, any idea where we should be heading?"

"That's for the Great General and the Mayor to decide, surely?"

Donal nodded. "I may be out of line, but I don't think either of them is thinking too clearly at the moment. Might be as good if, I don't know, two epically talented and legendary figures gave them a nudge?"

"Perhaps."

Donal pointed to the left. "Over there, the ocean. There are lots of coastal Cities and Towns where we could lose ourselves." He pointed to the right. "That way . . . not so much. Scrubland and empty plains. Maybe a few rural homesteads. Neither makes my socks roll up and down. So which way?"

Daine smiled at Donal explaining the local geography to her. Then a rattling noise began in her head. By Donal's reaction he heard it too

"By the sound of things, I'm not sure it matters which we choose," she said grimly.

And then the dice were rolled once more.

*

Eliud settled them down in a clearing just at the edge of the Capital, grumbling all the way.

"A man of my power and station in life, reduced to being a donkey!"

Kirstin stretched her back, which had become stiff during their flight. "We've been over this," she said, "no matter how dim a view you take of those at Court, there is a reasonable chance they will have noticed the appearance of the Sky Keep above them. This way, we have a decent chance of sneaking in."

"The Duskstrider does not sneak. He does not creep. He does not lurk. He arrives with fanfare!"

"He could also stop referring to himself in the third person if he doesn't want me to shoot him with an arrow."

"She makes a fair point."

He bent to pick up Savage, who yowled in complaint until she was released to her usual place on Kirstin's shoulder. "Yet another betrayal in the Duskstrider's — in my — tragedy-filled life."

He looked towards the wall of the Capital, lights glinting softly in the gloom. "So, we've tried this the honest way before — going through the front door — what say we do something more innovative this time?"

"I like innovation."

Eliud closed his eyes, seeking a presence as familiar as breathing. He surrounded it with his power and pulled, dragging it through space and time until he appeared in front of them with a soft pop.

The tall man with a beard stared around him in bewilderment for a moment until his eyes alighted on Eliud. Then he groaned and shook his head.

"El, what on earth have you done now?"

Kirstin looked at the richly dressed figure up and down. Expensive leather boots. Intricately brocaded trousers and tunic. And that familiar face . . .

"Eliud, please tell me this isn't?"

The Duskstrider smiled back, clapping the bearded man on the shoulder.

"I thought, let's cut out the middleman. May I present our Lord and Master, King Hanya Rendell. He and I are going to have a little talk."

If you enjoyed this book, please leave a review at your favorite online retailer's website!

Enthusiastic reviews from readers like you are incredibly helpful.

Thank you!

ACKNOWLEDGEMENTS

For all their help bringing this project to life, I would like to thank the team at Nef House as well as all the countless, tireless readers on Royal Road who have been invaluable at every step. Thank you!

ABOUT THE AUTHOR

BardLyre hails from the Midlands where they teach English. When not writing or teaching they can usually be found in the library. They own more books than is strictly necessary.

Visit BardLyre on Patreon for exclusive content:
https://patreon.com/BardLyre577

Discover more epic fantasy and LitRPG at
www.nefhousepublishing.com

NEF HOUSE PUBLISHING

www.ingramcontent.com/pod-product-compliance
Lightning Source LLC
Chambersburg PA
CBHW060241030726
47493CB00024B/1491